# Kerrie's Secretive Duke

## Naughty Book Six

Christine Young

ISBN: 978-1-62420-849-2

Cover Art: Designs by Ms G
Editor: Amanda Armstrong

# Chapter One

1838

The wind caressed her face, sending her hair flying behind her. The exhilaration keen. Hooves pounded, thundering beneath her. Kerrie Johnston pushed the horse harder, faster. She was one with her horse. Thrills chased down her spine with the exciting race through the forest. They would fly out on the meadow soon, headed for home. The huge stallion sired by her mother's favorite horse, Fiacre, trampled the grass. Battered the ground beneath his hooves. She lay flat against the big stallion's neck urging him to race faster. He leapt the log lying across the narrow woodland trail. She felt as one with the magnificent animal. Soon, she would need to slow him, walk him. Allow him to warm down. They would both breathe again. She sipped deep the forest air she loved. The fragrant smells were a deep part of her. Living in this manner was good. Thrilling. Free.

"Good boy," Kerrie whispered to the stallion stroking the animal, his hide sweaty. After they returned to the stable, he would need tender attention. As she understood the necessity, she slowed the pace to a walk, praising the animal as they continued. A deep breath of air filled her with the scent of pine. Four days were left to her. If she could enjoy every second with her horse, she would do so. She treasured the time alone with her thoughts. Sometimes she was a solitary soul. Loved the moments she had to herself. Was not looking forward to the next stage of her life.

The London season she didn't wish for awaited her. She was no débutante. Nor did she wish to call herself on the shelf though she was. Her stomach churned at the horrific knowledge of what was going to happen to her. Dancing with fops at the ball who had the sole purpose of shopping for a wife was not on her favorite to do list. Riding the wind.

Feeling Dex beneath her. Those were what her dreams were made from. Her parents didn't know she had taken this slight diversion into the hills far from the country estate where she was supposed to become a lady. She would never simper. Would never bow down to man's whims. She was independent, a free thinker. Taught to be so by her parents.

If her father discovered she had left her entourage in the village below, he'd be furious. Maybe her father wasn't part of that instruction. Even angrier if he discovered she was alone with no one to protect her. Kerrie didn't need or want babysitters. Didn't need to be protected or sheltered from the big bad world. She wasn't a helpless female. That's all her entourage was. Guardians of her virtue. Hah! The guards he sent as traveling companions weren't needed. She understood they were a precautionary tactic. Her father suspected she would do something to deviate from his plans. He was spot on with that assumption. Before riding up the path to the Montgomerie hunting lodge, she sent Aunt Ella a note as to her plans, telling her the anticipated arrival would be delayed a week. If she dared postpone her appearance in London further, she would do so. If she could put her debut off forever, that would be better. She anticipated with glee the time alone. Time to collect her thoughts then figure out a way to avoid a marriage, any marriage. She didn't have room for a man in her life.

Fathers always worried about daughters. Hadden had two to worry over. Though Kelsey, her younger sibling, always did what she was told. Kelsey was a father's perfect daughter. For the most part, so did she, do what was expected. This was not one of those times. Before she was whisked into the carriage, she told her father this was not what she wished for in her life. Her parents thought she needed a husband. The devil, she turned twenty this year. She didn't care about the label on the shelf. If and when she ever wed, the marriage would be for love, not to gain a title or wealth. A love like her parents experienced was what she was holding out for. Kerrie understood she would never find that type of love at a *dèbutante's* ball. Wouldn't find love anywhere in London either. She needed a real man. What did she want with a dandy? She needed a man who would stand up for her. Would allow her to continue with her dream...a stable of race horses all her own.

Nothing.

It wasn't as if she didn't have a few suitors. She did. Their kisses did nothing for her that would send her heart soaring. The caresses never sparked anything within. While the kisses were nice, that was it. Nothing else. No flicker of desire. No flames she couldn't resist. Kerrie wanted something that would cock her toes up. She understood that was what her mother and father relished. What her married cousins enjoyed with their spouses.

Kerrie leaned over to caress Dex, stroking the animal's neck. She'd been surprised when her mother allowed her to take the stallion with her. She also realized the allowance was to ease her into the acceptance of her destination. She had no choice except to go. Telling her mother she didn't care about a husband would never hold water. The words would be a lie. The fact was she wasn't about to settle. Most of all she didn't want a man with a title. That was the last thing she wished to have. A title would inhibit everything she longed for in life. There were too many rules that went with a titled aristo. She didn't like rules or regulations. Didn't need the obligations. She saw what Aunt Ella went through. Her aunt was a duchess. That title was just down the line from the king and queen. No, no man with a title would be hers. A man like that wasn't about to give her a second look. She was, after all, a *wee* bit, no, a lot rough around the edges. Her manners weren't lacking. The problem was that she had her own way of doing things that were not wifely by today's standards.

London... She was going to live with Auntie Ella, now known as The Duchess. The one and only Duchess. Her aunt was in charge of all the female relatives who were sent to the city for their coming out. So far, she had sponsored three of her cousins. She was the fourth. As far as Kerrie was concerned, she didn't want a season. Didn't want to be sponsored by anyone, even The Duchess. Back in the little village at the bottom of the hill were three trunks filled with all the new clothing her mother ordered to be made special for her introduction. Kerrie thought the expense was a waste of good money. Though her father had more money than he needed. Money that could have been spent on the stables or purchasing new horseflesh to breed. That's what she wished for. A stable of her own...not frivolous gowns. One that would be renowned throughout England as well as Scotland.

At the end of the trail, she found a boulder to sit on. This was one of her favorite places to reflect on her future. The idyllic spot overlooked a canyon that fell away to a stream far below. Yesterday, she walked down to the stream with a fly rod in her hand. She caught two fish for her dinner that night. Since she didn't bring the cook from her entourage with her, she cleaned then fried the rainbow trout herself. What she did would allow her travel guards to help her bring enough staples to last the week she planned to stay here.

The food was plentiful. She could also fish in the lake next to the Montgomerie hunting lodge. She possessed a clean aim, hitting a rabbit or bird with her rifle. However, cleaning and skinning an animal was not enjoyable. While her family had permission to visit the lodge whenever, they always wrote of their plans ahead of time to make certain they would be the only ones staying. Didn't find sharing amenable. This time for Kerrie the visit was unplanned. Knowing what was expected, she did write. Nonetheless, she was afraid someone would be at the lodge. When she reached the village below, she knew she would be fine. All the servants who worked at the lodge were at the village. No one was expected. She would be alone. Exactly what she needed to prepare herself for the dreaded season.

Thinking of the boring days ahead of her, she tossed a small rock over the edge of the cliff listening for it to land even though she understood she wouldn't hear a sound. The drop was too far. In this spot the stream tumbled across large boulders. The water rushed down to the sea. She breathed in deep feeling the mood. The scents of the forest as well as the beautiful scenery touched her soul with promise. Moved her. This serenity was all she needed. Balls, dinners, recitals, held no happiness for her. The crush of the season was horrendous. She cringed thinking about all those perfumed bodies in one area.

The noon hour had come and gone. She was hungry. For a few more minutes she leaned back, the autumn sun beating down on her face. From the summer, her skin was tan more so than what a lady wanted. She was no lady. Never claimed to be. Her best friend in the whole world scolded her for forgetting her bonnets. A bonnet got in the way of riding in the manner she liked. Dex moved restlessly beside her. She wished she could ride forever. Riding was her one and only true joy.

With a heavy sigh, Kerrie looked at the horse she adored. Smoothed her hand along his neck. "Time to get back, Dex. Are you as hungry as me? There will be something special waiting for you. After you eat, I'll bring you apple slices as well as the carrots you so enjoy. First thing though is a good rubdown. I did work you hard. You deserve my best efforts."

After she stood, she smoothed her hand down his long nose. Except for the white mark running down the center of his nose, he was pure black, his coat glossy from the tender care she gave him. His dark brown eyes stared at her, waiting for the treat he knew he would get. The juicy morsel would come later. The stallion knew that fact. He thought if he stared at her with his big brown eyes, he would get it sooner. Today, if she had apple slices or carrots in her pocket, he would receive his reward.

"You're such a fine fellow. Every lady's dream. Too bad there isn't a man out there as special as you are." Kerrie reached into her jacket pocket coming up with pieces of a carrot. She smiled at him. Until now she forgot about the treat. "For your good behavior." Dex had been right. She always gave into those deep dark eyes. Would give the big stallion everything since he always gave her his all. If there was a man such as that...good god, she might be able to give him her all.

Dex gobbled up the treat. Using a log, Kerrie mounted, swung her leg over his back. The movement hiked up her skirts to her knees. She didn't care. They were alone in this small piece of paradise. Not that she would give it a second thought in other circumstances. Riding near her parents' property she rarely met anyone. They lived away from the small town close where she grew up. She bent close to his ear. "Shall we race one more time? As soon as we leave the woods for the meadow, we will test your strength. Your stamina. A brisk race across the field is in order. You are in need of a *wee* bit of exercise. Not that you haven't outpaced your usual workout." The smart trot she set him to brought a bob of his head telling her he was just as ready as she was. Dex understood every word she spoke. He was an incredible animal. He would be the means for her to build her stable.

He shook his head, nickering approval. She kept the pace slow through the woods. Dodged fallen logs. Jumped over ones that lay across the trail. Once they reached the meadow in front of the lodge, she gave him the go ahead to sprint. The hunting lodge was a small dot in the distance. She inhaled as they set off. Her heart raced, the thrill of the run inherent in every part of her.

Exhilarated.

The grin of enjoyment swept her from the inside out. Wind tore at her hair as his speed increased. Leaning over, Kerrie urged the big stallion faster. Faster still. They flew over the grassy field. Together, they challenged the wind for the second time today. Next year Dex would race with the three-year-olds. Dex would win just as his father won every race her mother entered. Would become a legend. This horse was unstoppable. He belonged to her. This was all she wanted from her life; the horse, a stable that would be hers. A husband to demand things of her was not something she wished for. Did not want to be the oldest *dèbutante* for the season. Didn't need to be humiliated...scorned.

Hoofbeats that weren't Dex's thundered behind her, too close for comfort. Her heart lurched. Deep inside she panicked. She was supposed to be alone. No one should be here. Who the devil could be shadowing her? Kerrie turned to look over her shoulder. She grimaced at the sight. He was chasing her. His mount gained on her. She needed to urge Dex faster then faster still. This wasn't right.

A man...

No, it couldn't be. His face was stern. His lips pressed together in a tight line. What she saw of his expression before she turned her attention to the race of her life was anger. This unknown person had no reason or right to be furious with her. No reason to speed after her. What the hell did he want? Fear thrashed inside. Wind stung her cheeks. Her hair whipped around her face.

This man was the interloper. He didn't belong.

"Faster, Dex, please, please. Faster. Go! Our lives might depend on your speed. You're the fastest horse in the British Isles. I'm willing to bet on that fact." Kerrie's heart leapt.

She cringed against the horse trying to make herself small. Dex was tired from his earlier run. He might not win this race. Her confidence no longer soared. He was up against a formidable enemy. One she didn't wish to confront.

Seconds ticked by, one after the other. Hoofbeats still pounded behind her. When she peeked again, the man was closing on her. She bent closer to the horse's neck, knowing the stallion didn't have more to give. He was exhausted. Earlier, she put him through his paces. His big body heaved. Would want his oats as well as that good rub down she promised him. He would give her everything he had. This time his valiant heart wasn't enough. She needed to face whatever was in store for her. She would never run her horse to the ground. About to pull up on the reins, she felt the man beside her.

The shriek cried out from deep inside her when, without warning, she was lifted through the air to land hard on the stranger's thighs. "No!"

Kerrie pushed at the arm that circled her waist, holding her against a hard chest. Squirming, she twisted, pushed, kicked as well as hit the man. She punched him hard in the jaw. His head snapped back. She didn't care if she fell. This was far worse than finding herself trampled.

"Stop it!" He shook her as the stallion slowed. His words were furious. "Stop it! I don't mean to harm you. What the bloody hell do you think you are doing? That horse was out of control. He's too big for you. Too strong."

Kerrie swung again. Frantic. Her fist hit his jaw. His head jerked back for a second time. He dumped her on the ground. She landed on her backside so hard air rushed from her lungs. Moisture rose to her eyes. "Hellion! I saved you! What do I get for my efforts? A broken jaw!" He rubbed where she hit him. Stared down at her as if she was insane.

Kerrie couldn't help from gaping at the audacity of his words. Her feet firmly planted on solid ground, her hands on her hips she felt a bit of bravado. This man was an arrogant bastard. "Saved me from what? Just what exactly do you think your highhandedness saved me from!" The tenor of her voice rose. "You could have killed me! Could have been thrown beneath the hooves of your horse. You are too wild. Too reckless. Arrogant."

He swung his leg over then dropped to the earth beside her. Good

God, he was tall. Broad shoulders. Narrow of hip. Thighs muscled. Blue-grey eyes simmered with heat. Flashed sparks of fire in her direction. His enormous fury evident in the set of his jaw. She was taken aback by his words. Despite her determination to stand her ground, she stepped back from him. His stance was too overpowering. She couldn't meet him eye to eye. Would need to find some other way to state her case against his bravado. He had no rights here. He intruded.

"Your horse was running wild. You are a *wee* bit of a thing. Scrawny arms. No muscle. There was no way in hell you could keep that huge stallion in line," he spoke with infuriating calm. His voice held her enthralled for a moment. Talked as if he knew what was what. "Before you broke your pretty neck, you needed help. I came to your assistance. No thanks from you. I rescued you." He threw up his hands a scowl on his handsome face. "What the hell were you thinking?"

"You're crazy! I'm no damsel in distress who needs help from the likes of you. I had everything well in hand! Didn't need a man to save me from the horse I've ridden for two years. Dex obeys my commands. He understands everything I tell him." She didn't intend to back down from his tirade. The man was wrong.

"Could have fooled me." His fury was no longer flashing sparks of fire.

The eyes that stared at her turned smokey. His gaze ran over her as if he assessed her abilities. *Scrawny arms. No muscle. I'll show him muscle.* He seemed more annoyed than anything.

"Come along, I'll take you wherever it is you need to go. Are you one of the servants here? If so, you shouldn't be playing super horsewoman while there is work to be done in the house. Imagine you have chores that have been left undone."

*Come along? Not on his life or mine. How dare he speak to her in that manner? A servant? Never!*

Kerrie didn't have words to combat him, his highhandedness. His smug grin. His arrogance. Her anger had not died. "I did. I fooled you. Now I'm the one who has to walk back because of your overbearingness. I hate walking. Always ride."

She began the trek to the lodge. Which wasn't that far. She could have ridden into the stable. Because of his actions, she walked. Brushed Dex down. Given him his evening meal. This man kept her from attending to her stallion as he should be tended to.

"You're telling me you had everything in hand? That you weren't in trouble? I don't believe a word. That animal has to be sixteen or maybe seventeen hands. He's huge. All muscle. A little slip of a female can't handle an animal that large. Besides, if you were taking everything in hand, you were running the animal into the ground. A good horseman would never do that."

A wave of nausea swept through her. In all her life she'd never overtaxed an animal. In this case, his statement might be too close to the truth for comfort. Only because she was running from him. Unable to say anything else, she made an unladylike snort. "How would you know? You were chasing me. I feared for my life. Thought you were a madman. Still do." Kerrie felt more than ready to blast the man out of the water. Instead of giving him what for, she held her tongue after that last statement. She'd said too much. Arguing with this beast of a male would get her nowhere. She still didn't know his intentions. What the devil was he doing here?

"I know. Now, come along. Let me give you that lift to wherever you're going. You don't have to walk unless you're so stubborn you'd defy my generosity. Didn't you just tell me you abhorred walking?"

*Come along.* Infuriating beast.

Self-absorbed masculine animal.

"Would rather walk than be anywhere with you."

Kerrie was beginning to dislike this man with intensity surprising her. This handsome man, she amended, wishing he weren't so arrogant as well as annoying. Wishing he didn't believe his every word was gospel. Wishing he didn't intrigue all her senses. He was too handsome...too masculine...too male.

"No?" he questioned her. One more time in less than five minutes his hands were on her waist. He tossed her onto his horse. With no effort on his part, he leapt up behind her. The reins were in one hand. His arm was around her waist pulling her close. He guided the animal toward the lodge. In a different life, she might admire his skill with his horse. Might enjoy the heat pervading her body when he touched her.

No!

At his obvious destination, she groaned. He couldn't be going to the lodge. Where else would he go? There was nothing up here except the lodge. While she had permission, at the same time she didn't have authorization. Ella wouldn't have known until today or possibly yesterday maybe not until tomorrow she was here. The duke might have given this man permission to vacation at the hunting lodge. Her note would have reached Ella only a day or two ago. He would have arrived this afternoon while she was out exploring the territory. The servants from the village would begin to assemble. Her long-awaited relaxing vacation before the London season would be over.

"Seems your horse..." the man began but he cut himself off. His huge arm squeezed against her stomach.

"Dex."

"Seems your horse is headed for the stable. Did you steal the animal? Gives me more reason for concern. Are you a thief?"

His audacious question infuriated her more than his highhanded assumption she needed help.

The bristling couldn't be helped. He made too many suppositions to satisfy her. She meant to set him straight. "He's mine. My horse. No, I didn't steal the animal. If you want proof, I don't have any. Never thought I would need a document. Raised Dex from the moment he was born. My mother gave him to me."

"How would you...?" He looked over her clothing, ran his hand along the fabric of her skirt then down the length of her leg. "How would you afford that fine of an animal? You're dressed in clothing suitable for a servant. Not the owner of as fine an animal as that stallion. Believe you lie. Care to speak the truth? Could summon the law. Hold no respect for females who lie."

The groan she hid behind her teeth. He wouldn't send for the law. The sheriff in the village knew her. Knew her family. Would give her away. His question was legitimate. Dressed as she was, his rush to judgement didn't surprise her. "I don't always wear old clothes. Dex needed to be put through his paces. I dressed for work, not a day of leisure. Not for a ride in the park or down a country lane. Don't wear my, 'ride in

10

Hyde Park', ensemble when working out the animals. No reason to dress up when I'm putting Dex through his paces."

The air from his bark of laughter ruffled her hair. This was too much. She sucked in a breath of air when his arm tightened around her again. "Snippy little thing, aren't you? You need to learn to curb your tongue before it gets you into trouble you can't find a way out of." He spread his fingers across her belly. Heat flared in her. He took liberties he had no business taking, just like a bloody aristocrat.

"Stop calling me little! I'm not. I'm grown. A woman. Not a child. I'm not small!"

Kerrie didn't understand the burgeoning anger. The fury his words elicited. Understood the way he acted coupled with the words coming from his mouth had a way of irritating her. Rubbed her wrong. He talked to her as if she had no brain in her head. She was a woman grown.

This time he chuckled. His arm pulled her closer to him, pressed below her unfettered breasts. She pushed away to no avail. "When the description fits, I'll use it. When a person acts like a child they'll be treated as one. You, my dear, were acting as if you had no wits about you. A child would behave in that manner. Not a grown young woman." He moved his arm up. Her breasts pushed against his forearm. By his actions, he should be able to tell she was no child.

He made her feel like a hoyden. Just what did he expect her to do when she turned around to see a stranger chasing her? She needed to approach this from a different angle. It was time to learn a few things about this man who was invading her space, her life, her future. "What are you doing here? If you don't mind my asking?" she questioned hoping to get some information from him that would dispel her fears. He was still an unknown entity in her life. The man could force her. Have his way with her. She had no protection this far from the village and her entourage. The devil, she couldn't point that out to him. If she said as much, her words might put ideas into his head.

"You took my question right out of my mouth. I'm assuming you work here or in the village below. You've taken privileges that were never meant for you. Presuming you are getting ready for my arrival. Am I wrong?"

He steered the animal they were riding toward the stable. Kerrie straightened trying to keep her back from touching him. Everywhere he touched, heat flared.

"You're wrong on all counts. You know nothing about me. Your assumptions are all wrong." She cringed when she thought about tonight. He would persist until he discovered what she was about. Who she was. While this wasn't meant to be a secret, neither did she wish to broadcast the fact she didn't travel to London where she was supposed to be. Kerrie understood this man deserved the truth. Giving him her truth would not be forthcoming until he proved himself to be trustworthy. He could be the worst of the worst. The man could be a titled aristocrat.

"Enlighten me then. What am I wrong about? I'm a reasonable man. I'll listen. Decide what to believe as well as what not to credit." He persevered with the line of questions that she wished to ignore.

The man let her slip to the ground. She stalked to Dex's stall where she began to rub him down. Kerrie didn't want to look at this infuriating person let alone acknowledge his presence. She needed to ignore him. Pretend he wasn't there. Knew he wouldn't be here without the duke's permission. A man took the reins of his horse. She supposed all the servants she'd told had the week off would be up here working. So much for her wish for peace and quiet. Under these circumstances, she might as well have gone straight to London.

Talking to him was not an option at the moment. Any words that would fly at him from her mouth would offend him. Her standing in his eyes would diminish. While he watched over her, staring at her as if he wished to devour her, she couldn't think. If she offended the man too much, she would be sent back down the trail to the village. If she desired to remain here, she would need to find a way to coexist with him for her remaining days. She could charm as well as any woman. Flirting was second nature to her. Used the ploy only when necessary. Though she loathed doing so. This was for her good...not his. She didn't want anything from the man except to be left alone. If she were to find a *wee* bit of luck, she might be able to send him packing.

Minutes later when she finished seeing to her horse, she strode to him intending to bridge the widening gap between them. Kerrie held out her hand. With a deep breath, she began, "I'm Kerrie Johnston. Who are you?" This introduction seemed prudent. A name for him was a necessity. She hoped he didn't have a title behind his name. Men with titles were loathsome. Give her a peasant any day over a lord of the realm and she would be happy.

"Nice to finally have a name for you. Sterling Talmage at your service. My friends call me Tam." He brought her hand into his. Instead of shaking it, he brought it to his lips to kiss the back. He then turned it over to stroke the palm with his thumb.

Shocked, outraged by the strange feelings that centered inside her, Kerrie tugged. A man should not take wicked advantage of a situation...of...of a lady. He let go with a wide grin that pronounced the cleft in his chin. "Mr. Talmage," she acknowledged with a slight quiver to her voice. Glad that he bore no title in front of his name. "Believe we have quite a few things to discuss. I..."

"You don't belong here, lady. If you are not a servant then who are you? Some usurper who found a cozy place to call home? A woman who needs to hide from someone? Perhaps a lover? That still doesn't explain that magnificent horse you tell me is yours." He stood with his feet braced apart. His beautiful silver-blue eyes shot daggers at her. This man wasn't going to credit anything she said.

Obviously, yes, he didn't appreciate her any more than she liked him. "A friend of the family, the Montgomerie family. Ella is my aunt on my mother's side. Drake is my uncle by marriage to Ella. You understand. Right? My mother and father have a standing invitation to visit this hunting box. I took the invitation to heart which is why I'm here. Didn't wish to be in London." She was about to tell him too much. "What about you? Why are you here?" She tried for bold as well as brash.

"You're here without your parents?" The voice of disapproval flashed at her. "A lady doesn't go someplace like this without a chaperone. You are quite the risk taker. Maybe you're not as innocent as you are supposed to be."

Kerrie bristled. "That obvious? Nope. No parents for me. They trust me to say no to a cavalier man. Unless you don't take no for an answer to anything. Quite capable of taking care of myself. I'm an independent thinker." She couldn't help the sarcasm ebbing from her. "I've never needed a chaperone. Don't need or want one now. If you are applying for the job, there isn't a job. If you think I might want you, you are sorely mistaken. Don't need some unknown person in my presence to tell a man no."

"A little slip of a girl with no protection. Don't believe the duke and duchess would approve of you being at this hunting lodge by yourself. I'll wager they don't know you are here. Nor do your parents. Do you have a husband?"

She coughed, shocked by his assumption. "Good God, no!" She bit out before she could bring the words back behind her teeth. Whether she was married or not wasn't his business. The fact he asked was rude beyond anything a gentleman would enquire.

Bloody everlasting hell, he sounded sour, even bitter. Right before her eyes his disposition changed. Even with the ardent disapproval in the tone of his voice coupled with his words, his lips seemed to be twitching as if he held back a smile. What could he find in this conversation that was amusing?

*Unless the blasted man laughed at me. I am old enough to be on the shelf. I should be able to go anywhere by myself that I please. I'm not going to give him more reasons to chastise me.*

"I'm twenty," Kerrie blurted out again then wished for a second time she'd kept her mouth closed.

Before she told him her life story, she was going to have to curb her impulsiveness with this man. She didn't understand what was happening to her. Never acted this way before. She was quite capable of keeping her story behind her teeth.

"That old." His chuckle rumbled up from his gut, the grin he sported broad. "So young. Still..." He rubbed his chin with long sculpted fingers as if thinking. His neatly cut nails were buffed as well as clean. "A woman of your wild nature should have a chaperone despite your advanced age."

"Yes. That old. My age is not your business. Neither is a chaperone. I'm self-governing." She didn't like the tone of voice or the deep base laugh she heard after her words. Kerrie went back to rubbing down Dex before she gave more of herself away. She needed to keep her mouth shut. When he started talking again, she turned a bit.

"Means you're well versed in a great deal of things. Am I right? You are of such a great age. You must know men well. What they want. All about their needs."

His gaze lingered a little too long on her mouth then her breasts. Dropped lower. Brazenly assessed all of her. She bristled.

Kerrie whirled when he first began to speak, now facing him. She didn't wish to see into his eyes. Didn't understand the second meaning to his words. Knew there was something wicked underlying those innocent phrases. What the devil did he mean by what he said? Her face heated. She set her hand on her blazing cheeks, hoping she could cool them.

"Yes, I'm proficient at many tasks. For starters, I ride quite well. I train horses to race at Newmarket as well as other places. I'm an experienced..." Her shoulders squared. She tossed the brush into a barrel. Her hands fisted on her hips, she shouted at him. "What do you mean by that?"

His grin grew wide. His white teeth flashed in the dim light. "Good to know you're experienced. Maybe you can teach me some of those tasks you merit applauding at. You could always give me pointers on riding. Something a man likes to understand all the intricate details along with the subtle nuances of sitting astride the right mount. Might make my stay here more relaxing as well as interesting if you offered a few lessons...in riding. Could use some new knowledge of the carnal type. A woman who doesn't have a chaperone...my, my, my. This must be my lucky day."

Not wishing for this man to see the heat of embarrassment staining her cheeks, Kerrie turned away from him and once again concentrated on the grooming of Dex. Picked up each hoof to check for pebbles. This wasn't at all what she anticipated for tonight. Relaxing. Bah! That was also the circumstance she looked for by traveling here before moving on to the city. After she felt a bit more in control, she resumed the conversation. Stupid of her.

"I've no idea what you are saying or implying. Don't understand why you find humor at my expense. I'm going into the lodge now. After I've changed my clothes, I'll start dinner. I can make enough for two if you wish to eat with me. If not, you're on your own. I don't care what you decide. I'm trying to be polite."

"You're not staying in this lodge tonight unless it's in my bed." His voice was bland as well as irritating. "I haven't believed a word that has come from your sweetly kissable lips. A mouth I would like to taste among other places on your lush, well-rounded body."

Her back stiffened. She stepped away. Bumped into the back of the stall. Stumbled. Righted herself. "I am staying. Won't be lying in your bed." The nerve of the conceited man. She made a note to start down the trail tomorrow. She understood when she...no...she wasn't going to give into his dictates. Wasn't going to run. She would stay. Fight. What authority did he have to kick her out? Demand her presence in his bed? None over her. If she didn't allow him authority, he couldn't force her to leave. He was bluffing.

By the time she was out the stable door, she heard his curses. Kerrie smiled. The man was just as she imagined, all bluster and orders with no backbone. When faced with an unwilling victim, he didn't know what to do. Willing or otherwise she wasn't going to become his prey or fall at his feet. Nor was she about to join him in his bed.

Mr. Talmage caught up to her by the time she stepped inside the lodge. He grasped her by the shoulder to turn her around. She faltered. Managed to keep her balance by bracing her hands on his chest. Confronted him with her intentions. One more time, "I'm changing my clothes. After that, as I said, I'll fix dinner." By the looks of him, she doubted if he could cook.

"No, you won't. The chef Drake employs is in the kitchen as we speak. Fixing my dinner. If you wish to eat tonight, you should tell him he needs to make enough for two people. The man doesn't allow interlopers in his domain, the kitchen. You will have nothing to eat if you don't do what I've suggested. Whether you eat or not makes no difference to me. You will still be in my bed."

She was flummoxed. Perhaps he did have a bit of backbone. All Kerrie could do at this time was nod her head. This was a nightmare. She did as he told her then walked the stairs to the master chamber where she left all her belongings. She would have to move to a different room. That was fine. Sharing a room or a bed was unacceptable.

Shock hit her in the gut when she saw what he did while she was out riding. A few unladylike curses left her mouth. From behind her, she heard unconcealed laughter. He followed her.

All her clothing was lying on the floor outside the door. She whirled, her hands fisted at her sides. He stood at the top of the steps leaning against the balustrade, relaxed, arrogant. His little half smirk told her he enjoyed her discomfort. Seemed he trailed behind her to see her reaction. Kerrie found herself shaking her finger at him with disbelief. "You didn't. Of all the conceited...over bearing..."

"I did. If you want this room you have to share. Share with me. As I told you earlier, I'm willing to make concessions. You can even put your clothing back. There is plenty of room for two people."

"You've..."

His brow arched. He had every right to kick her out of the master chamber. No right to tell her she had to share his bed. While she fumed, she caved. Picking up her clothing, she marched to the guest bedroom at the other end of the hall.

"You've dropped your drawers," he laughed.

Kerrie marched back, grabbed her pantalettes from him then retraced her steps. Her back stiff. Her face flamed. Mortified. Humiliated.

"Wouldn't mind sharing. If you change your mind, you do know where to find my bed," he called after her retreating back.

A wise woman would leave in the morning. Without trying, the haughty man got her hackles up. She was stronger than that. More determined than he could ever imagine. She made plans to stay the week. Stay she would despite her misgivings. She wasn't about to back down. Before she changed her clothes, she needed a bath. A dip in the lake would make her feel clean again. Kerrie hoped he wouldn't see her sneak down the back steps. She gathered soap and a towel along with clean clothes. Her heart hit a rapid stride as she picked up her pace gathering the necessities for a quick washing in the chilled water.

Opening her door a crack, she peaked out. There was no one in the hall. On silent bare feet, she whisked her way to the back steps then down. She stopped for a moment to slip on a pair of slippers then quick-stepped her way to the end of the lake, the part that couldn't be seen from the front windows.

Kerrie understood she might have only a few minutes to take care of her bath. In the cold water, she wouldn't wish for more than those fleeting moments. With speed born of desperation, she stripped to her chemise and pantalettes. Didn't dare submerge herself naked. With her favorite soap in hand, she walked into the water. Dipping under so her hair would be wet, she lathered the soap through the long strands. It seemed to take an eternity to wash all of her. Afraid he would see her, she kept her back to the house. Didn't know what she would do if he discovered her bathing in the lake. Another confrontation so soon would be heart stopping painful. This bath in haste was far from relaxing. She needed a soak in a hot tub. If she asked, he might have ordered one for her. She wasn't about to go into the kitchen to heat her water or take a bath in the scullery as she did the night before as well as the one before that. Hauling buckets of water upstairs was a difficult task. One she needed to avoid.

After she realized she'd been daydreaming as well as wasting time, her heart lodged in her throat. She raced out of the water to the towel she left on the bank. Thank goodness it was still there. While she knew he'd not left the house through the front door, there was always the possibility of the back. Once she pulled her gown over her head, she heaved in a deep relieved breath of air. Naked, well, dressed only in her underclothing, she was too vulnerable. No man ever saw her without clothes. He thought she gave her favors away. How stupid of him. She didn't tolerate ignorance. The man was also judgmental. Rushed to conclusions.

The sun was now dipping behind the trees surrounding the property. As she walked back to the house, she saw him standing in the upstairs window of the master chamber. Heat spread across her face. How much did he see? He might have been watching her bathe. Another inferno blazed. Her gut clenched tight.

He was still watching. Biting her lip, she straightened her shoulders. She wasn't going to give him the satisfaction of witnessing her humiliation. Thinking again of him watching her bathe sent another wave of heat, flames licking all over her body.

By the time she reached the servant entrance, he was there, holding the door open for her. The smile on his face was wicked. He would think the worst of her. Would make more comments she didn't understand.

"Enjoy your bath, Miss Johnston? Must have been chilly. It's the wrong time of year to bathe in the lake." His voice was solemn which surprised her. "If you asked, I would have ordered a hot bath for you. Much more relaxing. If you were sweet, I might have joined you. My bath was hot. Took the liberty of informing my chef there would be two for dinner."

His formality surprised her. Behind her breath Kerrie muttered a few choice words she hoped he wouldn't understand. "Thank you. Didn't wish to put you out. After what you said earlier, I had no idea how you would respond."

"I had a bath," he told her again, his voice whiskey smooth. "We could have shared. Wouldn't have put me out at all. I would enjoy sharing most anything with you." He didn't wait for her to answer. His hand was placed with firm possession at the small of her back. "Come along now, dinner will get cold if we don't attend to it soon. I've been waiting for you. I'm famished. Been a long day."

*Come along. I am also famished. I've not eaten since breakfast.*

Her hair was wet. Needed drying before she wanted to eat. It didn't seem he was giving her a choice. He pulled the towel from her hair then made an attempt to towel-dry the length. Her hair was too thick. She would need to sit in front of the fire and comb it for the strands to dry. Doing so would take most of an hour.

"After we finish our meal, I'll brush your hair for you." He ushered her into the dining room. "Would enjoy that."

Brush her hair? That was the last thing she wanted him to do. The man was too handsome. Too intimidating. Too exciting. Worst of all he set strange notions stirring inside her body she didn't understand. If she were with Aunt Ella, she would ask about those feelings. She wasn't. She could never ask this man who would either smirk or laugh at her questions. Who might take advantage of her lack of knowledge. She didn't trust him. Not one *wee* bit. If given a chance, he would run right over her.

"No...no!" Holding up her hands as if the tiny gesture would sway him from the course he was set on. "Y-you c-can't brush my h-hair. It...it w...wouldn't be proper." She stammered out the words, berating herself about letting his presence get the best of her.

Again, the brow was lifted as if he speculated about another idea she wouldn't understand. His expression told her if he thought it best for him to brush her hair, he would do as he pleased. "Whatever pleases you. It is a tangled mess. I'm very good at brushing hair. Used to brush my mother's when it was so tangled a comb couldn't be drawn through the length. She never had the patience to do it herself. With my lovers when we finish, their hair is always smothered in tangles. Love the feel of the silken strands while they glide between my fingers. Ever had a man brush your hair? I would be your first?"

Her body quivered at his words. The thought provoked. "You brushed your mother's hair?" *His lovers? When they finished? What did they finish?* She choked. His statement took her by surprise. Her eyes widened. He didn't seem like a man who would care so much about a single person that he would brush anyone's hair.

"Yes. The fact surprises you. I can see it in your eyes. Mother was older. Her arthritis was terrible. When she was tired, she had trouble holding a comb or brush. With my lovers...they enjoyed the additional attention. My fingers gliding along their scalp, well that always led to more fun. We'll start with a comb. It's easier to untangle hair with a comb than fingers."

The man had her steaming again. It seemed to be a constant state when he was nearby. "You're not brushing or combing my hair!"

She found herself yelling at him. Mortified that he would believe he could say the words and expect her to allow whatever it was he commanded.

"We will see." He held out the chair for her. "This dress is much more fashionable than the last one. The fabric is acceptable as is the modest decolletage. You look stunning by the way."

"Thank you, I was pining for your approval." She managed to bite her tongue wishing she could hold the sarcasm back. If she meant to stay her allotted four more days, she would need to do something about the way she replied to Mister Talmadge. Nicer, even more polite would work. Sugar coated words were too obvious a deviation.

His snort of laughter told her he didn't care about sarcasm. It seemed he enjoyed her antagonism. A challenge she didn't want to give him. She didn't know why he brought out the worst in her.

He splashed wine into her glass then into his own. Holding the glass high, he said, "I propose a toast." He waited for her to reciprocate before he continued. "To a few more congenial days together. May they proceed in much the same way as this afternoon." He added almost as an afterthought, "I came here to relax. Would like to believe it's possible."

"Mr. Talmage," she paused while she thought of the right words, "if we stay out of each other's way, I'm certain this arrangement will work for both of us. Relaxing is what I also wished for when I arrived."

She grinned at his scowl of displeasure. It seemed he didn't want to stay away from her.

"Call me Tam."

She nodded, "Mr. Talmage," delighted in the second scowl he shot her way.

She saw that he gritted his teeth.

~ * ~

Even though she was the most disagreeable woman he ever met, Tam had no intention of staying out of her way. For some reason she intrigued him. Fascinated all his masculine senses. More than anything else, she irritated him with her unladylike behavior. For all he knew, she could be the spawn of the devil. Nonetheless, he saw something refreshing, unique in the way she tackled life. She made him smile when he least expected it. After that she scared him near to death with her antics. When he first saw her tearing across the flat meadow, afraid for her life, his heart leapt to his throat. He did believe she needed help to keep the huge stallion in line. The lady was so tiny. Too small to be riding that stallion or any stallion. If it was possible to feel scared to death, that would describe his reaction. If he had a say about the animal she rode, he would never allow her on top of a huge horse such as Dex. As things stood now, he didn't have a say. That could change.

Once he set her across his thighs, he was mesmerized by her bare legs. An immediate need to run his hands along them flooded his senses. His masculine nerves twitched. Her legs were long, slim and white. He imagined them wrapped around his flanks. When he spoke to her, his callous speech surprised him. It wasn't his habit to degrade a woman's reputation as he did hers. Much to his chagrin, this woman brought out all his worst instincts. Even at that baiting as well as teasing she was enjoyable. She never seemed to take him with the seriousness his words deserved. He adored the way her cheeks turned rosy with embarrassment. If he didn't miss a guess, she was clueless to the challenges along with the not so subtle innuendos he tossed her way.

She didn't like him. That part puzzled him. In his recollection, he'd never met a woman who acted this way toward him. If she knew he was a titled aristocrat, a marquess until his father passed, she would change her mind so fast it would make his head spin. Women were like that. Tam didn't doubt that salient fact for a moment as he admitted to himself he was jaded where women were concerned. The mere mention of his title had women dancing attendance, fawning over him, hoping to catch his attention. As of yet, he never met a woman who didn't worship a title along with his money. Whenever he could, he kept his aristocratic inheritance to himself. Doing so wasn't easy. Most places he traveled he was recognized. It was obvious this woman didn't know who he was. Tam meant to keep their relationship that way. He wanted her to know him. To understand who this man was, with or without a title.

For his part, he wished to learn as much about her as he could. What he did understand was The Duchess was her aunt, the duke her uncle. That would make her what...? When she introduced herself, she didn't put the title lady in front of her name. No, she was Kerrie Johnston, plain and simple. He wondered if she was related to the Johnston shipping magnate living on the eastern coast of England. That might be attributed to the fact she owned that magnificent animal. Once at Newmarket he heard a reference to the Johnston stables. Heard also it was run by a woman. Could that woman be her mother? It certainly could not be her. She wasn't old enough. No matter, obvious to him, the girl was given everything she wanted. Was spoiled from the top of her pretty little head to her tiny toes he'd not seen yet. He could imagine tasting her toes.

Interesting.

What could he do to change her dislike of him...perhaps lust for him? Lust was a heady thought. He reminded himself he didn't like the way she acted or the risks she took even though in too many ways to count she was adorable. A few tumbles in the big bed upstairs with her would be entertaining. Would get her out of his system. He would have to use all his available charm to sweet talk her into his arms, after that beneath the sheets. Doing so would be hard unless he could change her aversion to him to something a bit more positive. He would need to temper his speech. Hold back on the commands. Tam had to admit he got off to a bad start when he snatched her from her horse. As things now stood between them, she wasn't going to fall into his waiting arms anytime soon. Where it concerned him, her hackles were up, all her defenses in place. She bristled when she saw him. Turned her chin up. Stubborn little thing. The woman persisted in a battle she didn't need to fight. One she couldn't win.

While Tam stood at his window watching her as she disrobed then bathed, it took all his strength of will not to join her in the swim or bath as it turned out to be. Nothing could stop him from observing. A gentleman would never stare. Where this lady was concerned being a gentleman would never do. The sight of her slim body was just as delectable to his senses as he imagined while he held her this afternoon. Staring at her backside, her well-shaped butt as she waded into the lake, sent all his senses reeling. On the other hand, when she left the water, her camisole as well as the pantalettes she wore plastered against her feminine curves inflamed every masculine part he possessed. She was rounded in all the places he appreciated the most. There was enough moonlight to point all that out to him. He wished he could see the color of her nipples...in time.

While she dressed, he decided he would meet her at the back door. Her knowledge that he watched her bathe then dress seemed necessary for his plans to move forward. Let her wonder how much he witnessed. She would never be certain. He wouldn't say. The meal was quite good. The chef Drake employed was a master. The man created palatable dishes from everything imaginable. Though he couldn't help but wonder at Kerrie's cooking skills. He decided he would send the chef back to the village for more vacation days. Spending a bit of time in the kitchen with this woman might be fun. Working side by side would prove interesting. Tam imagined many different scenarios that would keep them busy.

He would maintain the maid. Needed to keep someone to tidy the lodge. Send the cook home, yes. The stableboy needed to stay. Without one...he paused in thought. Kerrie was a tiny woman. The top of her head didn't reach his chin. For that matter didn't reach his armpits. Her stallion was huge. She must saddle that big horse of hers by herself. The beast stood at least seventeen hands. Until he arrived with the stableman, there was no one to do the duty of saddling for her. Her ability left him in awe. Unless she had some trick, she would be hard-pressed to heave a saddle onto the stallion's back. Her arms were not that big around. Muscle was lacking.

A trick.

She would have some gimmick.

Across the table from her, he watched. Her light brown hair was streaked with touches of the sun, red in places as well as ash blond to white. Her pert little nose tipped up at the end. The lips he wished to taste were full, almost

Too full for a woman her size. He would like to see them swollen from his ardent attention. Her eyes were the same color as the whiskey in the crystal glass he poured himself while he watched her. When she strode from the lake, he noticed the firm round globes tipped with hardened buds. They were the size of fresh peaches ready to be plucked. He was the man to do the plucking.

After she finished the first glass, he refilled both his as well as hers. She slanted him a cross-eyed stare which produced a short chuckle he would never hide. This woman was his delight. So different from the women of his acquaintance. Pushing his plate away, replete, he leaned back in the chair. Rested his hands on his belly.

"If you are finished with the meal, would you wish to retire to the sitting room? I'm ready to comb out your hair. It is beginning to dry. All the strands will be tangled together. Quite a mess. I can fix that for you." To his surprise, her hair was curly. The few tendrils that dried while they ate dinner curled with beguiling tenacity around her forehead. He needed to feel the texture, run the stands between his fingers.

She choked on a sip of her wine, sending a few drops from her mouth. With the napkin at her plate, she wiped the tiny red drops away. "Didn't I tell you I don't want you to comb my hair? Do you have trouble recalling facts? Perhaps your hearing is lacking."

"You don't need to be rude. I'm just trying to be nice. Come along, now. Sit by the fire." Tam stood. Held out his hand. The maid he hired turned up with both her brush as well as her comb. He held them as he motioned toward the door. "If I don't do the honors, no one does. Not even you. Your locks will remain a tangled mess. Is that what you want? In the morning, they might be impossible to comb out. Would have to cut your beautiful hair."

"You've confiscated all my combs? How rude?" She muttered the last words while stomping off to the sitting room.

A gentleman Tam never claimed to be, though he could be gallant from time to time. What she told him implied she might have more than one of each. His maid assured him she did not when he excused himself from the table for a brief chat with the woman. He grinned, charmed by the flash of her amber eyes that deepened to a whiskey hue when she didn't like something. There was no further protest. Kerrie understood she lost this bout with him. If he had his way, he would allow her the win every now and then just to keep life from becoming a bore. He didn't want her to believe she would never get her way. He could afford to be generous in order to keep life interesting.

She did plop down on the hearth. He wanted her between his legs. Cuddled right up to his groin. He wished for her to feel his arousal. The proof of his willingness to bed her. If she noticed, he would enjoy the flood of color to her face. At this juncture in the building of their brief but pleasant relationship, she would never succumb. The fight was on because he did want her...and...he wasn't about to lose the battle.

"Not on the hearth."

Tam sat down. While he was leaning against a chair facing the fire, he patted the place in front of him. Shaking her head as if he was giving her a choice amused him. He would seduce her his way, not hers. This would take time, since to him, it was obvious she still held doubts concerning his charming self. He still believed she was disagreeable as well as annoying. However, she captivated every male part of him.

"Why? You don't like me. Why would you wish to do any of this?" she asked, the puzzle in her expression as well as her eyes there for him to read.

"I've never said that I didn't like you." He wasn't going to point out to her that she didn't care for him very much either. "You're a beautiful woman. I admire stunning women." That was a fact that could never be argued. Like was such a tepid word to use between two passionate individuals. Some of the women he bedded before, he didn't like. However, he never slept with a woman he didn't lust for. This woman made his heart pulse too fast. Heated his body with his imagination of what was beneath her gowns. He imagined since she was a niece of the duke and duchess, he should be careful how he approached her. If he didn't take precautions, he could find...hell, he was risking a marriage by pursuing this course.

Rethinking would be prudent.

Tam didn't believe he could do anything less than pursue his immediate plans. Damn the possible consequences. If something happened, he could sidestep as well as any man. Duels were illegal. He would never fight a duel with Drake Montgomerie. Never!

Kerrie blinked a few times as if she tried to understand the gist of his comments. Tam patted that place in front of him where he wanted her. In lieu of speaking, she sat where he insisted. One small step at a time. As much as he wished to hold those ripe peaches of hers in his hands, he wasn't about to caress her with intimacy until she begged. His hands around her hips, he pulled her close. She touched her body against his. Her little rump delighted him as she wiggled to get comfortable pushing against his inflamed sex.

She cleared her throat. "How long are you staying?" Kerrie asked with a soft sigh as he began to comb through the tangled strands. Inhaling, exhaling with each gentle stroke she supported herself against him. Her hands were on his thighs.

"Depends."

He held a strand in his hand, working his way from the bottom until he untangled the length. She sipped her wine. The pattern repeated until he was satisfied with the job. He put the comb on the hearth before picking up the brush.

"On what?"

To Tam, with no apparent reason she sounded angry. For the time he was combing her hair, he believed she relaxed. Felt the softening, of her body. She was stiff again.

"Don't be so vague. You owe me a decent answer. I came here to be alone. Your presence put a decided damper on my plans," she snorted as if she didn't like the gist of his comment.

That was something else that intrigued him. Her tiny unladylike snorts of disapproval. This wasn't the first one she gifted him with. Now he understood what she wanted from him. She wished for him to leave. Not until he'd seen this relationship to the proper conclusion. With a smile, she couldn't see, he said, his voice soft close to her ear, his lips touching. Whispers floating along her flesh. "I'm leaving when you leave. Won't have any female going down that trail alone. A woman needs protection. Even if she doesn't think she needs a guard at her back, she does."

He wasn't going to elaborate about thieves as well as the possibility of an abduction. Kerrie should be brilliant enough to figure out something of that nature. Also, some of the other consequences of going it alone she might encounter.

"No, you're not!" She recoiled, turning to glare at him, breaking the subtle mood he created. "I won't have it. You are not going with me!" Each word was punctuated with a jab of her finger on his chest.

"Look at the fire, little one. We will see. My company is not so bad."

Her return to her uncle, a good friend of his, would be done his way. Not hers, no, never her way. She might not return with her innocence intact. Nonetheless, she would return alive, unscathed in any other way. Drake wouldn't appreciate losing a niece to cutthroats of any kind. Hell, even the animals could be dangerous to her wellbeing.

He kept the chuckle to himself when she obeyed his command. Perhaps this little lady was more biddable than he thought. When he started brushing her hair, she settled into him again. A lady who enjoyed her creature comforts. From what his mother told him, the strokes were soothing, calming her when the day was at an end. He pushed her long hair over her shoulders so he could continue brushing while she leaned on him.

"This feels so good," Kerrie murmured, seeming to forget her aversion to him.

That was fine by him. She came both ways, hot and cold. One moment she bristled as well as glowered at him, the next she sighed in contentment. Kerrie wasn't as immune to him as she let herself believe. "There are a lot of things we can do together that will make us feel this good. With your go ahead we could explore all the different possibilities. Tonight, if you like."

"What things?" She'd pushed away from him again, her golden eyes taking on a bedroom, dreamy kind of look. He imagined that's how they would look when she woke in the morning or after good sex. "What are you implying? I'm not..."

It seemed she wasn't at all certain of herself or what he wished for. "We could start with the discussion about the bed in the master chamber. Take the wine upstairs along with a few of those delicious cakes," he spoke close to her ear. Felt the shiver of delight pass through her. The female part of her body hummed to life. Once she agreed, Tam held no doubts about her passion. She would be a delight as a lover.

"I'm not sharing your bed if that's what you are getting at. I'm not..." She stiffened again, retreating to the chilly voice he wished to have no part of experiencing. Kerrie resumed her position against him. "Remember, I don't like you. Don't lovers have to like each other first? I don't have any intention of giving into carnal pleasures."

"No, just lust for each other. Like plays no part between lovers. That is all that is needed. Lust. It's a wonderful condition. Hot. Wet. Sex." Inside he was chuckling at her naiveties.

"Mr. Talmadge?" Her tone was one of outrage.

He ignored the bristling. "When you leave here, where are you going? Did you tell me before? If you did, seems I've forgotten." He asked, trying to remember if she mentioned a destination. He would escort her wherever it was she was headed. He wasn't about to leave her to her own devices that would get her into more trouble than she could handle.

"Don't recall if I mentioned my destination to you. None of your business. Since you asked and you were nice, to London. Supposed to find a husband. Don't want one. Especially one with a title. Want to marry a man who can do a good day of work. One who doesn't believe he is entitled just because there is a title in front of his name. Who doesn't mince around at balls or hold his handkerchief with the dainty tips of his fingers. Don't wish to have a dandy as my husband. If I did want to marry someday, I want a real man."

Tam kept his yowl of laughter behind his teeth. No, he needn't tell her he was about to become the next Duke of Sherburn. She would run the opposite direction. Good God, what she described was not that far from the truth. He would have to show her not all titled aristocrats were dandies. He found he was pleased she didn't want a husband. Though, from what he'd seen of her so far, the little piece of baggage needed someone to look after her. Recalling how she rode Dex, it seemed she didn't have an iota of common sense. To keep her safe. A husband would do the trick. Didn't all women wish to marry? Have children? Why didn't Kerrie? He wasn't thinking straight. Needed to learn the truth.

"Why don't you want a husband?" Tam asked, curious if she would give him a good reason. "All women wish for the security a husband could bring, a meal ticket."

He laughed while he felt her back stiffen. Wished he could watch her eyes flare as well as her brows knit together. What other emotions danced through her female brain? They were suited in many different ways. He didn't want a wife, at least not yet. He had a few more good years of bachelorhood in front of him.

She didn't turn around. The sight of her expression would be nice. He imagined her flashing eyes. Full lush lips thinned in displeasure. From this vantage point he recognized the tilt of her chin.

"I've a million and one reasons." She wiggled against him, adjusting herself, inflaming him further. "I don't need to explain my reasoning to you. You mean nothing to me. I don't even know anything about you."

"Why don't you enlighten me as to one or two reasons. Assuage my curiosity. I'll be certain to let you know if I believe them to be valid."

Tam ran his fingers through the silken length of her hair, brought a few strands to his nose to catch the scent she favored. It was something he would tuck away in his memory. The fragrance was vanilla. Unusual. Most women seemed to like something stronger.

"Well..." she paused, moved again, caressing his hard length with her backside.

He was tormenting himself. Wouldn't do anything different. Though he couldn't guarantee where his hands would roam. He felt a male urge to cup her breasts, test the tips. See if they hardened with his caress.

It seemed she was experimenting. Trying to figure out things. A sudden flash of possible insight caught him. "Do you have siblings? A brother or two? Younger? Older." An answer to this question could give him a few clues as to what she was doing with her sweet curvaceous butt.

"How many questions are you going to ask me? I haven't answered the first one yet." Her indignant huff brought more amusement to the forefront. Kerrie turned the question back on him. "Do you have siblings?"

"If that's how you want to play this, let's start with siblings. We can get to the husband question later. It's not a topic I'll ignore." His hands settled on her shoulders. A light massage would relax this little bedeviler of men a bit more. Her head fell forward as his fingers orchestrated more magic. Dictated her reactions. He heard the soft sigh as he worked the knots from her muscles.

"Don't understand why that would matter. If you must know, I have one sister. Her name is Kelsey. Oh...that feels so good." Kerrie sighed again.

She was falling into his plans with seeming ease. He never thought her seduction would be this easy. Perhaps he deluded himself. As of this moment, he held no proof she was seduced.

"No brothers, then you wouldn't have seen..."

Tam decided not to go that route. They would be here for several days. He didn't want to shock her until she liked him.

"None..." Her little mewl of pleasure made him grin.

Tam wondered what she would sound like in other circumstances begetting pleasure. He set her away from him, intent on putting distance between them before he took something that wasn't offered. If he wasn't going to find relief tonight, he didn't need more sexual stimulation. She should retire for the evening. For Tam, a swim in the cold lake would help ease the heat building to an inferno.

Placing her on a large chair facing the dying fire, he filled both their glasses with the sweet wine that was stocked in the kitchen. "Here, you can give me all the reasons you don't want a husband."

She pushed hair from her face. "I don't appreciate being told what to do. Imagine you've noticed. A husband would have rights I'm not willing to give to another person let alone a man. To do so, I would have to trust the man. Except for my father as well as my uncles, I've never met a man who could be trusted."

"That's only...relatives don't count." If she were his, she wouldn't ride Dex unless he was on the horse's back with her. She would never like that dictate. His word would stand. As to Dex, his command would be law. He couldn't think of anything else. The need to protect this tiny female seemed to be in the forefront of his mine.

"Well..." She drummed her fingertips on the arm of the chair. Her face turned the rosy hue he enjoyed.

She was about to embarrass herself. How she would do it would please him. "Well?" he parroted, anticipating an enjoyable answer.

"I heard these two women..." She downed half her glass of wine then a bit more. "I wasn't eavesdropping, you know. I don't make a habit of listening to conversations that don't involve me. They were talking about..." She looked up, stopping then blinked a few times. "I'm not telling you this." She finished her glass of wine made to stand up, wavered then sat back down.

"Embarrassing?" He grinned anticipating what was yet to follow.

"Mortifying," she stated with a firm voice. "I don't understand what they were speaking of but what they said was strange. A man poking...never mind." Kerrie waved her hand in the air. Her face turned the color of a beet. "They were loud, laughing. I wasn't listening in on a private conversation, mind you."

"If you can't speak of sex maybe there is a third reason you don't want a husband." He sipped his wine watching the play of emotions on her face. Her eyes widened. "Is that what they were talking about? Sex?"

"Imagine so."

Tam didn't intend to say anything more to this delightful innocent. He was going to have to rethink his approach along with his intentions. With each tick of the clock, he liked this lady more than she annoyed him. "A third reason?"

"Don't want to share a bed with anyone. A man would take up too much room. I'd end up on the floor if I wasn't careful. Men snore. I'm certain it's difficult to sleep with all that noise next to your head."

She would end up beneath her husband more often than on the floor. If she became his, he would never push her from his bed. He would pull her close. Hold her tight. Explore all her feminine delights. "Is that all? Beds can be made to fit two people with lots of room left over."

"Why don't you want a wife?" she asked, holding her glass out inviting him to pour more wine into it. "Don't you think it's your turn to answer a question or two? I've held up my share of this question and answer interrogation."

"You're going to get foxed if you keep that up."

He evaded the question. Poured more wine for her enjoyment. He would never complain if she became a little tipsy. Would enjoy the possibilities. Maybe she would giggle. Some feminine giggles he enjoyed.

She lifted the fragile shoulders he'd been massaging a few minutes ago. The gesture was delightful as well as intriguing. Some of the best parts of her moved with the uprising of her shoulders. Tam found himself fascinated by the view. They'd gotten off to a rough start today. Tonight was turning out better. The conversation was interesting. The possibilities were intriguing. He began to make plans.

"I don't care," Kerrie told him. She was leaning back, her head settled on the back of the chair. With her eyes closed she seemed to enjoy the small conversation between them. "Why don't you wish for a wife?" She persisted.

"I do want a wife. It's my duty. Need an..."

Tam didn't want to get into the part about needing heirs. He was twenty-nine. His father would pass soon. The duke questioned him many times about a possible woman in his life. To this date he never met a woman he could live with or wanted to live with the rest of his life. When he did wed, he meant to be faithful. He understood enough about himself that while he might not love his wife, he would care about her. Tam wasn't certain if love existed or how love felt. As the new duke when the title became his, he had a duty to continue the line. Before he left for the hunting box, his father reaffirmed that fact. His father hoped to see a wedding then a grandchild. Just as Kerrie was going to find a husband she said she didn't want, he was going to London in search of a wife.

"Duty..."

She sat up staring at him with a puzzled expression. "Don't tell me you're one of those fops? An aristo playing at being a man?" Kerrie paused for a beat. Looked at him. "You don't..." she cut her words short. He wondered why.

He took umbrage at her assumption. "I would never presume to tell you that. A fop? Do I look like a mincing dandy? Have you ever seen me hold a handkerchief between my fingers then bring it to my nose? Granted you haven't known me very long...a day." Tam didn't understand why he was offended by her questions. Nevertheless, he was hurt. "I've never played at being a man." He was all man. Male to the tips of his toes. He never needed to pretend in any way.

Kerrie relaxed back in the chair. Her breath left her as a soft release. "That's a relief?" she sighed again. "No, doubt if you would have to make a game of being a man there would be repercussions. If I discovered you were titled, I'd leave first thing in the morning. Would make certain to leave without you knowing."

"Why? Do you have thoughts of marriage with me?" Tam grinned wondering how she would respond.

She took her time. Slipped her tongue across her bottom lip soaking up a few errant drops of wine in the process. She was foxed. He didn't have one doubt in his mind. She sat up seeming outraged. Her shoulders shook. "Good...God...no! You don't like me. If I did agree to marriage with a man, it would never be to one who didn't like me."

They were back to that. Tam reminded her just to point out a noticeable fact, "You don't like me either."

"True...though I do enjoy the way you brushed my unruly hair. Could get used to the attention. I did like the massage too. Every night would be nice... My legs...they would love that kind of attention. The muscles do get a workout controlling Dex. Sometimes they cramp."

She flushed when she mentioned a massage on her legs, seeming to realize after she spoke about the placement of his hands that might entail.

At the thought of any part of this delicate woman getting a workout on that horse left his stomach sour. Tam understood for the time being, he needed to hold his tongue on this matter until he was ready to make a decision regarding his possible relationship with her. Enraging her would set his plans back. If he kept her from her horse, she would be furious. Her safety was more important than her anger. He cared about her. How much he didn't yet know.

His mind wandered to thoughts of massaging those legs every night. He knew what would happen when he did. She didn't. By the rosy blush tinging her cheeks Kerrie might have some idea. He doubted that fact.

"It's best you go to bed before you imbibe too much." He took the wine glass from her hand. "Can you walk?"

She pushed against the arms of the chair before falling back. "Of course, I can walk."

Grinning, he waited to see the result of her efforts. He meant to allow Kerrie to come to her own conclusions.

When she tried again then failed, he swept her into his arms. Hers went around his neck. By the time he reached the second floor her head was nestled against his chest as were the soft curves of her breasts. He pushed the door to her room open with his foot then set her on the bed. Stepping back, Tam watched her wondering what she would do next. He was leaving everything up to her.

When she didn't speak or make a move, he said, "Unless you want me to help you with your nightgown, you will have to sleep in your clothes." His hands were on his hips as he waited for her answer. In this possible endeavor, he was a willing man. All she needed to do was say the words.

She twisted then leaned forward presenting her back to him. "Just undo the back of my gown. I can take it from there. I accept your help."

Tam stepped back, shaking his head as if to say no. Instead, he swore beneath his breath. Did her bidding then stomped from the room slamming the door closed on his way. The simmering anger was not something he understood. He alone orchestrated this scenario. If he'd left well enough alone, he wouldn't be hard as steel. Needing to be deep inside her. She escalated his desire without attempting to do so.

Downstairs, wishing she was in his bed, he gazed into the fire. His fingers threaded through his hair. Not many of the burning embers were left. Instead of finishing off the bottle of wine, he poured himself a generous amount of brandy. Unless he got foxed, sleep wasn't going to come to him tonight. Maybe by dawn he would sleep. His body whirred with life. If he could find a suitable woman besides the one upstairs, he would take her to his bed. He adjusted his pants then stared at the ceiling while he inhaled long deep breaths. This lady was working her way into his heart. He didn't want a woman in his heart, just in his bed.

The only relief in sight was the lake. Tam hoped the water was cold enough to slake the lust burning in him. Frigid would be perfect to relieve his needs. Shirking out of his clothes as he walked, they landed wherever they came off. By the time he reached the dock, he was ready for the cold plunge.

A long shallow dive brought him into the water. He swam beneath the surface until he could hold his breath no longer. After he surfaced, he gasped for air. The lake was damn cold but not frigid enough to ease his need for the enchanting woman upstairs. When she bathed a few hours earlier, she gave no indication how cold the water was. His little Kerrie was tougher than she appeared at first glance. He still wasn't about to reconsider her horse. If she was his... She would be his, she wasn't going to ride that beast. The decision was made. Like it or not, he would make sure she didn't ride Dex.

Since he was immersed in the coldest water he'd been in for years, he made the most of the event. He swam across the lake before returning. When he climbed out, he stretched out on the dock. He watched a few clouds ghost the moon. Stared at the twinkling stars. Tam loved it up here. Wished this lodge was his. He meant to buy a place like this for himself. Decided he would look into the matter as soon as he returned home.

His laughter echoed across the lake. What would he do if she came down for a swim? He was butt naked. Brought no towel with him. His clothes were scattered from here to the house. Imagined he could dream about making love in the lake with only the water separating her body from his. That was one place he never tried. Wondered how it would feel to only have a thin layer of water between them. A fantasy, one or two, might be nice. Might keep him going through the night. If he fantasized enough, he wouldn't walk to her room to find out if she was as soft and warm everywhere as she looked.

~ * ~

"What are you up to this time, Ella?" Drake, duke to The Duchess of London, asked with a wicked grin. "All I have to do is look into those beautiful eyes of yours and I know you're having wicked thoughts. You're plotting something. Can't keep secrets. Need to tell me or...might not make love to you tonight."

She would know he could never keep that promise. So, she continued in the vein that she thought would reap the greatest rewards. Ella plucked at her skirts, keeping her face down, her lashes lowered. When she looked up, she said with innocence in her voice. "Why ever do you ask? You believe I'm up to something? What could that be, I wonder?"

She was smiling through her teeth as if secrets abounded in her head. They usually did. His woman possessed a lively imagination. It seemed once she decided to accept her nieces as charges for their seasons, she became an extraordinary matchmaker. Ella handpicked the man she hoped would work for each of her charges. Funny that she always made the best decisions. For Ella nothing was left to chance. She researched. Dug into the man's background. Of course, she knew her nieces from birth. Understood all their likes along with their dislikes. She was astute while dealing with *amour*. Ella understood their needs too. Something far more important.

Drake recognized the look. His wife was plotting the next wedding. They just managed to get Tara wedded to Case. Now it seemed

Kerrie Johnston would arrive soon to begin her journey to find a husband. Kerrie never made a secret of the fact she didn't want or need a husband. Just like her mother, she was happiest tending to her horses. She despised men with titles. No one understood why.

Indeed, her carriage should arrive in a few days according to Kerrie. That was odd because he remembered the missive from her father, Hadden, who told him the arrival date. The two didn't match. He received two different messages. The one from Kerrie arrived a day or so ago telling him she didn't leave as soon as expected. She would arrive a week later.

An idea plummeted to his head. He wasn't positive but things were no longer adding up. Ella must also understand that. He tapped a finger on his chin. "Did you know, or did you read the correspondence I had from Sterling Talmage that was sitting on my desk?"

The little sneak. There wasn't a doubt in his mind that she read every word. He scrubbed his hand across his jaw still thinking, still wondering if some shenanigans weren't going on here. Chance might also have a hand in his imaginings. He would never put it past his wife to put these two in the line of fire. They might well be perfect for each other. He had to admit to that. Tam wanted a woman who wasn't after him because of his wealth coupled with his title. Kerrie didn't wish to be burdened with a title. If they fell in love, both could be assured what they felt for each other was true love. The if was a big one. The lie would be even bigger if it was continued.

Ella's smile was all sugar. "Should I have? Did you want me to read it? Would be pleased to do so. Only if that is what you want."

Ella had that devious innocent look he learned about years ago. With her head tilted just a bit to the side, he acknowledged the significance. She was plotting a union. It must be Stirling and her niece Kerrie. They might not appreciate her efforts. If they fell in love, they would thank her later. Drake knew Stirling was far too serious for a woman with such boundless energy as Kerrie possessed. He did need a woman with backbone, a woman who would laugh with ease. That was Kerrie. So far, Ella pegged every match right. Her record was unblemished. Not that there hadn't been problems that needed fixing before the happy couple could say, 'I do.'

"You know better than to tamper with the papers on my desk."

He would laugh except this was an issue he needed to make certain she understood. They'd been married too long for her not to comprehend all the delicate matters that crossed his bureau. Reading the wrong paper could possibly put her life in danger. He wouldn't stand for that. He would need to take better care of the paperwork.

The look of outrage on her face brought out a bark of laughter he would never hide. She snorted, very unlike a duchess let alone The Duchess. She did have her reputation to uphold. "Would never touch one piece of paper on your desk. I'm shocked speechless to hear you ask that question." Her apparent indignation caused him to chuckle anew. He knew she lied. Ella wouldn't touch but she would manipulate.

Now he was getting the gist of what happened. One of his letters must have drifted to the floor or his chair. Provoked by a wave of her hand or unprovoked...didn't make a difference. He would never know the truth. She might have had the maid sweep her feather duster over the top until something fell off. If that happened, his wife would have no qualms about reading whatever flew away from his desk. She would be innocent of all but curiosity. She didn't lie.

"What is it you did, Ella? I know there is something I will have the answer to sooner than later. Something I will have to explain away." Drake imagined that Ella would have all bases covered. Not only was she a passionate woman she was also very intelligent. She did love seeing her nieces wed to acceptable men. Men who would complement the woman, love her as well. Taking over her Aunt Charlotte's job was the joy of her life. She had so many nieces that would come to London for a season. That didn't count all the nephews if they failed to find suitable wives on their own. Ella was more than willing to urge the progress along with each new recruit.

Her bright smile could still send him to his knees. At this juncture in time what he wanted was to toss her skirts then have her here on his desk. He would do the sweeping of the papers despite the fact that afterward he would have to sort through all the ledgers.

She lifted small feminine shoulders, "Just set the wheels in motion. That's all. Promise you, they will find love together. The letter fell on the floor. I couldn't help myself. I did read the missive. Nothing from all your secret dealings. Nothing important."

"You gave Kerrie the go ahead to stay at the hunting box even though you knew someone else would be there." His words were not a question. He understood for a fact that was what she did.

"No, Kerrie never asked. Her driver sent word that she intended to take a week at the lodge. I never wrote back that it would be occupied by Sterling, letting chance take its course. Whatever could be wrong with that?"

Ella looked so proud of herself. He wasn't going to tamper her enthusiasm.

"You understand our niece despises titled lords. It's one of the reasons she was loathe to have a season. Sterling Talmage is a marquis, soon to be a duke. He will not be to her liking. Mark my words, Kerrie will reject him without giving the poor man a chance."

"Sterling isn't the usual aristocrat. Something happened to Kerrie she won't speak of. Storm was certain it had something to do with the viscount, whatshisname, that visited the village last year. She is quite lovely. Exceptional. Unique. The man made a pass at her. She snubbed him. The next time he saw her he tried to force her. From what I've heard, one of the village lads stopped the rape. Now she believes all titled lords are cut from the same cloth. Except you, of course."

"That's the way of it. Don't think she was violated? Not that it would matter to a man who fell in love with her. She would tell him. Wouldn't she?" Drake paced the room, looking to his wife then his desk. From now on, he would have to be more careful about his correspondence. If it was that easy for his wife to peruse his desk, what would happen if someone meant the government harm. Sensitive papers still crossed his desk. Two years ago, their home was ransacked by a man seeking information. He had his enemies. Wouldn't do to put Ella in harm's way or his children. He thought of the count who despised him. The man threatened him. His son was a known assassin.

"What do you think is happening at the hunting lodge?" Ella asked with that dreamy expression on her face telling him she was thinking about love. Also remembering their stay at the same place. The ultimatum that brought them together.

"I hope the two of them are not scratching each other's eyes out. I fear for Sterling if Kerrie discovers he's about to become a duke."

"Kerrie will suffer if he gets all autocratic about her riding. It's not normal for a woman to ride a horse such as Dex. You would never have protested if I rode him," Ella poured them both tea. Set a lump of sugar in each cup. "She will rebel. We both understand Tam's archaic notions about females. I believe Kerrie is just the lady to set him straight about those outdated notions."

At everything his wife spouted, Drake groaned. "I need brandy, not tea. Do you think we should pay a surprise visit to the hunting box? Help ease the tension we know will grow between those two?" Drake asked while he splashed a generous amount of brandy in his cup.

"Heavens no! We might interrupt something important. Something that might embarrass all of us." Ella's demure smile didn't surprise him.

Little minx, Drake didn't think anything would embarrass his wife. She would always find a way to turn the situation around. "That is why we should interrupt. We don't want the babe before the right amount of time." As if he'd cared when it came to his relationship with Ella.

Ella peered over the rim of her tea cup with an impish grin on her face. "If the two are right for each other, there is nothing wrong with a dalliance before the wedding to cement the relationship. We cannot be judge or jury given our relationship in that same hunting box."

When she looked up with brows drawn together Drake understood he was about to be reminded of his sordid past along with what he did with her in that same lodge.

He held up his hands in surrender. "I concede."

# Chapter Two

Kerrie woke with a start. After she sat up, she pushed hair from her face. Thoughts of the morning she planned yesterday left her thrilled to get on with her day. She was going fishing. Her rod along with the lures were in the shed near the trail. Her rifle was loaded and ready. She never left anything to chance when she was going into the woods. The narrow path she would take wound down to the stream below. Time alone with her thoughts was something she needed after last night's confusion. Those precious moments alone were the reason she came here before going on to London became apparent again. Tam intruded on those moments.

She snorted, what she understood about the man invading her thoughts. The prude, Tam, wouldn't like her going off by herself. He would protest. What he didn't know wouldn't matter. There was no doubt in her mind that if he knew her intentions, he would either verbally object or try to find a way to stop her. He would even walk with her. Kerrie didn't want company this morning. She needed to sort through all that happened yesterday. Her feelings for him puzzled her. Disturbed in ways she didn't understand. Knowing the man less than twenty-four hours she shouldn't have feelings.

What the man didn't know would never hurt him, she reiterated to herself a second time. She would bring back fish for their breakfast. Just thinking about fried rainbow trout, her stomach rumbled. With haste she pulled on the britches he would complain about then her shirt. Found her hiking boots and socks. After that she braided her hair to keep the flyaway strands from her face. A quick glance in her mirror told her she was presentable.

At the door, she breathed in a deep breath of air then crossed her fingers. Kerrie wasn't certain what she would do if the man was awake. Nothing about him surprised her. He was an enigma. Brazen it out, she supposed, would be the best way to move forward. Well, if he did catch her on her way out, he would need to come along with her. She wasn't stopping for any reason. Not even to argue the pros along with the cons about her adventure. To keep her from her mission, he would need to hog-tie her.

Kerrie didn't meet resistance in any form. No one was about when she walked through the kitchen. Last night Tam sent most of the servants home. She grinned. He sent the cook. He must believe her. She did tell him she could cook. Nothing fancy. The chef last night regaled them with delicacies she would never be able to recreate. She didn't need food meant for aristocrats though she appreciated Uncle Drake along with the fanfare he surrounded himself with. Didn't care if he was a duke. Her uncle was different than most aristos. He worked hard. Spied for the country when he was younger. Put his life on the line for England. That fact was enough to redeem him in her eyes. Now he delegated. Still, he worked. Something he didn't need to do. He had access to more money than he could spend in several lifetimes.

The shed offered all the gear she needed. The sun was beginning to rise enough to cast a few shadows. Fish were easiest caught in the morning. Kerrie scrambled down the hill. The incline was steep but not too difficult for her agile feet. She found her favorite spot from past visits then began to fish.

She loved fly fishing. She was always doing something. All the flies she used, she tied. It took skill to catch fish this way, much preferred over dangling a line in the water then lying back to sleep. She supposed if she wanted to relax and sleep, fishing that way might be preferable. During her childhood, she and her father spent meaningful time fishing the streams near their home. They discussed politics along with horses. She told him her dreams including the horse farm she wanted to establish. For her everything revolved around horses. Hadden understood because for her mother her life revolved around horses until she met her father.

Two hours passed. The sun was now above the tree line. She had five rainbow trout ready for cleaning and cooking. Why, she didn't understand the thought but she hoped to surprise Tam. Didn't know what to think of him. On one hand he was autocratic, demanding, infuriating and on the other he was gentle, sweet at times. The way he brushed her hair last night left her mind spinning with wayward notions she had no business thinking about. She hoped to know his true character before she left for London. This wasn't the actual season, more like the off season. There wouldn't be as many people. That was in part why she selected the fall. Once this idle vacation in the backcountry she chose was over, Kerrie understood she'd never see Tam again. He would never be part of her life. A long-term relationship with anyone wasn't for her. She had goals that didn't include a husband.

When she arrived back at the lodge, the kitchen was all hers just as the stream was hers this morning. Five fish were cleaned and dredged with flour. She scooped some butter into the pan then set two of the fish to sizzle. The other three were ready to go. In a bowl, she whipped up some eggs, added milk along with a pinch of salt. The second pan was for the eggs. Whistling she cut potatoes to go into a third pan. On the fourth burner, water heated for tea.

Kerrie hoped he was hungry. This was a lot of food for two people. She was hungry enough to eat half of this. He should be able to do the other half justice. What she didn't understand was this unbidden need to please the man.

Kerrie didn't hear him approach. She was turning the fish over, the butter sizzling then scrambling the eggs. When his hands settled on her hips, she screeched and jumped at the same time. Droplets of eggs flew from the pan. Tam turned her, his hands on her waist. The blue of his eyes darkened while he stared from her to the pan of fish. Thoughts of a kiss flashed through her brain. She shook off that idea disgusted, reminding herself he didn't like her. He would never kiss her. Besides, his scowl told him he wasn't pleased with something.

"What are you doing? Thought you would still be in bed." He let her go before backing up a step. His gaze swept the length of her. Only if she was blind, would she miss his unmistakable look of disapproval. He was such a killjoy. He could be a prim spinster with no problem.

She told herself she wasn't disappointed he no longer touched her. Even though her heart skipped a beat when his hands settled on her hips. She sent him the widest grin she could muster. Kerrie set her hand on his hard chest. "What does it look like?" Her sarcasm oozed. "I'm making us breakfast. Told you I could cook. Are you hungry? If you recall, you sent Uncle Drake's chef home. You have anything against fish?"

She had the distinct feeling sparks would fly if he questioned her about the fish and how they got into the pan. He would take umbrage over her solitary venture down to the stream in the early morning hours. That was when his autocratic nature would kick in and turn this semi-sweet greeting into something she would rather forget. As she remonstrated earlier, the man had two different sides to him.

"Starving." He poured himself a cup of tea. Pulled out a chair then sat. Resting his forearms on the table, he looked back to the fish. "Where did you get the fish? Don't recall any being here last night." Now his expression was a deep, very dark scowl. "Did I miss something?"

Disappointed she anticipated this reaction correctly, she heaved in a huge breath of air while waiting for the consequences. Sooner was better than later in this case. Get this over with. Tell the man the truth. They would have their disagreement. After that they could enjoy the meal. Honesty. No hedging. He would tell her what he thought. She would tell him her opinion. Already knew what he would say. He was so predictable. She would ignore him or better yet tell him that his notions were antiquated. Which was the truth. Better suited for a different age, the Middle Ages. What could be better than that?

Tossing the eggs onto a platter Kerrie tried for nonchalance. She added a smile in hopes she could sweet talk him into seeing this her way. Sifting in a huge lump of air while endeavoring a large grin, she spoke. "I went fishing at the crack of dawn." She braced herself for the explosion that didn't come.

"You fished the lake? Didn't know there was much there. The best fishing is in the..." His gaze seemed to catch the fact she was putting the last three fish into the frying pan. The air around him heated then froze as he rumbled the last thought around in his head. His eyes darkened. Sizzled just as the fish were doing in their butter. Kerrie braced herself for the explosion she expected.

The man figured it out. Didn't take a genius to do so. Answering him yes or no about the lake fishing wasn't going to happen. Kerrie surmised without any doubt he realized where she'd been. If he asked, she would tell him with straightforward sincerity. There would be no lies between them. Would have to have gone to the stream to catch five fish in this short time. In another pan the potatoes browned. It was time to set the record straight. Get the disagreement over with then enjoy the meal.

"Kerrie!"

She jumped, dropped the spatula then grimaced at his tone. She picked the fallen utensil up, rubbed it on her apron hoping that would annoy him. The volume with which he shouted her name made her cringe. Spatula in hand again, she turned to shake it at him. Coshing him over the head with the cooking instrument would be preferable. "You don't have to yell at me. The fact is, yes, I went fishing. The second fact is that you are the recipient of my labor. You do enjoy fried fish? There is nothing else to speak of. Not going to argue about something that is in my past."

"Going to the stream by yourself was foolish...out of the question." He waved his hand in the air. "Correct me if I'm wrong. You tackled the path while it was still dark. If you had asked, I would have gone with you." His lowered voice did not bode well for the next few minutes. The tone was more menacing than she'd heard so far from him.

"Semi-dark. Wanted to be alone."

"Picking at straws. I've been down that trail. You could have hurt yourself. No one...I would not have known where to look for you. Bloody everlasting hell! Didn't you think to let me know what you were about? You can't just wander off on a whim. You're female."

Tam turned away from her, strode from the kitchen. He was gone for at least a minute before he returned.

"You noticed. Imagine that," her syrupy smile didn't help the situation.

He seemed to be ignoring that statement. His face wasn't as red with bottled anger now as when he left the room. Calm was always good. She set the platters of food on the middle of the table. Sent him a cheeky grin then what she hoped was a flirtatious smile that would quench his anger. She was pleased this was the extent of the spat. She'd expected more. "Help yourself." Kerrie poured herself a cup of tea and added cream as well as sugar to the brew.

Tam hadn't moved from the spot inside the doorway. His brows were furrowed. The lines around his eyes deep, menacing. With instinct born from watching the arguments of her mother and father, Kerrie understood this wasn't over...not by a long shot. Trying to ignore him for the time being, Kerrie lifted the covers on the food then dished him a generous portion then just as much for herself. The conversation muted. She told herself to breathe. Needed to enjoy the meal. Before his appearance, she was starving.

The early morning exercise made her ravenous. She wasn't about to let him ruin her breakfast because he was in a ridiculous pique. He sat down in the chair across from hers. She ate until she was satisfied. When she finished, she sat back, sipping her cup of tea replete. Throughout the time taking them to eat, nothing was said.

His plate was also empty. Kerrie didn't think she would be hungry again today. She'd have to figure out something for the evening meal. A few snacks should be enough. Maybe he needed more food. Realizing she hoped everything that was going to be said had been said.

"Now that we've finished eating, we need to discuss your behavior."

He drummed his nails on the table. The look on his face was far too serious. Tam acted as if he had a say in what she did or didn't do.

*My behavior? Of all the insane, ridiculous...she didn't have words at the moment to describe her reaction.*

"Did I tell you I don't like you? Loathe the way you think you can dictate to me. I will continue to do as I please. There is nothing to talk about. You have no hold over me. None whatsoever." Here she was arguing when she didn't want to talk about her activities. Holding her breath, waiting for the explosion she thought would have come earlier, she rose to collect the dishes.

Tam's hand shot out to stop her. His fingers gripped her wrist hard. "Stop! That's what the remaining servants are here for. Come along."

Kerrie was getting fed up with that phrase. *Come along.* She didn't want to come along with him anywhere. To no avail, she tugged on her arm. His grip held fast. "No." She objected that he would think to command her. He had no right to do so. She dug in her heels to stop the forward movement. Seemed to do nothing.

"Yes." The underlying tone in his voice was too calm.

"No!" She yanked again. "I'm going riding. You can do whatever you wish. I don't care." He still held on to her arm. Was still pulling her in the direction he wished to go. It didn't matter that so far, he was going where she planned. Kerrie didn't appreciate his tone or manner. This was the man she didn't like.

"We are going on a walk. You and me. We are going to discuss what you, a female, can and cannot do. While I am here with you, you are my responsibility. We will come to an understanding or all privileges will be curtailed unless you are with me. Your father should have taken a sterner hand to his daughter."

*Privileges? Sterner hand? What did that mean?*

"If he did, he would have had my mother to answer to. While I was fishing, I wasn't in danger. My rifle was with me."

"That makes me feel better? Can you use it? If you were confronted with a person, could you shoot the man? Can you aim at a person knowing if you pull the trigger he might die?" The censure in his voice didn't go unnoticed. He let her go content to shadow her.

"No problem, I can shoot. The best marksman in my family. What about you? Right now, with a rifle in my hand, I could shoot you," she told him while his angry strides took her from the kitchen then out the door. She strode to the stable. Nothing or no one was going to stop her from enjoying her early morning ride on Dex. He needed his exercise. So did she.

Kerrie stopped in front of Dex's stall shaken. She gasped. So stunned she was rendered speechless for a few seconds. So, that's what he was doing while she was fishing. A padlock graced the gate. Her hands fisted, she whirled on Tam who stood behind her. He wasn't the least bit surprised or contrite. His arms were across his chest, his feet braced apart. The scowl on his face more apparent than ever. What infuriated her more was that his frown was changing to a wicked smile. One she would love nothing more than to wipe off his smug countenance.

When she found her voice, she yelled. "You didn't! How could you? You've no right to keep me from my horse! What unmitigated gall!"

Her anger spilled from her. Dex nickered as if he sensed her distress. He bucked. Kicked the wood behind him. If there had been room, he would have reared. "Unlock that gate right now!" Her anger boiled over. She was so furious her body shook. "Dex is my horse. Not yours. You can't lock him away from me." While her anger wasn't fading the level of her voice was.

"As long as I'm the only male here to supervise you, I'll assume that right. I told you as much earlier. This is a decision that comes about because I don't want to be responsible for a woman who is fearless as well as witless. Too ignorant of herself to realize she doesn't have the strength to control such a huge animal. Your behavior this morning clarified the truth to me even more. Nothing is going to happen to you on my watch."

"I'm not fearless. Never have been. I just understand my limits. Riding Dex is...is..." Moisture began to clog her eyes then her throat. Crying in front of this despicable man was not something she could do. Instead of allowing him to see her distress, she turned, running from the stable. She ran until a pain hitched in her side. He wasn't following her. He couldn't be so mean. The man was intractable. To think that earlier in the day her feelings toward him were softening. She even went so far as to dream of a kiss.

*Not any longer! I loathe all he stands for. Despise his actions. Wish him six feet under. Horrible despicable man.*

Kerrie didn't know if he would respect her need to be as far from him as possible. She didn't care. Yes, she did. Seeing him or talking to him would be impossible. Slowing to a walk, gasping for air, she kept walking. Continued to put one foot in front of the other. Even though it would take her some time, she was going to her favorite spot overlooking the stream. The stream she was now forbidden to fish. When was he going to forbid her the solitary excursion to the cliff? What hidden dangers lurked here? He was sure to get around to demanding she remain in the lodge. Somehow, she would have to find a way to ignore his plans for her. She could do that. Ignore him then do what she wanted. Sneak from the house when he was busy with something important.

Sterling Talmage was only a man. He couldn't watch over her all the time. Sometimes he needed to sleep.

It would be best if she left. He told her he would leave when she did. No matter what she did, she couldn't get away from him. Damn his handsome hide! Where she was concerned, he now overstepped his boundaries. Kerrie stepped into a hole. Fell flat on her face. Didn't even get her hands out to break the fall before she hit hard. She spit out dirt, cursing him. Her ribs screamed from the contact. That was the moment when she knew he was shadowing her. Heard his footsteps. Tears streaked her face. She pushed herself up. Limping, without looking behind her, she continued as fast as she could. Realized she would never escape him.

When she found a walking stick, the added support helped. She could take some of the weight off her strained ankle. No way, no way was she going to stop. Lord help her, she remembered last night. Sinking into his embrace while he untangled the long damp strands of her hair. Last night when he was brushing her hair, she was beginning to like the gentle side of his nature. In her estimation, the massage brought him up a notch.

With this recent confrontation, the scene brought the horrible man down more pegs than she could count. As far as she was concerned, he had a great deal to answer for.

This morning all those tender thoughts about the man vanished. Changed. He was a man *sans* redemption. She disliked him more now than when he spirited her from her horse assuming she needed help.

That was a mistake. She could forgive mistakes. Today there were no mistakes. Just an arrogant man bent on dictating his wishes. Bent on making her miserable. If wretched was his intention, the ploy worked.

This was flat out mean. Intolerable. Unforgivable. She would never understand his way of thinking. The man didn't believe a woman was capable of doing anything for herself. Thought women to be weak as well as thoughtless creatures unable to make decisions without a man's influence.

He was flat out wrong. She would prove this to him.

"You are foolish to keep going. Walking on a sore ankle can serve only to make the injury worse. I will have to look at the damage done by your impulsive behavior. After we return to the lodge, I'll wrap it up for you. Your ankle could be broken. Though I doubt if it is. Nonetheless, in that case you will not be able to use your limb for some time." Tam was beside her now, slowing his pace to match hers. "You are hurting yourself by attempting to defy me. That's the action of a child, not a grown woman." Tam reiterated, rubbing salt into her wound. He set his hand on her shoulder. She brushed the offending fingers off not wanting him to touch her. Desperate to ignore him, she looked away.

Talking to him would make her cry harder. *Autocratic men! Unbearable men!* There had been one other in her life. She'd let him dictate to her until he showed his true colors. If not for a friend, he would have forced her that day all in the guise of love. She didn't love that man. Had sworn off any man bearing a title. That man didn't love her either. He just wanted her, wished to be her first lover.

Tam wasn't titled. That man was a...she didn't even remember. Thought he might have been a viscount. Didn't make a bit of difference. For a brief time last night, she thought Tam might be a man she could come to like maybe even love. This morning, he dispelled those ridiculous thoughts with his infuriating behavior. She loathed all he stood for. The prude. He irritated her.

She reminded herself that he didn't like her either. She detested him. Nothing between them was different. They felt the same way about each other this morning as they did when they first met. They weren't compatible in any way.

This morning would have changed all those tender feelings that might have blossomed if he'd been nicer to her. She caught as well as cooked breakfast for him. Shouldn't there be a thank you in there somewhere?

"Come along now, Let's go back to the house. I'll carry you. Don't want you walking on your sore ankle."

"No! I'm going to the cliff. You go back to the house." She kept walking. Knew at almost the same moment she would never make it that far. Unable to stop the cry of pain, she gasped. He swept her into his arms.

"Don't be stupid as well as irresponsible," he told her with quiet menace. "If you had waited instead of storming off in a pique, you would not be hurt and you would have seen the mare I brought up here for you."

"Mare?"

"Yes, she is a beauty. The little lady is brown with four white stockings. Spirited too. A bit like you. Nonetheless she is an animal you can handle." Tam adjusted her in his arms, bouncing her until she put her arms around him, embraced him as she did last night. She didn't want to like the feel of his arms around her. "You can ride her anytime you would like. Though I would appreciate a bit of thought be put into where as well as when. Would like to know your whereabouts when you decide to ride..." Tam paused. "In case you don't come back, that is. Need to be able to locate you."

"I always come back," Kerrie was quick to say.

"A thank you wouldn't go unappreciated," he told her as they approached the lodge.

She wanted a thank you too. He would get his after she got hers. A beat of her heart passed. Another thought about the future days here with him. She gave in, understanding she would never receive that tiny acknowledgement. "Thank you." Riding this horse would not be the same as riding her stallion. She would accept this truce for the time they would remain here. Kerrie wasn't ready for a return to society. He must have acted early this morning or even last night to get the mare up here so soon. How the devil did he accomplish that?

Before she left, Ella sent her an itinerary. There were far too many balls, too many recitals and luncheons to attend. Events where she would have to make idle conversation. Pointless chatter was not her forte. She hated recitals. Disliked the thought of dancing with men who were strangers. Wished she could stay here…with Tam…oh dear.

"You're welcome. Here we are." Tam stepped up to the porch then into the main room. He set her on the same chair where she sat last night while they sipped wine. He stared at her before he spoke. "Stay put."

"Where would I go?" Kerrie mouthed back.

He grunted as if he wasn't certain what she meant. "I'll be right back with some hot water and bandages. Need to look at the damage you caused yourself."

Tam was right on some counts. Racing out of the stables then continuing to walk when she was hurt was stupid. She was not an imprudent or injudicious person. He made her crazy. She couldn't think rational thoughts when he was near. The pain from the ankle stopped the need to cry. Kerrie hated tears for any reason. Physical pain was different from emotional pain. One she could handle the other she could not.

While he was gone, she removed her boot and stocking. The bruise around her ankle was dark blue turning close to black in places. She did do this up good. For the next day or two, he wouldn't have to worry about her sneaking off to fish. There wasn't any way she could walk down that trail. Fishing in the pond seldom brought in fish. Riding would be difficult too. Now that her boot was off, her foot was beginning to swell. Returning the boot or any other shoe to her foot would never be possible.

After he kneeled down in front of her, he lifted her foot. His hands were gentle while he probed the swollen area. She flinched. He looked at her knowing how she felt. "Not broken. Just a sprain. You will have to keep it elevated. Stay off it."

"That should please you. I won't be able to walk for a day or two. Won't be able to ride. You won't need to wonder where I'm off to," she bit out through clenched teeth. "You won't have to keep Dex locked away from me." He was such an irksome man.

"Whatever you think about me personally, seeing you hurt does not give me enjoyment. I would much rather you were able to walk. We could fish together. I would be with you to keep you from harming yourself. Whatever you might think about me, it was never my intention to keep you from enjoyable pursuits."

There was an underlying note of anger in his voice. He set her foot in the cool water while he readied the bandage for her. "I will bind your ankle. I'll get you another walking stick. Believe I saw one in the coat closet. You can use that. If you stay off your injury today, you might be able to get around tomorrow with a slight limp. Today, I'll carry you wherever you need to be."

A rush of heat spread on her face when she thought about the close proximity between them when he cradled her in his arms. "No, no, I can get around the house by myself. Don't need help." She was thinking of trips to the water closet. How mortifying if he carried her there? That just wasn't going to happen.

"Suit yourself. It will serve only to make the recovery time longer. If that's what you wish..." He was holding her foot in his hand. His thumb rubbed across the arch. She shivered.

The sensation that small caress created, unnerved her. Longer recovery time was not coveted. If that was going to happen with a few steps, she would try to bury her pride. "All right. I will stay off my foot today. If it becomes necessary, you can carry me."

"Glad to hear you've come to your senses." Tam grinned at her, a smile that left her insides quaking as well as her heart beating out of control. When he smiled everything about him changed for the better.

"When can I see the mare? If you carried me to her, I could ride. Couldn't I? That wouldn't hurt my ankle. Would it? What's her name?" Kerrie understood she was reaching for something he wouldn't give. He wouldn't know she could control her mount with her thighs.

"Not today. Believe we've had enough excitement for one day. Don't you? The mare's name is Blaze. If you don't like the moniker, you can change it to whatever would suit you. While we are here the horse is yours. When we are at home, you can ride her anytime you like. You would have to visit me to do so. I'll bring you one of my socks to keep your toes warm."

The maid he kept at the lodge brought a tray with tea and a few cakes. After all she ate this morning, Kerrie wasn't hungry. He poured her a cup then one for himself. Tam grimaced when he sipped but didn't say anything.

"Are you going to leave me alone now?"

Kerrie didn't wish to be left alone with her thoughts all a muddle. That in itself was a contradiction. What she didn't understand was why she coveted time with this vexatious man. He bedeviled her at every turn. A simple touch of his fingers created havoc she'd never before felt.

"Tell me what brought on your dislike of dandies or aristos as you call them."

Tam leaned back. Relaxed. Confident in the extreme. He set his folded hands on his hard belly. Ever-watchful he waited with what appeared to be patience for her answer.

Her fingers wound into each other. He didn't have a right to know. Yet...yet for some unfathomable reason, she wanted to tell him. Needed for Tam to understand about her. "Two years ago, I was the recipient of a distasteful run in with a lord of the realm. Don't recall his title. Might have been a viscount. He thought that because I was nothing more than a mere peasant, his words not mine, he could do whatever it was he wanted with me. Believed I would pant for his attention. He wanted more than that. Seemed he wished for me to service him. Those were his words."

Tam stiffened. A scowl shuddered onto his face. "Why? Did you do something to make him believe you favored him?" The corners of his mouth twitched as if the question was distasteful to him.

Perhaps he found the story amusing. At his question she stiffened. Kerrie didn't want to hear him accuse her of doing something to provoke this so-called lord of the realm. She bristled with rightful indignation, her senses screaming. Wasn't it just like a man to ask such a question? "It wasn't my fault. I smiled at him, yes. Does that give a man some rights I don't wish to give? I've smiled at you too. Once perhaps. You don't believe I should service you, do you."

He held her foot in his hand, rubbed the arch. "A fair question. No, not in my mind. I'd like it if you would smile at me once or twice instead of glower. Scowling seems to be your preferred expression. Will give you wrinkles before your time. If what you say is true, that you smiled once. Don't recall. I would never ask for anything of you except your smile back," he told Kerrie as he began to wrap her ankle.

Her heel rested on his thigh. His fingers were gentle as he wound the material around her ankle as well as her foot. The man was all business. "Tell me if it's too tight. Wouldn't want to cut off the circulation."

She winced when he touched a tender spot. The bruise was growing. "I smiled at you when you came for breakfast," she told him, lowering her lashes. "Think I smiled yesterday a time or two. Hard to smile when you make it impossible for me to ride my horse. When you are so annoying, I want to scream at you instead of grin."

"Not anymore." He let a long breath of air out before looking at her. "Don't want to make your life miserable. Just trying to keep you safe from yourself. That horse is too much animal for a woman to handle. Any woman. Not just you. Have you looked at yourself? You're a tiny whisp. I can wrap your upper arm without my fingertips touching."

She brought in a deep breath of air before she spoke. "You take things from me. You dictate what I should as well as what I should not do. Order me around as to your whims. Command. You say you don't wish for me to be unhappy. Think again. You are not my father. You have no say about what I can and cannot do. In fact, I just met you. How many times do I need to tell you this?" Kerrie found herself shaking her head, wishing he would just let her be herself. "You've no idea."

"Never wish to be your father. When you are about to hurt yourself, yes, I will step in to right the situation. Now, what else did this viscount do? Is there more to this story?" Tam set her foot on a stool he brought over for her use. "Stay off it and keep the foot elevated. The healing will be faster."

"He thought...I don't know what he thought. He wasn't nice. I didn't like him at all."

Kerrie found herself hedging. She didn't plan to be explicit. Couldn't tell him how the man touched her places he shouldn't.

"You don't like me, " he reminded her." A wry grin on his handsome face, the smile made him look handsome as sin.

The devil take him.

She winced at the words that were true at times then not true at other moments. "He was nothing like you. You can be gentle..." she sighed remembering once again the night before as well as these last few minutes. Giving too much praise would serve to make him more arrogant. "What am I going to do the rest of the day? Why don't you tell me what brought you here. If you've already told me some reasons, you can remind me. I didn't listen well yesterday. I was too upset at having my solitude intruded upon. My bed, stolen. Ripped off my horse. Everything I planned, destroyed in one beat of my heart."

"I spend my days working. I've two estates that were left to me by a great aunt and another by my uncle. Neither had living children to pass the property to. They were crumbling eyesores to the nearby villages. I enjoy working with my hands as well as seeing something become beautiful under my care." He seemed to study the length of her leg.

Kerrie rubbed her hands along her legs. "You are fixing them up?" Kerrie asked eager to talk about something other than the horrible man who was relegated to her past. She hoped to learn more about this man who alternately enraged her then captivated her.

"Yes, but I've only been to one. In the next year, I'll put my efforts into renovating the estate in Cornwall. The mansion looks over the sea. Rains a lot though. Not real partial to rain. The scenery is beautiful. You might enjoy Cornwall. Have you ever been?"

When she moved to the side, her ankle hurt. She winced from the stab of discomfort. When she switched positions to get more comfortable it ached. Throbbed. Tam seemed to notice the uneasiness. He left. When he returned, he held a glass of brandy in one hand and a pillow in the other. One of his socks was draped across the pillow.

"Both for the pain," he told her. "Drink up. Can you put the sock on by yourself...of course you can. I'm going to check on a few things outside. Try to relax. I'll take care of dinner tonight."

~ * ~

Last evening, when he closed the padlock on Dex's stall, Tam understood she would be angry. She was a fighter. Perfect for him if he could ever stop making her incensed. She had a wealth of names she called him. Tam never expected tears. He hoped the little mare that would be delivered here tomorrow morning, would ease some of the rage blinding her. Instead of the fury he expected to be blasted with, she cried. He also understood why she ran. She didn't want him to see the tears. Her pride was the motivation that sent her tearing away from him, hiding within herself. If he didn't feel it necessary to protect this female, he would have never been underhanded in his dealings. This intense protective feeling for a woman was something overwhelming as well as new to him.

What he'd seen of Kerrie so far was that she was used to getting her way. She'd been coddled by her parents. He held the sneaking suspicion she expected to start her own stud farm with the big stallion she called Dex. Dissuading her of that notion was uppermost in his head. Tam understood he had a long way to go. Given the necessary time, he would figure this out. As of now, his mind was a blank slate.

Tam decided he would find a means to make his domineering decisions up to her. He figured by tomorrow she would be able to get around a bit. As she suggested, he would carry her to the little mare he had delivered here. She could ride for a bit. That might erase some of the sting of not being allowed to sit atop Dex for a long run. As wishful as he was, Tam also understood this wouldn't end all the pain. He felt certain she also felt betrayed. A long breath of air left his lungs. More than anything he needed to change that feeling of betrayal to something else. That's where he wasn't certain.

She was so beautiful. Kerrie stole his breath from him every time he looked at her. She was slim and curved nicely everywhere a woman should be curved. Kerrie moved with fluid grace when she walked, when she rode, when she bathed. No matter how hard he tried, he could not erase the vision she made walking from the lake clad in her shift. Nothing else. He saw more of her than a man had a right to see of a maiden. Still, he needed to see more. Touch more. Kiss every part of her.

That night his sleep was restless. Every time he turned over, he relived the moment she walked from the lake. In his dreams, he held her in his arms.

This morning when he woke the sun was shining on the hills. A stiff breeze blew down from the craigs. The time was early. He sat on a chair looking over the lake, a cup of steaming coffee in his hand. Last night he carried her to bed. He had a bath ready for her. A smile formed when he imagined her with her bum foot on the edge of the tub to keep the bandage from getting wet. His grin widened when he imagined her naked except for the wrapping of her ankle while she wore his sock. After seeing her emerge from the lake that night, he didn't have to do a lot of imagining. With those errant thoughts, his body thrummed with sexual energy.

He decided he would give her a few more minutes to get downstairs by herself. He left the walking stick beside her bed. She was determined to do everything on her own. Determined to the point of risking life and limb. Asking for help even when needed would be distasteful to this female. He would have to figure out a means to meet her half way. He wasn't accustomed to doing anything halfway.

First, they would ride wherever she wished to go and as long as she wanted. She could show him her favorite place. The cliff overlooking the forbidden stream. She told him about the spot last night. She was heading there to nurse her wounds when she twisted her ankle. He believed she might be softening a bit to him. Tam hoped there would be no more setbacks. If there were, he would deal with them one at a time in a manner befitting his station.

"Tam?" Kerrie stood in the doorway, breathing hard and leaning on the walking stick. She didn't call him to help. What did he expect? "What are you doing? Thought you would...well, I don't know what I thought. I was lonely by myself."

*Lonely without him?* "How's your ankle?" He grinned while he stood to help her to one of the other chairs on the porch. He poured her a cup of tea from the pot he put there for this purpose. "Milk and sugar?" He waited on her. Tam liked to watch her as he did things for her. "I'm going to look at your foot again. Need to see how the swelling is. We could always go down to the lake. The frigid water would bring the inflammation down."

She accepted the chair sitting down then closed her eyes. "Plain, nothing in it. Sore but better than yesterday. I'm not going to sit on my rear all day today. Need to cook you something for breakfast. Too bad there aren't any more fish. What would you like?" Kerrie pointed out with a kittenish grin.

Tam liked that playful side of her. Enjoyed the teasing part that didn't come out enough. "We shouldn't have eaten everything yesterday. Though there is bacon, still eggs and potatoes. Pancakes are a possibility. I can make pancakes. Can we work as a team? You me, a team?"

Tam liked the idea of working with her...beside her. So far, it seemed everything that happened worked against her wishes. If he could, he would give her anything she wanted. He would even resign the dukedom, if possible. Doing so wasn't in the realm of possible. He hated the title more than she did. *If that was conceivable.* When she discovered his title, that would be another setback to his plans. He would need to deal with the eventual discovery before he could make her his. There was a distinct likelihood he could keep the information from her until she committed to him. He would have to figure out how to do that.

Kerrie wanted a man without a title. A man who was not the next step down from royalty. The thought of that made his blood boil. Didn't like the idea of another man being near her, holding her, kissing her. Using this time to his advantage was a necessity. It would not be long before they would need to leave. He had duties as did she. She was supposed to be looking for a husband. What she didn't know yet was that she found him where she least expected. That thought stopped him for a moment then he grinned.

"Pancakes sound good as long as there is syrup. Don't want to stand too long. Can we ride after we eat?" She was staring at him with her beguiling amber colored eyes. "Dex...you can't keep him from me forever. He is mine. You do understand that fact. Mother gave him to me when he was born."

Tam wasn't certain how to tell her that a wife's property became the husband's when they wed. She would tell him when pigs fly if he mentioned a wedding this soon into their fledgling relationship. "True." Was the extent of the words he had to say on that topic. When he made up his mind, she would be his wife, he wasn't certain. "You can put your foot up on a chair and watch me work. I'll do everything. You can give me directions if that would please you. Drink your tea."

"After that we can go for a ride?" she repeated the question he forgot to answer.

"Yes. You can ride pillion with me on Dex or by yourself on Blaze. It's your choice." He enjoyed seeing the smile blossom on her face. Made his heart stop for a second. He wondered what she would do if he kissed her. Would she be receptive? Would she think he was like the other lord who took liberties she didn't wish to give. Until he heard more positive replies, he didn't dare test his concept.

"I do like it when you say yes instead of no." She told him while she sipped.

He understood what that smile did to him.

He tapped her on the nose. "Don't do anything foolish or stupid and I will always tell you yes. Keep in mind, I also appreciate that sentiment more than the other. Come along." Tam scooped her into his arms, taking long sure strides to the kitchen, where he plopped her down on a chair. "Going to make those pancakes. You're going to eat your fill." Yesterday at breakfast he never saw a woman eat as much. She was willow thin. How? He didn't understand. Realized then she didn't eat anything else the rest of the day.

It didn't take long to have breakfast on the table. They spent a few minutes eating, then he carried her to the stable. She pushed her face into his shoulder, laughing while he jiggled her. Tam's actions were far from innocent. He needed to feel the softness of her breasts pushed against his chest. Her slender arms wound around his neck. She let her fingers slide through his hair. Maybe a kiss was not too far off base today. Perhaps later if she continued to be receptive to him, he would test the water. Maybe, if she didn't call him any more derogatory names.

"I can walk. You don't have to carry me everywhere." Kerrie pushed a lock of hair that had fallen into his eyes away. "I'm far too heavy."

He wasn't going to prevaricate. "You are as light as a feather. Besides, holding you is nice. More than nice." He saw the rise of the rose-colored hue on her cheeks he liked to see. He was honest. The first time he held her across his thighs after the unneeded rescue, he had a premonition that he always wanted to be the man to hold her. Earlier, Tam arranged for the horses to be saddled. They were waiting. "Hope you don't mind my riding Dex. He does need to be exercised. Yesterday, while you were sleeping, I rode my horse." He finished with that last piece of information to avoid an argument.

The look on her face told him she was having difficulty adjusting to the fact someone besides her was riding her stallion. She would need to get used to the notion. The only way she would ride that beast was with him behind her, his arms around her. He meant to stand firm in this decision.

They rode for a couple of hours. Tam enjoyed watching her ride. He didn't understand, now that he knew her, how he could have ever thought she needed help. Her grace was fluid. Her body in tune with the animal. Confidence radiated with every movement. Kerrie was a remarkable horsewoman. She was still too slight of build to handle a stallion of Dex's size.

When they stopped at the cliff, she leaned over to stroke the mare's nose. "She is beautiful. The name Blaze isn't right for this lady. I'll come up with something else. You don't care if I change her name if only for a short time?"

Tam was pleased to hear the compliment. She was one of his finest. He planned on giving the mare to her as soon as doing so would be deemed appropriate in their fledgling relationship. Saying something to that effect today was too soon. Kerrie didn't know yet that in all respects the horse was hers. Also didn't yet understand that she was his. He sent a message to his father to arrange for a priest to have special papers written for a license so he could wed her without the saying of the banns. He didn't want to wait that long. The marriage needed to take place as soon as possible. Before she understood who he was. He had very little time to spare. Couldn't wait for a normal wedding to proceed.

She would protest.

She wouldn't be given a choice.

"Tell me something about your life in the village. Your parents? What would they say if they knew I was here with you? Alone? Unchaperoned?" Tam wanted to understand everything about this woman who would soon be his wife. He was used to getting his way. She would have to understand he had a title but he was nothing like the man she had the previous encounter with.

"You really want to know?" Kerrie sounded surprised.

"Yes."

"Oh my...another yes. I might faint if you tell me yes again. Swoon. Fall down right at your autocratic feet."

Sometimes her dry wit was more than he wished to deal with. This was too taunting for his likes.

"Don't be sarcastic. If you don't wish to speak of your life, then don't."

Tam was exasperated by her constant mockery. Hoped for a new beginning with this lovely woman. As far as he could tell, he wasn't going to have any more unpleasant surprises for her until he revealed who he was. Until she knew he was all that she loathed, he was safe. By then, he prayed she would harbor a few tender feelings for him. By then...they might be tied together...bound by the vows of holy matrimony. Might even have conceived his heir.

She leaned forward to touch his arm. What he heard next was sincerity. The smile on her face seemed hesitant. "I...well...I didn't...I don't mean to always be mean spirited. It's just that I never understand if you have some underlying question or meaning to your words. I'm sorry. I'll try to do better. Is my apology accepted?"

"Always." He tried to avoid the use of the yes word. Making her happy was important to him even while he knew he could not constantly do that. He paused wondering about his next question. If he understood more about this woman, he would deal better with her. "So, tell me, how did you spend your days?"

"If I tell you, you'll be either angry or annoyed. Seems everything I do gives you reason to withhold something from me."

"Let me be the judge of that. I am in favor of an independent woman but not if she doesn't comprehend her strengths along with her weaknesses. It would be obvious to anyone with eyes that you spend a great deal of time around horses. You know them. Handle them with expertise."

Tam supposed that to be the truth. Some of what she did would revolve around the stable of racehorses he knew about. She would train them. That thought didn't please him. That is, if she was the daughter of Hadden Johnston. She might be a different Johnston. The name was common. Where did she live? Close to Berwick Upon Tweed? If so, he had her parents pegged right.

Her bright smile sent his heart into a tailspin. She tossed him a flirtatious wink. "Just don't start yelling at me when I tell you something you will take umbrage with. I know you well enough now I could avoid speaking about that which will raise your ire. Nonetheless, I'm assuming you would like honesty. Withholding truth is dishonest. Can you promise?" Her head tilted to the side as she seemed to study him.

"Promise I won't yell. Doesn't mean I won't be irritated or angry. You have the ability to frustrate a man to death."

Tam understood what might be coming. He'd asked for the information. Thank God if this truth was what he was thinking, she would not be in jeopardy after they married. He supposed he should never be as confident as he was. To convince her might not be too difficult if he found a way to charm her. So far, he failed at that feat. For him, charming this lady was impossible. Didn't mean he wouldn't keep trying.

Lowering her eyes as if thinking when she looked at him, she nodded. "Very well. I'll trust your word. Won't be too surprised if you turn red with the effort. Bottled up anger always makes my father turn red. Don't believe it will be any different for you. Let me see, believe I'll begin with the most mundane of my adventures. Even that, I've a feeling you won't like what you hear."

"Mundane?" Tam didn't believe this woman would do anything ordinary. "Go ahead."

Holding in his breath, he plucked a piece of grass. Rubbed it between his fingers thinking of plucking the tips of the soft round breasts he felt earlier. Breasts that reminded him of peaches. Peaches needed plucking. Hers were ripe as well as ready.

"My father has his children, not biological, but adopted children. They live near our home, close enough so we can visit every day. Once a month we would drive to Edinburg. We would spend time in the worst part of the city looking for abandoned children. As of today, unless he's found more while I've been gone, father is taking care of twelve children. During my entire life he's found children, adopted them, cared for them, taught them trades so they could live healthy happy adult lives. Loved them. He adores children. What do you think of children?" Kerrie stopped talking to watch him. After a few seconds of silence, she poked him in the chest. "You're turning red. Suppose that wasn't mundane. Was it? It was the least...well if I'm going to anger you, that was the one thing I had confidence in that you wouldn't be angry when you heard."

This time holding his breath for the count of ten, he hoped to calm himself. When he felt the words would not come out in a yell, he spoke, "You...spent...time...on the worst streets of Edinburg?"

Tam found he was fuming. She told him this would be the least troublesome to him. What was the worst? He couldn't imagine. He wondered if it revolved around training the racing horses. While he didn't like to think about her riding more stallions than just Dex, he expected to hear about the training of horses. This about the children along with the worst streets was unexpected.

"Father was always with us, mother and Kelsey and me." Kerrie found heat rising to flush her face. "I never thought looking for lost children was dangerous. Can't imagine why you believe so. It's apparent you would forbid me if you had a say. Which you don't."

"Worst streets...my God! Does your father...?" His fists tightened with the effort to control himself. He stopped, realizing this part of her life was over. To berate a man, a father who she loved, who wasn't there to defend himself would put him steps back in his attempt to win over Kerrie. "Why don't we abandon that topic before I put my foot in my mouth and annoy you further? What else did you do?"

"Remember you're not going to yell. You came pretty close just now in breaking your promise." She pulled her long braid over her shoulder. Played with the end for a few seconds as if her attention riveted on the braid. "Should I go on? Would you rather tell me something about yourself? It is your turn."

Tam couldn't think of anything to tell her that wouldn't point to him as a man with a title, a man of leisure. Though he wasn't. He did have numerous business ventures. He would have to think on the notion. "Let's get the worst over while my temper is only on a low simmer."

He was formidable. Could rage out of hand in a blink. He'd been told that numerous times by both his mother and father. If the time did come to be his turn to share, he could speak of his mother. She was gone now. Wouldn't take exception to anything he said about her. Not that he held anything but fond thoughts for his mother. "Talk to me about what else you did."

"I would help father at the docks with the scotch shipments. Father owns ships, lots of them. They sail all over the world. Mother's family distills scotch. That's how they met. Father shipped the Graham scotch. Mother threatened him with the business when she needed to marry the richest man in the village."

"Reckon he didn't take too kindly to the proposition."

Tam was hard pressed not to hoot with laughter. Like mother like daughter, he mused. He could see Kerrie threatening him to get her way. She didn't have anything to hold over his head. He liked his life that way. Intended to keep things on an even keel. Though, he would never allow her to get the upper hand in something he felt would harm her.

"He married her. They fell in love. Don't believe either one thought love was possible. The relationship was supposed to be a marriage of convenience. That couldn't happen. If they didn't get pregnant, a very bad man meant to have the marriage annulled."

"Hmmm.... What else? That was about your parents. What keeps you busy during the day?"

Tam understood she was hedging her bets. Knew if he pressed her, the talk would come around to horses.

Kerrie cleared her throat. Her expression was hesitant. "My mother owns the stable, not my father. She loves her horses. Dex comes from Fiacre. He was my mother's most famous stallion. It's a stud farm. We breed and sell horses. Dex is going to be the backbone of my stable. First, he has to win a few races. Newmarket in a year will be his first major test."

"I remember Fiacre when I was younger. The stallion won wherever he raced."

His mind was spinning. It was her mother's stable, her mother who raised the famous racehorse as well as several more after that.

"Most of my days were spent helping her. Father took little to no interest in the business. In fact, he dislikes horses. Will only ride when there is no other choice. We breed horses. That's how Mother makes most of her money."

She repeated as if he didn't hear her the first time. What he was trying to do was ignore the consequences. Could not hold his thoughts back. They tumbled from his mouth.

"We?" he questioned; his voice harsher than he wished. "We breed horses? Please tell me you aren't in the stable when the stallions..."

The look on her face coupled with the beet red coloring told him all he needed to know. Still, he asked again in hopes his first inclination was wrong. "Were you there?"

Her back stiffened. Her chin rose a notch or two in the air. Her defiance was obvious. "Yes. It was expected of me. Both my mother..." she cut herself off, turning away from him.

Bloody everlasting hell! She'd seen...how was he going to get around that bit of information. No lady should ever see the breeding process. His Kerrie had seen them...the horses...the stallions couple with the mares... He couldn't utter words even in his head. His mind was blown. His nerves shattered. He promised he wouldn't yell.

Tam had to leave to garner his senses as well as tamp his fury down to a low simmer. If not, he would break his word to her. He would yell his anger as well as his fear. Striding down the narrow path for a few minutes, he turned around to return. After he reached her, he stood at the edge of the cliff. Rocks fell away. A tumble from this spot would result in severe injury or death. This was a place he should forbid to her. Shaking his head, he couldn't get around all the dangers this little lady encountered day to day. Couldn't wrap his mind around the fact she was oblivious to all that could harm her. If he had his way, he'd enclose her in a glass bubble...No!

*Watching the breeding of horses! Good, God. Bloody everlasting hell!* If the stallion got out of hand, anyone could be injured. That wasn't all. She shouldn't watch the breeding process. She was innocent. At least he assumed she was. That wasn't something a young female participated in. What would she think? What could her father have been thinking?

*That wasn't done! Never!*

To his surprise, Kerrie's hand rested on his shoulder. When he turned to catch her attention, she smiled. "You did better than I expected. Knew you would be in a rage. What I don't understand is why."

He tugged a huge breath of air into his lungs. Flattered by her assessment but still perplexed to think about what she did. "You think so? In a rage doesn't begin to describe my feelings."

She had no idea. He could shake her father as well as her mother. How could a man allow his wife to be present at the breeding of horses?

*His girl child.*

She didn't understand a damn thing.

"Yes, of course, I thought you would lose your temper. I'm not stupid. Understood you would believe it was not appropriate for me to see the breeding process. For a woman to see... What's worse for you to know is that Mother and I didn't just watch. We oversaw the breeding. Every part of the process. Father is always busy with his shipping business." Her sigh was soft, genuine. "It's your turn. Don't believe you could take anymore from me today."

Unable to stop himself he turned her, lifted her chin. He had to ask. "You understand what goes on between a man and a woman when they have sex?"

Perhaps he was too blunt. She didn't redden further. With this question, Kerrie paled.

"No, no," she paused in thought. "Not exactly. Is what the horses do the same as people? They mount...from behind. Don't believe I would like that too much. Though I never intend to marry. So, it doesn't matter. Not ever going to let a man do that to me."

What was he thinking? Relief swept through him. After that anger at the fact because of what she witnessed, she didn't want to make love with her husband. Didn't want to marry. He would change her mind.

When they did make love, she wouldn't be the one in charge. She didn't comprehend what a man and a woman did behind closed doors. Speaking of it, Kerrie appeared mortified. If he could see her toes, he was certain they would have turned red then would have paled just as her pretty face did.

"Suppose this conversation should travel in a different direction. What do you think? Would you like to see if we can catch something from the lake? A few trout for dinner? You're in no condition to trundle down to the stream. The trail is too steep for me to carry you without further danger to your person. So..."

Fishing would be an easy way to relax with this woman. They could take the little row boat out. Drift. Nap. Skinny dip.

"No, think...I don't know. I'm tired. This little excursion of ours along with the conversation has taken a great deal out of me. Might like to take a nap."

Her color was returning. She would be her normal self soon.

A nap seemed out of character for her though he did put strain on her nerves. He was certain about that. Perhaps she wanted to hide for an hour or two, nurse her wounds. He could allow her to do so. Maybe he needed time away from her to cool his temper which flared out of control whenever she acted with no thought. Even though he didn't yell, she comprehended his anger. He was hanging on by a mere thread. At least in this he wouldn't need to forbid her from doing something she loved. He wasn't in the business of breeding horses. Where riding Dex was concerned, he passed the worst of tests that would rise between them. Kerrie accepted Blaze as the horse she would ride while they were here.

What she didn't understand was that he wasn't going away. He would always be a part of her life. If he had his say...and he would...she would never ride Dex again unless it was pillion with him. "Come along. We'll go back to the lodge. If a nap is what you wish for, a nap is what you'll get."

"What are you going to do?"

*Ducal things.*

"Going to attend to some long overdue correspondence." He couldn't tell her what he intended. A few notes to his retainers would bring about more changes in her life. He was going to let Drake know they would be returning in a few days. The ball the Montgomeries planned for her would be attended by them. They had two more days remaining here then two days of travel time. He was going to make the most of those four days. His carriage with the ducal emblem emblazoned on the doors was sent ahead. They would ride to London in her carriage.

"Who are you writing to?"

"Friends. Family. Colleagues."

*Messages to her retainers in the village below. A note to my father to make certain everything will be ready for their wedding. A letter to her parents telling them what would transpire soon. Another one to The Duchess explaining to her she would still be able to plan a huge celebration of their wedding.*

"Oh. That's vague. Suppose it's not my business."

"No. Let's get you back where you can rest. You want a nap? A nap you will get."

Now, he was sitting on the dock at the lake. Kerrie was in bed sleeping. He thought that was where she was. With Kerrie he might never be certain. Somehow, he still didn't see her as a woman who took naps. Maybe she needed to have some alone time. That was why she came here by herself. He told her he would be fishing or riding. Dex could use a bit of exercise today. Told her he would occupy himself for the next few hours...while she rested. She would not be expecting him.

Bored to the tips of his toes, Tam tossed a rock into the lake. Watched the spirals of water spin out from the center. He wanted to be with her even if it was to argue. He enjoyed sparring with her. She lit a fire in his soul. Caused him to burn. Created deep emotions he never knew existed. She was too brazen, too bold. She risked her life with no concern. An end to her outrageous behavior would be stopped. Even thinking about coming to an isolated place such as this one was over the top for a well-bred young lady.

This spontaneous adventure of hers was beyond the pale.

His Kerrie wasn't brought up as a well-bred young lady. She was brought up to think for herself as well as do for herself. She wasn't a lady. In her words, she was a peasant, a commoner. Didn't want anything to do with nobility. Being sheltered was never part of her life. He realized he couldn't change her. Didn't want to do anything that would make her different. Enjoyed her the way she was. Tam understood he would have to do some changing if he was going to make this marriage a success. He didn't know how. Going into this, he understood she would always challenge him. Needed to make her happy. Must come to terms with her wants versus his.

The little lady intrigued him. Fascinated him. Captivated his senses. Moments after the rescue, he understood this was the woman meant for him. Her mercuric personality was part of her charm, simmering deep inside, possessing her. The danger she seemed to tempt came with her just as her beautiful smile, willow thin body, the way she challenged him when he least expected a challenge. After that there was a fire in her eyes.

Pulling out his pocket watch, he discovered two hours slipped by while he mulled over his position with her. When he entered the room Drake used as an office, he heard her off-key singing.

The sound came from the kitchen. Maybe she was having tea. Perhaps thinking of dinner. It was nearing the hour. He strode to the kitchen wondering what he would do or say.

Wicked ideas flew to his head when he saw her elbow deep in gooey bread dough. This was a situation he couldn't resist. Fantastic notions flashed through his head.

~ * ~

So, my son wants me to procure a special license for him to wed this lady he just met. He wants to get married," the Duke of Sherburn said with a pleased smile to his man, Talbot. "It's about time the boy settled down. Good God, he's twenty-nine years old, nearing thirty. Seems he's to have a birthday in a month. A birthday as well as a marriage. An old man couldn't ask for more. There will be grandchildren. An heir. Gives me something to live for. Love to have a grandson to dangle on my knee."

"If it makes you happy, Sir, I'm also pleased. Does he give a name to the girl? Is she someone we know about? Has the boy mentioned her before."

"Those are all serious questions. Ones that need to be answered. The gel's name is Kerrie Johnston. Doesn't hold a title. Parents are wealthy. The father owns a veritable fleet of ships. I know of the man. No, he just met her. Seems she stole his breath away the first moment he laid his eyes upon her. He's been panting ever since. He didn't use those terms. Those are just an old man's way of interpreting the words he wrote. I was that way with his mother. The moment I met her, I couldn't think of anything accept her in my bed."

"Wonder what made Tam change his mind about going to London to find a débutante," Talbot asked deadpan. "He was determined last time you talked to him. Said it was time he settled down."

"My son doesn't enjoy balls and such. Didn't wish to meet simpering ladies just out of the school room. Tam was going because he was desperate. None of his acquaintances would work for him. Suppose he met her somewhere else. Where was he headed? A hunting box? In Scotland?" The duke tapped the letter on the arm of the chair.

"Wasn't he going to the Montgomerie hunting box? He was going to stay a week before he left for London. Had some heavy duty thinking to do." Talbot pointed out seeming to dig at his memory. "You don't think he met her on the way there? Do you? Would he take the girl with him? That's beyond the pale."

"Yes, it's a scandalous thought," the duke laughed thinking of his son. In his day he always enjoyed setting tongues wagging. His son wasn't like him in that respect. Tam was everything he was not. Tam was a prude. Well, in his younger days he did act more like his son. "Yes, scandal can find a person when they least expect it. Don't suppose he loves her. Do you?"

"Didn't he say the gel stole his heart? No, he must want her. It's lust he's feeling. Good enough to beget heirs. The itch is always a good thing to feel for one's wife. Why doesn't he make love to her and get her out of his system?"

Talbot laid it on the line. "Maybe he has. She might not be the type of woman a man can get out of his system."

"Here, Tam says this lady is related to the duke and duchess. The Montgomeries. So, her line is better than just being a peasant."

"Seems so."

"Well, we will just have to get on with this special license he wants. When he gets back to London in a few days, we'll see what has transpired."

# Chapter Three

Kerrie hummed as she mixed the bread dough. The spoon became sticky, the dough growing stiffer. It was time to slip her hands into the dough. Sweat slipped between her eyebrows to run down her nose. With the back of her arm, she wiped away the moisture. She started with her sleeves rolled up to her elbows. Paused to think this through. Tam told her he was going fishing. Would be gone for hours. Might ride Dex. That thought sent a simmering fury through her. Dex was hers! How dare he? He didn't even ask. He should at least ask her permission.

Tam wasn't going to be here.

The room was too hot. Way too hot!

Before she thought further or put her hands in the dough, she slipped from her blouse letting it fall to the floor. Ah...that was better. Relief from the heat. A warm breeze caressed her, dried the sweat on her forehead and between her breasts. Kerrie understood what she did would shock her mother. It was just too damn hot in the kitchen. If she were alone, this wouldn't be an issue. She was alone now.

No one was around.

Tam was otherwise engaged. Fishing. Wouldn't be back before she finished with the bread dough. She was safe.

She told him she wanted to take a nap. She never took naps. When she tried to sleep, she was restless. Her thoughts about the man varied to such a degree. She didn't know what to think about him. On one hand he infuriated her. On the other, she wished she could learn more about him. She needed to be closer to him. A sensation she didn't understand flitted through her every time he was close. A kiss from the cocky man might also be nice. He was far too standoffish.

The man was so tall, broad of shoulder. His hair was thick, curling at his nape. He needed a haircut. She wished to run her fingers through the dark strands, see if it was as soft as it appeared. She brought in a long, very deep breath of air before shaking her head. Thinking about this man wreaked havoc with her muddled brain. He did so many things to infuriate her. How could she harbor tender feelings about him?

Kerrie didn't understand why she thought about him nonstop. He was nothing but a thorn in her side with all his dictates. His arrogance. The only reason his will won out was because he was stronger. He didn't have the right to padlock the stall to keep her from her horse. He did though. She couldn't fight the supercilious man. For now, she needed to accept what he did since she had no recourse to battle him and win.

They were here for two more days. He told her he would travel with her to London. By the time she arrived, she would have her stallion back. Her life would then be in her control. She puffed a strand of hair that dangled down her forehead and into her eyes. Kneaded the dough. Added more flour. A strap slipped from her shoulder. Wiggling with her arm, she managed to put it back where it belonged.

He did well earlier when he didn't yell at her. She understood he would be angry with what she told him. A smile crossed her face thinking about the expression on his face. The way his eyes burned hot. How he reddened. He did pose a few interesting questions. Never expected a blush the color of the sunset. The red didn't come from embarrassment but from anger.

She added more flour. Baking always had a way of soothing her spirits. She needed a bit of comforting now. Eating helped too. When she baked, she talked to herself about things that bothered her. Tam bothered her in a myriad of ways.

He troubled her more than she wanted to admit even to herself. For the first time in her life, she wanted to learn what a real kiss would feel like. Tam's kiss. No, she sighed, thinking about what that might lead to if she allowed something so intimate as a kiss. Sometimes one kiss led to more. That sage advice came from her cousin, Nicki. When Ian kissed her, Nicki told her she couldn't think straight. Wasn't able to do anything except feel. Ian took full advantage of her weakness. Nicki ran away with him. Sailed from London. Her aunt and uncle sailed after them. Caught them. Threatened to hang Ian from the yardarm of his ship. Nicki didn't regret one moment of the adventure with her now husband.

Anyway, in this instance, the man didn't want to kiss her. He didn't like her. She didn't like him. Oh...but that wasn't true. Except when he acted autocratic, she liked him a lot. Except when he put the padlock on Dex's stall, she wanted to discover what kisses from him felt like. Thank God he wasn't titled. If he was, she'd have to rethink her feelings. A man who held a title wasn't for her.

Tam told her he renovated an estate that was left to him. He also had another one in...she couldn't remember where. There were two. His family must have some wealth. She didn't care about money. She had enough to last her a lifetime. Told her he would write to colleagues, family along with friends. Maybe he needed to order supplies. Nails and wood. What did one need to renovate property? Paint? She didn't have any ideas. He might tell her if she asked. The man was closed off as to who he was along with what he did to make enough to be friends with the duke and duchess.

Appalled, shocked, what were the emotions flying through his brain when she told him about the breeding of the horses? He took umbrage with her actions. She took the work for granted. It was what she did. She loved working with her horses. Hoped someday to have a stable of her own. Her mother would help with the studs. Kelsey, her younger sister, didn't like to work with the horses. She spent her free days helping their father with the ledgers.

Kelsey loved numbers.

She loved horses.

Kerrie added more flour; with her forearm, scratched an itch on her nose. Noticed a light dusting of flour on her cheek.

"Oh!" She thought she jumped out of her skin.

"Hush...it's just me." His words feathered across her cheek. With the tip of his tongue, he touched the lobe of her ear. His hands settled on her bare shoulders, playing with the straps of her chemise.

Shivers crashed all the way to her toes. It couldn't be him. She was nearly naked from the waist up. She didn't expect the man. What was he doing here? Her blouse lay on the floor. Oh god, she thought again. She was almost naked. His fingers trailed with slow finesse across her shoulders then down her arms, taking the straps of her chemise with them. The fabric of her chemise clung to her nipples. Her body trembled at the tender caress. Quivered as if searching for something more. What that was, she didn't know.

"Tam...?" Her breath caught in her throat when his lips touched the nape of her neck. She froze, her fingers covered with sticky dough. She should be done with this part of the kneading. Her mind wandered. "You are not supposed to be here."

Her mind had wandered to Tam…and here he was.

"I am."

"You have to go away."

"Not now. I like the way you are dressed. Did you take your blouse off for me? Hoping I would find you here with nothing on except a sheer chemise. I can see your beautiful breasts. The tips are rose colored. Just the way I like them. I'm a man who can appreciate the color of your nipples." His fingers touched on one then two vertebrae continuing down the line of her back until he reached the last bone. Through her clothing the caresses were muted. Still, the impact threatened her knees. They trembled. His hands stopped at her hips. He pulled her against him.

She felt his hardness against her. "Wh-what are you doing? You need to go away. Tam...I."

He didn't reply.

With teeth, tongue, lips, he caressed her shoulder with tenderness. She stiffened, quivered, trembled with each touch. Wanted him. His teeth tugged on the strap to her chemise. Taking his time, he guided the fabric so it slipped further down her arm. She felt the touch of his lips on her. Bold as well as gentle, Tam continued his assault.

He nipped.

Laved.

Sucked on tender flesh.

Her skin prickled. Heat flashed as if lightning bolts collided against her. A stunted breath of air caught in her throat. Kerrie closed her eyes, leaning against him. Soaking up his warmth. The energy that was him. She thought she dreamed. Didn't wish to wake up. Tiny sounds. Mewling. A moan here. A sigh there. Her finger squeezed the dough. Flexed. The wet dough slipped between her fingers in a gooey mess.

Tam turned his attention to her other shoulder. Repeated the process. The straps hung at her elbows. Her chemise clung to the tips of her breasts threatening to slide lower. She would be bared to him.

"Tam...don't...you..." She licked her parched lips. "Can't..."

"I can...tell me no, honey," he whispered, turning his attention to her ear. He touched upon the lobe. Bit. Sucked again. Laved. "I would suck your breast into my mouth. Would you like that?"

Kerrie whimpered. Her words were a soft plea that held no strength. She wanted...didn't understand all the things she wanted. Remembered Nicki's words of warning. Lyssa's too. "Please pull the straps up."

Kerrie thought her knees would give way. If they did, she would sink to the floor. There were no other words to describe what was happening to her. She was melting, flowing like warm honey.

With his feet, he pushed hers apart. As if he understood the precarious position she was in, he set his massive thigh between her legs, keeping her upright. His hands on her hips, steadied her. "You taste like warm honey."

*Warm honey?*

Again, he caressed her shoulders with his lips. His fingers traveled along her sides. Explored each rib. Ripples of heat skidded through her. Flashed. Heated. Butterflies danced in her belly then lower. Kerrie didn't know what he was doing to her. Never thought a man's caress would heat her to flames. She would ignite in a few more seconds.

Tiny bites. Sweeping touches with his tongue to soothe followed. She didn't think he would stop. Felt the backs of his hands beneath her breasts. "My straps..." She was panting and breathing hard. "They..." speech was not easy. "Fall..."

His finger beneath her chin, he turned her head. Captured her mouth with his. Swept his tongue across her lips then pulled away. His eyes shimmered in the light slanting through the kitchen window. "You have the fullest lips, kissable, begging for attention. I want to give them all the consideration and kindness they need."

He took a seat in front of her. Watched. She thought to pull up her straps. What would a little bread dough harm? She could wash.

He stopped her, his hand on her wrist. "No, I want to look at them. At you. At your perfection. Humor me."

"Look at them? They are covered. There is nothing to see."

"Not for long if I give a little tug here or one there." Tam pointed to the spots. Didn't touch. There was so much implied.

"D-don't... Tam," her voice came out a thin wail. "I'm a good girl..."

Kerrie didn't want to be a good girl. A little bit naughty would be nice. She wished he would ignore her. Wished he would cover her. Now that he stared at her she wished for more of a kiss.

*Kisses lead to other things.*

"Of course, you're a good girl. I've no doubt about that. Your breasts remind me of peaches; full, firm, succulent. The nipples are ready to be plucked. Would you like that? I would pluck each one for you." He set a finger atop one, "See, they are hard. Ready for my devotion. I would pick them." Tam brought his hand away. Now, ignoring her. "You should finish with the bread. We can move on to other more pleasurable pursuits when the dough is rising."

"I...c-can't. My chemise... If I move, it will..." She would be left uncovered. Exposed.

"Ah, a little problem." His eyebrow lifted as if he speculated the problem. "A minor inconvenience."

Tam moved away. Kerrie watched him slicing an apple then a few pieces of cheese. He held a slice to her lips. "Open. Bite."

Unknowing what to do or what he wanted she did as he asked. While she chewed, a drop of juice slipped from the corner of her mouth. He sucked the drop away with his lips. She shuddered. Tried to knead the dough. When she added a cup of flour, one strap slid lower. She cried out in a slight whimper. One breast was bared. Nothing covered the tip. With wide eyes, she looked at him studying her.

Tam sat down. Stretched his legs out in front of him. Smiled. Chewed on a thin slice of apple. He set a piece of cheese on her lips. She bit. Kneaded the dough. The other strap fell lower. Keeping her forearms high helped. The strap seemed to stop there. Both breasts were uncovered.

With each little movement, they swayed.

Beside herself, Kerrie didn't know what she wanted. More kisses? A real kiss? Her straps pulled back to her shoulders where they belonged. She added more flour. Her chemise clung to the spot below her breasts. She tried to grab air. When she almost finished, he set her straps where they belonged.

"Meet me outside when the dough is rising. We can explore this a bit more." Whistling, he left her with her thoughts.

Heat flushed her cheeks, the tops of her breasts. Her body ached in ways she never imagined as well in places she never thought about. She should have told him no. Should have made him stop. The way his lips played over hers...

Kerrie understood she needed to get a hold of her emotions. Needed to guard herself. What would he do outside? With a vengeance she finished with the dough. Did as he said. Set it to rising. This was for dinner. She should have never, ever, removed her blouse. By doing so she invited him to take advantage of her state of *déshabillé*. He was supposed to be somewhere else.

He could have done so much more.

She wanted him to do so much more. Wasn't supposed to want more.

Needed to know what would come next. Just as when they spoke about the horses, he piqued her curiosity. She was a virgin. Giving herself to this man was something that would be frowned upon. Tam would think less of her. No man would want a woman used by another. Wasn't that what she wished for? Marrying was not going to be a part of her life. She hoped to be used by him. When that happened, she wouldn't have to worry about another man wanting to marry her. After she told her aunt, she would never be required to attend another stupid *débutante* ball.

Dear God, what was she going to do?

She was going to tell him what she thought of his maneuvers, his high-handedness. He had no right to touch her. She could have told him no. Oh...but the way his kisses made her shiver. Angry with herself as well as Tam, Kerrie grabbed her shirt from the floor then strode to the porch where he told her to meet him. She should have run to her room so she could hide. That wasn't to be. She didn't hide. Hiding wasn't in her nature. She met obstacles head on. With her shoulders squared, she would stand up to him. Tell him what she thought.

When she stepped onto the porch, she was buttoning her shirt. He smiled at her with that all-knowing arrogant, infuriating smile that left her gritting her teeth. He was far too self-possessed. Never doubted himself. She did like that about him. Hated it too. Held the shades of aristocracy.

"If you strive so hard to protect me, you should keep me safe from you!"

She plopped down on the empty chair before accepting the glass of wine he held out to her.

"More apple?" he asked with innocence that seemed feigned. "Cheese? Me?"

When she took the apple with stiff movements, wine sloshed from her glass. She licked the drops sliding down the sides of the glass then along her fingers.

"You've the pinkest little tongue I've ever seen. I'd like to play with it...your pink tongue. Your fingers too...other delicious parts of you."

His words disarmed her. She jerked. More wine spilled from her glass. Kerrie had no idea what he meant.

*Play with her tongue? Her fingers? What did that entail?*

"You're supposed to drink the wine, not spill the contents of your glass." He smiled at her. The grin was an indulgent one. Self-satisfied.

"What are you doing?" she snapped out trying to cover the desire for this man that ragged inside. If he touched her again, she would surely melt, dissolve into nothing. One kiss would lead to another. *Stay strong*. She didn't know how. "You've no right to touch me. You *dinna* have my permission."

A half-smile touched his mouth. "I never heard a complaint. Never heard the word no. Your body heated when I kissed you. Saw the flush of fire in your features, especially your eyes. Did I not do enough? Is that why you are so angry with me your eyes are crossing. Did I stop too soon? We could remedy that little problem. Tell me what you would like? I would deliver on any quest. Would keep you happy as well as content."

Chewing on a piece of apple, she studied the lake. To ignore his question would be prudent. Kerrie didn't know how to answer. Did she want more? Yes and no. Maybe. The sun would go down in another hour. Dinner would be ready. She'd found ham in the pantry. The bread would be good coupled with the cheese.

"Would you like to sit on my lap? We could explore your anger along with the reasons for...the annoyance. If it's more kisses you need, I'd be happy to oblige. If not, tell me no. I'll never take anything from you that you don't wish to give."

Kerrie rounded on him. "You don't like me!"

His hoot of laughter sent a jolt of irritation through her. "Honey, I've never said that. As it turns out I like you more than I should. You are the one who keeps telling me I don't like you. Why is that? Are you afraid of me?"

Those words didn't appease her. Neither did the challenge. She wasn't going to sit on his lap though the notion appealed to her. "What does that mean? More than you should? Don't understand half of what you say." She needed answers. He was too illusive.

"Why did you take your blouse off? If you didn't want my attention given to those parts of you that were revealed? I would understand the truth."

He was sipping his wine as if this was a typical daily conversation.

Seemed he wished to change the subject. Push this disagreement back on her shoulders. Were they having a disagreement? She wasn't certain. His question had her wishing she could vanish into the air. "Why...? The fact is simple. The kitchen was hot. You weren't supposed to be anywhere around. Imagined I was alone for the duration. By myself. Thought you were fishing. Would be gone until dinner." Her voice was prim. She didn't wish to admit to the fact that removing her blouse was a mistake.

"Did fish. Did go for a ride. Was bored. Wished to check on you. A nap was what you told me. If you had been in bed where you told me you would be, I would never have stumbled upon you in the kitchen elbow high in bread dough. You invited my touches. Though..." he paused, tapping a long slender finger against his chin. "You never asked me to... If you don't want a man to touch you, you should tell the man no. Did you tell me no? Did I miss hearing that word? I apologize if I did miss the word. I've never forced..."

Admitting she wanted him to touch her would not be prudent at this time. Still wanted another kiss. Staring at the lake she tried to ignore him. With a tiny pent-up brush of air, she replied, "I was too surprised to say no. Shocked. Never had a man..." she bit off too much, said too much.

"Did you tell that lord of yours no?" he queried, his voice harsh, his hand tight around the stem of his glass. "Maybe that's why he took more liberties than you wished. A man needs to know what a woman is thinking."

At the realization of what his words meant, the air she breathed caught in the back of her throat. Talking was not possible for a few seconds while she gasped for oxygen. "Rest assured. I told him no. Screamed the word no! More than once. Struggled to get away from him. He was too strong." That was all this wretched, provoking man needed to know. She crossed her arms, sitting back on the chair. Sipped her wine. Took a long drink. Sipping was not what she needed. Downing the entire glass would make her feel better.

"I gather, since you didn't tell me no, you enjoyed what we did together. Can I come to that conclusion? You didn't scream or struggle. You whimpered with the pleasure my lips on your naked flesh created. Moaned. Sighed. Even leaned against me with your head tilted back to give me easy access to more of your delightful body parts. I never thought you disliked what we did together."

He smiled at her when she drew her brows together in a fierce scowl. Her lips thinned.

"There was no 'we' involved in what happened. I didn't do anything."

"I disagree." He reached over then brought her to sit on him. He held her as if waiting for her to push herself away or to give him the one word that would set her free. "You responded to each caress as if you desired another. Is that why you are angry? Because I stopped? Because you wanted more?"

Tam ran his knuckles down her cheek. She leaned into the caress then sighed, the whisper of her breath soft in the deepening shadows of the day. With one finger he turned her to face him. "A kiss before dinner?"

His eyes darkened while he looked at her assessing the moment. Blue-grey eyes turned to dark blue. "This is your call," he prompted. "Do you wish for a kiss? If so, I'd be pleased to deliver what you ask for. Don't want any questions as to your most ardent desires. Afterward, don't want you angry with me."

Kerrie wanted this kiss then another one after that. Still uncertain of herself, she nodded. "Y-yes."

His thumb ran across her bottom lip. Her tongue touched upon the sultry path he took. Inviting moisture followed. "Do you know how to kiss a man? You seem eager enough." Leaving his thumb on her lip, he looked into her eyes.

That was a strange question. Yet in truth, he must not...must not believe she was experienced. Did he wish for a woman with experience? That wasn't her. Kerrie needed to be honest. "No... I've never kissed a man. The man the one who thought he was above me because of his title, kissed me. I bit him. Is that the same as yelling no?"

"Ouch! Yes, more so." He chuckled before asking the question, slanting her a half-smile that didn't quite reach his eyes. He seemed to contemplate the bite. "Are you going to bite me?" he asked. "A tiny nip or two is always nice. However, a full-on bite..."

"Bite you? No!" *A tiny nip?* "What do you mean?" On his lap she squirmed. His hand tightened where he held her.

"I'll show you. If you wish to reciprocate, I would never say no."

His fingers swept into her hair. Cupping her head with his hand, he brought her so close their breath mingled. He blew on her lips. Touched for a beat of her heart. The caress as light as a feather. "Moisten them for me. Run that delectable pink tongue that I wish to taste across the fullness of your mouth. Leave your taste behind. I wish to savor it. Let me teach you, honey. Need to taste as well as cherish you. Learn from me." He ran his hand along her arm then back down. Caressed the curve of her hip then higher to a point just below her breasts.

Lowering her eyes for a second, she waited. Did his bidding wondering what would happen next. When she looked up, his smile was broad. His eyes dark. His lips captured hers in a searing caress. She felt his tongue move between her lips, touching her teeth, pushing forward. Kerrie wasn't certain what he wanted her to do. She heated. Flushed. Felt the bombardment of sensation. The motion born of instinct, she opened wider for him, felt the gentle glide of his tongue inside her mouth. His rubbed against hers, touched her inside. His hands settled on her ribs just beneath her breasts. She burned. Caught on fire.

Feeling bold, she touched his with hers. Heard his deep masculine groan. With another instinct surfacing, Kerrie understood the groan was born of pleasure, not pain. She brought her hands to his shoulders then around his neck, clinging to him. Her nails bit into his neck. She needed to get closer.

Her body responded. Flared to life. This was ecstasy. She'd never thought something like this could be so titillating.

She ached in places foreign to her before Tam.

With his tongue, Tam played inside her mouth, explored. Danced. Bit with gentle ease on her lower lip. Tugged on the sensitive flesh. When he pulled away to look at her, his smile played havoc with her senses. He ran his hand along her side. Up then down. Stopped beneath her breast. With another groan, he set her on the chair that moments before he plucked her from. She was left bewildered, wondering what she'd done wrong. For several seconds she lowered her lashes, wondering.

"Tam...?"

Kerrie was mortified with her brazen behavior. She'd been too bold. Gave him reason to set her aside. A wave of nausea swept her insides. Fear followed. "Did I do something you didn't like. I...?" She reached out to touch him. Needing. Wanting. "I would have an answer. If you would, tell me."

He stuffed his hands through his hair. "No!" He groaned again, stomping from the porch as she watched him walk away. His strides were long, his back stiff as if he couldn't escape her too soon. He didn't look back. She sat in the chair feeling forlorn as well as unwanted. He didn't like her. She knew that for a true fact. This was an example of his distaste for her. Didn't enjoy what she did. A man would want to be in charge of all situations. Wouldn't he? He wouldn't enjoy a woman who was audacious or forward. She was that. Should have told him to stop.

What was wrong with him? What was wrong with her? Confused, she stared at her blouse. Fastened the three buttons that were undone. Kerrie wondered if she didn't button them when she walked out here to obey his order. No, they were all fastened. He wished to undress her. Why did he stomp away?

Standing at the end of the dock, Tam looked as if he wanted to dive into the lake, clothes and all. She thought to walk out there to question him again. Put her hand on his shoulder as she did earlier today. Thought better of the idea. By the looks of this, Tam didn't wish for anything to do with her. Kerrie turned to the kitchen. She went back for the glass of wine, downed it then poured herself another. Took solace from the heady taste. Needed to drown her feelings for this man she didn't understand. Didn't want to think. Didn't want to feel.

Her emotions strained. Sensations shattered. All she thought before kissing this man, she questioned. Understanding Tam would never happen. She would see to dinner. Forget what just occurred between them. Perhaps later tonight he would tell her why. Why he stormed off as if she set a fire beneath him? Men! Who could understand them? Sometimes she heard her mother swear the same words.

The bread was ready to go into the oven. She sliced ham as well as additional cheese. Sat down on a kitchen chair to sip wine. Walked back to the porch to check on Tam. Restless, she paced the length. She couldn't see him anywhere. She picked up the plate of apples and cheese. Wished to throw them.

For the next hour, Kerrie wandered around the lodge. She walked upstairs to change her gown. Her ankle was much better this evening. The sprain would heal soon because of his tender attention. She poured more wine. Took the bread from the oven to cool on a platter. Looked at the clock. In the main room, she plumped pillows. Moved the sofa to a new spot before moving it back to its original place.

An hour had passed since the kiss.

She touched her lips. *Why did I make him angry?* She thought he wanted the kiss as much as she did. He acted as if he did before he didn't.

*What a fool I am. He needed someone who was experienced. Either that or he decided he truly didn't like me. I can no longer say that about him. I like him too much. If he meant to sweet-talk me into his bed, the deed would not be difficult*. It did seem he desired her in carnal ways. She supposed that was good. Could that need be bad? Yes, of course it was bad. Ladies didn't do those things with gentlemen.

"My boldness scared him off," she murmured, wishing she knew the horrible extent of what she did. "He'll have to come back when he gets hungry. Won't he?"

While her intention in coming here was to be by herself, she was now terrified of being alone. What if something happened to him? There was so much she didn't know about Tam.

She stood on the porch watching, waiting. When she walked to the dock, she was afraid he might have fallen in and not been able to get out. Could he swim? She wrapped her arms around herself to stave off the sudden chill encompassing her. Rocking, swaying, moisture rose to her eyes. She tamped it down. She never cried. Damn, she cried yesterday when she found the lock to Dex's door.

The sky began to darken even more. Clouds on the horizon built higher. A storm was on the way. While the day had been hot, a cold breeze blew against her heated skin. She should go inside. Wait for Tam.

Where was he?

That moment she saw him racing Dex across the hillside. Wild. Untamed. Free. He gave no heed to his safety. The scene was vivid. Stirring. She understood the thrill of racing. Many times, she raced her stallion across the hills where she lived. Tam was bent low, his chest just above the stallion's neck. His hair blew in the wind. When he saw her, he stopped. Dex reared on his hindlegs. Tam stared at her before he turned the horse. Headed to the stable. He would come back. He wasn't hurt. She breathed in a deep breath of relief. Couldn't decide if she should run to the protection of her room or stay on the porch to wait for him.

Her hands were clasped beneath her chin. Watching. Enchanted by the magic the two created. The scene was thrilling.

Once the vision ended, Kerrie wanted to rail at him for making her worry. After that, she needed to run to him. Wrap her arms around him so she could feel his heartbeat against hers. Afraid he wouldn't wish for that type of attention from her. She held her ground, remaining on the porch while she watched him lead Dex into the stable. She was still on the porch ten minutes later when he walked to the house.

He stood in front of her, his hands on his lean hips, his lips twitching with what appeared to be a smile. Her mind felt blank.

"Dinner is ready if you're interested. If not, you can go to the devil!" She couldn't mask her anger any longer. He owed her an explanation.

~ * ~

The events of today tried every nerve he possessed. When he saw her standing at the counter kneading bread wearing her chemise and skirt, his body went rigid. Every part of him soared to attention. He'd not thought to be put in a position such as this. It was all he could do not to toss her skirts then and there make her his. It took all his restraint to leave her in the kitchen with the bread dough when he would rather carry her to his bed. When he set his course, he had the intention of wooing her as she deserved. What he did today was attack her. He wasn't going to apologize. Kerrie tempted him beyond his wildest dreams, beyond anything he ever experienced. When he wanted a woman in his bed, all he needed to do was ask. Women made themselves available to him...because of his title coupled with his wealth. They wanted marriage. She liked the attention he gave her. Never told him no. Didn't protest in any way. If she had, he would have stopped despite the cost. The whispered kisses, the soft caresses. The little female sounds she made when he caressed her told him she enjoyed what he did. Told him he gave her pleasure.

She was so damn tempting. Beautiful. Intriguing. Frustrating. Annoying as hell. Her body teased. He was right when he saw her breasts more fully revealed. They were ripe peaches waiting for him to pluck. Her nipples were a dusky rose, tight hard buds that begged as well as tortured every nerve ending he possessed. Her breasts weren't large. They weren't small either. Tam wasn't a man used to denying himself his pleasures. If this had been another woman, he would have finished what he began. This wasn't another woman. This was the woman he hoped to make his wife. Would make his wife. If he didn't scare her away, she would be his.

With Kerrie, he needed to take his time. He didn't know if his body would grant him the time to court her the way she deserved. She was innocent. Wasn't at all like the usual woman he took to his bed. Bloody hell, her untried kiss sent him over the edge. When she slid her tongue into his mouth, he thought he'd gone to heaven or hell since he couldn't finish what he began. Tam understood the second time around with her that if he didn't leave, he would be deep inside the coveted heat of her warm inviting body. He wouldn't wait for the vows to be said, for her agreement to be his wife. He would make her his in every way that counted.

He didn't know how he was going to wait another day or the three weeks necessary for the banns to be read. He prayed his father procured that special license for him. If she continued to tempt him, he would have her in his bed before it was proper. Distance was all that would keep them apart. In this small hunting lodge, there was no way he could keep distance between them.

She didn't understand what she did to him. She believed he didn't like her. Never understood how flirtatious her smile was when she gifted him with it. She didn't even try. Thank God, he irritated her often enough the smile was rare.

She didn't understand when he set her aside. She looked confused then annoyed, frustrated too. So was he. After that she looked hurt. Her cheeks turned a beautiful shade of embarrassment. He didn't want her to feel humiliated.

She would not understand why he raced off as if the hounds of hell chased him. He would never be able to explain how the sight of her, the taste of her inflamed him. One kiss left him mindless with desire. Hard. Wanting. Tortured with need.

"Dinner is ready?" he asked, surfacing from his thoughts when she walked into the room. Now, when he looked at her, his memory kicked into overdrive. He knew the shape as well as the size of her breasts. Knew the tantalizing curve to her hips. The sweet scent of her...vanilla...all woman. Her breasts were enough to fill his hands. Not overlarge and not so small he would have to search for her curves in the dark. The taste of her plump lips...ah...he would never get enough of tasting. Relishing their softness, he found on all parts of her body.

It was underhanded of him to slip the straps of her chemise down her arms when her hands were buried in gooey bread dough. To take advantage of a moment he was not supposed to witness. He didn't feel guilt or regret seeing first-hand what her body had to offer. While she didn't know his plans, she would marry him soon. Time was all that stood in the way. There was no alternative.

Tam didn't want to frighten her. All he managed to do was to hurt her feelings when he stormed out. Bloody everlasting hell! He couldn't stay on the porch, Kerrie on his lap sweetly compliant, kiss her, touch her without taking more than she was ready to give. Explaining to an innocent maiden his reasons for his mad dash also was not plausible.

He had no doubts he could seduce her. Charm her to his bed. He'd had enough practice. If he willed it that way, she would fall into his arms with no hesitation tonight. Her response to him this afternoon was quick as well as passionate. He felt raw desire rip through her. Through him. Straight to his sex. Dear Lord, when she rubbed her tongue across his, he thought he would explode at that second.

Somehow, he would have to explain. The words for an explanation weren't in his head. How did a man tell an innocent how much he needed her? That he needed to make love to her. Wanted to feel her surrounding him. All she wished for was a kiss then perhaps another one. He didn't think another kiss would be possible without taking more than she was able to give.

"Yes," she breathed, her eyes shimmering with unshed moisture. "Dinner is ready. We could eat in the kitchen or on the porch. You make the choice since I've no idea of your way of thinking."

"The kitchen would be nice," Tam told her, hoping there might be more distance for him. Two chairs separating them. A table between. The chill of the air. Tonight, there wouldn't be a storm. What appeared to be billowing clouds were blown away. While the sky wasn't clear, there was nothing that would bring on a tempest. With the lack of a breeze the evening turned sultry, too warm. He pulled at his damp shirt. Maybe the heat was caused by thoughts of her delectable little body beneath his while he thrust into her. When he closed his eyes, he remembered the way the tip of her breast pebbled when he touched the hardness. He swallowed.

Tamped down the burgeoning lust at his groin.

He knew the curve of her hips.

Tasted her.

"Wine?" she asked, her voice wobbling a bit. "I would..."

"I will carry the tray along with the wine. Why don't you go to the porch. Make yourself comfortable? Bring one of the comforters. Outside it might grow chilly. Don't want you to be cold."

Her voice was hesitant. She was doing everything she could, to keep him happy. She didn't need to. He was a man who had gone to heaven and back. "If that's what you want."

It was. He followed her, watching the gentle sway of her hips. Intrigued by what she might do the rest of the evening. She set the tray on the table between them. Splashed a bit of wine into the glasses. He needed more than a tiny spill. He filled the glasses to the brim.

The meal was strained, silent. No words were said. Kerrie held herself aloof. The line of her back remained stiff. Her attention focused on the lake. He didn't blame her. She was guarding herself against more hurt or awkwardness. Tam didn't know what it was she felt for him.

*She didn't tell me no. Responded as if on fire. Melted against me as if she was made of warm honey.*

Yes, the lake beckoned. A swim would cool him off. Once the sun set and Kerrie left to go to bed, he would go for a swim. Cool off. Just being with her, not even touching her, he stood at attention. The next few days might well be the longest of his life. The carriage ride to London would be strained. Tam didn't know how he was going to stay away from her. Didn't know how he could withstand the two days in a carriage with her.

She tempted beyond endurance.

Teased without knowing what she was doing.

Once the sun went down and the evening grew dark, he said a silent prayer of thanks. Tam watched her walk up the steps to her room. She glanced over her shoulder. The amber of her eyes picked up the candle light. He should go to her. Explain. Explaining wasn't possible.

He should go to her. Somehow, apologize for his behavior. Doing so would get him into more trouble. Deep water would close over his head.

He would drown.

Tam waited in the main living area hoping she would not return down the steps. Once he felt certain she was in her room and not coming out, he grabbed a towel. He stripped on the porch until he wore only his buckskins. At the dock, he tugged his pants off. Once he reached the dock, he ran. Dove into the cool inviting depths. His body eased. Sweat from the day's sultry heat washed away. Cool water caressed him. He breathed in a deep silent breath of relief. Already, he felt better.

Beneath the water he swam until his lungs felt as if they would burst. After surfacing for air, he dove again. Water caressed his heated flesh. Came up for air. Dove. Tam let his mind wander. Roamed to the woman with chestnut hair washed with hints of the sun. Turned to the breasts he desired. Taste. Touch. Scent. He required all of her. He needed to find a means to keep images of her out of his head. Impossible.

With sure strokes he swam to one end of the lake. Sat on a rock for a few minutes before disappearing under the water again. He immerged. Shook his head watching as drops of water flew from his hair. Turned onto his back. Floated. Felt a small ripple against him. Alerted him to someone in the lake. That person had to be Kerrie. There was no one else around. He tread water in order to watch. He waited. Tried to control the raw hunger for the woman from taking over his senses.

Darkness encased the lake. A shadow slipped into the water beside the dock. Swam with sure strong strokes across the lake.

Kerrie? She disappeared then resurfaced.

She was here to torment him again. Torture a man in agony. This was cruel. Kerrie didn't know her presence tortured him. Drove him mad with lust. Did she know he was in the lake? That was doubtful. When she left to go upstairs, she looked as if she wanted distance between them too. Confusion was still the expression on her face. She came here to cool off as well as think. Just as he did.

He didn't wish to frighten her. She must not know he was in the lake. Wouldn't be aware he watched her.

"Kerrie," he called out his voice soft. He heard the muffled gasp. Splashing from her strokes stopped. Would she be as naked as he was? No, she would wear her chemise as she did the night she bathed. Close enough to naked. His body hardened. His thoughts escalated faster than he could assimilate them. She was erotic, evocative. He could make love to her with only liquid between them. If he wasn't mistaken, this would be her first.

"Tam? What are you doing in the lake? You're not supposed to be here. Just as you weren't supposed to be in the kitchen." She sounded both angry as well as annoyed. "I...wished to be alone. You can't...have to go."

Powerless to stop himself he barked a laugh. He needed to be alone too. "Swimming? You? What is it that you do in the lake? Something other than swim? I would know. It might be entertaining. Fun. Can I watch?"

"I...needed to cool off. I was sweaty. The day was hot as well as humid. Didn't wish to heat water for a bath." She sounded apologetic. "I'll leave. You must wish to be alone. Don't...no...intrude on your space."

"No!" He swam toward her. Knew doing so was a mistake. His muddled brain didn't think with clear vision when she was near. He thought of all the reasons he should hold her, kiss her, explain. Forgot the reasons he should not. "Don't go because of me. It's a big lake. We can both cool off from the heat of the day."

Knew with her in the water the lake was not big enough for both of them. Tam wished he could enfold her in his arms. Wished for her long legs to be wrapped around his flanks. He could make this happen. No one could stop him except Kerrie. If her earlier behavior was indicative of now, she wouldn't.

"If you say so..." Kerrie swam toward him. She was a good swimmer. Confident. Strong. She stopped a few feet in front of him, treading water. Light from the moon showed him her smile. If he didn't know better, he would call the brilliant grin mischievous. Wicked. Tempting. She was a naughty girl. He jerked when she sent a spray of water straight to his face.

"Little witch!"

Tam was stunned for the moment. Never expected that. He wiped the water away. Watched, fascinated, waiting for what would happen next.

As soon as she splashed him, she turned to race away. Her kick sent more water into his face. Tam bent his strength with one purpose, to catch her. She was fast. He was faster. Tam caught her foot. Pulled her toward him. Her laughter turned into a giggle. A delightful sound that heated every sense he possessed. His hands were on her shoulders. Her upturned face stared into his eyes.

The moment was his. He meant to capitalize. "Hold your breath." After he was positive she did as he said, he pushed her underwater. Held her there for a couple of seconds. Backed away after he let go. Waited for the revenge that was certain to follow. The naughty lady would want the last say. She wouldn't have it.

When she came up sputtering, it was to lunge toward him then put her hands on his shoulders. Her breasts touched upon him. He caught the slight vanilla scent that identified her. They both went beneath the lake. His hands on her small waist, he pulled her up. The shore was close. He stood. Tam was naked. For all the good it did her, she was all but naked in her wet chemise. The beautiful rose blush at the tips of her breasts drew him. All the reasons he had for swimming vanished. Assaulted by his masculine needs, he continued.

"Wrap your legs around me, honey." He knew he was in a wealth of trouble when his member pulsed against her with intimate exactness. Felt the sultry heat between her legs. Her core open to him. Deep inside a groan rumbled from his chest. She was close yet so far away. He could bury himself inside her. Could touch her womb. He could not!

"You're naked?" There was question in her voice. "I feel...I feel...is that?"

Tam didn't wish to hear the words she was about to say. He knew what she felt. His sex was eager, over eager to seek her warmth. He burned. She set him on fire. Even though she sounded in awe. His lips captured hers in a long drugging kiss. He swept his tongue along the outside of her lips, once then twice. Felt her heat everywhere. Her breasts pushed against his chest. Nipples moved with her body, against him, pushed upon him as she pulled herself closer. Firm curves he needed to hold in his hands pressed closer and closer still. He didn't dare. She opened for him. With brazen need, he thrust his tongue inside her open mouth. She reciprocated. Brazen. Audacious. She tasted of warm Kerrie and wine as she melted over him. He pulled her closer, his hands at the small of her back. Lowered to cup her bottom. She wound her fingers into his hair. All that separated their bodies were a fine, flimsy chemise and a slide of water. Heaven to this drowning man.

Enchantment filled him. Her magic made him feel complete. Reality rushed to the forefront. He needed to think of her first. Remember his ultimate goals. Didn't wish to frighten her. His lips ran along the column of her neck. Touched the pounding point at the base. Slipped along her collarbone. She was fire in his arms, in his soul. The magic of her enchanted him. By himself, he could not hold himself in check. To pull away from the heady touch of her sultry lips, he needed her help. Willed her to tell him to stop.

Kerrie tossed her head back, giving him permission to explore.

"Tell me no." He needed her words so he could put an end to this before he couldn't. "Tell me no before it's too late. Before I do something we both might come to regret. That might cause you grief."

Sex before marriage wasn't the proper order. That was what he was about. The right way to proceed with his future wife. He never proceeded the wrong way.

Stopping now would hurt her again. Going forward would also hurt her. The last thing he wished to do was give pain to this woman he was coming to adore. The explanation couldn't be made as to why he stopped. His arousal was obvious, pulsing against her, touching the heat he needed to explore. How would he tell her he intended their first time together to be as man and wife. In his bed at his ancestral home, was supposed to be the first time. Unable as well as unwilling to stop himself, he pushed the straps of her chemise down her arms. He must taste. For him there was no alternative. The tips of her breasts touched upon him, hardened further. He was besotted. She was all he ever wanted in a woman, a wife. His future. All his past dalliances were just that in the past. With her in his arms, he was no longer a single man. He needed to be with her as much as he needed air to breathe.

"Yes," she said as he tested her breast with the palm of his hand. Touched upon the hardened tip.

The need to suckle overwhelmed. Tonight, she could be his. In his mind, if that happened, there would be no question as to a marriage. In her mind...that would be left as a question. He was certain. She would refuse.

Tam gritted his teeth. Distanced himself. Restraint was everything. Had to put her aside before he gave in to his building lust. "Come along. The water is chilling you. Don't wish for you to get sick. You need to get dry then warmed by the fire." He prayed she would comply. Would not feel the sting of rejection. The devil knew he didn't wish to end this seduction of both parties.

"I'm heated from the inside out. Doubt if I'll take a chill. I'm never sick." She protested his treatment as did he. "What about you? Are you cold?"

Her words were whimsical then hard. If he could do so, she would know true fire. He would make certain she burned from the inside out. In time, "It's the kisses, honey that have warmed you. We need to dry off. You go first. I'll wait here." He paused for a few moments. "Did you bring a towel?"

"Two," she giggled. "One is for my hair. I don't want to stop... Like playing in the water with you."

It seemed she realized he wasn't giving her a choice.

He loved the sound of her girlish laughter. He adored playing in the water with her. Needed to hear more of the laughter. Until Kerrie, he never liked a woman's giggle. "I'll wait for you in the water. Take your shift off. Wrap the towel around you. As soon as you are in the house, I'll follow." He was doing everything possible to keep Kerrie's virtue safe from him.

"If that's what you want. I was having fun," she murmured, sounding stunned that playtime was over. The sound of her voice sent a chill through him. Again, she was feeling the sting of rejection. There was nothing to do about that.

"So was I. Thought you might need to rethink..." He cleared his throat, choking on his thoughts. "Rethink what was about to happen."

"Do I? Rethink?" She swept her tongue across her lips. "Did I do something wrong? I would know. Am I too bold? Men don't like bold or brazen. Fun...what we did was fun. No? You didn't have fun?"

"Nothing wrong. You're perfect. Too perfect. Alluring. We just need to stop before it's too late to end what we are about. Don't want to take something from you you're not ready to gift me with." Tam thought he might have said too much. He needed her to understand that he was about to take her virginity. She wouldn't want that.

Her expression seemed strained, her lips turning down. He swore in silence. She didn't understand. "I'll be right there. Hurry. Go quick so I don't take a chill. Can't claim I've never been sick."

Powerless to stop himself, he watched her swim to the dock. She used the ladder then walked away from him, from the water. Moonlight caught her slim form, her narrow waist, the curve of her hips. Saw the chemise flutter over her head then pool on the ground catching the light. Watched her wrap the towel around her body then one around her head after she wrung water out of her hair. She paused then looked for him in the darkness as if waiting for some signal.

She stopped midway to the lodge. A glance over her shoulder told him she would wait for him. Tam didn't believe she would be ready to see a naked and fully aroused man. He gestured with his hand. "Go on. I'll be right there."

Stiff strides, back straight as if laced with starch, took her to the porch then into the house. Tam didn't know how he would find her disposition. Following in her wake, he dried himself then wrapped the big towel around his waist. He picked up his buckskins.

Stepping inside the lodge, the main room was empty. The fire in the hearth still crackled, the embers snaping. A candle burned, wax dripping down the side. Tam added a piece of wood. Dropping the towel, he slid into his buckskins then put his arms in his shirt sleeves. Next when he saw her, he saw her toes first. She paused at the top of the stairs as if debating. With a long heft of air, seemed she made up her mind. As she walked down the stairs, the robe she put on opened with each step. Her legs were bare then covered. The sight tantalized every nerve ending. The vision did nothing to tamp down the raw passion he felt increasing since knowing she was swimming, almost naked, in the lake with him. He wanted her more now than he did when he first realized where she was. Wondered what she wore beneath the robe. If he had his wish, she'd be naked.

Kerrie sat down by the fire, brushing out the length of hair that shimmered different shades of red and gold in the firelight. He stood beside her. Intense. "Would you like me to brush your hair again?"

Several seconds passed while he held his breath hoping Kerrie would be agreeable. Tam didn't know if that was something he could do and remain steadfast to his plans.

The smile she graced him with sent another bolt of fire to his loins. "It was nice the other night when you brushed my hair. You were very good. Yes, if you would like. Don't wish to do something that will send you racing away from me. Don't understand why. If you could explain..." As if she didn't wish to hear the answer, she let the statement fade.

More than she could guess, he needed to touch her. Once again, he pulled her between his legs while he leaned against the couch. Minutes ticked by as he gave tender attention to her hair. Spread the length through his fingers. Let the silken strands sift through the sensitive parts between them. After it was dry, he pulled her against him. His arms were wrapped around her, crossed beneath her breasts. It was all he could do to restrain himself from taking this intimate moment with her farther. He didn't dare. Another bout of rejection from him would not advance his cause.

She sipped the wine he poured before they sat down, snuggling closer to him. With each innocent move, she pressed against his arousal, stoking the fire that needed no help to flame to life. "I like the way it feels when you touch me. Why did you leave this afternoon? Why did you stop while we were in the lake? I didn't say no. I said yes. Wanted something..." This time her words held a wealth of accusation. "Don't know what that was. Hoped to discover the truth."

"You should have told me to stop," he ground out through clenched teeth, understanding what she wanted but she didn't understand all that entailed.

If she wasn't the woman he meant to become his wife, he might have answered her needs. She was right. She didn't tell him to stop. Though that fact pleased him. "You should tell me no. Next time I might not be able to stop on my own. I might take something you've no intention of giving." More words, curse words were on the edge of his tongue. She didn't need to hear them. Tam bit them all back furious with himself. If he said what he was thinking, he would shock her.

"What if I don't want you to stop? Shouldn't I have some say in what is going on between us? A relationship takes two people. Doesn't it?"

She turned. Set her finger on his chin, trailed the tip along his jaw. She moistened her mouth as if preparing for his touch. "Would you kiss me again? I do like how it feels deep inside when you touch your mouth to mine, when I feel your tongue touch inside me."

He couldn't answer her with honesty. Of course, he wanted to kiss her and so much more that her toes would curl if she knew all he hoped to experience with this woman. Not tonight. No curling toes yet. Soon...more than her toes would twist then bend with the way his hands moved on her body.

His brows drew together. She caressed them from the middle outward. "I promise. I want another kiss. Maybe even one after that. Would you mind terribly?"

Tam groaned a deep husky sound that told of his lust for one special woman. The question was absurd. He didn't mind at all. Compromising her might be the way to deal with her. "One kiss, after that you will go to bed. I'm not going to make love to you tonight. Tempt me no further."

He wanted to take hope in the crestfallen look she sent his way. Prayed she would accept his words. Tam bent close, intending to make this kiss as chaste as possible.

"If that's all I can hope for then so be it," she told him, sounding resigned to accepting one kiss, nothing more.

His lips brushed with light strokes across hers. She swept her tongue along his mouth. Opened for him begging for his entrance. He was a man enamored of his future wife. Her magic was potent, the enchantment overwhelming, too strong for his weak male body, the heat burning inside. Mercuric. Bearing down on him straining his resolve. Tam was not going to set aside his plans. They would remain in place. His fists squeezed against her.

Trying to smile he pulled away. Ran his knuckles along the softness of her cheek. Allowed them to travel the length of her neck. Tam wanted to push the fabric of her robe down her arms then explore the soft exquisite curves he would find. Wished to discover if she was wet with her need. His voice was husky with raw desire when he spoke. He was hungry for his woman. Not tonight. "Go to bed, Kerrie. I'll see you in the morning."

He was taken aback by the tears in her eyes. A single drop slid down her cheek. His resolve almost ended.

"Yes, the morning. I remember now. You don't like me. You wouldn't leave me like this if you cared anything for me!"

Her brows furrowed. Anger simmered. She pushed away from him flying up the stairs with her robe hiked to her knees.

"Bloody everlasting hell!" he swore violently beneath his breath.

His fist hit the wall making everything shudder. The candle rocked on its base. The clock on the mantle swayed. When the last thing he wished to do was cause tears, he hurt her again. Tam strode outside then around the lodge to where he could see her window. A candle burned. Flickered. Went out. She went to bed. That was what he needed her to do. He just didn't like the tears. The hurt he inflicted while trying to save her from his lust was damning.

He rubbed his hands along the back of his neck. Shaking his head, he walked to the dock, thinking about another swim. All he wanted was to shield her from pain. Instead, he caused the heartache. Caused her tears. While he was pleased she wanted him, he understood he still had an uphill battle to wager. It would be so easy to give into his need for her small soft body. To go to her then teach her pleasure.

If he went to her then apologized, all would be lost. She would be in his arms. Beneath him. His control was fleeting. He returned to the porch then into the main room. Needed to court her the right way. All he'd done so far was wrong. He sat staring at the fire with his glass of wine between his fingers dangling between his legs. If he thought it wise, he would drink until he couldn't keep his eyes open. Sleep on the sofa. As the night drew on, he steadied himself then attacked the stairs.

When he walked by her room on the way to his, he heard her muffled sobs. His heart shattered into thousands of pieces. Tam couldn't allow her to cry. While he understood his reasons for rejecting her, she didn't. He wasn't certain what to do. He couldn't leave her this way. He couldn't go to her without doing the same again.

Unable to leave her in the state she was in, Tam knocked on her door. "Kerrie? Honey, can I come in?"

She didn't answer. With caution, he pushed open the door. When he saw her curled on her bed, a pillow clutched to her chest, his heart broke. Shattered into thousands of pieces.

Kerrie sat up, pushing her hair from her eyes. "I don't want to see you. Don't come in here. All you do is hurt me. Reject me. You hate me. I can't live like this. One minute feeling ecstasy from you then the rejection. How do you really feel about me?"

Powerless to stop his feet from moving, he strode to the bed. After he sat down, Tam pulled her into his arms. Her cheek pressed into the hollow of his shoulder. He ran his hand along her back, hoping the movement would sooth the pain, stop her tears.

"Don't cry." He heard her hiccup then snort. "Please, don't cry. The last thing I want is to hurt you. I'm trying to protect your innocence. I want you more than I've ever wanted another woman. Won't take your virtue. I'm not..."

How could he tell her what he wanted without...? Maybe he could just hold her until she slept. Don't kiss. Don't touch where you shouldn't.

The words he searched for didn't gather momentum. The clock on the shelf ticked. A lone candle burned down to a nubbin. She must have lit another one. Wind whistled with a soft sound along the eaves.

She pushed away. Tears slid down her cheeks. With his fingertip he collected a drop. "I'm sorry, honey."

"Why don't you want me?"

An honest question, one he couldn't ignore. "I've told you over and over again. I do want you. Need you more than any woman I've ever met." Tam wanted her more than anything, more than any other female he'd made love to. In the few days he knew her, she became a fever in his blood. He hungered every moment for her.

"Then...why do you turn away from me? Why do you kiss me then act as if you disliked the kiss? As if you don't want to..." Kerrie caught her bottom lip with her teeth. "Why?"

His gut turned over. All his protective instincts came into play. "Can't explain. In time..." Hell, in time, he wouldn't have to give her the words. Maybe he should break through her maidenhead. Get her pregnant. If she carried his child, even if she discovered he was a marquis in line to be the Duke of Sherburn, she would have to acquiesce then marry him. He wasn't a man to carry on in the wrong order. If a man was going to marry, he would wait for the wedding night. There would be no child conceived before the ceremony that would bind them together for life. He couldn't explain his reasoning. In this modern era, his beliefs seemed to be obsolete. Even Drake and Ella had relations before they wed. That was about twenty years ago. Maybe he was obsolete in his thinking. A man could have a change of opinion. He was known throughout the ton as a prude. The label fit. This little sprite was changing him.

In retrospect, Tam didn't want that for her or for him. He needed to do this right, with respect for the woman he knew she was. Everything in the proper order. To dishonor her would also dishonor him. The right order of events was far too important to ignore. She would remain a virgin until their wedding night. There was no other way for him.

"Go to sleep. I'll stay here with you. Hold you, tell you to sleep."

"Why? You don't like me."

Her words hit home. Shattered his composure. He told her over and over again, that wasn't the case. He didn't know what else to say. Understood with mere words he'd be unable to convince her. She was stubborn to her Scottish core.

"I'll stay here because I caused your discomfort. I'll hold you until you go to sleep because I need to make amends."

Tam pulled her back into his arms as he lay down beside her. Stroking her hair, he let out a long breath of air. This well might be the longest night of his life. Never before had he denied himself. A beautiful passionate woman in his arms was willing. This was a first for him. Until this moment, he realized that he always took what he wanted.

Her face was nestled against his chest. His arm was around her holding her close. He pulled the covers on the bed over them while he listened to her breathe. Tender feelings assailed, washed into him. Tam understood what he did was right. Even though sleeping on her bed with her in his arms was far from proper. After his actions today, she needed comfort. She was willing to give herself to him. Kerrie didn't know she would despise him if she learned the rest of his name...names...the multitude of names that told the world he was titled. He had a horde of names. The name he didn't wish to share with her.

Sterling Talmage, heir to the dukedom, was always proper. Serious. Upstanding. Never created a scandal. Why did this fragile slip of a lady run him astray of his convictions? She turned him upside down. Inside out. Didn't know if he was coming or going. His restraint lacked power. If he spent much more time in her company, he would lose the battle he was fighting against himself. He had to marry her as soon as possible. How would he go about convincing her to bind her life to his? She was positive he despised her.

Wind rustled around the eaves.

The ticking of the clock told him time passed.

He knew when she slept. Her breathing changed. Her body relaxed into his. She no longer held herself stiff against him. He needed to leave soon. One leg of hers was bent over his. Her hand rested on his belly. He imagined many future nights like this. There would be differences. They would spend the night along with the morning making love. He smiled. Felt her lashes flutter on his nakedness.

Without waking her, he moved her. Settled her head on the pillow. Tomorrow was their last day here. He would have to find things to do away from her. Taking her into his arms for a kiss no matter how tempting was forbidden. He put this in motion the afternoon he found her half-naked, her hands buried in bread dough.

At the door, he stopped to look at her. She slept...peaceful slumber. Now he wondered if he would be able to sleep. Not for a while. With a soft snick, he closed the door. Barefoot, he padded down the steps to the main room. Tam poured himself a full snifter of brandy before sitting on one of the chairs facing the dying fire.

He closed his eyes, remembering the day, the kisses, her body so close to his he felt her sultry heat caress him. Kerrie Johnston was a woman to look forward to knowing more. Wished to understand all of her thoughts. Hoped he could compromise enough to keep her content. He trusted his father had the special license. He needed the marriage before she learned of his title. She would be his duchess. How long could he last as a Mister before she discovered his truth?

This marriage was something to look forward to. He sipped the brandy and watched the fire while plotting his path tomorrow. He would do all in his power to make certain he didn't hurt her. Intimacy was forbidden. Distance was hoped for.

She might be disappointed when she woke up alone. He would leave her a message at breakfast. Words that might make her smile.

~ * ~

Early the next morning, he would make a huge breakfast. Would leave the eggs and bacon warming in the oven along with potatoes. He whistled while he composed a short letter to her. Pleased his idea might make her happy.

*Kerrie,*

*Enjoy breakfast. I will exercise the horses. If you wish to help, come to the stable. You can ride Dex with me. If you would rather stay indoors, you should please yourself with whatever you like to do. Drake has an extensive library in his office as I'm certain you know. You are welcome to peruse the books.*

*I will be back for lunch. At that time, we can discuss plans for tomorrow. I would like to get an early start as I'm eager to reach my home. I'm certain you are also eager to see your aunt and uncle.*

*If you decide to make bread, it might be best if you keep all your clothing on your delightful self. If I witnessed you in your déshabillé, I would be tempted to taste you again. Where you are concerned, I've no willpower. Let's not tempt a man who is not a saint. Shall we?*

*However, I do expect to see you in the stable sometime. Do you enjoy mucking out the stalls? No? Neither do I. Suppose you've had ample opportunity since your mother breeds horses. You must know your way about the horses along with their needs.*

*I will see you sometime today. If not at lunch, perhaps sooner.*

*Tam*

He understood he needed to stay at least two steps ahead of her if not more. When or if she showed up to ride, he would need to be unavailable. Her sitting in front of him on Dex was not a good notion. At lunchtime he would be late or early, hoping she was finished. Getting everything ready for the trip to London was his primary concern. Notes needed to be written to his retainers in the village below confirming his earlier instructions. In the interim, he didn't wish to hear even one 'Your Grace.' He had to make that perfectly clear to everyone who he employed. Heads would roll if there were mistakes.

His personal carriage needed to be nowhere in sight. By now, that ducal emblazoned vehicle should be in London. She would be none the wiser. None of his retainers would be nearby to thwart his fake identity. They would travel via her coach to London. Understanding how fast the sight of her sent fire coursing through his blood, it would be best for him to ride one of the horses most of the time. The two of them cooped up alone in the carriage was dangerous to his well-being...more to hers. She would not be pleased if he rode Dex instead of being with her in the coach. Something else he'd need to deal with.

Finishing his drink, he let out a long sigh, wishing it was morning. Taking the steps two at a time, he headed upstairs. Stopped at her room with his ear to the door. Nothing. He wasn't going to risk waking her to peek into the room. She could still be sleeping.

In his bedchamber, he stared out the window. Sleep, he needed to sleep a few hours. Slipping from his clothing, he lay down. Closed his eyes.

Muted light filtering through the window woke him. Looking out the single pane of glass he noted the gray skies. Rain pelted the window. He groaned hoping the deluge would cease before the path down the mountainside was running with water, a river, as well as too muddy to travel. A low rumble of thunder, a blast of wind hitting glass told him the storm would not let up soon. Yellow-blue light flashed across the sky. Padding naked to the window, disheartened he stared out at the early morning storm. All his plans would be put on hold.

If he mucked out the stalls, he would be too smelly as well as dirty to take Kerrie into his arms, kiss her senseless, hurt her. He clenched his teeth together, willing himself to more control, more restraint.

Tam poured water into the basin. Washed his face and chest. He pulled out clean clothes then shifted the thoughts in his mind and donned the ones he wore yesterday. Heading for the kitchen, he put an ear to her door, hoping to find the room still silent.

Good, he would fix breakfast, eat then take himself off for chores just as he described in his note to her. Tam was glad arrangements for tomorrow were made ahead of departure. All he meant to do today was to confirm those preparations. With the rain pouring from the skies that would be impossible. He would have to keep his fingers crossed no evidence of his status was left in the village.

Stepping into the kitchen, he stopped midstride. His plans changed a second time in the few minutes he'd been awake. Kerrie was stirring the eggs then flipping the pancakes. Potatoes simmered in another pan along with bacon. He was not going to get a respite. There would be no distance unless the barrier could be the kitchen table.

"You're up early. Did you sleep well?" she asked, a smile parted her sweet, kissable mouth.

"Not as well as I would have liked." *Not as well if you'd been in my arms warm against me.*

"Should have expected you to leave my bed. Nonetheless, your presence was pleasant while it lasted. You were warm. Your arms around me felt like a boosting place. You did make me feel better." She poured more batter into the pan. Other than those words, it appeared she meant to ignore him.

*Boosting place? What did that mean?* "You and I...we cannot sleep together. Has nothing to do with whether I like you or not." Tired of explaining himself, his words were harsher than he wished.

"You don't want to hurt me...my feelings. Rest assured, I understand how you feel about me. You won't hurt me again. I won't let that happen. I've wrapped a hard shell around me."

It seemed they were of like minds...yet they were not. Her back was stiff, her nose in the air proving her point. Her words were true. She built a wall around them. He felt the unfriendly distance opening between them.

The pain in her eyes coupled with her words told him she was going to hold herself aloof from him for the rest of their stay. It was obvious they weren't feeling the same. She had no idea. For now, that was good. They still had today as well as two more before he could begin to court her in the proper manner. He needed a chaperone at all times though he knew himself well enough to understand he would seek some alone time with her. There would be a ball. The next day he would call on her. Meant to ride with her. Show her a few of his favorite places. That would be their alone time. Seemed safe enough.

"You have no idea how I feel about you. You don't listen to a word I say. Are you always this stubborn?"

He was tempted to pull her into his arms for an early morning kiss. The action would lead to more, then even more kisses. He couldn't risk touching her in any manner. Even a chaste kiss would lead to more than what he deemed proper without marriage.

"Why don't you tell me?" Kerrie was quick to ask as if she hoped for a confession.

"Seems we've a thunderstorm rolling down the mountainside. Hope the tempest doesn't change our plans for tomorrow."

Tam searched his head. Staying here one more day alone with her... No, he wouldn't let that happen. Even if the storm dumped water on them, they would be able to leave by noon. They would reach the tiny village below. Start out making up time by riding until dark. That was not his original plan. The second, ill-advised scenario would have to do.

"Seems that way." She spooned eggs from the pan, dividing them then placing more food on his plate. Kerrie handed it to him. Stood by him for a few seconds before she ignored him again. "There you go."

"Suppose we can't ride Dex today...if it rains...a storm." Tam searched for more conversation, falling short on ideas. He would spend the majority of the day cleaning out the stalls. Dex would remain locked up. He'd be dirty, smelly. She wouldn't wish to be anywhere near him.

"Suppose we can't." Kerrie sat down opposite him. "If the rain does let up, I'll be in the stable ready as well as eager for that ride. Decided Blaze wouldn't do for a name for the mare. I'm going to call her Briar, if that suits you."

It suited him just fine. Though he didn't tell her yet. The mare was hers.

~ * ~

Ella stood back, her arms crossed in front of her looking at her handiwork. The bodice was too big on Kerrie. Her breasts were too small to fit into the gown that had been sized to her younger sister. The corsage should have fit. Obviously, the gown did not. Well...it worked a different time. It would work now. The ploy had too. She handed Kerrie several scarves then several more. Kerrie appeared perplexed by the entire scenario.

"What are these for?"

Ella was quick to say. "Stuff those in the bodice. That should do the trick. Fill you out quite nicely. This little maneuver worked for your cousin Nicki. She got the wrong dress too. The one meant for Lyssa. We both know how well-endowed your cousin is. Don't understand all the mistakes coming from the modiste. She didn't used to make so many..."

Ella tossed her hands in the air frustrated beyond measure. The ploy never worked for Nickie. She was trying to make light of the situation for Kerrie's sake.

"I don't like this. Don't wish to deceive anyone." Though she did as Ella bade her. Kerrie stuffed the scarfs inside the gown to fill out the bodice. "Don't want anyone to notice me," she mumbled.

"Are you thinking of your Mr. Talmadge?" Ella asked, laughing.

She received stern orders from Drake that she wasn't to let on that Mr. Talmage was a marquis soon to be a duke when his sick father passed. Tam would rather have his father alive than the title he never wished for in the first place. Ella was pleased when she saw the flush of rose color sweeping across Kerrie's chest to rise to her cheeks. "Trust me, he won't ever know." Ah...but the McInnis noticed the scarves in Nicki's bodice. Pulled them out. Ella gave a silent prayer that Tam wasn't quite as observant. The man shouldn't be peering down the front of her gown. Drake did warn her that was what all men did given the opportunity.

"Was he invited? A man with no title?" Kerrie sounded incredulous. "Will there be men there who aren't lords of the realm? Is it just because he is wealthy? He did tell me that much. Inherited some estates."

"Yes, and yes." Ella was smiling with fondness for her niece. She'd become a lovely young woman. No wonder she caught Tam's eye. The man was lucky he discovered her aversion to titles before she discovered his. Before he let the cat out of the bag, so to speak. If Tam's plans worked out, Kerrie would be a countess in the next few days. Later she would be his duchess. The marquis would have a great deal of explaining to do. Might be fun to watch him backpedal. He would trip over his tongue before he succeeded in his endeavor. Sometimes men such as the marquis as well as her husband the duke needed to be brought down a peg or two. Backpedaling was good for their highhanded ways, their inborn arrogance. A retreat would be in order before another advance.

"Tam will come to the ball? Be surprised. Didn't give me the impression he liked these affairs any more than I do," she snorted her dislike. "I would rather go out and ride Dex or Briar. Suppose they both need exercise. I believe in this, Tam and I are of like minds."

"You are right. Tam doesn't like these types of affairs. However, I do believe he wants to see a certain young lady he became acquainted with in a most inappropriate manner... unchaperoned. Your Tam doesn't like to do things in the wrong order or create scandal. He's quite stuffy. You do know that. I'm surprised you like him. The two of you are so different. You're a free spirit." Ella was rearranging some of Kerrie's curls. Giving added touches that weren't needed. She wanted to keep her hands busy so she wouldn't spout something that would undo all Tam worked for. She didn't want to be the one to give him away. That time would come soon enough. When it did, sparks would fly.

# Chapter Four

Kerrie stood in the ballroom, flanked by three cousins, Ash, Liam and Colby. Aunt Ella and Uncle Drake stood at the door, greeting all the guests after they were announced by their butler. The ballroom filled. Chatter threatened to drown out the arrival of each new guest. Music played. Glasses of wine were served from trays carried by servants hired for this special occasion. She'd never been to an affair such as this. Overwhelmed by all the fanfare, she wished she could hide behind one of the potted palms purchased for this event. She didn't know a living breathing soul except for the relatives.

"Mr. Sterling Talmage."

The entire room stopped chattering. All was silent.

Startled, her gaze shot to the door. At the sight she beheld, her breath caught in the back of her throat. Hearing his name called out, Kerrie realized she'd been holding air in her lungs until he arrived. She needed to admit to herself she didn't expect the man to turn up even though he accepted the invitation, Aunt Ella told her she sent his way. Following the announcement then the initial silence, a low murmur swept around the room. People seemed to know him. Appeared as surprised as she was that he attended the ball. As Tam glanced then seemed to glower at the guests, the murmuring stopped with sudden abruptness. He seemed to hold some power over the people whispering his name. Seemed rather strange to Kerrie. She blinked a few times while she continued to evaluate what just occurred.

The moment he saw her, she knew he came for her. His broad smile swept into her heart. Understood if she wasn't being introduced to the ton, he would not attend. A giddy feeling ran through her. Her breath wedged inside. Her heart skipped a beat then another. Kerrie attempted to pull her emotions into some manner of control. In his evening clothes, he was so handsome. With no effort at all, he stole her breath again. She gulped as much oxygen as she could manage as it seemed to burn her lungs. Tam looked resplendent walking toward her. She blushed recalling how much of him she'd seen.

Taller than most in the room, he strode in her direction. His eyes fixed on her. She tugged up on her bodice, crossing her fingers that the scarves were well concealed. Ella had been positive this would work. He would notice. She knew he would. He would make some comment that would embarrass her. That was a given fact. She would turn red from mortification. There was no way to get around this horrible predicament. She could never wear the dress the way it fit *sans* scarves. There was no time to fix the top.

Colby stole that moment to ask her to dance. "I..." she murmured, looking back and forth from Tam to her cousin. Somehow, she understood Tam wouldn't like her dancing with him even though he was a close relative. Thought Colby might be egging him on, daring him in some underhanded way. As he walked toward her, his mouth was set in a grim line. An expression that should scare Colby. It didn't. Her cousin seemed pleased with the sight. Grinned at the man then proceeded to walk with her toward the dance floor.

"It won't do for you to seem too eager to dance with that man. Put him in his place is what I say."

Colby nodded his head in Tam's direction. "He's far too possessive. I can tell from his eyes. The man believes he owns your time. See, my sweet cuz, now the man is scowling. His brows have become one. He will be furious when I pull you into my arms for this waltz. What do you say? Should I hold you too close for propriety?" Colby hooted a laugh.

To Kerrie it was obvious he enjoyed baiting Tam. "It would do him good to be jealous. The man doesn't know I'm not a threat. That I'm your cousin. I've never met him." Colby chuckled, giving her a quick kiss to the cheek. "I'm looking forward to bringing you back to your other cousins while Tam is watching. Before he can step in politely, you'll have at least...wait, there is Kane along with Stephen. We can keep you occupied for the next several dances. The ton doesn't look down their nose when relatives dance more than once at a *fête*."

Kerrie didn't like what he was doing. She wished she had some say in this sneaky maneuver of his cousin's. Would have liked to voice her opinion and have someone listen to her. If Tam cared, she would be surprised. "He won't be jealous. Sometimes..."

She wasn't going to say he didn't like her again. He told her several times in the last few days that wasn't true. During the day of the storm along with the two days of travel he remained aloof, distant. His eyes pierced with an intense gaze she didn't understand. Now the way he walked, the stiff set to his shoulders coupled with his expression, she didn't know what to think.

Most of the days since their return, he rode Dex. She joined him in the afternoons on Briar. They didn't talk much. She reiterated that she didn't want to do the *débutante* thing. Didn't think of herself that way. After all, she was twenty. Most of the girls at the ball were just out of the schoolroom. They were seventeen or eighteen at the most. Any of the young ladies who were older would be participating in a second season having not found the man of their dreams their first time around. This was her first season as well as the last. She was so out of place she needed to laugh.

Tam told her about his younger brother and sister. They were special to him. Would have to make extraordinary considerations to take care of them. His brother was twenty-one, a friend to Ashcroft, Drake and Ella's son. His sister turned ten-years-old a month ago.

"Yes, that man you covet is beside himself with both jealousy as well as a simmering rage. He can't stand the fact I'm dancing with you. His fists are clenched tight at his sides. His brows drawn, lips thinned. There are strain lines around his eyes. He thought you would be in his arms, not mine. You need to be careful, little one. Whatever happens, don't give him your heart. He's dangerous. Believes he owns you. I can see that in his eyes." Colby whirled her around so she could see the man.

Kerrie understood Colby's advice came too late. Her heart was his to do with as he pleased. "His face is red."

"No, he is green around the edges. If that's not jealousy, I, my darling cousin, don't know what to call the expression. Tam expected to get this first dance with you. I stole it from him. Might call me out. He is boiling as well as envious. I do believe he means to manipulate your time. Can't have that, now, can we? Maybe we can maneuver you just right so Ash gets the next dance. After that there is Liam, Kane, Drake as well as your other uncle who I'm certain will not mind being part of this. After all, neither the duke or The Duchess will appreciate a scandal connected to their name. They would never step in to give Tam what he wants. With all your relatives here for your support, the man will have to work just to gain one dance with you."

"I don't understand why you think he's come here for me?" she retorted hoping Colby was right. Though she would rather dance with Tam than her cousins along with the other men Colby listed. The last thing she understood were the crazy rules set down by the ton. Why shouldn't two people who liked each other dance more than once? Nothing here made sense.

"Why not? You are a beautiful woman. You spent several days at the hunting box together. Tell me, were you a good girl? Were you naughty with that stuffy...man? He's a prude. Known for doing everything in the proper way. No, that man would never do anything to create a scandal. He's a stuff shirt. A killjoy, prim as well as proper in a man's body. You didn't have an iota of fun. Tell me. What did the two of you do all day, every day? I do think from what I know about you, you might be as prim and proper as the good man over there who seems to be making his way to us. He's not going to let me have my way."

The music ended. Colby brought her back to where they'd been standing. Ash was there as was Liam and Tam. Colby handed her over to Tam whose hand was outstretched, while his eyes were narrowed. He accepted her hand then bent over to kiss the back. When he stared at her, his gaze was hard. When he spoke, his voice was harsher. Colby was right. He didn't like the fact she waltzed with another man.

"My dance."

Tam didn't give her a chance to refuse or accept. Before she could blink, she found herself dancing too close to him. His hand rested with unwavering possessiveness on the small of her back. "Who was that man?" He bent close, whispering to her. "You best have a good answer for me."

He threatened her. Her chin went up. How dare he? Now, she felt the way Colby did. He could rot. "A friend of mine...a longtime friend. Known him forever." Maybe he was a bit covetous. She intended to play the game Colby started. "What would you do if that isn't good enough for you?"

"No longer." His harsh, unexpected words surprised her. "He's no longer a friend of yours. I won't have it."

She bristled, angry with him. Kerrie knew she needed to reply with honesty. Though she didn't understand why he was angry. Wasn't a ball for dancing? "Tam." She touched his neck with her fingertip. "You've no reason to be angry. Colby is one of my cousins. He was keeping me entertained if you must know. Now, take me back. My dance card is full. The last time I looked, your name wasn't on it."

He did sound jealous. The thought pleased her. Maybe he did like her a little bit.

"No. It's not! However, other than family, I'm the only man who will dance with you tonight. Best you get that into your pretty head. I'm not sharing you now or ever. You're mine."

That would create a scandal to out scandal anything before. A man didn't dance with a woman other than his wife more than once or twice. That's what both Aunt Ella along with Colby told her. "You can't mean..." Kerrie didn't want to be talked about. She didn't want to find herself the new gossip of the ton. If he had his way, they both would be on the lips of all who attended. "I won't...what happened to the man who needed to preserve distance?"

"Kerrie, I don't want any other man holding you in the shelter of his arms." He was shaking his head, his lips in a sneer. "Doesn't matter that the card is full. No one will dare go against my wishes." He whirled her around the room. The music changed to another tune. He didn't take her back to her family. Nor did he stop dancing.

*No one will dare go against my wishes?*

*What did that mean?*

She tried to forget his anger. His threats along with his possessiveness. She loved the way he felt so close to her. Adored his body pressed against hers. He held her way too close. Kerrie didn't mind that either. While the waltz continued, she closed her eyes, floating in his arms with the rhythmic flow of the music. He moved with grace. The tap on his shoulder surprised them.

"No!" In a low voice Tam stormed.

"Yes." The man was her uncle tapping him on the shoulder, signaling that he would have the next dance. "You will behave yourself, young man. My niece's wellbeing is important to me as well as The Duchess. Don't intend to have scandal attached to her good name. if I'm not wrong, you also abhor scandal." The threat was implicit. "One dance. Since Kerrie is under my supervision, I'll allow two."

Tam let her go, seeming to understand the tone as well as the tenor of Drake's voice. They moved away. "Don't let the man intimidate you," Drake whispered. "He won't embarrass you. I have it on the best authority."

"Is The Duchess the authority? You know," she paused looking into her uncle's stern features, "he doesn't intimidate me. He wouldn't let me go. I did tell him..." Kerrie was pleased with the discovery. At the hunting lodge, she never understood what to think. One moment he was kissing her, the next pushing her away. The constant rejections stung. She remembered the tears the night he held her.

"Perhaps tonight it will take all your cousins to help keep the besotted fool in line. Though his actions are out of character."

When the dance ended, he brought her back to the small group whose main purpose here was to protect her.

Tam smiled. By the look on his face, he wasn't about to heed Drake's command. Ella gave him a nudge as if to encourage him to do something. If Ella didn't change her tactics, she'd soon be called The Matchmaking Duchess. "We can get something to drink and not set tongues wagging about us. Don't wish to be the next *on dit*."

*"On dit?"*

"As I'm certain your uncle told you, dancing with me too often will take a toll on your good name, your reputation. Don't wish for that. The Duchess has given her approval to visit in the guise of eating. Nonetheless, no other, non-relative is going to whirl you around that floor and hold you too close. Now, I would like to get you a glass of punch or wine. Whatever you like. After that I would find a nice table on the balcony. We can visit. Catch up on what you have been doing the last two days since we parted ways. Need to know all you've been doing...thinking."

"As you wish."

Kerrie smiled to herself and hoped he would try to kiss her. Seemed forever since the lake, the kiss, the touches that set fire on her. Since the night he held her in his arms while they lay in her bed, she thought of little else. On the terrace they might get a bit of privacy. Time for themselves.

"You're agreeable."

"Yes," Kerrie nodded.

She meant to be all things agreeable tonight. Hoped to start from the beginning with this confusing man. Wasn't going to bring up the fact he didn't like her. "I'd like something to drink as well as eat. I was so nervous for this evening, I didn't eat all day. I didn't expect you to be here."

"Eat then drink whatever looks appealing. Don't wish for you to waste away. Like you just the way you are." His hand at her elbow, he guided her toward the food. He trailed a finger along her spine. She shivered at the fleeting contact remembering another time. Remembered being almost naked in the lake with him. The way he held her. The feel of his body pressed against hers. The kisses.

"What would you like? Anything look good?"

Tam grabbed two plates, filled them with a bit of everything before she could answer. He handed them to her while he brought glasses of wine. With his head he motioned to the terrace. "Let me know if you get cold. The day was warm though. If you take a chill, I will give you my jacket. Women don't wear enough clothes," Tam mumbled as if speaking to himself.

She smiled at his words. Seemed he liked it when she wore less rather than more. Of course, that was when they were alone. An empty table beckoned. They sat down. He grinned at her. The expression was an all-knowing look that sent a vibration of desire throughout. "You dance well." His pause seemed calculated while he thought. "As well as you swim. Bake bread. Kiss. I do like your tongue..."

He also remembered their exploits at the lodge. Thoughts of those moments heated her with mercurial magic. An enchantment that would never leave her. He mentioned them for a reason. What that aim was she wasn't certain. "As do you." Her face flushed. "Don't know how well you bake bread. Can you?"

The lump in her throat stuck. She sipped the wine. It was delicious. She coughed when the liquid went down the wrong way.

"Never in my life. You could teach me. We could recreate the moment. We would both be bare from the waist up...or...with nothing on at all."

Heat from his words flushed her face. "Oh...when? My..." She thought her eyes would cross. *Naked from the waist up? Nothing on at all.* He taunted, teased until she felt dragons setting an inferno coursing inside.

His gaze focused on her bosom, stared hard while he appeared to study, to scrutinize. One dark eyebrow arched upward while he appeared to be speculating, a wolfish grin lit his features. She wanted to cover herself. Her hands rose before she let them fall back to the table.

"What is it that you have stuck down the front of your gown?" He reached out as if to touch the offending article before bringing his hand back. "Don't dare do what I wish to do. Whatever...? Why?"

The increasing flush heating her face sent her hands to her cheeks. She wished she could crawl beneath the table. Hide until this went away. He knew. Without blinking, he knew. Aunt Ella lied. Told her Tam would never notice the scarves. He did observe. Did question. He did mention them. Didn't like what he saw. "No...nothing."

Tam looked around the private space. No one was there. Brushing the back of his hand across the rounded tops of her breasts, he tugged on one scarf. Pulled it from the gown. Let it float in the air for anyone to see. Her hand covered the tops of her breasts as if she could stop him from taking away more of the scarves before she became quite humiliated. This should never have happened.

"Nothing?" he asked incredulous that she dare tell him there was nothing between her and the gown. He waved the scarf again. "This stuffed between you and your gown is nothing?" His voice rose. He was angry.

The scarf fluttered to the tabletop. She didn't understand this new anger. If not for the scarves...well...anyone would be able to see to her bellybutton. "Scarf...why yes. If you must know...it's...it's the latest fashion trend."

She tried to sound as if everyone stuffed their gown with scarves. As if this was normal. She couldn't get the right tone. Her mortification ran soul deep.

"Why? Why?" Tam repeated. His voice softened as if he realized her humiliation. "Why when you are perfect the way you are? I don't need more than enough to suck into my mouth. To taste. To savor."

She gasped at his words. *Suck into my mouth.* She looked down, played with the fabric he left on the table. Saw the gap its departure made in the bodice. She saw the hardened tip of one nipple. Wheezed. Her gaze flew to his. "Can't...you tell...why? You are not a novice when it comes to women's clothing. I'm certain of that. Must you discomfit me more? You should be able to see why."

Tam tapped his fingertips on the table. "Yes, I know. Yes, my experiences with women's clothing is extensive. You are correct." His eyes focused on her bosom. "Your pretty peaches aren't as big as the space made for them? Ella didn't do her job this time. She failed. That must be new to her. It's delightful now that I think about what I'm seeing. Didn't expect that tonight. I'll put the scarves back...scarf." He reached for the material. She clung to the small scrap. If he put the fabric back into place, he would touch her.

"No!"

Shaking, Kerrie grabbed the material, turned then stuffed the scrap back into its rightful place before he could do so, adjusting her gown. She was mortified to the tips of her toes. Her face was hot to the touch. She flamed, not because he seduced but because she was so far out of her comfort she couldn't breathe.

"I've touched you there before." His voice was gentle as if she would accept his caress without question. "I will again." He looked as if he contemplated that thought. "You've no need to feel embarrassed. No one but me saw you."

She would not. Could not. Not while they were in a public place. Yes, more than likely, he would touch her again. Heat her body with the tempest generated by him, by Tam alone. Kerrie didn't believe anyone could reach her so very soul deep that she longed, ached with anticipation.

"Was." A gulp of air helped with the rest of the words she wished to say to him. "Was told you were proper. How is it I've never seen that side of you? Prim. Around me you've never acted proper or the least bit restrained. I want you to act stuffy as well as the prude now. Right now!" Her fists tightened. She had no intention of letting him tease her here with the promise of a caress, even a kiss. A kiss would lead to...

His slight bark of laughter unnerved her. His grin was wicked. He reached out to her, ran his knuckles along her neck. "I find it devilishly hard to be stuffy or prim and proper when you are around. For the life of me, I cannot be restrained. The order of things vanishes from my head. The brain you muddle with a smile. When I see you, I like to see color sprout on your beautiful face, paint the rounded tops of your breasts. Need to touch as well as taste. Relish all of you." He trailed a fingertip along the line of her bodice. His fingers were long, tapered, nails clean, manicured. "Who told you that? Who dared call me those names."

"Colby. You asked who danced with me. Colby." He could not mean to object. "Colby is my cousin."

"Does Colby have a last name? I would know if this boy is indeed your cousin. He appears a bit young for you. Unseasoned. Not some imposter."

"Gray. Colby Gray. He is Nicki's brother. He is older than me. Much older."

"Oh...heard a few rumors where those two were concerned. Naughty. Very naughty. Are you naughty too? I do believe I've seen that side of you, the unrestrained side. Would be nice to explore further with that in mind. You were very naughty when you stripped to just your chemise and skirt to make bread. You tempted me. It was all I could do to keep my hands to myself. I did...well I tried very hard."

The man didn't keep anything to himself. He teased her with his mouth, his hands. She flushed again thinking about the moments he kissed her. All the times she wished he would do more. She did all but beg.

Mischievous. "You know the answer to that as well as I. Never planned that you would see me in my *déshabillé*. It was hot in the kitchen. You were supposed to be out riding. Fishing. Didn't expect you."

"Surprises are the best. The back of your neck as well as...well...all of you was tasty. Delicious. Anyone else I should know about? Wouldn't wish to make a fool of myself when there is a cousin or a cousin's husband around that I don't know about. My plan is to keep you all to myself. Yes, all to myself. Won't share. Never was good at sharing. What is mine, I keep."

"Aunt Ella told me that Kane and my cousin Lyssa will be here tonight. They..." He stopped her answer when he cut her off with a wave of his hand.

"Also heard about the little ditty Lyssa sang at a recital. Naughty. Very naughty. Something about pussies, I think. Maybe stroking them. Ah, I'll have to search my head for the words. I could repeat them to you in time if you ask nicely. A month or so the two were together, alone out at his country estate. When, I might be so bold as to add, Kane was her chaperone all that time. Ella arranged this so-called guidance. Quite handy to be the chaperone to the woman you want to fall in love with. Though I was told, Kane wasn't wishing to fall in love. Wasn't that the time while the duke and duchess were chasing after Nickie? Very naughty. Are all Ella's niece's...naughty?"

Her face heated more. Flushed. "Suppose we...all the females...know our minds. Wish to think independently from protocols. Understand what we want. Been brought up to speak our mind. To do what we deem right for us. If that is naughty, then yes. So am I." Kerrie was thinking about the stable, Dex, breeding her horses.

"Do you want me?" he asked, his voice soft, beguiling, mesmeric, fascinating. "Do you wish for another kiss? Out on the terrace, I could give you one if you ask."

"Yes, all the time you are not doing something that infuriates or annoys me. When you do...well...sometimes I don't like what you do. There are times you dare too much."

Kerrie stopped to think as she figured out what she needed to say, how to answer his question with undeniable facts. "Don't like much of what you do. Locking my horse away from me, forbidding me to go fishing, or using a certain trail because it might prove to be dangerous for a woman. I'm certain there would be more if we stayed at the lodge another day. You would find things to tell me I cannot do. Don't much appreciate that aspect of you."

Tam grunted as if he didn't agree. "Finish your drink. We'll go for a short walk in the garden. We can return to the dance floor after I've kissed you. Must have one kiss from your delicious lips. Remember the taste. I'll let you dance with any man who is related to you. No one else. Doesn't matter if you protest." His confidence on that subject infuriated her. "My scowl of dislike will turn every possible suitor away."

"You have no say as to my dance partners! Autocratic beast! I should walk away." she retorted, her voice rising with each sentence. She held up her hand with the paper dangling from her wrist. "I have a dance card. There are names. The men will expect a dance. It wouldn't be right for me to tell them no. To ignore them."

"We will see." Tam grinned then picked up her hand. "This card means nothing to me." Turned her hand over. Placed a soft kiss on the palm. "We will see who dares attempt to dance with you when I'm standing by your side," he repeated as he stood tugging her to her feet. For the walk to the stairs leading to the garden, he tucked her fingers into his elbow. "Come along now. After all that food, a walk in the garden will suit both of us. When we find a secluded place, I will taste my naughty lady. Bold as she is, she will kiss me back."

"Only when you make me naughty," Kerrie mumbled, wishing she could think of some words that would put him in his place. She couldn't. "I don't like that you call me naughty. I'm not. Don't disobey."

His soft chuckle burst from his chest. "Are you a good girl then? No, don't want you to be too good. You would show me up. We can be naughty together. Wicked is more fun than good. Let's be wicked together."

Once in the garden, he set his arm around her waist making sure she walked close to him. "How are you going to stop me from dancing with someone on my card?" Kerrie was curious how he could be so certain. He wouldn't stop her though he believed he could. "If someone comes for their dance, I'll comply."

"Believe my scowl will keep all comers from seeking out a dance with you. If a man is so stubborn to ignore me, I will try some other means to convince him you are off limits. Besides, don't believe you wish to dance with anyone except me. Do you?"

She giggled, turning to touch his chest with her hand. He challenged her. He was right. She didn't care about any man except Tam. "Audacious man. Infuriating. All-knowing."

He stopped. His way was not how tonight was supposed to be. "Your scowl is so ferocious that grown men will turn away? Cower in their boots?"

"Yes."

"As you said earlier, we will see. If you don't intend to kiss me, we should return to the floor. Aunt Ella might send Drake out to find us. That would be embarrassing. He...might do something you would come to regret."

"As in hang me from the yardarm of one of my ships?" Tam smiled down at her, his hungry gaze searing into her soul. "The duke would not come. Ella would never send him out here to find us. She understands we need time alone to strengthen our relationship. She encouraged me to take you outside for a bit of fresh air. A kiss behind the roses. Perhaps a touch here or one there." Tam's hands rested on her waist, slid so they caressed her backside. When he pulled her to him, he was hard. She felt his sex against her. Remembered the feel of him pressed intimately against her the night they swam.

She gasped at the evidence of his desire. His hand beneath her chin, he lifted. "You can feel how much I want you. That won't change." His lips captured hers. His tongue filled her. Danced. Played. Sweet passion rose to a crescendo. She heard his groan of desire. Felt one hand beneath her breast cupping, testing.

With a deep breath of air and what seemed to be regret, Tam set her aside. Her lips were damp. He touched them with his thumb. "Time to go back inside. One kiss, nothing more despite the fact the night is warm. We could dally longer. But... If I play with your breasts the scarves will slide out. Don't want anyone seeing that which is mine."

Kerrie wasn't unhappy with the comment. However, she needed to set a few things straight with the man. "My breasts are not yours. They are mine. You cannot claim something so preposterous."

"We will see. Now come along." He held out his hand to her.

Denying contact would be perverse of her. Even though there were things he did she took umbrage with, she liked him. Wished to see more of him. Was coming to adore the man. Whatever physical contact he initiated she would never tell him no.

Kerrie imagined she was naughty just like her cousins. He knew that. Played upon the fact. Enticing her to act the way she wasn't brought up to act. Only gave into his maneuverings because she adored him. Hand in hand, they walked back inside the ballroom. She was pleased to see Lyssa as well as Chauncey dancing with their husbands. When they noticed her, they ran to each other. Hugged and laughed. Kane stood behind Lyssa, his hands on her shoulders. Stephen behind Chauncey. They all touched with possession, their gazes never departing the woman they vowed to love forever.

Hoping to prove this arrogant man wrong, she smiled at the man approaching her. She hoped the grin was flirtatious. One look at Tam, he turned to make his way in the opposite direction. She whirled, pointing her finger at his chest. "What did you do? His name was on my dance card. You sent him away. Why?" She was miffed at him again. Once, just once, she wanted to be right, about something, about anything. He said she wouldn't dance with another. She told him she would. It was obvious now to her that Tam wasn't going to allow her to do so.

"Told you my scowl will send any man hoping to dance with you running in the opposite direction. Face the relevant fact. I was right. You were wrong. Come now, let's have another turn around the dance floor. The scandal won't be too bad. This will only be what...our third time dancing? I need to hold you close. Can't seem to get enough of holding your softness against me."

The arrogant man didn't give her a chance to accept or reject. He caught her in his arms then joined the people whirling around the ballroom. "You are incorrigible."

"Arrogant, as you've told me numerous times. Now incorrigible.

A despicable beast. What other names will you call me? I'll have to make a list so I can remember."

"We are going to create a scandal. You don't care. Are you so impervious to the morals of our time you can ignore the dictates of polite society?"

"Yes. Have to make my position clear to these young peacocks who are looking for a *débutante*. You are my *débutante*," he told her as they mingled with the crowds. "No one else can lay claim to you."

Ash was the next to dance with her. Stephen danced after that. All the while Tam, with his hands locked behind his back, rocking on the balls of his feet, watched. Glowered. Kane took the next dance. Seeming frustrated with the situation, Tam danced with her again. This was the fourth time.

"How many is that? Three or four?" she asked him. "Is this your intent? A public humiliation of me? I hear people murmuring. Their hands are over their mouths. I've heard your name as well as mine. As well as how do they dare? I think that lady with the magnificent bosom almost fainted."

"My only focus is to keep you out of the arms of any other man except me or your family members. Nothing nefarious about that. What is it that you want?" He bent low, touched the tip of his tongue to her ear. "Do you want me as much as I want you? If I asked you tonight, would you come to my bed? Lay in my arms as you did the night at the lodge?"

She pushed back, gasping for air. Her hand pressed against his chest. "Don't tease me. Rejection is not something I enjoy. If you will not let me tell you yes, don't tempt me with seductive words. Evocative words that make me want you. That is one of the things I dislike about you. Playing fair should be one of those rules you seem to have so many of. You shouldn't be able to have this relationship the way you want it. At your whim, you shouldn't be able to tease me then leave me."

"Sorry." This time he sounded contrite. "I never meant for you to feel rejected. Bloody hell! I want you more than I need to breathe. Burn to have you in every way. Cannot help myself. When I'm with you my hands and lips won't behave themselves. My restraint vanishes. I have to push you away or I'll ruin your reputation."

She didn't believe this man would ever be contrite. His seeming remorse must be an act. He danced her back to the little group standing beside the potted palm she wanted to hide behind until Tam arrived. After he returned her to the group, Liam danced with her. She enjoyed Tara's step-brother. While he was a notable rake among the ton, he was a delight. The man smiled and joked. He never seemed at all serious.

Kerrie smiled at Tam as they passed by then mouthed the words, "Cousin." Tam nodded and waited. She saw a woman approach him. The pair spoke for a few minutes. They appeared to know each other.

Another second or two passed before Tam swept the young lady onto the dance floor. He held her too close in Kerrie's mind. Kerrie bristled with jealousy while she watched them weave in and out between the couples. The two were so at ease. So familiar.

The realization that he played her, used her, swept through Kerrie. With the snap of two fingers, Tam could have any woman he wanted. Kerrie knew of this woman. The lady in question was the daughter of a marquis. Kerrie was nothing. Had no title. Tam was exploiting her to get what he wanted. He must want a title. If he married this woman, would he have a title? Wanted to be a lord of the realm. She couldn't give that to him. The other woman could. If that was the case, why did Tam act so possessive of her? Nothing Tam did made sense. All his actions were at odds with what she knew to be true about him.

Problem was, she couldn't figure out what he wanted from her. If it wasn't sex or the coveted title, what was it the man played her emotions to gain? She had some money, more potential than fact. She possessed a small dowry. Tam didn't need money. She once more reminded herself he was far too handsome as well as charming. He could have any woman he wanted. Cancel the charming part. He'd never been appealing to her except when he touched her, kissed her, made her melt. He was always charismatic. Always debonair. Irritating. Autocratic. Annoying... the list of opposites continued. She couldn't keep her mind from him.

What was he using her for?

After Liam returned her, Drake took the next dance as his. It seemed they all understood no one would ask her to dance. Kerrie had questions for her uncle. Wasn't at all certain he would answer. "You know

Tam well?" she asked, watching Uncle Drake nod in the affirmative. "What can you tell me about him? I would know what type of man I'm attracted to."

"Where Mr. Talmage is concerned, you've nothing to worry about. If you're afraid he will hurt you in some way, he won't. The man is steady as well as true. Loyal to a fault. He abides by all the rules. He would never take you away on one of his ships for an adventure."

Drake must be thinking about Nickie and the McInnis. He stole her cousin away. Broke all the rules of courtship so he could have her alone. Kerrie wasn't so certain Tam wouldn't do the same. "You've nothing bad to say about him? You've never noticed his arrogance, his demanding nature. He's forbidden me to do several things. I find that reprehensible as well as overbearing. He is nothing to me. No relation. Not a husband or a father. What right does he have to set rules?"

"He has only what's best for you in his mind."

"Tam placed a padlock on Dex's stall so I couldn't ride him. He has no right to do so."

"He has his reasons."

Well, that was that. Kerrie wasn't going to gain information from her uncle. Drake was on Tam's side in all things. Wasn't that just like another male to side with another man without understanding the facts? When she turned to look at Tam, the man's scowl kept all eligible men at arm's length. What was it about the expression on his face that warned possible suitors to turn then run in the opposite direction? Well, she didn't come here to find a husband. Perhaps he did her a favor. She wasn't going to have to meet the dandies looking for a wife, for a female with a large enough dowry they could continue to gamble as well as whore.

After her conversation with Uncle Drake, she understood nothing. Her uncle touted Tam, praised him. Found nothing bad to say about him.

When Drake finished the dance, Tam whirled her around the dance floor again. She was doomed. Helpless in his large hands. She couldn't refuse him anything. "My uncle seems to think you are the greatest. Why is that?"

"I'm flattered," was all he said as he dipped then swayed to the rhythm of the music. "I appreciate all your uncle's talents." Tam was audacious.

He kept her in his arms for two more dances before surrendering her to the potted palm. Keeping her hand in his, he pulled it behind his back as if hoping no one would see.

Tam couldn't hide from the crowds gathered there. Why they cared what Tam did was impossible for Kerrie to understand. He wasn't even titled. What power did he have over the others? Did he have so much wealth that he could sway opinions. Did he know scandalous secrets about these people that if revealed would hurt them in some way. Watching the clock, Kerrie felt as if she counted down the minutes until she could leave the dance floor before returning to her room. In some respects, the night was enjoyable, she didn't wish to have another one such as this one. Didn't intend to be present at another gala such as the one she endured tonight. This was her last one...first as well as last. She was going home. Would tell her aunt tomorrow about her planned departure.

When the clock struck midnight, she felt like Cinderella fleeing from the ball. In this situation, the handsome hero followed her. She stood with Tam, sipping wine, talking. Possessively, his arm snaked around her as if he owned her. Tonight, his ownership was a fact. He let everyone there know she was his. No one disputed that fact.

He bent low to speak to her. His voice whispered against the nape of her neck. "I'm going to walk you down the stairs then to your room. Need to make certain you arrive at your bed in one piece. Tomorrow, I'll be here at one o'clock. We'll go riding. Spend the afternoon together, hopefully in my arms."

"Dex?" she asked eager to see her horse, to ride her magnificent stallion.

"Yes. That was my plan. Only if you wish to ride pillion with me...do you?"

With her hands clasped tight beneath her chin, she agreed by nodding then speaking. "Yes, please."

He held her close, his body so warm, so intriguing. All negative feelings seemed to vanish from her mind. "There might be other men coming to call tomorrow afternoon. I've left instructions with both the duke as well as The Matchmaking Duchess that no one is to be allowed your company. I'm thankful for your aunt's talents." Tam didn't elaborate on that piece of information.

Kerrie couldn't help but put her hands on her hips to better glare at the man. "Again... How... You won't be there to scowl at them. Why would they stay away?"

Tam stopped her tirade with a finger to her mouth. His grin sent a warm rush of liquid heat into her. "Hush now, we both understand you wish to be with me. You don't want other men clogging up your free time along with mine. True, I won't be scowling. However, believe this evening, I've sent a clear picture as to my feelings for you. If you didn't care for me, I... Never mind. I still would."

"You can't know that. I'm not your pawn to place wherever you please. This is what you do that angers me. This is what I don't appreciate. You make decisions for me. Don't ask me for my opinion. No one makes...decides for me." She was panting, breathing hard. "I want to understand how you can make so many assumptions then expect everyone to adhere to your wishes."

"No, you're right about what you are telling me. You're my woman, not a pawn, never a pawn. There are no assumptions being made here. Facts instead. Truths. By now, you should understand what I expect. Don't believe I've left doubt in anyone's mind except yours. In time you will accept what is destined to be."

She didn't have a chance to breathe before his lips enclosed hers, brushed, touched upon her, delving exploring. Firing the storm. Tempest flared. Just as always happened, his kiss sent a river of heated liquid rushing through her. She flowed into his hard body. His hand cupped her breast, held steady, flitted across her nipple. Scarves slithered to the floor. He found intimate territory. The kiss went on and on. Her heart raced faster with each stroke of his tongue, his fingers. Mercuric energy spilled into her. She turned into his touch, his lips, teeth then his tongue. Being wayward had its advantage now that she understood he didn't wish to pull away from her. There would be no more rejections.

Kerrie's fingers sifted through the soft strands of his dark hair. Nails clung to his shoulders. She delighted in the masculine groan of pleasure rumbling from his chest. Her whimpers and sighs seemed to give him reason to deepen the kiss, to make the caresses continue when he should have stopped. Heat coiled deep, again then even more with each stroke.

Behind her, the clearing of a male throat sent a bucket of ice into her. They were no longer alone. Stiffening, he pulled his hand free of her corsage.

"Mother sent me to chaperone the two of you. She was afraid Tam might follow you into the bedroom. There is only so much hanky-panky mother will allow to go on under her roof. Seems the way the two of you are going at this kissing, you need a helping hand in order to behave," Ash said with a chuckle, appearing to eye the door. "Kerrie, you need to go inside your room. Lock the door behind you. Don't let this rascal inside. I'll stay out here with Tam until I hear the lock. Tam and I will talk about his intentions toward you. I need to make certain my cousin is taken care of in the proper order."

Her hands on her heated face she turned to do her cousin's bidding. Tam held her arm. "I will see you at one tomorrow. Don't forget. If any suitors brave their way here, you will turn everyone else away."

She nodded.

"That was quite a kiss," Ash said laughing as he watched his cousin with jaded eyes. "Are you certain the man has not taken more liberties?"

Kerrie gasped, shaking her head, unwanted heat flushing her cheeks. "No, nothing I wasn't willing to give."

"That's what I was afraid of."

~ * ~

When Sterling Talmage showed up at one o'clock sharp the next afternoon, The Matchmaking Duchess met him at the door. He bowed low. Kissed the top of her hand in greeting. "Good afternoon, Duchess. Is Kerrie ready for that ride I promised? Dex is prancing, eager to be on his way. Needs his exercise. You know."

Tam thought a bit sardonic; he was prancing too, more than eager to see what today would hold for the two of them. He did have plans. Big plans. Holding her in front of him was something he looked forward to doing. Her small but curvaceous body nestled next to him would be delightful. Though he couldn't take wicked advantage of her as he would like. He would need to restrain himself more than he was used to doing with her. At least until they reached their destination. Exploring certain parts of her he'd yet to touch was part of his plans today. She would be pleased with the arrangements he made at the waterfall. Two more days of limitations with her if his luck held. The wedding was in the planning stages. He'd yet to ask.

"Hello, Tam. I take it you've come to see Kerrie. She is excited. Looking forward to the afternoon. Where are you escorting her? After last night, somewhere safe I hope." When he bent so Ella could reach him, she kissed both cheeks. The brush of her lips was soft yet chaste.

"We are to ride. If you must know, I'm taking her to the waterfall in the north pasture. As you also know, the fall is beautiful. The roar of the water exquisite. Though this time of year it is not as delightful as the spring after the snows have melted." The day would be pleasant, the outing beneficial to his cause. One step closer to the woman he meant to make his wife would be taken. At least he prayed it would. Marriage plans were on his mind. Didn't see a reason to wait. Not when he knew she was the woman meant to be his. Today he would begin to coax her to see things his way.

"Take care, Tam. Your actions last night stirred up a hornet's nest of rumors along with innuendos you will need to deal with. Kerrie's name... Did you see the news this morning? Your conduct made the headlines. Kerrie is the one who is blamed in unflattering terms. She was called a harlot several times. A woman out for your wealth as well as the title. We both understand that is not her way. Because of this, I'm going to need to keep the paper away from Kerrie. If I can't, your ruse is up. One slip, she will comprehend who you are. She will fly home in an instant. What you seek will be much more difficult to attain. I promise. I'll do my best to keep the news away from her."

The fact this damaged her good name more than his, angered him. He felt no guilt as to his actions. The guilt came from hurting her again. Tam slapped his riding gloves on his leg as he looked up the winding staircase to the floor above. "There won't be any more rumors or gossip.

We won't be off the Montgomerie property or the Talmage land today. No one will be around to see me with her. The privacy I crave will be ours." He held up his hands so he could continue speaking. "We don't need a chaperone. I promise you. I've no thoughts of making love until we are married folks. Rules...you know. Do everything by the rules. Known as the prude. Nothing has changed. Tomorrow afternoon, Ella. The wedding will take place then. If I thought I had a chance of convincing her that marriage to me would be the best for both of us, we would marry tonight. Be prepared." He paused searching the stairs again. "You will make certain this wedding gown she will wear fits her? I won't be pleased if her bosom is stuffed with scarves that I will need to pull out."

"Her measurements have been taken." Ella spoke in her defense. "Because the two of you were a day late, there was no time to see the gown fit properly. This one was meant for her sister, Kelsey, who is larger..."

"Good...don't appreciate mistakes."

He tested the stairs again, searching for her. She was late. Was this a ploy? Had she changed her mind at the last minute?

It appeared Ella wasn't prepared to give up. "Reporters can follow the two of you today. If they do, will that make matters worse? Are you certain no one trailed you here? For that matter, who wouldn't expect you to show up today to take the young lady you were rumored to be smitten with for a ride somewhere? You monopolized all her time last night. I'm positive you were shadowed. They are very good at dodging footsteps."

"Since that is a distinct possibility, we will leave by the back. Maybe Ash could create a diversion." In this adventure, he didn't need or want company. The little waterfall on his land where he intended to take her was ready for them. The wine, the food, seclusion where he could work the magic he hoped to use to convince her to wed with him. Everything was prepared to his description. She would say, yes. The special license waited. Tomorrow... Couldn't arrive soon enough.

*Tomorrow.*

"You jest." Ella laughed. "Ash won't be up for another hour or two. He had his fun last night after the ball. Won't tell me what it was he did. What he doesn't understand is that a mother knows. I'm letting him play for a few more years before I find the perfect woman for him. Settling down now would be disastrous for my son. A man must be seasoned. Must be prepared to leave his single life behind. Until then a man should not look at marriage as something he needs."

"Hope the boy doesn't become a wastrel," Tam muttered while he continued to process his plans for the day.

Ella chuckled, her thoughts obvious on her expressive features before replying to his comment. "With Drake as his father there is little to no chance of that happening. He's a good agent though I wasn't pleased when he showed an aptitude for spying. His father is proud of the boy. Grants him a bit of leeway when he is home. His trip to Paris with Tara was eye opening. My son did well. He did enjoy the intrigue along with the adventure."

Tam found himself frowning, thinking of strategies when Kerrie stopped at the top of the steps. She was lovely, dressed in an amber-colored split skirt meant for riding that sent his mind forming numerous possibilities. He felt certain she would show up in britches. For some reason he was getting used to her tiny bouts of defiance, even enjoying them. This morning, after last night, he'd expected a small measure of rebelliousness. Was pleased with what she chose to wear. As he told her before, they would find compromise.

The rounded curves of her hips caught his attention first. Appreciating the view, his gaze remained there longer than it should. The white shirt she wore was covered with an amber jacket which hid her breasts and matched her eyes. When they were alone, he would discover more of them later. If she dressed as usual, she wore only her chemise beneath the blouse.

After he thought about Ella's words, he felt certain at least one reporter would attempt to follow them. Even riding pillion with Kerrie, he had no doubt the strong stallion would out-distance any pursuit. Kerrie would never be afraid of the speed. His thoughts flew back to their first encounter. The misadvised rescue. She was furious with him. Came to understand he had her best interest at heart. She did forgive his intrusion to her ride. Thoughts of those first moments gave him good reasons to smile.

Her hips swaying with each provocative step, Kerrie traversed the stairs. She knew what she did inflamed him. He'd never been able to hide his instant attraction to her. His sex swelled as he watched her move down the steps. A cape was tossed over her shoulder. Even though the day was sunny, there was chill in the air. Summer was over. Leaves were beginning to color heralding the beginning of autumn. They both understood the weather could change in an instant. A storm could rise as if from nowhere.

"Are you ready to go?" he asked, unable to keep his bold perusal from her. She was beautiful.

Tam appreciated the care she took with her appearance. Rose tinted lips, shadowed eyelids, along with a light dusting of powder on her cheeks. She darkened her lashes. Her hair was tied back with a ribbon.

Ella cleared her throat as if realizing he was about to make another spectacle of himself. Granted, so far, she was the only person watching. "You do need a chaperone, Tam. I might come along. Though we both understand three is a crowd. Need to protect my niece from you." Ella gave a small sigh. "Though I don't believe Kerrie wants to be protected. Neither did I when Drake set his sights on me."

Tam almost laughed when Kerrie's eyebrows drew together and her lips thinned to show her distaste for the proposal. She would have something to say about the suggestion. "No, we don't," Kerrie was quick to volunteer. "If you thought we needed one, there would be one here. We would bore you, Aunt Ella. Tam won't do anything I don't wish him to do. Never has."

"Ah, well, that fact is what I'm afraid of. You wish for his attentions. Suppose that is good in this situation," Ella said with a slight lift to her shoulders coupled with an all-knowing smile. "A chaperone can get in the way of an honest courtship. Don't believe Drake and I would have done half so well with chaperones."

It seemed years ago everyone in London knew the tale of the courtship of the duke and his now duchess. Also, many young *dèbutantes* told the story when they hoped to gain more time alone with the man of their dreams. Drake gave Ella a choice. Go away with him for a week at the very same hunting box where he met Kerrie or he would never call on her again. Ella was so in love with the duke she gave in to the horrible threat. Drake rented a hot air balloon for over half the distance. After the fact, no one in London believed Drake would have never called on Ella again. He was smitten by her beauty along with the sweet personality. After the fact, what anyone else thought didn't matter. Ash had been conceived during the stay or shortly after. No matter, the young babe came before the appropriate time.

Tam didn't wish that for Kerrie. Proper, in the right order, he reminded himself every waking moment. Didn't mean he couldn't initiate her into new erotic sensations. Today, he would take their relationship one step farther. Today, the love of his life would feel ecstasy at his hands. What would one day change? If she conceived today, who would think twice? He would.

He was far too stoic for the impulsive Kerrie. Despite the fact they were so different, she was never far from his mind. It was said that differences attracted. He would need to marry her soon. If not, there could well be a child arriving before nine months. Every time he was with her, he expected his control to vanish. Luck, so far, was on his side. His question to himself was how long would lady luck visit him.

Tam held out his hand for Kerrie. She accepted. He placed her fingers in the crook of his arm. She leaned into him. Her sweet curves pressed against his chest. "Dear Ella, thank you for arranging our introduction. Don't much care how you knew Kerrie would be at the hunting box at the same time. We are off."

He headed for the back of the house. They passed through the terrace then on to the stable. A soft breeze flitted around them. It would be too cool to test the water in the stream the falls created.

"Where are we going?" Kerrie asked, her breaths difficult at the rapid pace. "Could you slow down? This isn't a foot race. Is it?"

Contrite, he swore to himself. He should be more considerate. His eagerness to be alone with Kerrie was out of hand. "Sorry. I am in a hurry to have you all to myself. Seems as if it's been a bloody long time since we were at the lodge. Last night there were far too many people for my taste. Don't much like those affairs. Needed to put in an appearance though."

"Yes, you forget your long legs. I feel as if I'm forced to run to keep up with you. Now, I'm looking forward to time alone with you also.

I won't be witness to all your scowls along with the narrowing of your eyebrows. I must ask, where are we headed and why the swift pace? Thought we have all day to get to our destination."

He laughed at her question, putting his hand on hers, squeezing. Her hand set in the crook of his elbow was nice. He needed more contact. "I'm going to show you some of my family's property. I've a picnic lunch set up near a gorgeous waterfall just waiting for your inspection. Would you enjoy a swim? Ah...but you would need to strip down to your chemise. Seems you've done that once before. I would guard your privacy."

Her less than lady-like snort caught his attention. She stopped to speak her mind. "If you intend to embarrass me at every turn, I'm going to turn around then walk back to the house. Tell me now your intentions," she told him in a huff. "There will be no swimming today. Not stripping down to my chemise. You're not going to catch me naked. As you well know that night was an accident. Didn't know you were swimming in the lake."

"If you left me, you'd miss the ride on Dex. Doubt if any small awkwardness would cause you to forgo this little excursion of ours." By the drawing together of Kerrie's brows, Tam knew he hit the mark. She would never give up the chance to ride her animal even if it was pillion. She would wonder why her stallion wasn't stabled here at the Montgomerie estate. As to the state of her clothing, he had ideas.

"When are you going to give me back my horse? My horse," she repeated as if for his benefit. "You've no rights to the stallion. I've talked to Uncle Drake. He's put me off with one excuse after another. It's not right. Dex is mine."

She still didn't understand. To date he made no mention of a union between the two of them. After they tied the knot, Dex as well as everything else she owned was his. For as long as necessary, he meant to avoid her questions about Dex. "Here we are, saddled. After you, milady. Would you like help up?"

The question Kerrie ignored. She was bent on a different activity. Introducing herself to her horse, Kerrie brushed her hand down Dex's nose. In the palm of her hand, she held a carrot to his muzzle. The horse nickered his pleasure at seeing her as well as the treat. Tam needed to admit she did have a way with the big animal. She could ride without peril as long as nothing startled the huge horse. If something happened, she would never have the needed strength to control the stallion.

Tam lifted her. She was so light. In those few moments, his pledge to keep her from riding Dex alone was reaffirmed. Tam mounted behind her. Wrapped one arm around her waist. Felt the sudden shudder. Her heated response. She was so passionate. He cared about her. She fascinated as well as intrigued him. From the first sight of her, he wanted to know her...all of her.

Bending, he touched his lips to the lobe of her ear. Nipped. She leaned closer to him. Puffed a sweet sigh of pleasure. There was no distance between them. For the ride they were joined together. No space separated their bodies. It was what he wished. "We will enjoy this time together. Promise. I will kiss you as well as hold you. Caress you in familiar as well as unfamiliar places that will delight you. Would you enjoy that? I will. In return, you can touch me anywhere you would like."

Tam felt the shudder of her small body as she acknowledged his words. Just as Kerrie mentioned to Ella, she would never tell him no. In all they did, she was a willing participant.

"Yes. I would like that. Would touch you...? Where?"

As if she wasn't guessing the correct answer, he tossed his head back, his laughter loud and clear. Tam sported a good idea as to where she almost told him she wished to touch him. He wanted that too.

As they passed through the gates of the Montgomerie estate, Tam saw a lone rider in the distance. *A reporter.* To misplace the man, they needed to race the wind. The newsman didn't have the look of a well-trained horseman. Tam didn't wish to take a chance on being wrong. It might be enough to report that the heir apparent and the woman he embarrassed at the Montgomerie ball were riding one horse. Headed into the countryside with no chaperone. He sucked in oxygen. His nerves strained. Just because of this, her name would be on the tip of everyone's tongue tomorrow morning. Even if he lost the man, there was no recourse. The ensuing scandal inevitable.

"We have a shadow. Do you mind if I let Dex have his head? We need to lose the reporter," he whispered in her ear, knowing he didn't have to ask.

All he needed to do was inform her when along with why.

When she whirled to look behind them, his lips brushed across her cheek. If they'd been alone, he would have taken a moment to kiss her. If she gave him an opportunity, in any other situation he would have taken advantage.

"A shadow?" she queried, sounding puzzled. "What do you mean? We have a shadow?"

"Yes, a shadow, if you will. Someone is following us. Seems we piqued a few people's interest last night at the little party your aunt held. Reporters are always a nuisance. We did create a bit of a scandal. If we are to be alone today, we need to distance ourselves from this person so he doesn't know where we are."

"Ella warned you about too many dances."

"I would do the same today," he growled.

"Do you think you can do that? Escape the man?" She gripped his forearm, her fingers tightening as if she prepared herself for the race. "Dex will win," she told him, her confidence in the big stallion showing.

The first question was innocent. The second statement held a wealth of truth. Though Tam took umbrage at the fact she appeared to be questioning his riding skills. "It's Dex we are speaking of. Believe the horse could lose Pegasus if that's what we wanted. Do you doubt me?"

Her grip on his forearm still circling her waist tightened while her knees clenched hard against the horse's sides. "Anytime you wish, go. I'm ready." She laughed her delight at this sudden turn of events. "We will lead him a merry chase, the three of us. This will be Dex's first test. In a year, we can try him at Newmarket." Kerrie tossed her head back. Before he could start, she turned to face him. Her eyes flashing with boldness. "Kiss me hard then go!"

His breath caught at her brazen words. He wouldn't wish to have her any other way. His mouth seized hers. His tongue brushed inside as she audaciously invited him inside her fire scented secrets. She reciprocated each move. The dance of tongues was short, sweet as well as heavenly. As soon as he pulled away from her, she gripped his arm again. Nodded as if giving her permission to race the wind. To sprint across the land. Tam was certain the kiss would be reported in tomorrow's paper. It was just as well nothing else they did today would be seen. She cried out with excitement as Dex picked up speed.

Five minutes turned into ten then fifteen. They raced across Montgomerie land then Talmage territory. Tam used the shortcut between the two properties to weave through the trees. He slowed Dex to a canter. The big stallion was winded from the wild ride. Kerrie was laughing her delight. Tam recalled his untimely rescue the way her cheeks flushed with the excitement coupled with her anger when he plucked her from Dex. She loved the exhilaration of a fast ride. How would he ever keep her happy if he refused her this excitement she seemed to crave? He could not. Would have to find a means.

"Do you think we lost them?" she asked breathlessly, twisting her body so she could see behind him.

"Believe so." Tam whistled, pleased with the way the last fifteen minutes played out. The reporter was left far behind. Would have no idea where he was headed. With Kerrie mounted in front of him, they were going to have a marvelous afternoon, playing, talking, discovering each other. He would return her to the Montgomerie estate before dark. Thoughts of taking her to his home flashed through his head. Knew if he did, the ruse he played would be over before it was prudent. Chances with their future could not be taken. Deviating from his plan, he would never do. Before the wedding she could not learn of his title. If she did, the marriage would be put on hold. The setback would be devastating.

Once again, he reduced the stallion's speed. This time to a slow walk. Questions in her eyes, she tilted her head a bit to look at him. Long wisps of hair fell loose from the ribbon she held the silken strands back with. "What are you doing?"

The question was fair. Now that they were alone, he meant to begin a leisure exploration of her. An excursion meant to seduce. Charm. Torture him. Needed to see the winds of the tempest he intended to create inflame her. He would begin with gentle yet bold touches. Ones she was accustomed to enjoying. Today he meant to taste her breasts, suck and lave until her little sighs of pleasure flitted in the secluded glen. Wanted her to melt all over him as if warm honey. Until the winds of the tempest he created blew hot. Until the storm raged. He meant to touch her more intimately. Introduce her to more pleasures of the flesh.

His forearm rested beneath her breasts, lifting them. He felt the weight of their pressure against his arm. Dex was well-trained. He had to give Kerrie credit for that feat. With his knees he controlled the big horse. His fingers flicked one then a second button opened on her shirt, exposing the line of her neck. The rest followed. Kerrie gave no protest, verbal or otherwise. As if she knew what was coming a puffy breath of air left her. A little sigh trailed after. Tam felt the rise and fall of her chest as she heaved in air.

After her blouse opened, he tugged on the ribbon holding her chemise closed. In a matter of seconds her breasts were bared to him. With his hands he cupped both, brushed his thumbs across the tight hard buds. She shuddered. Her nails bit into his arm. She scooted back until her sweet butt touched upon his arousal. If he wasn't careful, he would deflower her today. He didn't think that such a bad idea except doing so went against his basic nature. When he did take her, she would have no protest about becoming his wife in every way. He would tell anyone, if necessary, what they did in order to achieve her compliance.

After he pushed her hair aside, his teeth scraped across the nape of her neck. She gasped when he bit. Today, he needed to feel her heat, touch the sultry moisture between her legs that would rain down on his fingers. Feel her most intimate dark secrets. He didn't want to proceed too fast though. A climax today might startle her. Kerrie would harbor no thoughts on the culmination of lovemaking. He needed her to understand everything. The first time would cause some pain. After the pain would come the ecstasy. When he had his way, she would relish all he did.

One hand held a breast. His free hand traveled across her thighs. She squirmed when he pressed against her mound. "Your sweet pussy. What do you think? Did your cousin understand what she sang?"

"Tam... should you..." Ran her sweet little tongue along her mouth. "You... I don't know. No, I guess. What are you talking about?"

Tam hoped this was the closest to a protest she would make. "I should. Would rather test naked flesh. Want to feel how soft you are right here." With the heel of his hand, he pressed against her. With no hesitation, she opened her legs wider giving him better access to tender parts, to intimate parts. To the dark humid heat he needed to feel. "You want me to touch you here. Don't you? Tell me true."

"Yes."

A wispy little breath of air sifted through her lips. He bent low to catch the hem of her split skirt. His hands slipped beneath fabric, traveled until he met her drawers. Cursed. Still, he continued to find the small opening at the crotch. Slipping one finger through the opening, he felt her warmth, the heat, the wetness. Honey rained down. "Do you like my fingers here?" He slid them through her softness. Caressed.

"Yes."

Tam withdrew. From the distance he heard the thunder of the water cascading on to the ledge. He settled the skirt around her legs. He couldn't have done that if she'd worn her britches. He was pleased.

"What else are you planning on today?"

With his damp finger he touched her cheek then the long column of her neck. She would wonder about the moisture. He wasn't going to explain anything today. "Food, wine, more pleasure than you've ever known." He returned his attention to her breast, twisting the hardened tip. Plucking the tip, wishing he could taste. "I'm going to teach you about a woman's climax. We are going to enjoy ourselves with no thoughts of tomorrow or the next day."

"Umm..." She wriggled against him, seeming to want more. "Are we almost there?"

He stifled a groan in order to speak, "Yes."

He brought his hand up to point. "There are the falls I spoke of."

They were there at last. Alone after too many days apart. The blanket was spread on the ground close to the falls but not so near the spray would hit them. The basket of food waited for them as did two bottles of his finest wine. A small table had been placed on the ground for their convenience.

Kerrie slid off the stallion before he could help her down. Tam followed her watching her run to the falls. Standing behind them on a path circling between the rock ledge and the tumbling liquid, she held out her fingers capturing the droplets. Her laughter filled him with happiness. He knew she would love this place. The glade was beautiful. Peaceful. To his knowledge, no one came here. They would not be interrupted.

Tam sat down on the blanket that had been spread out for them and watched her antics. She fascinated him. Kerrie was so unlike any other woman he'd ever known. Spontaneous as well as free, she lived her life the way she wished. When they wed, he would find a means to keep her the way she was.

Until he arrived in her life to create upheaval, she'd been a free spirit. He changed some of that. While he couldn't give everything back to her. He could...

...Compromise.

Negotiations were their means to move forward. They would find a middle ground to shape their future.

With the wine poured, he walked to her. She'd run from one side of the falls to the other. When she reached him, he handed her the glass. Her smile stilled his heart. She was everything to him.

"Here is to today and all the joy we can find here. To you as well. Will you drink to us?" he asked.

She clicked her glass to his. "Yes! Oh yes... What else have you planned? I can hardly wait. Tell me!"

Her back to him, Tam held her in his arms. The moments were peaceful watching the water tumble to the ground then move on to the sea. When the sun hit fine droplets, they sparkled as if they were the finest crystal. With Kerrie in his arms, he swayed. The motion was gentle, rocking her. He sipped his wine then led her to the blanket. He leaned against the trunk of a fallen tree. She rested against him. His eyes closed as he brought the vanilla fragrance of her into him.

Scents of the trees, the falling water, even the lush grass where the blanket lay, filled his senses. Still, he was afraid for them, for their future. The orchestration of his plan might infuriate her. When she discovered his lie of omission, the deceptiveness would be difficult for her to like him. Tam was determined to figure out a way to diffuse her fury. He would find a means. Had to find some tactic that would work.

Telling her now would end all his plans for a future with her. Explaining later might have the same effect. What he needed to make certain of was that they consummate the marriage. If they did, she could never ask for an annulment. He would never sign papers to give her a divorce.

Why was life so fraught with complications? He never wished for a title. The damn title was all that stood in their way of happiness. Tam was quite certain she cared for him. Kerrie allowed him access to her body. She would do so again today. If she told him to stop, he would do whatever she asked. That small negative word or words would never happen. Tam searched for a means to bind her to him. A child would help. A child before the wedding was not in the right sequence.

For the next few hours, they would find pleasure in each other's arms. "Are you hungry? I find I'm ravenous for the food in that basket as well as you. Which hunger should we deal with first?"

He waited for a reply of some sort. All he heard was the crashing of the water where the liquid hit the rocks.

Setting her glass on the circular table, she turned in his arms. Her smile ravished his heart. "Starved for a kiss."

"Ah, well...so am I. It's been almost twenty-four hours since I kissed you though..." he paused thinking, tapping her nose with his finger. "You did kiss me when we started out on this adventure."

Off the subject of hunger, "Do you think we lost that reporter?" she asked as his knuckles ran along her jaw then down her neck. He trailed a fingertip around each breast coming closer each time to touching the hardened tips. "You never fastened your blouse. Is that an invitation? If so, I'm quite willing to accept the invite." Beneath the short jacket she wore, he saw the swelling of the beautiful globes that teased all his senses.

Needed to see all of her.

That too would wait.

The kiss was first.

"I hope so. Would not wish to find us interrupted. Believe we lost that reporter during the first few minutes of our wild ride. Dex is too fast for most horses even while carrying two riders."

Kerrie was staring at him, her eyes wide amber pools of concern. "Interrupted? Are you telling me the reporter might have followed us? He could be spying on us? Right now?" Her hands went to her shirt. He stopped her. Held her hands within his.

Bloody everlasting hell! Tam never meant for her to worry over the man finding them. Dex out ran the other horse. "No," he said as he touched her chin lifting it so he could make certain she understood. "He would never be able to keep up with your stallion. We both know that. The man, when I saw him. rode like a *débutant* new to horses."

"Are you certain?"

"I am." His lips found hers, tasted of the sweet wine as well as the innocent woman. Tam never saw her confused or uncertain. Today, she was just that. With his fingers at the small of her back, he pressed her close. Felt her rounded breasts against his chest.

Looking at her, "I am positive he didn't follow more than a minute or two." Nonetheless, he would wait a bit. It would never do to be too eager. "We will eat first. Sip the wine. If I hear anything, I will tell you." The news about his escapades last night was too damning without adding fuel to the gossip.

~ * ~

"I tell you, Drake, I'm concerned about those two." Ella paced his office, fidgeting with her fingers. Tossing her husband looks of anxiety. "It's not because that man can't keep his hands off my niece. Though that could be a problem of magnitude if he wasn't so set on following the rules in the correct order. It's not because he wants so much alone time with Kerrie. A man deserves to have his time to learn about his soon to be bride. Even the reporters following them along with the gossip in the London Times isn't of grave alarm. I understand deep in my heart he would never cause her pain. If she wasn't willing, he would never..."

She was so beside herself, she couldn't sit still, couldn't stop the words from flowing with her fears. Moisture sprang to her eyes.

"What is it that has you chattering as well as pacing nonstop? It boggles my mind. You set this situation into play. What worries you now? Are you regretting this? I'm trying to be patient here. Should I make a guess?"

Drake tipped back the glass of brandy he poured himself,

appearing to study his wife.

"Don't be so obtuse. I'm certain you can guess. We both understand how Sterling has lied by omission. Kerrie has no idea he is not a plain mister. She's falling in love with a man she doesn't know at all. What is she going to do when she discovers the truth about him? She despises men with titles."

Ella fretted more, wringing her hands as she paced the length and back then did so again. She plumped a pillow on the canape near the door. Rearranged the figurines on the shelf before setting her sites on the mantle.

"You are right. In the end, nothing will be good for Tam. He's made a royal mess of this. All hell will break loose when your niece discovers upon marriage to the man that she will be a countess. To make this worse, if that could be possible, in the end she will become a duchess. Kerrie has always been practical, never sought wealth or a title as some women. She is happy with the breeding of her horses. He did take Dex away from her. Not quite certain how the man was able to do that. Anyway, Kerrie is content with a simple life. Though..." Drake let out a soft chuckle. "...a man does like to know that the woman he marries loves him for who he is, not what he can give her."

Ella whirled on her husband, hands clenched at her sides. She found herself furious with the man. Angry he could laugh at a serious situation. Both her husband as well as the marquis were thickheaded brutes when it came to a woman's feelings, "This is not funny! Sterling is taking her horse away from her. Did you not see the padlock on Dex's stall? I'm surprised he did not take the stallion to the Talmage stable."

He held up his hands in silent supplication. "He also gave her a fine mare. Perhaps they are equal." Cleared his throat as if the time would enable him to search for the right words. "I'm not as thick headed as I know you are thinking. I do agree with you, my dear. Though you do need to admit there could be humor in this situation. Look at the amusing side. Tam finds, after a few years of looking, the woman he wishes to spend his life with. A woman who doesn't covet him for his title along with his wealth. She cares for him, just him. She is enamored with him, just him. He's always wished to know the woman he married loved him for himself. As did I." Drake gave her an intense look. With an arched brow, he continued. "I was willing to do whatever needed to be done as is Tam."

"Bah!" Ella waved one hand in the air. "All you cared about was finding a passionate woman because your mother was such a cold fish."

"Not all I cared about. I too wished for a woman who loved me for myself. I found you. I've been pleased ever since."

Ella smiled at his words giving her a feeling of hope for Sterling. "Kerrie doesn't care about the wealth. She loathes men with titles after their names." Ella couldn't cease her fretting though. The ceremony is supposed to happen tomorrow. The marquis needed to convince Kerrie she wished to marry him on short notice. "What are we going to do?"

"Starters?" Drake's right eyebrow lifted as if thinking about her question in mockery. "We aren't going to do anything. This little problem needs to be solved between the two of them even though negotiating the terms of Kerrie's surrender will not be easy for Tam. He's chosen not to tell her the truth. It's up to us to hold our words behind our lips."

She set her hands on his desk, leaning close to him, and spoke with passion. "We need to do something. This is all going to fall apart. Kerrie will leave. She'll go home to her parents. They won't marry. Neither will ever find love. I don't like messes."

All Ella could think about were the worst-case scenarios playing out here. She wanted both of them to be happy, content as well as in love. Drake was right though. They shouldn't interfere.

"You cannot be successful with all your matches. You didn't pair up Nicki and Ian. Nor did you put Chauncey and Stephen together. Though, so far, the ones you did put together have worked out very well."

She huffed, thinking about the matches between her nieces and the chosen men. "The very fact that I brought Kane and Lyssa together set up the relationship between Chauncey and Stephen. So, I did have a hand in the marriage of those two. Tara and Case are a perfect match though it did involve heartache I never foresaw. Didn't expect the man to be such an ass!"

Drake hooted at her choice of words. "Nicki found her own man."

"No, Ian abducted her. He found his woman."

"Much the same. Nicki put up no protest in the abduction. One cannot call what happened between them resulted in a kidnapping. I did enjoy threatening the rake with a hanging from his ship. The look on his face was precious. Yes, that was a very good time for us. I did enjoy seeing the fear in the rake's eyes."

"Let's get back to Kerrie and Tam. How can we keep the information from her? If she gets up before the rest of us and sees the paper..."

Leaning forward, arms on his desk. "The girl would have to be up at the crack of dawn to read the gossip column. The servants have their orders to dispose of the evidence. There will be no papers available to her. Since you told me there was a reporter following Tam, I suppose there will be more gossip tomorrow."

"I do hope that man doesn't find them. I'm certain he plans a tryst at the waterfall on his land. Kerrie will not tell him no. I've seen that look in her eyes when she stares at the man. My niece is besotted with the marquis."

"He won't compromise her. The man is not known as the stuffy marquee for nothing. He earned the moniker fair and square. Tam won't change overnight."

"Kerrie has robbed him of all his stuffiness. Besides, when a man is around a beautiful woman, he doesn't think logically with his brain but with a different part of his anatomy." Ella snorted. "He could very well compromise her."

# Chapter Five

Kerrie licked her fingers. The food was wonderful. The day was amazing, sunny as well as warm. Tam smiled and looked at her as if he wished to devour her. Everything in her life was perfect. Her head was a bit fuzzy from the wine she'd been drinking. She felt relaxed. At ease with this man who surprised her at every turn. Would love to have him wrap his arms around her. Hold her tight.

Light winds rustled the leaves in the tree overhead. The waterfall shimmered in the light of the sun. Everything was idyllic. The peace she felt here was the same as at home when she visited some of her special places.

She lay on her back, staring at the sky thinking about Tam. She felt as if she'd known him forever instead of just a week. A few white clouds floated high above, changing shapes with the twisting breezes. Tam lay on his side, his head propped up grinning as he stared at her while he ran one finger up then down her neck. As he requested, she'd not fastened her shirt. The jacket she wore seemed to cover most of her.

Tam plucked a piece of grass. He trailed the piece of greenery down her neck then between her breasts. She rolled over to look at him. Her jacket opened. One breast spilled free. A rush of heat suffused her. She was shy around him even though she loved the way he touched her. He was smiling at her. With the backs of his hands, he was pushing the fabric of her jacket aside. The grass swept across the tip of one breast after that the other. At the light evocative caress, she quivered. Her body trembled with the sensations he evoked. There was magic in the air. Mercuric enchantment. Her body heated further.

He sat, slipped his shirt over his head. Her gasp of pleasure caught in the back of her throat. She recalled the lake. The darkness lit by a slender moon. She needed him to reveal more. He was broad as well as bronzed. Muscles rippled as he moved. The width of his chest tapered to narrow hips. She bit her lip wishing to reach out to touch him remembering how he felt when they swam. He'd been naked. That night she felt the hard length of him pressed against her stomach. She wanted to know more about Tam, the man.

"I've not seen you without your shirt...not in the light of day," she told him, mesmerized by the view. "I..."

Her hand on her chest, she didn't know what else to say. She couldn't think. The sight of him created a tempest of yearning.

"Did you wish to touch me?" he asked, his grin wide, the deep gray-blue of his eyes darkening until they were nearly black. "I would never tell you no. Do what you wish. Dance your fingers across my chest. Would you like me to touch you in all the places I know will excite you? I could do whatever pleases you."

Unable to speak, Kerrie nodded. Ran her tongue across lips that had gone dry. Her mouth parched. Anticipations soared. Tam waited while she tried to gain the courage to reach out to him. Her hand quivered. She stretched forward then brought her fingers back a couple of times.

"Are you afraid?" His voice was soft, gentle in tone. "There is no need for fear. I only bite a little."

"Oh!"

"Just a little in all the right places," he murmured, his voice tender, coaxing her to continue her exploration.

Shaking her head, "No...yes...well I suppose I am afraid. Nervous. This is all so very new to me. Yet you've touched me more than once. Held my breasts in your hands." Kerrie pressed her flattened palm on the middle of his chest. Crisp dark hair narrowed to his waistband. She moved her hand so the palm touched one of his nipples. "They are so small." She thought he might laugh at her. He didn't.

"Unlike yours... Your breasts overflow my hands. The tips are hard, as you say, much larger than mine. I appreciate that fact more than I could ever explain. Your breasts are soft rounded globes I delight in touching. To me they are the finest jewels a man could ever see," he said as his tone changed. "The crests I adore respond to my touch."

"We are so different. Imagine that's a good thing. Don't you think?"

Kerrie didn't know where they were headed with this conversation. She never wished to marry. Now thoughts of living with this man the rest of her life filled her with happiness. She didn't understand the change of emotions. She couldn't imagine not seeing him every day or sharing hopes along with dreams. Couldn't envisage a life without him to talk to. Found herself rethinking her earlier decisions.

"Are you cold?" he asked, a half-smile on his lips. "We can remedy that. I could..." he paused, stopping the sentence.

She wondered what he was about to say that he would stop so abruptly. "No...are you? I find I'm *verra* hot."

She thought with the sun shining, he would not be cold. Wasn't certain why he asked her the question. His chest was naked while she still wore the bulk of her clothing. Maybe he wanted to dress.

Tam was shaking his head, grinning, watching, touching again the lapels of her jacket. "Would you take this off? Need to see more of you. If you're not cold...that is. I wouldn't want...you to be cold. Don't wish for you to catch a chill."

Yes, he'd seen more of her but not all of her. Before there was always a little bit of cloth covering private places. He would ask her to bare herself to him. He did so for her. She gulped down a raw bit of air. Held the burgeoning panic at bay. She felt adventurous. This would be so much easier if he seduced her, removed the clothing in her stead. While she was so on fire, she couldn't think. Didn't seem he meant to seduce. By his question he insisted she make the decision.

Heaving in more oxygen, she slipped from her jacket, setting the garment beside his shirt. She wasn't naked yet. Though her chemise along with her shirt were unfastened. He nodded to her, one finger pushing material aside so he could see her. Her breasts moved as she fought for courage.

"Take it all off," he whispered, his voice husky, so different from the normal sound, so very deep. "Let me see you. All of you. I've been patient. As patient as any man can be. I've waited days for this moment. You are beautiful."

"Do you want me n-na—naked? I don't think I can do that even for you. Would need help from you."

Still, she slipped her blouse from her arms. The chemise followed. The piece of grass he teased her with earlier swished across the hardened and puckered tips of each breast. When she looked down, she wondered at the size of them. Her breasts seemed swollen. The nipples larger.

"Yes, for me naked would be wonderful. Maybe not for you. Did you know you've the prettiest ripe peaches I've ever seen. Want to taste them, pluck the tips with my mouth, fingers too, until you cry out in pleasure. Suck them deep into my mouth."

She flushed, felt heat rise to her cheeks, saw the tops of her breasts turn red. Watched Tam grin at the sight. She was baffled by his words. "You want to suck on me? That sounds strange. Is that normal behavior? You do abide by the rules. You've told me all has a proper order. You don't do anything that isn't proper." Strange as it sounded to her, she could imagine the sensations. Kerrie looked at him with narrowed brows. "This isn't proper. Is it?"

"Yes," he told her, his voice growing in volume as he explained what he wanted. "Yes, sweet one. I want to suck, bite, flick with my tongue. Do the same all over again. Want you so hot...so wet...willing. Rules be damned!"

The change in his voice startled...took her by surprise. "If I'm to be naked then you should also shed your clothing. That seems fair. Don't you think? I would like to see all of you also. Need to see that hard part of you I felt against me."

Yes, she wanted to see that part of him that touched her intimately the night they swam. Was surprised she spoke the words. Kerrie found herself both curious as well as afraid of the next few moments. She sipped air wishing. Somewhere deep inside she knew she shouldn't give in to his requests. The hell with shouldn't. She wanted to.

"You remember the night we swam in the lake?" His question stroked her nerves, shattered her control.

She nodded but, "You were naked then. I felt you... Is that the way I'll see you now? All swollen and hard. Is that...? You know I've seen the stallions." Fires flamed. Tempest thundered. Tam appeared as if he remembered the same moment. His heated gaze raked over her. Touched her with the knowing intimacy.

"You didn't see me. Today if you wish, if you ask, I'll be naked in front of you. Kiss me now. My hunger for you has grown. Don't believe this man can wait any longer for a kiss from you. Hold you in my arms. Feel you against me."

Kerrie understood this was not something she should do. Tam was right. She was daring as well as naughty. Brazen as well as bold. Her thoughts would be construed as wicked. Just like her cousins before her. She leaned toward him. His hand went around her head, fingers winding into her hair drawing her down to him. She sprawled on top of him. Against her she felt the crisp dark hair of his chest. Felt the heat of the man along with the enchantment he created with ease.

Their mouths united, his with hers. His tongue tripped across hers, rubbed, slid in then out. A whimper of pleasure left the back of her throat. One hand cupped her breast, warmed, caressed with possession. The kiss was long as well as deep. Hard and slow. Blood raced through her. Her heart pounded. The drum of her pulse echoed in her head. With his teeth, he tugged on her lower lip, bit with care. She moaned. Whimpered. Sounds rippled from the back of her throat into his mouth. Raw desire flowed. Felt lost when his lips left hers. He traced the moisture on her bottom lip with his thumb.

"So full. Plump. Red. Need to see if the rest of you tastes as good. May I?"

His fingers threaded through her hair, let the strands slide between them. He seemed to be waiting for an answer. She wasn't certain she could speak.

"Please..." Tam spoke about tasting her breasts, pulling them into his mouth. He kissed his way down her neck, across her collarbone. Teasing. Exciting. Setting fire to her. She shivered. Trembled anew. Raw sensations vibrated through her.

When his mouth closed over one nipple then tugged, she cried out, arching against him. Her fingers bit into his shoulders. Her teeth bit down on his arm. Butterflies danced in the pit of her stomach. The sensations rocked her. Shocked all the way to her toes. An ache grew between her legs, senses intensified where he touched her that night, and began to flourish. With each pass of his mouth, the tempest he orchestrated deepened.

She arched up, pressing against him when he pulled her breast deeper into his mouth. Sucked hard. Deeper still. He did just as he told her he would do. He drank the roundness into his mouth. She felt his teeth against her flesh, his tongue flick across her nipple. He drank in all of her. Sipped with strength. Took most of her breast into him. She whimpered. After he turned his attention to the other breast, his fingers caressed then explored lower. Dipped beneath fabric to explore virgin territory. Heat settled deep in her belly.

"You are a delight. You are fashioned exquisitely, just for me. You are mine, Kerrie. All mine."

His whispered words unnerved her. Unraveled all the tense nerves. He rose above her, looked down. "Your pretty little nipples are damp from my possession, pulled taunt begging for more. However, I've not tasted your lips enough." Once more he captured her mouth within his. Her lips were framed by his mouth. His fingers dwelled on her skirt, unfastening the ties. Pushing the fabric down her legs. She helped him lifting each leg so he could rid her of the troublesome material.

When his hand settled beneath the fabric of her pantalettes on her belly, she bolted upright, thought she would jump from her skin. Hit his chin with the top of her head. She panicked. His hand rested there, warmed. Stilled. He kissed her again, as he began to explore her intimately. Until he cupped her mound.

"Can I remove these?" he asked above her, staring down on her. "You will enjoy the reason. I promise."

Kerrie felt certain her eyes were glazed over. Felt as if she was out of her body looking down on the two of them doing unspeakable things together. The winds of the tempest he created howled. "Y-yes...I think so..."

"Ah, my sweet, honey. You must be certain. Tell me now. Yes or no? This is your decision to make, not mine. You must take the choice out of my hands. Won't do anything you don't tell me you want."

With growing impatience, his fingers dallied with the ties of her pantalettes. His knuckles brushed the sensitive flesh he was uncovering.

He bent to kiss her navel. Her muscles constricted as he moved lower pushing the fabric down without untying them.

"Yes..." The single word was a thin wail. "Yes...you must or I don't believe I'll survive. I ache. My body... I don't know what's happening to me. Do you?"

Her words were uttered in sharp pants. She was beside herself, her flesh hot, her body throbbing and arching with desire, hunger she didn't understand.

Before she knew what was happening, she was naked except for her stockings. On his elbows he was taking in his fill. Studying her. She thought to cover herself but, palm against palm, he held her hands beside her head. He bent to kiss her belly, to move lower. With each touch of his mouth on her, her muscles contracted quivering with need.

"So beautiful. Do you wish for me to stop? I will tell you now. Don't wish to stop until you cry out my name with your climax. I'm going to give you ecstasy you never knew existed. Want you to understand..."

She was beside herself with need. Arching. Writhing. "Don't stop! Please don't!" She didn't want to feel the painful rejection stopping would cause. He'd rejected her too many times. She'd never felt this intense need before. "I need you, Tam. Please, please don't cast me off now. Don't reject me again," she whispered, her breath a soft moan. "I want you."

"I've no intention of rebuffing you or stopping unless you say no. This 'please' you spoke is good. That is what I was hoping to hear."

His lips traveled along the inside of her leg to her knee, to her foot. All the while he was removing one stocking. Stopping at her foot, he massaged the arch, touched there lightly with his fingers then his lips. After that he turned his attention to her other leg until she writhed. Bowed. Whimpered. She was beside herself. Still, he prolonged this. Brought her higher.

Startled by his swift movement, he was kissing her lips again. His hand pressed against her just as he did earlier today. Her legs were spread wide. He was between them. His thighs pushing hers apart. One finger caressed her with tender care. He gave attention to her mouth, to a spot between her legs that sent her ricocheting higher and hotter than she could imagine. Her cries of pleasure filled the glade. She heaved against him, searching for more, for something she didn't understand.

"That's it, honey. Let it go. Trust me to bring you the pleasure you deserve. That which your body seeks. Give in to what you are feeling."

Once again, he bent his attention to her breast, teasing, taunting. Wild tempest. Lightening crashed into her.

She felt him, a finger glided smoothly inside her. Then two. He filled her. She felt as if she adjusted to him. Stretched. Moved inside her until she squirmed and shuddered with the intense sensations. Her body soared. Flew high then higher still. Her nails bit into his shoulders. She shuttered. Shattering into hundreds of pieces, she cried out. Pulses vibrated through her. The world burst upon her in a myriad of rainbow colors. Sensations swept within. She bucked, throbbed and sought everything.

"Tam!"

He continued to stroke her until she calmed, easing his fingers from inside her, cradling her in his arms. Rocking her with his warmth as well as his strength. She relaxed into him, reveled in his arms.

"What," she gulped air as her body calmed. She realized she'd never felt such immense pleasure or such intense sensations. "What did you do to me? I...I would know."

His lips brushed across hers with slowness that started another fire burning. "Gave you a woman's pleasure. In my arms, under my direction, you climaxed sweet, tender ecstasy. You can have that whenever you ask. Watched your eyes. You didn't close them. That was nice. Later we could do the same again. Would you like it if you climaxed another time? I love to rock you until you cry out my name again. Like that, hearing my name when you reach your pleasure."

She sighed as she realized he almost made love to her. Wondered if this was what it would be like when he sent his sex inside her. "Yes, though it's not fair. I would do the same for you? I would give you the same desire, gratification. You showed me ecstasy I never knew existed. Is that possible? Can I give you pleasure? Does a man have a...a climax?"

She wondered though, understanding he still wore his buckskins. He'd received no pleasure as she had. Surely, he must have felt something...nice.

"I would enjoy your embrace if you would like." He brought her hand to touch him. "A man can receive pleasure such as you felt as well as give it. If you touch me here." He pressed her hand against himself.

Kerrie felt his hardness against her palm. Even through the fabric of his pants, he was hot to her hand. "What do I do?" she asked her feelings open.

She didn't wish to sound stupid or innocent. This step she was taking was big. She needed to see him. Needed to understand what would happen to his body. Thought of the stallions she watched mount the mares. Saw them thrust inside. Heard the scream from the mares. Was that pleasure or pain? Oh my, would he be that big? Couldn't be. As large as a stallion? She wasn't naïve. Oh...but she was. In this, Tam might be right. For her to watch was not a good idea. Too late...

With a flick of his wrist, he freed himself. Brought her hand to his sex. With a will of their own, her fingers closed around his length. Tightened. Explored the hard length. Tested. Moved on him. She felt the satin of his skin, the fire and the heat. He was smooth against her hand, hard, wanting. After she squeezed, he groaned. The sound rough. He showed her how to move her fingers. Bending, she touched the tip of him with her tongue. When he jerked, she looked at him. He nodded.

"Honey, you couldn't do this any better."

She studied, investigated, and tried moving faster then slower. In not too many minutes she heard the husky cry as his body trembled and he released his seed onto his belly. "Tam...? Are you alright?"

Until she saw his grin, she was afraid she'd hurt him. "Fine...better than fine. You were perfect."

After a few minutes passed, he cleaned his belly with one of the napkins from the basket. He pulled her into his arms. She nestled against him, closing her eyes. The peaceful moments while he held her were almost as sweet as the climax. She wanted to be held by him forever. Never wanted this moment to end. It would. He would have to bring her back to the Montgomerie estate.

"I need to get you dressed," Tam told her as he braced himself up by his elbows. "Don't want you to take a chill."

"Is that it?" Kerrie asked, wishing she could snuggle against him until it was time to leave. Her nakedness no longer bothered her. She ran her hands along his chest, followed the line of dark hair to his navel. He'd not fastened his buckskins.

"We have something...a topic...I need to discuss with you. What I need to say to you is important. Unless something changes that is all there is for the moment. Later, well...though when we finish this conversation, we could do this again...if you like." He stood fastening his pants then pulling his shirt over his head. "Believe me, I wish there could be more right now. Important matters come first. Fun later. The proper order," he added almost as if an afterthought.

Seeing into his mind was what she wished for. That wasn't going to happen. She would need to wait until he said his piece. "A topic? What is it? What is so important that has you so serious?"

All manner of ideas raced through her head. She caught her breath, hoping he wasn't going to make some demand she would hate.

"Yes, I've a question for you." He brought her the clothes he scattered around the small space. Stood back, arms crossed appearing to wait for her to dress. "I wish I dared discuss this with you naked in my arms. Afraid that is far from possible. Don't want to take further advantage of you than I already have. If you wish to understand the truth about how I feel, I would like to be deep inside you. When that happens, all your choices will vanish. You must have a say in this. I'm not going to demand anything of you."

"Choices? Deep inside me?" She thought...speculating. Would her choices vanish? She wasn't positive what he meant. Though now she had a few guesses. No doubt he would tell her. "I'm not certain I would like to remain naked since you are dressed." She flushed, heated while he stared at her. "Feel too vulnerable this way."

"You are new to this sexual play. In time, you will get used to lying with me without wearing a stitch. We will enjoy your nakedness when we are together. Mine too."

Once she was dressed, everything fastened, he poured her a glass of wine. Kerrie drank. The wine was delicious. Her throat was parched. Famished, she ate a slice of cheese along with a piece of ham. Drank some more before he splashed additional wine into the glass. She watched him as he paced around the blanket. Tam was nervous. That was unusual. He was always so sure of himself.

"Did your cook pack anything sweet? I find I'd like something sugary." Kerrie was putting off this conversation which she was now coming to dread. He was taking too long, making her nervous. She searched through the basket of food coming up with a container of chocolate cookies. "Do you want one?" she asked, holding out the box for him.

"No, I'm pleased to watch you eat. Always like to see you indulge yourself. Will pamper you whenever I can. The fact that you enjoy food delights me. Most women are afraid to indulge themselves."

He sat back, the bottom of his wine glass resting on his belly. He looked relaxed as if the upcoming discussion was of little concern. Only a moment ago he seemed nervous. Which was it? While he'd dressed before her, he didn't fasten his pants or don his shirt. She saw the dark hair between the opening of his pants, knew what was below the waistband. She swept her tongue across her lips. He was no longer hard. He would be small now...until he was aroused again. Did she do that to him? Arouse him? How? She didn't know. Thought the arousal might have something to do with kissing.

The startling realization hit her. She stimulated him until he was... A sense of feminine power raced through her. Unable to stop herself, she licked her lips again. When she switched her focus from his sex to his eyes, she heated anew. Flushed to the tips of her toes. The look he sent her way was one she didn't want to acknowledge. It was obvious he understood where her attention was given. Tam grinned, looking satisfied with something.

"Oh, my."

"I'm pleased you are curious. Drink some more wine. Eat your cookie. I can wait for conversation until your other needs are sated. We will deal with one thing at a time. Go ahead."

"I'm satisfied." Kerrie downed the rest of her wine before pouring herself another glass of wine. By the look in his eyes, she was certain she would need the fortification. She bit into the chocolate delight. Savored. When she looked up, he posed the question that would begin the discussion.

"Will you marry me tomorrow night?" His voice cracked. He asked. He didn't demand. "I'm hoping."

She sucked in a fragment of air. A crumb of cookie caught in her throat. She coughed. He'd never spoken of anything permanent. One didn't get much more long-lasting than marriage. This was the first time she heard Tam sound insecure. She didn't understand. Why would he want to marry her? Marriage seemed so lasting. She reminded herself she didn't intend to marry. "Why?"

"You like me to touch as well as caress all those lovely sensitive female parts you have. You appreciate what we did here today. Why not marriage? We would enjoy ourselves. You fascinate me. Intrigue me until I can't breathe. Would never bore me. You are wild as well as unrestrained. Naughty, though you don't wish to admit to the trait. Your body is delicious, small and curvaceous. Small, except for your breasts. Now that I've tasted you, I know marriage to you would be exceptional. I want permanence with a woman. Why not you? You delight me."

Kerrie found herself bristling with indignation. If she were to marry, she wanted so much more than what he told her. Exceptional. Good. Pleasant. All those things...but...to her mortification she blurted, "What about love?"

"What about it?" Unperturbed, he sipped his wine, cast his gaze over her. Appreciating her. "I care for you. Need you by my side. Would like to have children with you. Love will come with time. We've known each other for a very short time. What about you? Can you say with any sincerity that you love me?"

Children? She'd never thought about babies since she never thought to wed. "I find that's not enough. Don't wish to share..." She paused thinking about the laws of their times. "Don't want a man to own all that is mine. When we part ways, my horse will be mine. Dex will no longer have a padlock on his stable door. I'll be able to ride him when I want. Not pillion with you. Why would I want to give up all that I have?"

His relaxed persona changed. He slashed his hand in the air as if trying to point out all the ways she was wrong. "What besides the horse is yours? What do you claim as belonging to you? Deep down you understand I'm right about Dex. A woman with less than substantial strength cannot control that huge stallion. He's all muscle. You know it. The facts are clear to anyone with a mind as well as eyes. Dex knows when you're astride him, he can do what he likes. So far, what he likes is to please you. Problem is, you won't admit to the fact." His words were harsh now. He wasn't pleased with her reaction.

Her back stiff, chin in the air, she went on to say. "I never planned on marrying. Never gave children a second thought. Suppose if I married, I would love to have a child or two." That was the only answer she could give him. While he might be right about the stallion, Kerrie wasn't about to admit that to him. She raised him. He never...but he could.

"There is more at stake here than you think. Concessions will be made for you. If you agree, I'll make certain all your dreams come to fruition. I'll compromise whenever I can." He touched her lips with his fingers. His voice softened as if he realized his anger wasn't getting him where he wanted to be. "Hush now. Let's not argue over trivialities. When we are wed, I will see that you have the best stable in all of England. Better than your mother's. Together, we'll race your horses. Breed them. The money you earn will be yours. I've no need of more wealth. I'm not planning to take anything from you. All I want is to give to you. Make every day of your life happy."

"Mother's?" Kerrie liked the sound of it. "A better breeding farm than my mother's."

Competing with family was not a priority yet the thought sounded quite nice. Kerrie always wanted to be successful in her endeavors. Her mother was a successful breeder. If her stable matched her mother's, she would be pleased.

"That is up to you. If you want to best your mother in this process, I'll give you the funds to do so." Again, he held up his hand. "You will pay me back from revenue gained in your business. Is that acceptable? If you need advice on the running of the business, you can come to me. We will hire men who are capable."

"I don't want your money."

"I know." Air rushed from his lungs. "That's why this proposition will work. I can trust you. If you agree to the marriage, I'll know it has nothing to do with my money. You will also understand I'm there for you, no matter your needs. A man likes to know if the woman he is married to wants him for more than what he can give her."

"You're not making any sense."

She was confused. Baffled by all he said. Why would he think she would marry someone for other reasons than love. She did love him. He didn't love her but he cared. Was that enough? There was something else going on here. Unable to read between his sentences, she shrugged.

"Will you wed with me tomorrow evening? Make me the happiest man alive?" His voice grew deep, husky almost the way he sounded when he was caressing her, fondling. Touching those places that made her wild, frantic with her hunger. "I will give you everything you ask for."

He warmed her heart in so many unique ways. Kerrie wanted to say, yes. She hesitated, wondering if accepting would make her happy. Wondering if agreeing would be the worst decision of her life.

It seemed to her he could see her hesitation then the possibility of compliance. He went on to say, "I could compromise you right here. Give you a few more moments of a woman's pleasure. Would you like that? I, however the stuffy person that I'm known to be, would rather wait until after the wedding for the wedding night, the consummation of our union. What do you say? Do you wish to have me bury all of myself deep inside you right now? Not just my fingers? Would you rather wait to have a proper night after the nuptials?"

Stalling for time, Kerrie held up her empty glass. "Another glass of wine, please. That would..." Her voice quivered. She would like to know how it would be when he did make love to her. She cleared her throat. Repeated the request. "I'd like another glass of wine, please."

Kerrie found that she'd downed the last one in two gulps. He sprang this on her. Shocked her mind. Discovered herself terrified to the tips of her toes. To answer him was impossible. She didn't know what to say. Even though she'd never thought to marry, she needed this man in ways she could never describe. As he said about her, she cared for him. Wanted him. Loved him even when he was acting autocratic. Needed to explore him further. He was all she wasn't. She was wild as well as impulsive. He was calm, proper. He was her opposite in most every way. Would she be happy with this man?

To her surprise, he filled her glass then his. While he leaned back against the log, he smiled at her. "Take your time. We have all afternoon. There is no reason to rush your decision. Drink up. Ella and Drake are waiting to find out the answer. Oh, did I mention the ceremony will be at the Montgomerie estate? Two o'clock tomorrow afternoon."

*No reason to rush?*

Ella and Drake are waiting for an answer? My answer? He'd already told them his plans. She felt both outraged as well as pleased. Seemed Tam always sparked two opposite emotions in her. He was winning her over one tiny bit at a time.

Didn't he just tell her they would hold the ceremony tomorrow? Kerrie leaned upon him. His arms surrounded her. The feeling delicious. Comfortable. If she agreed to his outlandish proposal, she would always be his. He would be hers. Forever. She realized she wanted Tam to be hers, only hers.

Kerrie couldn't think of anything better. She never expected a proposal. Never expected to meet someone she could see a life with. In so many ways, this man was perfect for her. He told her he would compromise. Wouldn't take anything from her even though by the right of the law he could.

Closing her eyes, she sifted through the days they spent together. There was so much she disliked about Sterling Talmage. He was autocratic. Domineering. Had a sense that he was always right. He never gave in to her demands. He commanded people without speaking. So very much like her Uncle Drake.

There were also many characteristics she loved about him. He was kind. Sparked heat. Gave her so much pleasure. Cared about her. Thought of her needs before his.

*Tam told me we could negotiate change. Could compromise when in disagreement.*

She could live with the ability to negotiate as well as compromise. Wasn't that what marriage was all about? Did he tell her what she wished to hear? So, he could have his way? Were his words the truth?

Wine flowed into her glass after she emptied it. Drank long and deep. Her mind floating, she turned to him, "Kiss me."

He did.

"Yes, I will."

~ * ~

When the afternoon began, Tam was terrified she would refuse. Terrified the outing would be disrupted by reporters. He wouldn't have a chance to be alone with her, to ask the question. She was so beautiful. Her hair glorious, thick, her lips now swollen with his kisses, her amber eyes, sparkling with the fever he created. Mercurial enchantment with each touch floated around them. Before they left the secluded glade, he brought her to two more magical climaxes.

*She agreed to my proposal.*

When she told him yes, he felt as if everything he'd ever wanted was before him, waiting now to claim. In fewer than twenty-four hours she would have his name. After the sun began to go down, he brought her home. Told Ella along with Drake their plans. The wedding was set for two, tomorrow afternoon. All her London relatives had been invited. His family would be there to celebrate.

Unless she heard about his title before the vows and the consummation, all would go as planned. Nervous, yes, his nerves were stretched to the snapping point. He wouldn't be able to relax until the ring was slid on her finger and they were pronounced husband and wife. He couldn't get the image from his head. Riding home, they were followed by a lone man.

*A reporter?*

This didn't bode well. He worried they might have been shadowed and seen. In this morning's paper not only was there gossip but also a drawing of the two of them dancing together. Rage filled him that someone might have watched them making love in the glade. The waterfall was on his property. The reporter would be trespassing, invading privacy. The man might have drawn them. He was still positive no one could have kept up with Dex. He shook off the feeling of dread. Kissed her neck. Cupped her breast.

"You need to fix your hair before I bring you into the house.

Everyone will know what we did. Would you like help?" Tam loved to run his fingers through her hair. He would do more harm than good if he tried to give assistance.

"Better do this myself," she murmured with a small laugh. She lifted her hands to finger comb her hair. "Don't want this day to end. Wish we could ride back to the glen. Spend the night there."

Tam pulled several leaves from the long strands. He teased her while she was occupied. "Neither do I, honey. Neither do I."

Tomorrow he would be a married man. He would have a countess. Holding his breath Tam prayed. The lone rider trailed them until they disappeared into the stable. Holding her breast in his hand might not have been wise. He couldn't resist. She was his. In a matter of hours all would learn their truth.

Kerrie slid from the horse without help. Tam leapt down beside her before tossing the reins to the stableboy with instructions to take proper care of Dex. He caught her hand in his as they exited. Her fingers so small, fragile. She would need to proceed with caution. He understood he could not keep her from the stallion. If he did, the action would be contentious. She would come to hate that dictate. Knowing her now, she would find any means possible to defy him.

A compromise would be in order. Negotiations, prudent.

There would need to be rules. He would discuss it with her. Bloody hell, he needed the ceremony to take place now! Before anything could backfire. Not tomorrow. Now! Tonight! His fists clenched tight, frustration eating at him.

Trying to relax, hand in hand, they walked through the back terrace. Elizabeth was there working on a needlepoint. When she saw them, she smiled as if expecting an announcement. She seemed to be waiting for them. On edge. Anxious. Ready to send for reinforcements.

"Where are your mother and father?" Tam asked, needing to get everything moving. Now, he felt impatient. Restless to his core. He brought Kerrie's hand to his lips. Kissed the back. Turned it over for more intimacy. Kissed the palm. Touched there with the tip of his tongue. Felt the small shudder shuffle through her body. Bloody eyes, she didn't have any business riding that huge stallion of hers.

"You have something to tell them?" Elizabeth asked, her voice filled with sugar. Her smile was all-knowing. Anticipating the announcement. "You can tell me. I can keep a secret."

"None of your business, Imp," Tam said as they walked by.

Elizabeth stuck her tongue out at him. He tweaked her nose. "Are they in the drawing room?"

He kept walking. Didn't wait for an answer he didn't think he would get. This time of night, he was pretty certain he knew where they would be.

"Maybe. Don't keep track of my parents. They do what they please when they please. Wouldn't be surprised to find them in bed."

She shot him a look that told him, after what he said, she wasn't going to tell him anything more.

Tam chuckled. He'd known the little she-devil her entire life. She could get into more trouble than his soon to be wife. Elizabeth was adventurous. A born flirt. Spoiled all the way to the tips of her toes. Thought she held the world in the palm of her hand. Expected men to bow down to her. She would find a man who wouldn't. A man who took matters to heart.

"You must be more familiar with my aunt and uncle than I thought," said Kerrie who looked baffled. "You act as if this is as much your home as theirs. You know where everything is. Assume you can..." Kerrie stumbled to keep up with him. "You don't have to move so fast. The house is not burning down," she told him while she tugged on his arm, a wasted attempt to slow his forward progress.

Tam stopped to say a few things to her. Yes, he was in a hurry. He didn't have to make her life difficult with his impatience. "We've been neighbors my entire life. We all played together. Ash is younger but as soon as he was old enough, we did things together. They know my house just as well. So yes, I'm familiar. I'm certain they are in the drawing room. Shall we? Hope we won't be interrupting something...er...intimate."

He tugged on her hand, eager for the meeting. For the culmination of his plans.

Stepping into the room, the pair were sipping brandy while they spoke. He thought he heard his name. Seemed they realized who came into the room. He nodded. "Ella, Drake. We've good news to share. The two of you will be the first to know."

He realized Elizabeth stood behind him. She followed them.

"Knew it!" Elizabeth stepped by them to take a seat near the fireplace. Her hands folded on her lap, she appeared the angel most people thought she was. Tam along with her parents knew better.

Tam couldn't stop the grin. His arm wrapped around Kerrie's shoulder, tugging her closer to him. He inhaled the tantalizing scent of vanilla. Oh, yes, just as Elizabeth could be an angel when she wished to get her way so could Kerrie. He believed Lizzy would go the way of the other female cousins. A little bit naughty as well as a little bit nice. Some sugar coupled with a whole lot of spice. Lizzy was beautiful. Had the look of her mother. She would cut some poor man a wild ride. In a year or two, Ella would be looking for a husband for her daughter. He wondered what she would allow. Certainly not the leeway she gave the nieces. Not for her daughter. Lizzy would be chaperoned day as well as night. Drake would see to that. There would be no unchaperoned rides to the glen.

"What is this news?" Ella asked, looking hopeful.

"Do we have a ceremony tomorrow? Can I be a bride's maid?" Elizabeth clapped hands she should have been sitting on. Her excitement was noted. Waiting for the official announcement, she folded her hands beneath her chin.

"At two unless you can manage sooner." He cast a hopeful look in Ella's direction. Questioning, "Ten perhaps?"

"Now, we know the two of you are impatient. Not everyone can get here earlier," Drake said with a grin. Ash won't even be up at ten. He will have to stand up for you unless you've someone else in mind."

"Did you have an enjoyable day? The time spent must have been..." Ella asked, changing the subject. She sent her question in Kerrie's direction.

The blush on his soon to be wife's face would tell the tale better than words. He meant to step in to save her. "Since I got a yes, the minutes we spent together were very enjoyable." He placed his hand over Kerrie's. Her face turned redder. "Wasn't it, dear?"

"Yes..." she mumbled, looking at her feet.

"That's all?" he chuckled, seeing her discomfort. Knowing what she must be thinking about. "Nothing else to say?"

For some reason his intentions changed from saving her from the embarrassment to seeing the rose color on her cheeks deepen a shade or two. He was delighted with her reaction to his efforts this afternoon.

"No." Her back stiffened. She stared at him as if willing him to silence. "No... nothing more to say. Believe quite enough has been said."

Her aunt seemed to take pity on her discomfort. Ella rose and came toward Kerrie, her hands outstretched. Tam let her go. Ella held Kerrie's hands in hers. "Come, let's leave the men to speak of whatever men talk about the night before a marriage. We've things to discuss as well. We'll have some wine then talk about your wedding. What can be accomplished as well as what cannot. Flowers? Cake? Lyssa and Chauncey will be here in the morning to help you get ready. I've mentioned the wedding might be a possibility. I'll send word this evening that you are getting married. Your parents will not be able to make it on such short notice. However, we will have a celebration in a week. That will give them time to get here."

"Never thought to have a wedding. Never thought... My life is taking on a different direction than I planned?"

Somewhat dazed, Kerrie trailed after Ella. Elizabeth followed behind her chatting nonstop.

"Are you happy about that?" Ella asked, stopping at the door. "You should be. Tam is a fine young man. He will make you a wonderful husband. Known him forever. He's a better big brother than Ash."

"Yes..."

Tam didn't appreciate the hesitancy in Kerrie's voice. He wished he could hold her, reassure her what they would do tomorrow would be beneficial to both. For his intended, this must feel like a whirlwind hit her. She told him more than once that she didn't intend to ever marry. Of course, she would have second thoughts.

He watched her leave the room with her aunt. Their heads were bent together whispering. He would love to know what they talked about. What he did know was that The Matchmaking Duchess would do all in her power to reassure his soon to be wife. Would make the wedding wonderful even though the ceremony wasn't months in planning. Tam didn't believe Kerrie would care about an extravagant wedding since she didn't care about wealth or titles. Never planned to wed. He couldn't wait months for her to become his.

Kerrie was his fiancée for a short, a very short engagement. At the thought, he swelled with pride. Knew he would enjoy showing her off in London. They wouldn't get to the city any time soon. He meant to spend the week learning all he could about his young wife, all of her. All the ins and outs of her beautiful body along with her mind. Taking her to all his favorite haunts on Talmage land would be next on his list. He thought to make love to her in every beautiful spot.

"She won't change her mind." Drake said with confidence as he too watched the women leave the room. "Kerrie has always been that way. Once she decides on the course she wants..." Drake lifted a shoulder before holding up a snifter. "We did anticipate good news. Brandy? Kane and Stephen will be here soon to help celebrate your upcoming nuptials. It will be the most eligible bachelor's last night of being single. What do you say? Should we celebrate."

His stuffiness came to the forefront. Prim along with proper denoted his behavior. "Don't wish to get foxed. All of you will strive to see me unable to walk. Under the circumstances, don't feel as if I can relax or celebrate until after the vows have been said. Don't wish to make a costly mistake," Tam mumbled, wishing, craving this was done. Fearing the revelation of his secret. Terrified of the gossip column tomorrow even though he felt certain they'd not been monitored. "Need to go home. Got to tell father the good news."

"One drink won't hurt anything. Wait for Kane and Stephen to arrive here. Maybe partake of two," Drake said looking up to see Kane striding with Stephen into the room. "Well, what do you know? Here they are as if they were watching for your arrival. Yes, two drinks would be better than one. Need to loosen you up a bit. You're as stiff as that bloody fireplace poker resting against the mantle. All will turn out just as you've planned. There is no need for worries. So far the hardest part is over."

Yes, he was stiff. Had good reason for his stretched nerves. Found more often than not, he was holding his breath. He didn't like surprises. The last week had been one surprise after another. He was certain that with

Kerrie by his side the rest of his life would flash by in much the same way. She had this way about her. Seemed she tilted his world on its axis.

"Never thought to see you wed. Always were holding out for someone who wanted you, not the title." Kane laughed as he accepted the snifter of brandy meant for Tam. "Was that way for me too. My issues were a little bit different. Wanted someone who didn't see a half breed when she looked at me."

"As we all were looking for a woman who loved us," Drake said, spilling brandy into a second glass also meant for the prospective bride groom. "A woman who could give unconditional love."

"Don't mind if I help myself. Lyssa tells me Kerrie is quite the horsewoman," Stephen said with a half-smile. "Hope she doesn't flaunt her skills." He slanted an all-knowing look in Kane's direction.

Tam recalled the rumors circulating about Lyssa a few years ago. Didn't want to even contemplate the thought of Kerrie doing tricks on that big stallion of hers. It was hell for him knowing she rode Dex, wished to continue riding him. If she fell, the brute would trample her. As to date, he hadn't seen anything that might indicate she was careless with her mounts. "She is, but if I catch her doing tricks of any kind, she won't be able to sit on her little butt for a week."

He would never hurt her even with a child's punishment. He would have to think of something, some punishment that would fit if she were to try to do something so stupid.

The padlock on Dex's stall came to mind. He would forbid her to ride unless she swore she would not do something so ridiculous as tricks that could backfire. Once they were wed, he would speak with her about the stallion. She would listen. Logic would win over impulsiveness. Perhaps not. Kerrie was wild at times. Spontaneous with every beat of her heart. One might say she lived for the moment. He found that trait both refreshing as well as terrifying.

Kane was tapping the crystal of his glass with his nails looking thoughtful. He tipped it back. Drank. "I supposed the same. Came to realize an explanation was indeed warranted. Lyssa's charming *derrière* hit the ground too many times to count. Her actions hurt her more than my hand ever could. To save my life, I would never lay a hand on her except to listen to her scream her pleasure," Kane said grinning as if remembering the last time he made love to her. "The fact was that she thought because I could do the same tricks only better that I would have no objections to her following suit. What she didn't know at the time was that I learned to ride that way to protect myself, not to entertain."

"Did the ladies go upstairs?" Drake asked, looking to the stairway. "It seemed he searched for a change of conversation."

The butler would have told the women where Kerrie and Ella were. "Dear God, they all know not to say anything about me...the title?"

One more time he thought his nerves would snap. So much hinged-on silence. Women chattering could bring out the truth. Women who were drinking, well, that was more frightening for his secret. "If even one word or suggestion meets her delicate little ears, the wedding will be off. All hell will break loose. If she hears one, 'your grace,' I might not ever see her again. Without thinking of the danger, I wouldn't be surprised to see her mount Briar and head home." Sweat beaded on his brow. He wiped it off with his arm. Felt moisture run down his chest. "Is it hot in here or is it me?"

"You," the other three men spoke in unison with laughter.

Tam spent the better part of the hour trying to appear at ease with everything that was going on around him. Something he wasn't...at ease. "I've never been so nervous in my life. What is it about lies of omission? Lies that would damn me if she discovered the truth. I understand the truth cannot be kept from her forever. Given some time, she might be able to come up with a few reasons she would enjoy being a countess then a duchess. The explanation as to why I never mentioned the damming fact is obvious."

"Both Lyssa and Chauncey understand what is going on here." Kane said, his voice soft as if he commiserated with Tam. "They won't say a word. Though watching you squirm does have its amusements. Watching you at the ball the other night was also entertaining. You did monopolize her time. Your scowl sent many a young swain scampering away in fear for their lives."

"Not so entertaining as that recital, Lyssa sang at." Tam retorted, teasing. None standing here in this room could say their courtship went with ease. "She did have a way with the tune. Heard the matrons were beside themselves. Gasping and coughing when she sang about the lady's pussy." Tam felt vindicated when he saw the flush of embarrassment cover Kane's face.

Kane held up his glass. "*Touché*, my friend. At the time it was all I could do not to roar with laughter. I had to get her out of there before she got to the next verse, which was more damning, if that was even possible. Hauled her out of the room as if it was going up in flames. Lyssa had no idea why. She is still such an innocent. She had no idea what she was singing. Not so sure she does to this day. Though she is always curious, asking pointed questions. I've never told her," Kane filled in with the humor surrounding wedded bliss at least the steps that would come before.

"Drink up," Drake said leaning back in the chair. His feet were propped on the desk, his glass of brandy rested on his stomach. It was clear he enjoyed the conversation and wasn't about to regal anyone with his courtship of Ella so many years ago. There was an ultimatum. Ella loved him so much she was willing to gamble on her reputation.

"Anyone else going to be here tonight?" Stephen asked. He sat by the fireplace, one foot on the hearth. It seemed he was about to contribute. "I had no such amusements. Chauncey almost died at the hands of the Sioux women the first day we entered the camp. Everyone believed her to be my white slave, not my wife. Had to deliver a bride price to the chief as well as her father. Again, she was beaten, lost our child while I, along with her brother and cousin, were corralling the horses."

Drake cleared his throat. "Since I was certain the wedding would be tomorrow, I sent invitations to Liam as well as Colby. Both said they'd be here in another hour. Ash is on his way from London, eager to see the two of you wed."

"Young pup doesn't know that soon his mother will find the perfect lady for him. He'll be leg-shackled as well as madly in love before he understands what is happening to him. I'll laugh when Ella finds the exact right woman for him. There will be no way for him to say no, he'll be so smitten."

"My Ella does have a knack where matchmaking is concerned. Says she knew I was hers the first second she saw me."

Drake sipped thinking about those first rocky days of his courtship. When she agreed to go with him, he'd been both pleased as well as shocked. "The original Duchess told her no touching below the waist. What was a man supposed to do except challenge that dictate. Spit my wine out when she asked me why."

"The two of you never had a courtship. You hauled her off to the hunting box in a hot air balloon," Kane said with a smirk. "Got just what you wanted. Didn't you, old man? You had everything your way."

"As did you," Drake shot back. "You were her chaperone. Bloody hell! What was my wife thinking?"

"Arranged by The Matchmaking Duchess. Ella pointed out that I owed her," Kane spoke up in his defense. "How can I refuse your wife? She pulls that 'owes me thing' on me every time she wants something from me. Though, I've got to admit that isn't very often."

"Seems you met Kerrie at the lodge quite by accident. At least the *rendez-vous* was a coincidence in your mind. Anything happen we should be aware of? Does the stuffy duke have an heir on the way as we speak? Will there be a *wee* duke before nine months is up?" Drake asked, drumming on him, testing his nerves.

He felt rattled from the inside out. "I'm not the duke."

"Yet. It's just a matter of time."

"Not that it's your business. Unlike you when we have a child, the babe won't be here early. I can guarantee that fact. Do things in the proper order. I do."

Thank God for that. With Kerrie he almost forgot about the proper order of life. One thing did not come before the other. She kept him so off kilter he almost forgot this afternoon.

"Just kisses?" Kane lifted a dark eyebrow as if he didn't believe the words. "Hope that wild lady of yours has a numbing effect on your standoffishness. It would do you a world of good to be a bit impulsive for a change."

The answer to that sent a rush of heat through him. The kisses were sweet but things did not go as far as they thought. He did not take her virtue. She was still complete. His flushed face would tell all his friends there was more than kisses that went on between them. He wasn't going to answer.

"Nothing that would bring Hadden to your place with a gun?" Drake asked with a wry smirk.

"No. I don't need to be forced to the altar if that is the direction your question is taking. The altar is where I want to be. The sooner the feat is accomplished the better I'll feel."

There were times this afternoon he felt certain he would have to force her to stand in front of the minister by setting the consummation before the nuptials.

"Saw the gossip column this morning," Stephen said, his voice taking on a serious tone. "Will there be more rumors in the column in tomorrow's paper? Did anyone see the two of you? Heard you were riding double. That would create another stir beyond the myriad of dances you had with her. Did you keep your hands to yourself?"

Tam cringed at the question. Didn't wish to answer but decided it prudent to do so. "Yes, a reporter saw us riding together. Kerrie rode in front of me on Dex who easily outdistanced the man. Nothing to see or report. That's all. No gossip in store for the paper in the morning." *I pray that is true.*

"There might be a drawing of the two of you together on the horse. I can imagine the headlines. Let me think on this," Kane sipped while the men stopped talking. "Oh...something like this. Stuffy duke abducts his lady fair. The rest of the column would make good assumptions about running off to a private glade where this duke, almost duke, takes her innocence. If the gossip goes as it did this morning, Kerrie will be accused of bewitching you, working her wiles to get you to wed her. It will say she is after a title along with the wealth. The two of you were riding a stallion. Who was her stallion? You?"

"I'm not the duke." His irritation grew. He wasn't her stallion either. Not yet.

Drake finished the discussion. "When the wedding is reported, all the gossip will be true. Hope you will have explanations for her."

"I will need to make sure she is vindicated," Tam said as he set his glass down then stood. "She doesn't know how to work her whiles on anyone. Nonetheless, she has bewitched me. I'm leaving."

"Need your beauty sleep, Tam?" Kane taunted.

"Something like that."

After his third brandy Tam decided it was time to go home. He needed to take Dex to the Talmage stable. Who knew when Ash would arrive. He couldn't stay. His father waited for the news from this afternoon. The true duke would be pleased. Had been after him for several years to find a wife. He couldn't wait for the other guests to arrive. They could drink without him.

Tam nodded to the men who would be his new relatives, saying again, "Going home. I'll be here at one. Keep the damn papers out of her line of vision."

He heard the clock chime eleven times. Tam didn't mean to stay so long. His father would be in bed. Would be angry if he didn't wake him with the news.

To his surprise when he reached his home, the duke was available but not awake. His father sat in the drawing room, his head nodding, eyes closed. His snore was loud. He'd waited up for him. A wave of tenderness swept through Tam. He did love his father. Wished his health was better. Before Tam woke his father, he poured a brandy for both of them. His father's butler, Talbot, of forty years waited for his return. He sat in a nearby chair. Relaxed but wide awake.

"Sterling," his father mumbled as he shook himself awake. "Glad to see you home. A bit late. Drake have a celebration or was it more in tune with a wake?"

"I woke you. Sorry I was so late. Been celebrating my good news with Drake along with a few friends. Kerrie agreed."

"You didn't tell her?"

Tam let the air rush from his lungs. Since he met her, he vowed to keep the truth from her as long as he could. "If I had told her, she would have told me, no. So...no, she doesn't know. Tomorrow as well as before I get her alone in my chamber, there can be no 'your graces' uttered to my father, to me or to my new wife." He stared at Talbot. "All the newspapers are to be destroyed."

"You understand that in time, she will discover the truth," Robert said with a hrmpf. "Don't much like lies. Untruths have a way of backfiring."

Pinching the bridge of his nose, he heaved in a staunch breath of air. "Neither do I. Wish I dared tell her the truth. I'm certain, if she knew about my title, she would never agree to this marriage. As it is, I'm on tenterhooks waiting for the sticky situation to be over and done with. Need to call her wife before I call her my countess. Need to bind her to me in so many ways that nothing can be undone. Wish she gets with child soon. That will help my cause."

"Well...pour me and Talbot a drink, son. We'll celebrate with a toast to you and your future bride then we'll get to bed," Robert told him. "It will be a long day tomorrow. Rest assured, we will back you in every way you ask."

They held their glasses up high, "To you, Your Grace and to the new countess. May you have a wonderful and long life together," Talbot said with a wink then a grin.

His father chimed in, "To well-kept secrets. Also, lots of little ones to brighten my days. I do wish to hold a grandchild or two in my arms."

Tam hoped for that too. "Thank you."

"To the truth as soon as you dare," Robert added as he tipped his glass. "Truth is always better than lies."

*As soon as I dare.*

He would reveal everything to her. Understood he would need to tell her before she discovered the ruse by accident. Before one of the servants slipped by calling one of them by their title of respect. Tam was shocked as well as pleased nothing had been uttered as of now.

Talbot wheeled his father to the downstairs room they set up for him when he lost the use of his legs.

Tam poured another glass of brandy. He walked up the stairs. Tomorrow evening, he would carry Kerrie up these stairs. He would set her on his big bed. He would make love to his wife. Air stuck in his lungs. His heart raced as he thought of the day as well as the night to come. His body leapt to life.

He didn't know how Ella knew Kerrie would be perfect for him. As he thought, any matchmaker would never put them together. They were far too different.

Wild instead of calm.

Stuffy versus unpretentious.

Opposites in every way.

Ella told him they needed each other. They would complement each other.

~ * ~

Ella bustled around Kerrie's room, pouring small glasses of sherry, setting out berry tarts. A few minutes ago, the seamstress arrived. She was making last minute changes on the gown Ella commissioned without Kerrie's knowledge. Taking tucks here and there. Elizabeth danced around the room, a glass of wine in her hand thoroughly enjoying her first adult event.

"Only one," Ella warned. "You want to be able to stand up for your cousin without a headache tomorrow. You won't..."

"I know, Mother." Elizabeth lifted her shoulders then sipped, her lashes lowered. "I won't embarrass you. I promise. Two might do me fine though. I'm ever eager to encounter new things. Life is worth living to its fullest. I intend to do just that."

Ella didn't have time to lecture her daughter about appropriate behavior in this new situation. There was so much to do. Though she didn't miss the last two sentences. Her daughter wanted to live life to its fullest. That was the sentiment that gave her reason to fear. Elizabeth was too spontaneous. She thought with her heart. She was too much like Kerrie.

Lyssa along with Chauncey swept into the room, bubbling about their cousin's wedding. The seamstress held Kerrie hostage while she pinned the bodice. Made tucks here then there. Another few after that. As to Ella's directions, made certain the bodice fit her. Didn't wish to be embarrassed again by adding scarves. If that happened, Tam would be furious.

Elizabeth splashed wine into glasses for the two ladies. Topped her own off despite the words from her mother. Lyssa and Chauncey gave cheek kisses to Kerrie who scowled back at them.

"Why?" Lyssa began looking thrilled to be attending her wedding. "You've fallen in love with the stuffy man. I love that Aunty Ella was able to see the two of you would be perfect partners. One, oh so proper, the other wild and free. The two of you will test each other every day. If you're lucky, the nights will be bliss-filled...a tempest of passion."

The look Ella sent toward the two newcomers was one meant to remind them they needed to keep their conversation bland in front of her daughter. A daughter who already knew too much but not enough. They should both understand how important these few hours would be. No one could reveal the truth to the bride.

Kerrie gulped down her glass of wine. To Ella she never appeared so nervous. This niece of hers always knew where she was headed. This was an obvious hiccup in her usual self. In some ways the couple were very much alike. "Not too much," Ella warned thinking she had two innocents to look after. "Don't gulp the wine down. Your groom won't appreciate it if you fall asleep on the ride home after the festivities." What she needed was to send her young daughter to bed before she over indulged on the wine. For Kerrie, relaxing tonight was important.

The knock on the door brought more snacks, an assortment of meat and cheese, seasonal fruits. There were three different types of bread sliced. Ella handed the bride food.

"How did you meet your mar...your man," Lyssa was quick to correct herself. Smiled. Frowned.

Ella scowled at her. Chauncey gave a nervous giggle. Elizabeth coughed.

"What's wrong with all of you?" Kerrie asked, looking around the room at her cousins. "You are all... I don't know...keeping something...from me."

Ella wasn't about to allow the discussion to continue in that vein. She spoke up to cover the near *faux pas.* "How much did you eat today, sweety? You need to wake refreshed. The wedding's at two. We've a lot to do before then. Let's talk about what you would like. In this short time, we will get as much done as possible."

Ella counted on both hands the arrangements. Flowers would arrive at ten. Talbot would help her arrange them in the third-floor ballroom. The cook would bake the cake along with an assortment of small individual cakes. The bridesmaids' dresses would arrive at eleven. The seamstress promised to work through the night with her employees. There was no maid of honor unless...Elizabeth. No, perhaps she knew Lyssa or Chauncey well enough to ask. She would have to ask Kerrie what she thought of that. If the wedding could have been planned, Kerrie's sister would have been the logical choice for the maid of honor. She would have to see to it. If Nicki were able to come, she would be the next logical choice. Ella knew Nicki and Kerrie were closer than the others. They lived near each other. Had spent some time on the small island the aunts used to believe they owned until Allura's husband put a stop to their visits.

She looked to Kerrie as if to ask her. Kerrie was sipping wine, swaying a bit as the seamstress worked on the gown. The bride had too much to drink. Ella supposed she would behave the same if she became the fiancée one day the bride the next. All of that after only a week of knowing the man. She might need fortification to sleep. There had been no time for Kerrie to adjust to this new turn of events.

What the devil was the man thinking? He should have been forthcoming from the start. Kerrie would have given in to her heart. They would never have this frantic rush to wed threatening and hovering over everyone's head. There might have been pitfalls. Ella didn't have a doubt the pair would overcome all of them.

The long sigh escaping told Ella she understood the haste. The man hated lies. Loathed the fact he didn't dare be honest with this woman who stole his heart. He also was an impatient man. Just like Drake he was used to having his way. Ella knew he loved Kerrie. Also knew the feelings were reciprocated. Despite whatever turmoil they encountered, the two of them would weather the ensuing storm.

Why did the title make so much difference? It was the heart of the man that counted. Kerrie would think so too if she stopped a moment to consider who Tam was.

Most women would have coveted the title, countess or duchess. Kerrie didn't care about the man's title or his wealth. She remembered that she didn't care either. It was the man she wanted. She would have done anything he asked even if it was outrageous.

Drake asked the outrageous.

She succumbed.

There might be sparks when Kerrie discovered the truth about her Mister Talmage. Ella didn't have one doubt that given time the girl would forgive as well as forget. She knew Kerrie loved him by the way she watched him, followed his every move. The fire that burned in her eyes. They'd shared more than kisses this afternoon. Though she believed they'd not... Tam wouldn't take her innocence unless he had no other means to convince her his way was the right way. Kerrie was still a virgin. No wonder she was so nervous she looked as if she could faint at any moment. She continued to drink. The girl would sleep until noon. That wasn't possible. She had to be up sooner than that in order to get ready for the wedding.

Shaking her head, Tam would never do anything out of proper order. Tam believed the wedding should precede the bedding. If the wedding did indeed take place, the order of things would go forth uncontested. If it didn't, Ella grinned, the order would be reversed. She was pleased with her pick for Kerrie.

The two would challenge each other. The pair would fight. Make up in the most delightful way. They were perfect life mates.

While Kerrie would find a man who would temper her wild nature, Sterling Talmage the next Duke of Sherburn would discover a woman who would push him out of his tightly closed shell. He would learn to live the life he was meant to live. Tam would no longer find himself bound to the dictates handed down to him by his father and his grandfather before him.

# Chapter Seven

Desperate for support, Kerrie gripped Drake's arm. He was her lifeline. Her fingers tightened around his forearm. Drake patted her hand as if that would still her throbbing nerves. She felt stretched thin. All this came about so fast. She was terrified. What she wanted was to run as far as well as fast as she could away from this moment. She told Tam she would be his wife. At the time, her promise didn't seem as real as it did now. Now, there was no turning back. She was stuck. With such a rush to the altar there had been no time for her to adjust her thinking. She never wanted a husband. Now, she was about to have one.

"It's going to work out," Drake bent close to speak to her. "You'll see. Sterling is the perfect husband for you. Impeccable. Even though he is your opposite in every way. You love the man? Am I right?"

"I know...it's just that... Yes, I love him. This is happening so fast, too fast. Mother and Father... I wish they could be here. This would all be so much easier if Mother was here. I was never quite... I don't understand the rush."

As if her wishes could conjure her parents, Kerrie looked behind her. They were waiting at the door. The distance between her and the altar seemed forever. She didn't think she could walk that far. She thought she was dreaming. Her wishes muddling her mind. They could not be here. They were here.

There weren't a lot of people to witness the ceremony. Though she thought everyone that was invited was there. Tam wanted a private ceremony. Most of her friends lived too far away to make it in time...excluding some of her cousins. Kerrie was grateful for the cousins who were here. Wanted to see her sister. Oh...that would make this so much more real. This was real. If she walked down that aisle then said the words, she would be Tam's wife. She was afraid. Her knees shook. Her heart thundered. Gulping air did nothing to ease the waves of fears encapsulating her.

She told him yes. He talked her into the answer he wanted. It had not been hard. Kerrie sucked air. Again, then again as if that would give her the needed courage to place one foot in front of the other. She didn't have that courage. When she turned as if to leave...

Drake whispered words of encouragement. "That man loves you. Think you know or guessed as much. Don't toss that away because you are afraid. Always thought you were as courageous as your mother. After all, Storm asked Hadden to marry her. Made a bargain he couldn't refuse. Ended up falling in love."

"He loves me?" Kerrie questioned, startled at her uncle's comment.

She had not dared to hope. Love was good. He told her he cared about her. She intrigued him. Loved her spontaneity. He gave a wealth of compliments. Never once told her he loved her.

"Believe this is my job," a deep voice rumbled from behind her. "You know, though, it was nice of you to stand in for me in my absence."

Kerrie's world righted at the voice she was so familiar with. Delighted, she whirled. What she saw wasn't a dream. It was real. "Father! Mother! Kelsey! How?"

Storm spoke up. "Got two messages about five days ago. One from Ella, the other from the driver of your coach. Didn't know there would be a wedding today. We were planning a visit soon. Ella said we should hurry. Guess she was right. Seems we got here just in time for the ceremony. Would have liked to help plan the wedding of my oldest daughter."

Kerrie's heart was in her throat. Now her life righted itself. "Thank you. Thank you for being here for me. Tam didn't wish to wait. Said he wanted to be wed as soon as possible. Oh...I'm so glad." She threw her arms around her mother then her father. "You'll be able to plan Kelsey's wedding. I'm certain of that."

"I'll take my seat with my wife," Drake said, handing Kerrie over into the safe keeping of her father.

"Wait," Kerrie reached out to her uncle. "If Ella was so smart, planning so efficiently, did she have a dress made for Kelsey? I would have her be my maid of honor. Do you think Elizabeth will be too disappointed?"

"Yes and no. Elizabeth knew as did the rest of us there was a real possibility that your family would show up. Understood if they made it here in time, she would be out one job. I'll see to the arrangement as well as let the groom along with the spectators there will be a slight delay. Would a half hour be enough time to get Kelsey ready?"

"More than enough," Kelsey breathed in a breath of church scented air smiling. "Not even that long. All I need to do is change into the gown. It should fit perfectly. The seamstress had my measurements from the last time we were here. I've not changed."

Kerrie started to go with her. "Stay here, sweetheart," Storm said. "I'll help her as will Ella. She just needs to dress. I'm certain the gown is laid out and ready. Wrote to Ella we would try our best to be here. You know your aunt never leaves anything to chance."

Hadden found a chair for her to sit. Elizabeth sat down beside her. Drake went to tell Ella. The rest of the wedding would go well. Kerrie recalled the gown she wore at the ball. Her sister was bigger in certain places. Recalled Tam pulling the scarves from her bosom. By mistake, the gown had been designed for her sister's measurements.

"I don't mind. All the time I hoped that your family would get here. You deserve to have your sister for your maid of honor. Everything else is turning out wonderful."

Elizabeth sat down beside her. Patted her hand as if to soothe her jangled nerves.

"Thank you. I'll remember this forever. Thank you. If there is anything I can ever do for you..."

She wanted to look down the aisle. Wished she could see Tam. The two men would have gone back to the waiting room. He would be impatient. Perhaps angry at the delay. He would pace. Maybe swear. The wedding was supposed to begin at two. It was now ten minutes after. She knew how punctual he was. She teased him about that flaw. Not that punctuality was a failing. Time danced around her as she waited. The clock downstairs ticked. Her heart beat then beat again. People chattered.

The organist played tunes. Her heart skipped a beat as her pulse seemed to stall in her throat. A few minutes later Kelsey stood in front of her ready to take the steps to walk down the aisle.

"It's time. Take a deep breath," her mother told her. "You are beautiful."

Storm hugged her then turned to wait for the signal for her to go to her groom.

Arm and arm Drake and Ella strolled to their seats. The music began. Kerrie drew a deep breath of air. It was almost time.

"Are you happy?" her father asked, bending down so he could whisper the question. "We can stop this if..."

"No! Yes, I'm happy. Very happy. I love the man. Doesn't mean I'm not nervous. Afraid of the future. What's to come. All is so different to me."

Though something deep inside her knew he was keeping something from her. She didn't like secrets. Never had. Did he lie to her? She tucked in a huge lungful of air. "Yes," she said a bit calmer. "I wish to marry Tam. He's kind and gentle though a bit autocratic. He told me we could negotiate any differences we would have. We can even have a discussion about my running the stable. He's going to start building it."

"Good." Hadden sounded as if he wasn't quite sure she understood the way things would be for her now.

She did. Kerrie understood more than her father thought. The men entered.

Storm walked to her seat in the front. Charlotte, Ella's other daughter walked down the aisle, tossing a few rose petals as she went. She was such a beautiful little girl. Then after that Cole, the youngest Montgomerie walked bearing the pillow with the rings.

Hadden bent to speak to her. "It's your turn. Are you ready?" The music changed to a traditional wedding march.

"Yes." Kerrie nodded.

Her arm linked with her father's, they stood at the entrance. Kerrie gasped in air when she saw Tam. He was tall, so broad of shoulder. In his formal clothing he had the look of an aristocrat. Of course, he wasn't. Ash stood beside him watching. For a moment Kerrie thought her rakish cousin would wave at her. Would tell some tale about her past that would embarrass her.

When Tam noticed her, he smiled then nodded. With her father at her side, they began the slow walk to the altar. The minister stood next to Tam. Ash stood on the other side. He grinned at her too.

"My stomach is doing somersaults," she whispered to her father. "Don't know if I can walk all that way."

"That's normal," Hadden told her. "I'll hold you up. When I give you to your groom, tell him if your knees are weak. He will hang on to you. Won't let you fall. I promise. He's there for you, to support as well as love you forever."

Her father was right. Tam wouldn't allow her to stumble. There were no more words for her. As they moved, she kept her gaze focused on Tam. He seemed to be doing the same with her. She stood in front of him. The music stopped. All was so silent...still. Silence echoed. It seemed all ceased breathing.

"Who gives this woman to this man?" the minister asked in a slow strong voice looking at Hadden.

"Her father as well as her mother," Hadden sounded grim, maybe resigned.

What if he didn't want her to wed Sterling Talmadge. What if...what if her father knew something she didn't. No, he would have told her.

They were giving her away to a man she knew little more than a week. What if he wasn't what he seemed on the surface. Panic swept through her. Kerrie clutched her father's arm thinking that running back down the aisle away from Tam might be prudent as well as wise.

"Steady girl," her father handed her to Tam.

His hands took hers. They were warm where hers felt as if they'd been stuck in ice for the last hour. He drew her closer to the altar. She handed the bouquet to her sister. She tugged in the most air she could find in the stuffy room. Her gaze drifted to Tam. He tightened his hold. His dark blue eyes gave her confidence. He smiled. She tried to smile back, and felt a dizzy wave assail her. She swayed. His fingers tightened.

"Steady now." In a whisper of air, Tam repeated her father's words. "I'll hold you through life. I'm here for you. Will always be here for you. You have nothing to fear."

Kerrie nodded, gulping as the minister began to speak. The words droned in one ear then out the other. She didn't listen. Heard she must obey him. She didn't wish to do so. Didn't want to say 'I do' to that. He squeezed her hands. She vowed to obey. Why would she do something so stupid?

Tam vowed to honor as well as cherish her. He would do that. She knew he would. Didn't understand how she would know something like that. He cared for her. She loved him. What was she doing? Ella told her Tam loved her. She needed to remember that tiny and so very important fact. Hold onto the detail for however long it took for Tam to say the words. Men were slow in that category.

He tilted her chin. His lips brushed across hers. So light, so soft, mesmerizing, heating. "We are married," he whispered as he drew away. He swept his thumb across her lips. "Can you walk? If not, I'll shock everyone by carrying you. Scandalizing people seems to have become a habit since I met you."

"I can walk. Don't want to astonish anyone. You shouldn't have to leap out of what is a comfortable place for you." She felt as if her words rang true. Now that the ceremony was done, she felt better. Her raucous nerves seemed to be settling down. "Am I your wife?"

"You made your vows, said I do. Did you forget saying them? Suppose you are my wife, for better or worse. Bring on the good times. Can't be backing out now. Won't allow something like that."

His soft chuckle gave her confidence as well as hope that her life would work out the way she wished. Though his words surprised her. Running wasn't her way.

She sucked in a deep breath of air. "Don't wish to back out."

"That's my girl," he told her. "We're done here. Shall we move on to the next part of the wedding? The celebration? After that, I'll see to your pleasure."

As they walked down the aisle, the guests fell into line behind them. Ash and Kelsey. Her mother and father then Drake and Ella, her cousins after that.

Drake's butler handed them a glass of wine when they ended the walk down the aisle. All stopped by on their way to the food, wishing them well. They hugged, shook hands, lifted their glasses in toasts.

"All I want now is alone time with my wife, Mrs. Talmage. How does that sound? I do like the sound myself. Mrs. Talmage."

Tam was still beaming. She was trying to get her stomach under control.

She leaned into him as they walked hand in hand.

In the ballroom they danced. "You can have as many dances with me as you want," she told him, thinking this was nice. So unlike the ball where he stared down all the men who approached her. "I don't wish to dance with anyone but you. Now, there will be no scandal attached to your name."

"Or yours," Tam reminded her.

"Yes, well, I don't care about gossip. Rumors as well as speculation mean nothing to me."

Kerrie was above that. She knew who she was. What other people said about her didn't matter to her.

"You will have to dance with other people tonight whether you wish to or not. Your father will want a dance. Drake too. I would gamble, Ash, my best man, your cousin will want to spin you around the dance floor."

"Let's get some food. This day has been trying. I've had more wine than I should. Eaten little. Think it would be best to rest as well as watch the fanfare."

"Me too," Tam agreed with a soft chuckle. They sat at a special table delineated for the bride and groom. Food was brought to them, wine too. It was a special blend from the winery in Bordeaux. Even though she was hungry, she did little more than push the food around on her plate. Nervous energy overruled her stomach's needs. The music started again. "This dance is ours. We will be the only ones on the floor. All eyes will be on you. Can you do that?" Tam stood, holding out his hand.

"Yes. Just wish to be with you. Alone with you. Need to leave. As soon as possible, can we leave?"

She accepted his hand. Pulling her to him, he twirled her around the dance floor. Held her closer than acceptable. "I've waited for this dance all day," Tam whispered to her. "I need to hold my wife close. So close you will feel me hard against you."

"I do."

She did. She felt his arousal. Remembered holding his sex in her hand. Moving on him until he spilled his seed. Yes, she wanted the same again then again after that. Tam created magic. He heated her until she moaned. She was married to this man. He was hers. Hers alone. This was the dream of her life. A dream she'd never thought would come true. Something she denied until she could deny it no longer.

"Yes, you said the words earlier. Now, you are saying them again. Did you mean it when you told the minister that you would obey me?" he asked her, sounding curious. "For some crazy, irrational reason, I didn't believe you to be sincere. A wife should always obey her husband. You know that. Right?"

She was shaking her head, grinning at him. "You do know me. Understand the way I think. If I agree with what you ask of me, then I will most certainly do your bidding. Otherwise..." she let her thoughts trail off.

"If you don't agree? What then? Will I have chaos to deal with? An argument? A bride who is running wild, doing whatever she wants, risking herself?" He squeezed her waist bending close to touch the tip of her ear with his tongue. "As your husband, I cannot allow that to happen. Trust in me, in my judgement."

"You said we would negotiate. I will hold you to your word." She felt as if he was going back on his promise. "You wouldn't do that would you? Go back on your word? You will negotiate everything we disagree on. I understand about Dex. Still, I would seek to train him. He responds to me. He knows the touch of my hand."

"We can discuss that later. Not on the night of our wedding," his voice was harsh as he danced her farther from the guests. "Don't wish to negotiate anything tonight. Just want to love you as well as feel your love surround me."

She found herself on the balcony. He stopped. Pressed her against the railing. "Negotiate all you want tomorrow. Make a list. We will discuss anything and everything if that's what you wish. Believe we are in perfect accord at the moment. For now, it's a kiss this man needs. A better one than the last one where we had an audience."

"Yes, that was just a brush..."

She moaned as his mouth claimed hers. Touched. Excited. Aroused to a fever pitch. She felt his tongue glide into her mouth then out, massaging. Burning with an intensity she was beginning to understand. He moistened her lips, tugged, bit with care. "Tam..." once again her knees weakened. Unable to stand by herself, she clung to him. "If you wish....to.... You're going to have to hold me up."

"Always. I've waited for this since yesterday. Remember the glade. There will be pleasure tonight. Not too much right here, mind you. Some though..." He set her atop the rail, stepped between her legs. Mindless, she couldn't think. Couldn't protest. Didn't wish to say no. Though she understood she should do just that. He looked down on her. His eyes were dark, eager. She touched him. His arousal was hard. A groan rumbled from deep in the back of his throat.

"When can we leave? I want to touch you, here. Feel you. All of you. Need to..."

She had trouble breathing let alone speaking. Kerrie wanted so much more than just touching. She understood tonight he would come inside her. Knew there would be pain. She also knew because of the time spent together yesterday there would be great pleasure.

"My little honey is eager to be with me. I appreciate that."

He nipped her chin. Followed the column of her neck with his teeth. Tempted. Lured to distraction. He found her lips. Swept his tongue across them. Deepened the kiss.

"Yes..." She breathed into his mouth while his tongue rubbed against hers. They played together. She whimpered. Kerrie wanted to hold his sex in her hand. Needed to feel the pleasure he taught her.

"You liked your climaxes yesterday. You wish to feel that immense surge of ecstasy again, when the entire world seems nonexistent. You want another one. Don't you?"

"Yes."

"When we are home." His hand cupped her breast, held it still for a moment. "You are a wicked lady. Wish for me to give you everything you dream of. Pleased there are no scarves between you and the fabric of your gown."

Kerrie didn't understand what he could be talking about. "Wicked? It must be you who brings the cheekiness out in me. I'm not wicked."

"You've no corset," he stated with a bit of something in his voice Kerrie couldn't identify. "I find I can appreciate that. Makes your bare flesh closer to mine. Makes everything I want easier to discover. If I lowered your bodice, I would be able suck, bite, lave the tips of your beautiful breasts. What else aren't you wearing? Dare I make a guess."

Heat flared. She looked down, noticed things she would have never thought about until yesterday. Kerrie lifted her shoulders a tiny shrug. She didn't understand at all the reasons for what her aunt suggested. "Ella told me you would appreciate the fact I've no underthings on. None whatsoever." She wished she hadn't been so brazen to mention that. He didn't look pleased. His normal scowl deepened. "I'm sorry. You don't like it," she was quick to say hoping he wouldn't remain angry. "That's not proper. No, you like proper. Don't want anything out of order."

"No drawers either?" He tapped his finger on a leg. One hand drifted to curve over her *derrière*. "Naughty." He caressed. "Wicked," he said. "Don't be sorry. Your unrestrained words make this man hungrier for you than I could imagine."

She caught a gasp of air when his fingers tightened. Caressed her backside, filled his hands. "You don't like..."

"Love knowing you've nothing on beneath your wedding gown. Adore knowing there will be nothing between you and my questing fingers on our ride home. What else are you keeping from me? Plan on taking advantage of the situation. You say Ella suggested this? Drake must be one happy man." He tugged on her bottom lip with his teeth. "I should let us get the obligatory dances out of the way. The sooner the better. Need you all to myself. We'll need to remain here to cut the cake. After that you are all mine."

"After the dances we can leave?"

She looked down again. Her gaze touched on his crotch which seemed to have grown since he started kissing her. "Do you wish to know what else she told me?"

His knuckles grazed her chin, swept her neck, ran across the top of her corsage. "What is this? More scarves?" He tugged on the handkerchief. "You had your fittings. Don't like...these." He held the fabric up.

"It's not what you are thinking. The handkerchief is a wedding gift. Storm told me it was worn by my grandmother on her wedding day. Mother sent it with one of the messages between her and Ella. My aunt gave it to me this morning."

"Tell me what else was said. What did The Matchmaking Duchess tell you? This man would love for you to tell me."

Kerrie cleared her throat, stared at him for a moment, her throat parched. She didn't know if she should say the words. Her aunt told her Tam would appreciate what she was going to do. "Ella said," she wasn't at all certain this was a good idea or that Tam would like this. Nonetheless she meant to brazen this out since she started the conversation. "Said...I should keep you guessing. For the first month I should wear nothing beneath my dresses. You would toss them just to see if I spoke true. After that I should deviate from that plan. Sometimes wear clothing beneath my gown, other times not." Kerrie heard him suck air.

After a lengthy pause, he spoke again. "The cake has to be cut." His voice sounded deep, dark and husky. So unlike the norm.

"Yes...the cake." Kerrie rubbed her hands along her dress. She felt the *faux pas* to the tips of her toes.

"The celebration goes on. We have to eat. Drink some more wine." His hand slid along the inside of her leg, touching bare flesh as he explored. He stood between her legs. Spread them with his. He could touch her as he did yesterday. Maybe...just...maybe he wasn't angry. As the conversation continued, she felt mixed emotions emanating from him.

*Yes. Eat and drink.*

"Do you think you can do that now that you are naked beneath your gown?" His fingers brushed against intimate skin. She squirmed. Moaned as he rubbed the tiny nub that brought forth burning heat. The one he told her about. "We cannot do this here."

He helped her down. Walked. They were on the main floor. She'd wanted him. Needed him to finish what they began. She understood why it couldn't happen.

Tam waltzed her to where Hadden and Storm sat. He handed her over to her father with a flourish. "Believe this dance is yours."

He didn't sound himself. Distracted. So very distant.

While Hadden danced with his daughter, Tam escorted Storm onto the dance floor. They disappeared into the crowd, laughing at something he told her mother.

She was looking into her father's eyes, his expression grim. He should be pleased she was married. After all, she'd told him she never wished to wed. He'd told her not to close her mind to the possibility. Where Tam was concerned, she was open. "Don't ask me again if I'm happy. I am. Tam is wonderful."

"He kept you from Dex. I heard the story about the padlock. Can you deal with that?"

He condemned before he understood the entire story. Her father would not have heard about the untimely rescue.

"It's a little late to be asking those questions. We are married. Besides, Tam said we would negotiate whatever we disagree about. I can do that. As long as he is willing to discuss, I will be able to present my feelings. He might compromise. I can pray he will do so."

"I hope so too. Sometimes there are things a man won't negotiate with his wife. He might talk to her but he will never give into her wishes."

The last words haunted her.

She was back with Tam. With her hand tucked into his, he led her to their table. They ate. Drank more wine. She felt dizzy in the nicest way. When the cake was cut it seemed the well-known proper man remained just that, proper, solid. Attune to all the societal dictates. She thought to smear the cake on his face so she could taste him. Did not. She wasn't prepared for possible retaliation. Did not relish the thought of the sugary confection on her face. Of his lips tasting all while everyone watched.

Ella told her she should try to see things his way once in a while. Doing so would help the marriage last in a good way. Kerrie supposed that was true. Though she wasn't about to do everything in Tam's fashion. She would need to assert her independent feelings some time. She was her own person.

If she could keep him guessing as to what was beneath her gown, she might be one step ahead. For the next month, Tam would understand she wore nothing. Ella told her men wanted sex. Her man was no different. If her husband gave her pleasure, she would also want to be with him intimately.

The rest of the evening was spent wishing she could leave with him. Everyone visited. Chatted. Asked for a dance with her. She met his little brother along with his sister. Was introduced to his father. Robert was his name.

His father seemed content to watch everyone dance and mingle. Sometime she would ask Tam about Robert. Why was he confined to a wheelchair?

She felt the tap on her shoulder. Turned to see Tam standing beside her. "Honey, would you like to go home now? We've done all the obligatory things. The guests cannot retire until we do. I want you all to myself in the carriage. Need to have you in my bed tonight." Tam paused for a few seconds. "Wish to hear you scream my name as I give you a woman's pleasure. Do you wish for that too?"

Kerrie nodded, having full understanding of what he spoke of. They stopped at their table. She drank down the remainder of her champagne, wobbling a bit as she stood. Tam wrapped his arm around her. "Steady, milady."

That was the third time she heard that word, steady. She did need to brace herself. Prepare herself. He wanted her in the carriage just as she was dressed now. Nothing beneath her gown. He told her he would be a bad boy.

Tam held her close. Waved to the guests. "We are off." His arm was wrapped around her waist. She leaned into him. Savored his warmth. She closed her eyes not wishing to walk. He would carry her.

Cheers echoed in the room. The chant started by Kane was continued by the other guests. "Kiss the bride," became a rhythm.

She didn't mind if he kissed her again. Knew he would later. Now, in front of all these people, Kerrie wasn't certain.

With a wicked glint in his eyes, he pulled her close, tipped her chin. "Don't mind if I do." He captured her lips with his. Probed and swept inside. She moaned. Sought more from him. Fire flamed within. The kiss went on and on. She wrapped her arms around him, absorbed in the sensations. Melted during the onslaught.

With bravado, thinking she could do as she liked, she thrust her tongue inside his mouth, moving as close to him as she could. Pressed her belly against him to feel his sex. Thought she heard the words 'Your Grace.' Someone must have been talking about Drake or Kane. They were both acknowledged that way as was Ella and Lyssa.

They couldn't be talking about Tam.

He was a mister.

Ending the kiss as abruptly as the contact began, Tam scooped her into his arms. "Hang on to me. Wrap those pretty arms of yours around my neck." He turned toward the exit. Before he could get more than a few feet, Ash and Kelsey stopped him.

"Not so fast," Ash said with a twinkle in his eyes. "We've a little send off for you. Can't go anywhere without this small gift. Mother would not appreciate me if I allowed you to leave without this moment. All her hard work would go to waste."

Kerrie felt the stiffening of her new husband's body. Tam wasn't pleased with this set back. Neither was she. That was all the time the well-wishers needed to assemble along the walkway.

When Tam and Kerrie exited, handfuls of rice were tossed at them finding places they didn't belong. She buried her face in his shoulder. He ducked his head. The rice went everywhere, inside her gown. Into her hair. By the time they reached the carriage she was drowning in rice. Laughing. Giggling. Tam laughed too.

Tam set her inside the carriage then jumped in to sit beside her. Breathless, she tried to dislodge the tiny particles. "I'll help."

As they started the journey to the Talmage estate, the carriage made a horrible racket. She'd noticed the words on the carriage. Cans bumped along the road behind them.

Just married.

Newlyweds.

Some things she couldn't repeat even to herself.

~ * ~

Tam was pleased. Except for a few minor misspoken words, the day went as planned. Kerrie went through with the wedding. For the entire day, he worried she would change her mind. He heard one 'Your Grace.' That was all. She could have thought the person was speaking about her uncle or any number of guests. They weren't. After she drank enough wine to feel a tiny bit tipsy, he relaxed more.

When he saw her standing at the doorway to walk down the aisle, her father beside her, he was stunned. Amazed. The sight of her caught at his breath, twisted his heart. She was dazzling. Best of all, her parents arrived on time. Ella apprised him of the possibility. If that happened, the wedding might be delayed a few minutes. Her sister was the bride's maid. It was everything Kerrie wished for.

She was more beautiful than he could have ever imagined. The wedding gown accented her beautiful breasts, the smallness of her waist. While he watched her walk down the aisle, she glowed with happiness. He couldn't ask for anything more. Tam understood how happy she would be to have her parents with her on this important day. Her sister was the maid of honor. Her father would give her away. The man scowled at him.

Ella must have worked her magic to get them here. The Matchmaking Duchess had a knack of putting events in order. No one dared to defy her wishes. Two days, that's all it would have taken. Still, when not expecting to travel, it would have been a remarkable feat to get them there. She told him when Drake approved his request to go to their hunting box, she wrote the first letter advising Kerrie's parents they should make plans for a visit on short notice. Told them not to be surprised if their oldest girl would be getting married.

When he discovered she wore no corset, he was in awe of her audacity. After she told him it was Ella's idea, the pieces of the puzzle fell into place. More surprises followed. Kerrie told him about what she would not be wearing the first month of their marriage. He grew harder, his sex aching to possess her. Tam couldn't imagine getting through each day with that image in his head. If she wasn't careful, she might find him tossing her skirts anywhere as well as everywhere he found her.

When they were cutting the cake, in his mind's eye, he saw her as he remembered from yesterday in the glade. All he wished for was to get her alone. Undress her. Explore. Taste. They ran through the gauntlet of people tossing rice in their direction. She giggled. He chortled.

The carriage door was open for them. He set her inside, wicked thoughts ruffling through his brain. Tam sat beside her. The driver closed the door. They began the trip to his home, their home now. He was excited. Pleased with the outcome. Expectant. Nervous as hell.

Kerrie seemed apprehensive. She was shaking rice from her hair. There were pieces embedded in the elaborate hairdo.

"Let me help." Tam didn't wait for her to answer. He pulled her across his thighs.

She yelped. Surprised. "How?"

"I'll show you." Taking his time, he began to pull pins from her hair, sifting his fingers through the long strands. Letting the softness caress the inside of his fingers. As he worked, rice littered the floor. Tap, tap, taping as they bounced. "Is there rice in here?" he asked as he ran the tip of his finger across the top of her gown.

"You know there is." Kerrie reached up to sift her fingers through his hair. Rice spilled on the floor and seat around them. She laughed. Tilted her head back. "Think I drank too much wine. You kept filling my glass. I'm a *wee* bit tipsy."

"That's the way you are supposed to be on your wedding night. Would you like another." He pulled a bottle along with two glasses from a basket across from them. He tipped wine into both glasses. "This is our time to enjoy. Drink, there is more. Ella packed food too. Though it's not food I'm hungry for. It's the taste of you I need."

One handed, Kerrie played with his intricately folded neckcloth until the fabric was undone, dangling in front of him. More rice scattered. She toyed with the fasteners on his shirt. It was nice she was not bashful about disrobing him. How far would she go? He was also pleased they had yesterday. Without that time, she might be timid. Wary of his every caress. Though he couldn't see his Kerrie at all shy. She was bold. Cheeky at times.

'Umm...'" a soft breath whispered, touching upon him. "I'm hungry for you. Seems to have been ages since you touched me...and...I *ken* you kissed me at the wedding but that just wasn't good enough. Not after what you taught me yesterday."

He agreed with the sentiment as her fingers floated across his bare chest. Touched here. Caressed there. Explored further...lower... She was wonderful. He was forever thankful for the day in the glade to prepare his innocent virgin for the wedding night. With her hair falling around her shoulders, he ran his fingers through the length. The silken strands flirted along his bared skin. Cupping her head in one hand, he brought his mouth to hers. She moistened her lips in anticipation.

The heat along with the potent magic of her seduced his senses. Stirred. Disturbed. His hands settled on her shoulders. He was far too tempted. His body quaked with anticipation. She moaned her desire. His bed was too far away. She pushed on his jacket and shirt until the fabric slipped down his arms. He should not take her this first time in a carriage.

"I love the way you feel, so hard everywhere, except your lips. Your mouth is soft..." She moaned again, a sight trilling from her open lips.

He covered her mouth with his. She pushed into him. He pulled her tiny sleeves down her shoulders until her exquisite breasts popped free from their confines. His hands gave the beautiful jewels the attention they deserved. A whimper. Soft sighs followed. She arched. Her breasts pushed against him, sashaying across his chest. He needed to take them into his mouth. Test the flavor.

Bloody, bloody hell, he loved the way she felt beneath his hands. Soft everywhere. Prepared to receive him, accept him into her body. Imagining the softness heated him, inflamed his senses. His heart raced with expectation. Eagerness. He was too enthusiastic. Needed to slow this down. See to her pleasure.

Tam tugged on the skirt of her gown. Ran his hand along the inner part of her legs. As if knowing what he wanted she parted them for his quest. He teased tender flesh. Taunted the sweetness he found. Felt the softness, the moisture. She rained on his fingers with her sweet nectar. He bent to take a breast into his mouth. Drank from her body, pulled her into him.

"Oh..." Her breathy sound of pleasure ignited him. Her body arced.

Curved to meet his. Tempted. Everything about her was aroused. Stimulated.

"Open your beautiful eyes, honey."

He wanted to see her when she shattered into pieces.

She obeyed without a blink while she undid his britches, pushing on them until she freed him. Her small fingers surrounded his shaft. Kerrie was so passionate, her body erupted with raw desire. They were just too far from his bed. He didn't know if he could wait. He had to wait. The proper in him wanted her first time to be in his bed not in a carriage though he knew they had time. Rocking her to her pleasure seemed more important than his own. Tam wanted to see the evidence of her virginity on his sheets. He wanted everything to be faultless. The unspoiled wedding night. All needed to be perfect. If he took her now, they would both be denied. The reasons for waiting, nonexistent.

The way her body pulsated, tightened, he knew he could bring her to a climax before they reached home. If she continued her seduction of him, he would also find ecstasy by her hands. Tam slid one then two fingers inside her, watching the ever-changing emotions on her face. Encountered the evidence of her untried status. With his thumb he massaged the pearl that would help along the climax. Her sweet body quivered, trembled. She kissed him with her eagerness to reach that ultimate high.

"Tam!" Her body quaked. Exploded into the torrent of wonder he orchestrated.

He felt her core throbbing. The pulses in unending waves. Felt the end as she erupted with her pleasure. "That's right, honey. Keep it going." Her head fell against him, relaxing as he soothed.

"You do that to me," she said after a few minutes passed. "I want you to..." She looked up questions in her eyes. "Does a man feel...these...do they."

His bark of laughter caused her to draw her brows together. "Next time will be even better. I promise. I will be deep inside you. My seed will fill you, warm you. Yes, it is easier for a man to reach that place..."

Kerrie moved her hand on his sex. He groaned. "I want to see your seed, Tam. Can I?" With an imp-like expression, she looked at him as if asking permission. He didn't think she was about to wait for his consent.

Tam nodded, feeling the explosion coming with the first touches. He felt the climax. Shouted with the pleasure of it all. "Vixen," he murmured at the end. For seconds he didn't move. Tried to even his breathing.

She smiled at him, tilting her head as if she wished to see him better. Touched the liquid. "Naughty, wicked, now vixen. Now what other names do you intend for me? I would know. You are my devil." Her eyes twinkled with deviltry. Life with this woman would never be dull. She was spicey. Could be sweet when the mood hit. She would never bore.

"I can think of many names that would suit. For now, those will do," He pulled her close. Her fingers spread across his chest with lazy strokes, drawing circles, pulling at the dark hair she found.

"Can we have more wine? I'm hungry all of a sudden. Famished for food rather than your body. What's in the basket?" Kerrie reached across him to see. Her lovely breasts touched his arm. His body quickened. They swayed perking up when she stopped to look at him. The tips were still long...hard...damp, glistening from where his mouth played.

"You see what there is. I'll fix your gown." Prudence now might ease his raging passions. He needed to stay grounded until he could have her alone in his bed chamber. His fingers brushed across satin flesh while he adjusted the bodice. "Temptress..." he mumbled. "You don't even understand what you do to me."

With a giggle coupled with a wide grin, she pulled out tarts. Held one to his lips until he bit. He poured wine. She sipped then winked at him. Bit into the tart herself. He could get used to her playful side. The sound of her girlish giggles made his heart thump hard. He never expected to wed such a person as Kerrie. As he grew older and no one stood out, turned his heart, exploited his passions, he thought he would wed just to beget an heir. Believed he would like the woman he married. Never thought to fall so deeply into her aura. Didn't realize such happiness awaited him. He discovered that Kerrie was everything to him.

Ella Montgomerie sent him to find her. Oh...he didn't doubt Ella would have introduced them if he'd remained here. This was so much better. He'd had a week with her alone. Got to know her in privacy. Knew he lusted for her. Hoped he would fall in love. Under any other circumstance, she would have learned of his title. What then?

Tam discovered with each passing hour with Kerrie he found it was more difficult to keep his hands to himself. Lust singed his body. He hoped a week in bed with this lovely lady would work somewhat to ease his cravings. They could slip out of the mansion one day. Return to the glade. This time he would make love to his wife there in that idyllic place.

His wife.

As he pulled her gown into place, his knuckles swept over the tight hard crowns he needed to taste again. "Oh..."

He made a second pass across them. It wouldn't hurt his plans to keep her aroused until they could fall into their marital bed.

More than a week, he would need a month perhaps. She reacted to his every touch with wildness. Bold when she reciprocated. Brazen then soft with womanly undertones. She flushed a beautiful shade of rose when he said something outlandish. He would call her delicate feminine parts by their name. She should understand once he consummated their marriage, she would always be his wife. There would be no way out when she discovered the hated title haunting him.

"There, no more playtime until we get to my room. Eat. Finish your wine. We need to hold off on our pleasure."

Maybe not. Perhaps what he thought earlier was the right way to proceed. He kissed her again. The kiss was light. He tasted the wine she drank. Her lips were swollen, red from the attention he bestowed upon them. He hadn't kissed her enough, tasted her enough. Filled her enough.

The carriage rolled down the long drive leading to Mayfair. As if eager to see her new home again, Kerrie was leaning out the window. His hands on her waist, he pulled her inside. He caressed her hips. Her soft sigh pleased him.

"If you keep that up, you're going to freeze," Tam told her laughing at the sight of her sweet backside in the air. "Get back in the carriage. We'll explore the land to your heart's delight tomorrow. Go for another ride if we can get out of bed."

Talbot met them at the door, his hands locked behind his back, rocking on his heels. Grinning as if delighted. "Your father would like to see you before you retire for the night. He told me he won't take no for an answer."

Tam cursed. This was not part of his plans. "He wishes to see me now? On my wedding night? This better be important. Should have taken her to the townhouse in London where we could be alone, without interruptions. The carriage ride would have been longer." Tam growled while he ushered Kerrie inside.

"Your wife too," Talbot said as Kerrie seemed to hold back, her eyes wide. She would be uncomfortable with this interview. No doubt, his father would say something to embarrass her. "I believe it's a celebratory toast to you as well as your new bride. He tired early on and was unable to remain for all the festivities. The coun..." He corrected himself after seeing Tam's glower. He cleared his throat, "Mr. Talmage napped an hour after we returned. Now he's fine. Wishes a few words with you along with your new bride. A welcome home, so to speak. He's quite eager to toast the newlyweds, his son as well as his daughter in law. He is looking forward to the possibility of a grandchild." The man paused. "Soon. He's hoping very soon."

Tam stopped a sigh of displeasure from filling the hallway. He could never ignore his father's wishes. The duke asked very little of him. Didn't want to. "In the library?" Tam guessed. The room was his father's favorite place.

"Yes. The glasses are poured. Brandy for you along with your father, sherry for your new wife unless she prefers the more potent drink." Talbot looked to Kerrie for an answer.

"Sherry is fine." Kerrie's hands wrapped around his arm, clinging to him. He placed his hand over hers. Her face was flushed with the sweet fire of desire they orchestrated on their way here. She was still aroused. He hoped she stayed that way. Time would tell.

He felt the wobbling of her legs as they moved forward. Any more to drink, she might pass out before he could consummate the wedding. Didn't wish to get her upstairs in the privacy of his room only to have her fall asleep. "Hope there is something to eat."

He wanted more food for Kerrie to counter the effects of the alcohol. A bracing cup of tea might do the trick. They weren't being offered tea. No, this was to be celebratory.

"If you wish, I'll scrounge a platter of cheese, meats to be coupled with slices of bread. There is also a tray of food in your chamber. As you know if there is something else you wish, just ring. Robert has paid extra for staff to be at the newlyweds' beck and call." Talbot gave a short bow. "Want all to be impeccable."

"Thank you. I give you permission to dismiss them for the night. If there are any needs not taken care of, I will see to them. Don't want anyone to invade the night I've planned."

Taking Kerrie's hand in his, he led the way to the library. He always marveled at how small her hands were with long delicate fingers. So much smaller than his.

Robert waved when they walked through the door. His smile of greeting contagious. "There you two are. Congratulations are in order. Wished I could have danced with the bride." He lifted his glass to them. "Grab a drink."

"Father—" Tam began but was cut off.

His father waved his hand in the air. "I know you are eager to get to know your bride a little better. You have a lifetime ahead of you. A few minutes with your aging father won't kill you. I would like to see your bride a bit closer. She is very beautiful. See why you wanted this one." His voice was gruff. Tam realized they would be here for far longer than he anticipated.

Tam picked up the filled glass for his wife then one for him. *I have been eager for this moment for more than a week.* To Tam, waiting a week did not sound that long. Perhaps he was being ridiculous. A normal courtship could have lasted months. With Kerrie he couldn't afford a normal courtship.

Robert cleared his throat. Looked to the couple then his butler of so many years they were on a first name basis. "To my son and his chosen wife. I wish the two of you all the happiness you deserve. Children as well."

They clinked glasses, drank deeply. "Thank you, Father." Tam was ready to leave, setting his glass on the table before reaching for Kerrie.

"Now, sit for a few minutes. Talk to an old man. Make him happy.

You are not the only one who wishes to get to know your young lady better. Under normal circumstances she might have spent some time here before the wedding. Had dinner a few times. I know you will keep her in bed for a while. So, humor me."

"You don't look old," Kerrie said, "Tam looks so much like you. What put you in the wheelchair?"

The older man's eyes grew dark, the smile vanished. She sat down, biting her lip. To Tam, she looked as if she wished to fade into the woodwork.

"I suppose you will find out soon enough. My condition is not a secret. An accident, a horrible one. Took my wife's life and rendered my legs all but useless. The horses were spooked. We rocked precariously. I tried to protect her...haven't been able to walk very well since that afternoon. I was helpless for hours until someone passed by. Now, even though I try, walking is painful. I'm told I need to try harder. For my health."

"I'm sorry. You don't need to say more."

Tam felt her distress as if it was his. His father never talked about that day. He kept the memory stored in his head. Tam reached for Kerrie's hand to tug her to her feet. "Father, we will retire now if this is all you wish."

"No, please sit...tell me more about how the two of you met. This has been such a whirlwind courtship." He turned to Kerrie. "I saw that your father and mother were able to arrive in time for the nuptials. Tam told me you wished they would be here. That was nice. Gather you didn't expect to see them. Your sister stood up for you."

"Yes, it was all Aunt Ella's doing. She told them they might wish to visit. Couldn't say anything else positive that would lead them to believe there was a marriage in the works. Though when they sent me here, they hoped."

"I see. Been told you don't like titled folks. There a reason?"

Father!" Tam was beside himself. His father was pushing this too far. If he didn't stop him, he might reveal who he was. He needed to complete the bedding before this could happen. "Don't be rude." He was ready to whisk her away in an instant if this went farther.

The duke gave a huge hrmpf. "Do be quiet, Tam. What is wrong with a man who has a title fixed to his name?"

"Nothing truly. It's just..." Kerrie paled beneath his father's scrutiny. She readjusted her position, obvious to anyone she was discomfited by the question.

"I'll tell him. Perhaps speaking of the incident is too painful."

She waved her hand in the air to stop him. "No...no... It was a couple of years ago. Suffice it to say, I was accosted by a viscount. At least that is what I thought he was. Don't recall if that was his rightful title. I didn't like the man to begin with. Told him to go away. He thought he had the right to have me because I wasn't a lady. I didn't agree with him."

"You've never been accosted by a duke or a marquis?" Robert asked the pointed question. "Perhaps a man with a higher title might behave in a better fashion. Perhaps he would adhere to rules of polite society."

Tam held his fists tight at his sides. Anger boiled inside. Simmered. Thought he would boil over if his father kept this up. He couldn't believe what his father was doing. "You are getting a bit too personal, Father. These are questions you have no right to ask." Tam ran his hand along the back of his neck. Both furious as well as worried.

"Just want to understand better. You know...not that it matters so much."

Kerrie looked from him to his father then back to him. It was apparent she was curious about the questions. Tam didn't want the wheels in her head to start spinning. She was too intelligent not to realize there was something unsaid. A lot unsaid. He found he was holding his breath. Thought for a moment his heart would cease to beat.

"Never been attacked by a marquis or a duke. I would hold that the higher the title the more arrogant the man would be. He would think a woman who does not have a title is free to sample just as the viscount did."

"Good, good to hear that. So, you've got nothing against those titles. Men with higher titles tend to be more self-contained, not arrogant. You understand. Follow rules to the letter, prim and proper to the extreme. They have been drilled in good behavior from the moment they are born. There are rules a man must follow. One might call most dukes stuffy."

Robert shot him a smug look.

"A woman doesn't need to marry an aristocrat to define herself. I don't need that. The man called me a peasant. Which I am. What does it matter?"

Her words were strained. Her body tight with anger he saw sweltering just beneath her skin. Tam needed to whisk her away before the incident turned incendiary.

Robert put his hands into a steeple beneath his chin as if contemplating her words. Tam was beside himself with the agonizing feeling his father would give his lie away. He found himself frozen in time.

"Did he say anything that isn't true?"

"Where are you going with this, Father?" His hands itched. Strangling his father now seemed to be a good idea. Kerrie looked to him as if seeking advice.

"No," Kerrie's voice was subdued. "No!"

Tam understood her anger would simmer. He hoped she would let loose with her annoyance. If left to smolder, this could ruin the wedding night. Sometimes anger could turn to passion. He hoped this was the case.

"We are headed upstairs now. Good night, Father. Talbot will see you to your room. Hope you have a good night of sleep. Won't see you in the morning."

Tam swept Kerrie into his arms. He'd planned this moment from the time she agreed to become his wife. All the foreplay was just that. Tonight, would be real. They might conceive tonight.

Tam heard his father chuckling as they sped up the steps. The old man had this planned. He wanted to unnerve him. His ploy worked. His nerves started snapping one at a time as he plagued Kerrie with his questions about dukes and marquis. Thought the gig was up. Afraid the marriage would never be consummated. If not, she would seek an annulment. During the interview he believed his father was going to tell her who she wed. Tell her she was now one of those hated aristocrats. There were no doubts in his head that when she heard the truth, she would explode. He would need to figure out a means to placate her initial worries as well as soothe her fears. Before all that happened, he hoped she'd fallen in love with him. His father was wise with his questions. She should not label all aristocrats the same as the fool who asked too much of her then refused to accept that she didn't want him.

The door Tam kicked in as he turned sideways. Leaning Kerrie against the closed door, he kissed her long and deep. His hands cupped her backside. His erection was hard and increasing against her. Tam knew she felt him. She moved her belly against his length caressing. Stimulating. Her body strained to meet his. She was intrepid as well as unabashed. With so little experience, his wife did understand how to arouse him.

"Sorceress," he murmured, his voice soft against her ear. "You enchant me. I'm sorry my father was so rude. He had no right to question you about something that was none of his business."

He needed to take his time with this first mating of their bodies. That was the proper and so stuffy duke thinking. The part of him that Kerrie was teaching him about herself, needed wanton and swift. Hunger. Fire. Passion. Maybe he could find something in between.

"It's alright. He was just trying to make conversation. How was he to know I don't enjoy talking about that time? I deserved the question after I asked him about his legs. Should have asked you first."

She ran a fingertip across his jaw. Unfastened the buttons on his shirt. Seemed to Tam she was as impatient as he was. Kerrie pushed both his jacket and frock coat down his arms. With a manicured nail, she scraped a path down his chest. She was learning. His male body was stimulated to its fullest. Brought to attention by her charmed fingertips. The magic of her flawless body, the enchantment, Kerrie was as wild in her lovemaking as when she rode her stallion. Soon he'd show her how to ride him.

"Kerrie, love..."

She nipped on his shoulder. Laved the sore spot. Bit again. She pressed her body against his. "I love the way you feel. Your strength. The muscles that ripple when I touch you. You excite me." Kerrie pushed her hand against his length. Rubbing him through the fabric of his britches. "You're hard."

"As steel."

"Hmmm...."

He took her hand away. Set the long delicate fingers on his chest.

She rubbed across the tips of his nipples. "If you continue, I will explode before I'm inside you."

"So...?" she questioned nipping him with her teeth. "Are yours as sensitive as mine?"

"Don't know about that. I want my seed to fill you," he said, placing her hand in the middle of his chest. "Need to see to your pleasure first."

His lips captured hers while he swept her into his arms walking with her. He laid her upon the bed coming down on top of her. Kissing her. She responded with the pureness that was in her. Kerrie was wild and sweet. Spicy and filled with honey. She was his now. Soon would be in every possible way. When she discovered the truth about him, there would be nothing she could do. No turning back. He would never grant her a divorce. After tonight, an annulment would be out of the question.

"Want that too," she murmured as she arched, her body curving to allow his hands to roam. Thrusting her breast up so he could touch as well as suckle to his heart's delight. Felt the shiver of her desire sweep through her in lingering ripples.

Her hair filled his hands. He wanted the long chestnut hair wrapped around him. He knelt beside the bed. Pushed her skirt to her hips. Before he finished this first time, he meant to kiss her from the top of her head to the tips of her toes. Everywhere in between. All the dark secret places he would know. At the glade, he held back. Didn't wish to frighten her. He initiated her into the ways of amour. Tonight, there would be no holding back.

His focus turned to her stockings. The garters. Rolled one silken stocking down her leg. Brought her toes to his lips. Kissed each one before turning his attention to the second stocking. Repeated the process until her soft feminine sounds filled his ears. Found sensitive spots behind her knees. The scent of vanilla swept through him. Her puffy soft cries told him how much she enjoyed the attention. Her beauty filled his senses. The heat of her swept into him.

"Stand up." He pulled her to her feet. Her gown fell to the floor. He kicked the fabric away. His clothing followed hers. Naked, he stood in front of her. Rigid. The sight of her sitting on his bed, wearing nothing bewitched all his senses. To his joy, she didn't appear shy or embarrassed to be naked in front of him.

Kerrie reached out as if to touch him. "You..." she sounded breathless. Her words crisp. "I could look at you forever and never grow tired of the view. Tam, I want you now. Show me what we missed in the carriage as well as yesterday at the falls. Need to feel your heat cover me. Want you...all of you. Don't keep anything from me. Make love to me."

"As...could I look at you and never grow tired of the sight." Before his eyes the tips of her sweet breasts hardened, puckering in the chill of the air in anticipation of what was yet to come. He needed to taste, suckle, explore. "You are made for my hands. Mine alone."

Tam covered her, spread her legs, came down on top of her. Felt all her precious softness against him, felt the heat, the arch of her body as she responded. Heard the breathy cries as he explored her secrets. His hands roamed. He would discover all her mysteries. Tempest escalated. Would learn everything about her.

~ * ~

Storm and Hadden watched their daughter leave with her husband, rice falling around them. On them. Into their clothing. She leaned into her husband recalling their marriage. Remembering the outrageous proposal. Her scheme caught his attention. At first, he'd felt sorry for her and tried to help with the issue at hand. Hadden never understood the complications. She couldn't tell him. Was too embarrassed.

Hadden told her more than once if some part of him had not wanted her, he would not have wed her. This man she loved to distraction showed up at their wedding with red-rimmed eyes wearing his work clothes...drunk. After the vows, he stormed off so he could continue drinking. It was not the way to start a marriage. Storm wanted a marriage of convenience. If Hadden was going to be married to the woman, he wasn't going to have anything to do with abstinence. Hadden needed her in his arms as well as in his bed.

"That just happened..." Disbelieving, Storm pointed at the vanishing carriage. "Our daughter is married. I have so many misgivings.

Too much haste. Too many questions. She doesn't comprehend who he is. He's keeping a huge secret. That's not right."

"Too sudden for my taste also. Though the deed is done. There is no turning back the clock," Hadden said. "She is...?" He paused to correct himself. "Has always been too impulsive. Too reckless. Our Kerrie says one thing then changes her mind and does something else. She's known that man for such a short time. He's lying to her. Not a good start for a new husband and wife. All hell will break loose when the truth is discovered."

"Let's hope she doesn't change her mind about this marriage. If she does..." Storm wrapped her arm around her husband's waist. "Ella told me our Kerrie doesn't know she's wed the heir apparent to a dukedom. She has no idea she will become a duchess upon his father's death. There will be a tempest of anger when she discovers the truth. He will have a great deal of explaining."

"Backpedaling."

"Apologies."

Hadden was repeating himself, unable to do anything different. "He lied to her. That doesn't bode well for the marriage," Hadden grumbled. "A man should tell his wife all she needs to know. Should tell her before they say the vows that will bind them forever together."

"I held back information from you. I had my reason. Sterling must have his."

Storm watched as the carriage zoomed away, cans along with other paraphernalia dragging behind making an ungodly racket.

"I was angry," Hadden added. "Angry you deceived me, threatened my livelihood. My shipping business, my reputation. You had it so well planned." He paused as if he tried to collect his thoughts. "This," he waved his hands. "I had no argument against this."

"You'd already fallen in love with me. You just weren't willing to admit it to either of us," Storm said, her voice soft while she remembered those first turbulent days of their marriage.

She put an abundance of cayenne powder in the mashed potatoes to give them more taste. She thought it was paprika. All the food was dry as well as overcooked because he didn't come to dinner on time.

"True, still wanted to shake you senseless. If it wasn't for that horrible man, sneaking around, I might have done just that. As the days passed, I knew without a doubt, I wanted you. Didn't know how to get you into my bed." He laughed as he seemed to recall other events. "You cut that dress so low I thought your breasts were going to pop out at any time. I could see your lovely nipples. What would you have done then if I used that gown as an excuse to seduce?"

"Never. You would never hurt me. I don't believe Sterling will hurt our little girl either. Ella would have never encouraged the courtship if the man wasn't both decent as well as honorable. I'm not saying he won't have to have a hasty explanation when she discovers the truth about him. With hope, they will be so far in love the truth won't make a difference. Though...I can see her walking out on him."

"He's supposed to be a real stuff shirt. The man has gone outside all normal bounds by marrying our daughter the way he did. A week...he proposed in less than a week. That is not what a man who follows all polite society rules does. This intrigues me. I would like to learn more."

"Ella told me he didn't want to lose her to the truth. He couldn't wait a moment longer. Surprised they weren't wed yesterday."

"How long do you think he can keep this a secret? It's a bloody big lie," Hadden said.

"Not more than another day or two."

"Depends on how long he can keep her in his bed."

~ * ~

"It's done, Talbot. Our boy is married." The two clicked their refilled glasses together. "My son can't keep his hands off her. That is good. Couldn't wait to get her to his bed. Want to see the fruits of this marriage sooner than later. I've only got so long left to me. Don't want my son to waste any time."

"You should be proud as a peacock, strutting around, spreading your tail feathers. This moment you've been waiting for has taken longer than you hoped. It won't be many more months before there is another little Talmage running around this big mausoleum. Nice to have the happy sounds of children in the house again. I'm so pleased."

"Hopefully, she'll be heavy with child before she discovers his ruse. Would have advised the boy to speak the right words from the beginning. She would have figured out all aristocrats are not cut from the same cloth as the first man she met. It's never good to make such hasty judgments. He will pay the price. I've no doubt about that. Though she loves him. One can see it in her eyes when she watches him. The girl wouldn't have married him if she didn't love him."

"In the poor man's defense, the woman is beautiful. He didn't wish to lose her for some petty reason that can easily be whisked away. In time, she will be so in love with our boy, she won't care what title follows her name or his. After all, her aunt is a duchess. Her uncle is a duke. She must understand they are in love. Must comprehend they don't look down on those of lesser rank."

"No excuse. Her beauty is what brought them together," Robert said with a smirk. "My son does know how to find a beautiful woman. Keeping her is quite the opposite. I do predict they are in for a wild ride." He was pointing his finger at Talbot. "She has a temper. That one does. Too many ups and downs for this old man to endure. Though I understand I'll see it all. Have a great vantage point. Could give advice if anyone wished to learn from an ancient."

"From what I've heard it was the wild ride he rescued her from that set all this in motion. Heard he yanked her off that beast she was riding, afraid for her life. Also heard tell the woman wasn't a damsel in distress. Beauty coupled with zing. Irresistible for your son."

"If I was younger and unwed, she would stimulate my interest." Robert stared upstairs. "Think he's consummated the deal yet. They'd been playing in the carriage. Knew by the look on her face he kissed her senseless. Her lips were swollen, red with his attention. Do you think my son did anything else? Suppose they could have done it on the ride here. Once the girl is wedded as well as bedded, there is no way for an annulment. Sterling would never agree to a divorce. No one is going to invade their space until they come up for air. Sometime tomorrow or next week by the look of the two of them."

"Why...there could be a babe from the first time. She might

conceive tonight." Talbot clapped his hands together.

Robert snorted his disgust with the situation. "He should have consummated the deal the afternoon he took her to the glade. I know they played. Dallied with each other. When she came here, she had a sensual flush about her. Almost the same look when they stopped to see us tonight."

"So very true." He touched his fingertips together. "Yes, the same look as just now," Talbot said grinning while he agreed with everything that was said.

"Not to change the subject, have you burned this morning's Times? That was some naked drawing of the two. Why, I almost got an erection from staring at the two of them together," Robert said. "That would have been the first in how many years? Shouldn't have seen my daughter-in-law in such a state. Not right. Not right a'tall. Nonetheless, the ton has seen the same picture. Mark my words, that little scene will come back to haunt the two of them. Bite my son in the butt, it will."

"All papers are burned. Are you certain the deed wasn't done? What man could...resist such a ravishing woman?" Talbot cleared his throat. "You get my meaning. She's a beauty. It would have taken more control than most men have to keep the dalliance from escalating to that point. We both know our boy has too much restraint. He should have let go then instead of waiting."

"Resist her? Good God why?" Robert asked, a silver brow arching. "My son, if he has a plan, he would resist her. Sterling always has been a man to act in the proper order. As was I along with his grandfather before him. The Duke of Sherburn must be above reproach in all things. That is why the wedding had to take place with such haste. He would have put the cart before the horse if left even a few more days."

"Yes." Talbot drank the last remaining drops of his brandy. "The two of you are much the same. Like two peas in a pod. It must be difficult to keep all those emotions behind your teeth...bottled up inside you and corked. If I recall, you did let loose a bit when you wed Amanda."

"With Amanda one had to be more spontaneous. While I don't know Kerrie well, I've the impression she's going to give my son that wild ride we just spoke of. Can't wait to see how it comes about. What she lacks in sophistication, she makes up for in every other way," Robert pointed out. "She will be flawless. A duchess of impeccable standing. She will be perfect. Just as Ella is a perfect duchess for the Duke of Richmond. Those two women are cut from the same cloth."

Talbot shifted his weight while he made a point of staring at the fire. "Sterling will not wish to restrain her. He will have to do so. I see that he padlocked her big stallion so she couldn't ride him. That must have made her furious. The beast is hers."

"They weren't wed yet. Now the big brute is his," Robert laughed. "That doesn't surprise me. My boy always believes that the fairer sex is also weaker. He would never believe she could control that animal. Wouldn't want to see her hurt."

"In some ways they aren't weak at all," Talbot said.

"You're right. Nonetheless when strength involves muscles that are pitted against an animal as large as that horse of hers, what woman would stand a chance? With little Kerrie riding him, that's an accident in the making. In this, I do agree with my son. Though he will need to be careful with further declarations that will infuriate his little woman."

"In many ways I'm going to wager on Kerrie being the winner in most of their skirmishes. She will smile. Sterling will melt, want to give in to her. Even now, it appears he will give her whatever she asks for."

"Except with the stallion."

Robert let out a long slow breath of air. "Except with Dex."

# Chapter Seven

"Tam..."

She never thought this lovemaking would be as wonderful as he made it. She was on fire. Burning. Shivering with each stroke of his sensual fingertips. He left no place untouched. Found every secret erotic spot she possessed. Sought the depths of her hunger. Raised her passion. She thirsted for him. Craved the feel of his flesh against hers. The raw mercuric passion he stirred in her left her breathless with need, her heart pounding. Dragons tossed fire deep in her belly. Her nails bit into his shoulders as he kissed her everywhere. Her body rounded to move closer to him arced against his. It did seem he gave his attention to all of her. His lips were everywhere.

Passion soared reaching to the heavens.

Enchantment flamed with the heat of a thousand fires.

The play of his mouth moving along her sent her soaring. Magic haunted her, ghosting across uncharted territory. She throbbed, pulsed. He created tempest and fire. The storm swept through her, raged. Her hips arched to meet him, needing more. When his fingers delved between her legs, touching sensitive flesh, she bit him. Sunk her teeth into his shoulders. Cried out. Clung to him with all she possessed. He touched secret places, dark sensitive places. His hard flesh rested on her belly. She wanted to hold him.

He growled deep in the back of his throat as if she did something wrong.

She was afraid she hurt him. She licked the small wound on his shoulder where she bit, ran her hands along his back. His teeth raked the tips of her breasts. Moving lower, he nibbled on her belly. The muscles contracted with each sensation. She burned. Ached. Longing filled her, pulsed with each caress of his large hands.

He knew what he was about. Understood what she wanted.

"Tam..." She needed all of him, needed that splintering of all her senses he could create with such seeming ease. Remembered how she came apart in his arms. Unraveled one tiny thread at a time. How he sent her so high she touched the sun. "Please...Tam...please." His body blanketed hers. His weight upon her was wonderful. She sipped air as he continued his descent down her body. He spread her legs. Lifted her knees. His mouth pressed against the insides of her thighs. The sparks intensified with each stroke of his fingers along with his lips, his tongue. Her body spiraled. Thousands of nerves seemed to pull apart. Began to collapse. Splinter.

His lips captured hers with an intimate caress. Touched upon her then swept her into the storm he orchestrated. She reached for the stars. Pounded on his back. Longed.

With one deft stroke he sent her over the edge. Shattered again. Fractured into thousands of pieces. She climaxed. Cried out with the pleasure he gifted. Sent her fingers into his hair as she clung to him.

After that he began again. He'd not entered her except with his tongue. When he kissed her, she tasted the wine he drank.

"I'm going to come inside you as soon as you..."

His lips captured hers again. His hands found all the places he aroused her before. She moaned as his body moved on hers. Felt the tip of his sex touch her. He stroked, the intimacy profound. Deepened with each passing second.

"Tam..." Kerrie whimpered. Sighed as one more time he brought her higher.

"I adore the little sounds you make in your hungry need."

Her fingers clawed his back, scraped against his buttocks. Feeling him, she opened wider, arching closer to his fire. Wanting him inside her, filling her. Needed him to become part of her.

With a slow measured stroke, he pushed inside her channel. She felt her body accommodating him, stretching. Aching with need. He filled her.

"I'm sorry." With that said he thrust hard.

Kerrie bit down on his shoulder. She held on to him as tight as she could. Her legs clamped against his hips. Tears stung her eyes, slipping down her cheeks. Deep inside her, Tam didn't move. He held himself still. Willed his control to overshadow his need. Pushing up on his forearms, he wiped away the tears with his thumbs. "I'm sorry," he told her one more time. "This will never hurt again. I promise you only pleasure. The pain will pass soon."

The pain vanished as if it never happened.

Tam caught her mouth with his. She opened for him needing to feel the ecstasy when he probed inside her. Touched with deep insistent strokes. His hands caressed her breasts, fondled, tugged on the hardened crowns. Once more, Kerrie began to spiral, feeling the flames ignite. She arched against him. Low vibrating sounds came from deep inside.

He thrust harder, faster. He moved slower. Thrust again. Penetrated. Retreated. Changed the tempo. Thought he must touch her womb. Her nerves began to fragment apart. Disintegrate into shards of ecstasy. She grabbed on to him. Wrapped her legs around his hips as he continued to make her spiral higher then higher still.

"Tam!"

He shouted too. She felt his warmth fill her. Tam lowered himself on her, bringing her to his side as he rolled over. He held her head. Wound his fingers into her hair. His long fingers sifted through its length.

"Silken. You are wonderful. Amazing. Honey to all my senses."

Kerrie closed her eyes. Shaking, her bones felt like mush. Her lashes fluttered on his chest. She set her quivering hand on his hard belly, caressing. She didn't know what to say. Didn't know if she should say anything. This quiet time while he held her close was almost as good as when her body fragmented into thousands of tiny pieces. His hand ran along her back to her bottom then back. He touched each small bone along her spine.

"What are you thinking?" he asked while he continued to soothe. Each caress easy, soft. Created magic in a different way.

She pushed up to look into the blue-gray steel of his eyes. Her breasts sashayed across his chest. He was smiling, pushing strands of her hair from her face. He appeared smug; his eyes tender. He caressed her with his gaze.

"You. I'm thinking about you." Kerrie said, unable yet to put coherent thoughts into her head. "What's in your thoughts now?"

"Thinking that you are wonderful. Ecstatic as well as lucky you agreed to marry me." He wound his fingers through her hair. "Want to wrap your hair around me. Don't ever wish to let you go. Could spend the rest of the night making love to you. Don't think I will ever get my fill. What do you think? Can we stay awake all night? Make love until dawn?"

"I, you too." She was thinking she might be falling even more in love with him. "Wonderful." What they did was something she never dreamed of before she met this man.

"I believe I missed a few places?"

"What?" Kerrie asked, "Missed."

"Wasn't able to hold back long enough to turn you over then kiss your little butt. Wish to sip on your backside as well as your frontside. Would you like that?"

She snorted a sound she made when someone said something audacious. "You would kiss my...?" She laughed at him, touching upon a lock of hair that had fallen into his eyes. Pushed the hair away from his face. "I should kiss yours."

"Yes. After we recover, I'm going to have to pay more attention to your backside. I need to taste you everywhere."

"You would do that?" Her cheeks flamed while she thought about the audacious places, he did kiss her. "You wish to kiss my backside?" Kerrie was incredulous. "Will it be as exciting? Think I might like to try that. Can I kiss your delectable little butt?"

He barked his laughter. "My butt is far from little. Might be delectable to you. Yes, you can kiss me anywhere it pleases you to lay your mouth. Want to explore as well as learn all of you. Not just certain parts. All of you." He rose from the bed, walking to the wash stand.

Heat rushed to her face while she pulled the sheet above her breasts. She marveled that he could walk naked without a care without being mortified. The man was magnificent, tall and strong. His broad back narrowed to trim hips. Long well-muscled legs... He must know his worth. Of course, he wouldn't be embarrassed.

He turned to her. She saw blood on his member. Her blood. She realized that would happen. Even though she knew, the knowledge didn't prepare her for what she was afraid he had in mind. "Would you like to wash?" Tam dipped a cloth in a basin of water left for their use. Kerrie watched him remove the sign of her innocence from him.

She was no longer a maiden. Between her legs she felt sticky. Knew what she was feeling was his seed mingled with her blood coming from inside her. "Yes. Could you leave?" She tucked her bottom lip beneath her teeth.

"I could." He paused as he looked at her. His smile grew. "I won't." With soft steps he brought the water along with the cloth to her. "You need to get used to me seeing you. If you don't wish to wash, I can do it for you." His voice was tender, filled with concern for her.

"In front of you?"

"I can do it for you." Those long fingers that caressed her everywhere, tugged on the sheet. He sat down on the bed, pulling the covering free from her breasts. "Would like to clean you. Want to see the blood on the sheet. This is the way a wedding is supposed to be. We are married. This was your first time. There is nothing about you that I won't know. The maids will whisper that you were a true virgin. They will spread the information. That will please me as well as the rest of the household."

"Must you be so blunt?" Kerrie was appalled at his words.

She needed time to adjust to this...this being a wife.

With a free hand he ran a fingertip down her neck then across her shoulders. Continued to the valley between her breasts, touching one rounded globe with his knuckles. "So soft, so much silken flesh for me to explore, to taste. There is so little time." He cupped one breast in his hand. Touched lightly upon the hard crown. "Later." He left the basin and cloth on the bedside table.

Padding naked across the room, he brought the tray of food left for them to the same table. She didn't understand how he could be so carefree about his lack of clothing. Didn't understand how he could expect her to wash with him looking on. He placed a grape in her open mouth. She didn't know she'd been gawking...staring at him.

He closed her mouth. His chuckle was soft. His amusement was embarrassing. "Try chewing after that swallow."

A few seconds later, he handed her a glass of wine then sat down next to her causing the sheet to move lower. Kerrie gave up trying to bring it high enough to cover the tops of her breasts. She was almost as exposed as he was. Though she did enjoy looking at him. He might enjoy looking at her. Knew he did. Didn't understand why she thought 'might.'

He handed her a glass of wine. "You are my wife in all ways." He sounded pleased with himself. His eyes were tender.

"Yes."

"We've consummated the marriage. I managed everything between us in the proper order...almost proper order. It was hard. Devilishly difficult if I don't mind saying so. Keeping my hands..."

"Yes." Kerrie didn't understand what he was attempting to tell her. She watched him close his eyes while he leaned against the headboard. He seemed pleased. Didn't understand what he was going to do next.

Sleep?

She wasn't the least bit sleepy.

"Tell me something about yourself I don't know? We haven't been together all that long," he asked as he appeared to be staring at the opposite wall. The bottom of his glass rested on his belly. He was still sitting on the bed...still without clothing. Nothing covered him.

She swallowed hard trying not to look at him, to ogle the most fascinating place. That part of him that was so different from her. He was magnificent. She wished to touch. "I don't know. What would interest you?"

"Why did you decide to stop at the hunting box?" Tam turned to her, an expectant look in his eyes. "Did you know I would be there? Did Ella play some role I don't know about? I surmise now she was playing at matchmaking."

"Neither. Nothing earth shattering. I needed a few days to think. It's a better place than anywhere else I know to be alone with my thoughts. The country is beautiful, the fishing divine. I love it there."

"You've been there alone?" His voice assumed an angry edge. His words harsh.

Of course, he wouldn't want her to go there alone. She'd never done so before. "With my family." Kerrie wasn't certain where this question was going. "Never until this one time...alone."

"What was it you needed to think about? Something so earth shattering you couldn't wait for someone to be with you? Someone to guard your interests?"

She blinked a few times. He was going to reprimand her. She didn't appreciate that. "My upcoming season." She felt indignant. Didn't understand why she felt the need to defend herself. "Seems I avoided that fiasco by meeting you. I didn't wish to be presented to the lords of the realm. I was attempting to figure out some way to get out of going to the events that were planned. Never wished to be a *'débutante'*."

There it was again. Her real fear of the aristocracy. Afraid to be taken advantage of because she was a peasant, a commoner.

Her aunt was a duchess. Her uncle never belittled Ella. She would have to think about that.

"Instead of marrying me, what would have happened if you fell in love with one of those lords you don't wish to have anything to do with? Something like that could have happened. What would you have done? Would you deny that love?"

She stiffened. Didn't appreciate the train of his thoughts. "Where is this going? Falling in love with a lord would never happen. I would detest each one I met. Would never allow them to get close to me. To know me. Once their title was announced, I would turn the other way. Would never talk to them. Dance with one? Never!"

He grunted, seeming to dislike her answer. "Because of the title or the man?" Tam was facing her now. Staring at her, his eyes narrowed, brows drawn tight.

Kerrie shot him a glare, growing angry with his questions. The man knew her feelings. "Both. I don't like this line of questioning. You know how I feel. Why do you torment me along with my thoughts?" Waving her hand in the air, "It doesn't matter. Didn't fall in love with a lord. Fell in love with you, a commoner. Just as I am. We are equals. I am pleased. I hope you are too."

"Are you in love with me?" His voice turned tender again. A half-smile curved his lips. "You just said you fell in love with a commoner. That's me. Is it not?"

The wine that went down her throat came back up. Red drops splattered the sheet. It was too soon to say. "That was blunt."

"Are you?" It seemed he meant to persist with the question. "Are you in love with me?"

She thought she might be in love with this man. Nonetheless, it was too soon to say the words. Making herself vulnerable to him was not what she wanted. She already said the words.

Trying to keep control of her emotions she meant to change the subject. "Will you negotiate with me about Dex. I've trained him. He knows me. Trusts me. Been the only person to ride him until you took him from me. He might not take to a new trainer. The stallion is important to my new stable."

"Not tonight. No negotiations on our wedding night. I've quite a lot of thinking to do on that subject before I can conclude what is best for my wife as well as her stallion." He rose, extending his hand to her, taking her wine glass from her. "Want to hold you by the fire. Just you and me watching the flames. Don't want the night to be tainted with a discussion that can wait for another day. This is our wedding night."

If she stood, he would see all of her. All the parts he touched, kissed. He would see the stains between her thighs as well as on the bed. She hesitated, pushing back the fear, all the embarrassment. This was so far beyond what she felt comfortable doing, she had to hold her breath.

"Take my hand." Tam encouraged, waited for a few seconds. Left to set the wine along with the food by the fire. When he returned his hand extended, she reached out to him.

Kerrie allowed him to help her to her feet. His gaze toured her body while he kept her hands from covering herself. After she sat by the fire, he returned for the basin. Without asking he spread her legs, touched her, washed the blood from between her legs. She was shaking, her body trembling as gentle strokes vanquished the signs of her virginity. Kerrie understood she should not be ashamed or embarrassed. He was her husband. Still...

Tam sat back on his haunches, looking at her. Smiling. A pleased smirk on his arrogant features. She managed to bring her legs beneath her.

"You will get over this shyness with me. Do you feel better? More comfortable?" He tossed the rag with her blood and his seed on it into the basin of water. Droplets splashed.

Unable to speak, she nodded. He pulled her into his arms. Holding her close. One hand rested on her hip, caressing. The movement was gentle, soothing, always tender with her. Kerrie closed her eyes, leaning into him. She brought in a breath of air before sighing the oxygen out. His warmth surrounded her. The strokes upon her body were not meant to entice. Was reminded of the night he combed her hair. She stared into the red-gold flames licking at the wood. Felt the heat from the fire as well as the warmth from behind her.

She heard the tick of the clock on the mantle. The candlelight died, flickered, casting the room into dark shadows. Cuddling into his broad chest, she must have dozed. When she woke, she was in bed. Tam was behind her, encompassing her. One of his large hands held her breast, teased the nipple. His lips fluttered against the nape of her neck. Fire ignited within her, swept through her as if a bolt of lightning flew through her, heating her from the inside out. He teased the dark secrets that sent her spiraling.

She gasped as he entered her. He was inside her now. Moving, slow precise strokes filled her. Created the magic anew. He brought her higher. His teeth grazed her shoulder. She climaxed as he shouted out his release. A huge breath of air caught in her throat.

"That was nice," Tam murmured as he withdrew from her. "Very nice. You do like your climaxes? As I enjoy mine."

"Yes." Tam turned her. Held her. Kerrie thought what he did was more than nice. She nestled her head in the hollow of his shoulder. Touched the tip of her tongue to his sweat sheened flesh. When she rose above him, the tips of her breasts brushed across his chest. He touched the nipples with his thumb, skimming, teasing.

If he continued, she would be aroused again. Would want to have him filling her one more time. She didn't know if it was too soon for a man. This time she wanted to be the one doing the seducing. Tasting each of his nipples, sucked then teased him with her teeth. She liked the sounds that greeted her. The masculine groan coming from the back of his throat. Needed to play and explore.

His hands tightened on her shoulders.

"Tam, let me make love to you."

"Bloody everlasting hell! Please!"

Kerrie rose above him, looked at him, moved higher to brush a kiss on his mouth. His hand formed around her backside. Pushed her against his swelling sex. She rubbed her damp swollen parts on him. She kissed his mouth again then moved lower. When she touched his belly with her lips, his stomach contracted, the muscles rippling with the need she shaped. She went lower until she set her tongue along his shaft. His hard member pulsed to life. Sprang solid against her mouth. She grazed him with her teeth.

Another groan rumbled from deep in his belly. He ran his hands along her ribcage. Cupped her breasts. She jerked when he tugged on the hard buds, twisted with tenderness.

"Do you like...?" she began then cut her words short needing to explore more of him just as he discovered her. She kissed his thighs, found the soft part of him below his aroused flesh. Ran her tongue around him then down the inside of his thighs, nipping, kissing.

"Magician, two can play this game." he murmured, his voice husky, whiskey smooth. A swift motion brought her to him. His mouth closed over one breast where he sucked until she whimpered. He turned his attention to the other breast. "I haven't kissed you enough. Need your mouth molded against mine. Give me your tongue. Send it straight inside."

She straddled him. His fingers wound into her hair, pulling her so his mouth met hers, fit over her lips. She opened for him. He kissed her hard. Deep. Kissed her again then again. Laved with his tongue. Hungered to be inside to feel the rain of her pleasure.

"Ride me, honey. Sit on me. Take me into you."

A tilt of her head, a soft questioning smile, "I don't..."

"Ride me, little vixen. It's what you want. I know it is. I need it too." He positioned her above him. "You want the control...to take charge. I give it all to you. Pretend I'm your stallion."

Kerrie felt the tip of him against her. Looked down to see the obvious. His aroused flesh hard, pulsing to be within her. Tam thrust into her while he pulled her down. His hands caressed the curves of her hips.

When she looked down at them, she saw how they came together, joined as one. Her hands were flat upon his chest. He tugged her down to kiss her again, thrust his tongue deep inside her mouth while he thrust farther into her. Against the tips of her breasts, she felt his crisp dark hair.

Moving on him, Kerrie realized he was letting her set the pace to her needs. He massaged the small nub. He told her his touch there would always give her immense pleasure. Her body shivered, vibrated with all the attention he directed to that tiny spot. It seemed she was sensitive everywhere he caressed. Hungered for more. Mercuric sensations swept through her.

When she reached that all-encompassing peak again, she collapsed on him. Her breath hard pants. He still filled her. Possessed. "Can't do this again."

"Would you like to ride the horses instead of me?"

"Ride? I can't move."

The man barked his laughter. "I think you can. In an hour you'll be ready for me again. I won't take you though. Not until I find some of my favorite places on my land to make love to my wife." He swatted her buttocks. "Baths first. If you would slip under the covers I'll ring for baths. I'm certain Talbot wouldn't mind seeing you in the buff. I would though."

She curled under the covers while he went about his business. Talbot did arrive on the threshold in a matter of a few seconds. It seemed to Kerrie he must have been waiting for the summons.

The stodgy old butler nodded. Grinned a grin that took hold of his entire face. Even his eyes shimmered with what appeared to be pleasure. "The water is steaming. Waiting for the two of you. I'll send up a tray of croissants and a pot of hot tea. Anything else you would like?"

"That will do for now," Tam said as he watched the man he'd know all his life walk from the room, a huge grin on his aging face.

"I don't have clothes," she said after the door was shut. "Can't go around naked all day even if you wish it. Where are my things? Aunt Ella must have sent my trunk."

"Naked all day? That sounds like a fine idea to me." He laughed, seeming to be pleased with the situation. "You can have the first bath. Ella did send over your clothing yesterday before the wedding. The trunk is in the dressing room." He nodded in the direction. "You will have to walk naked to get there."

She was still beneath the covers when the servants trundled in with steaming water as well as breakfast. Once all the extra people left the room, they were alone again. Just as he told her, Kerrie found herself forced to rise naked from the bed. This wasn't easier the second time. Though it should be.

Tam sipped hot tea while he watched. Seemed to study her. She tugged in a good amount of air before rising. With her chin tilted as high as she could manage, she walked to the bath. When she sunk down into the heated water all her muscles thanked her. She was sore...everywhere. Didn't realize it was so until now. Perhaps she'd overdone the pleasure.

Staying here until she was a prune, soaking up the heat would be nice. When she felt his hands on her shoulders, she jerked. Her lashes flew open. Didn't know she was lost in thought. Water splashed over the sides.

Tam ran a soapy cloth along her shoulders. With the unexpected contact, her heart pounded. "Lean forward." He soaped her back. "If there was room, I'd get in with you. I'll have to buy a larger tub. One that will fit two people. I would enjoy making love with my wife in the bathtub. Don't you think...?"

*A bath with Tam?*

"N—no need for that."

"What? You wouldn't enjoy bathing with me? Sharing the water. The heat. The pleasure." He left off, handing her the soapy cloth.

Tam put on a black dressing gown with gold trim. She finished washing, understanding he would also like hot water. She looked around for the towel. Kerrie couldn't reach it. One more time she brought a deep breath of air into her lungs. As she stood, water sluiced down her body. Head held high, she walked to the towel. Wrapped the cloth around her.

"I laid out a riding habit for you. Believe we should see to getting you a maid. Would you like help combing out your hair?"

"No. You take your bath. I can manage."

She didn't need a maid. Why would he waste good money on another servant? He had so many. She tried to count them all. Doing so was impossible. He did tell her he was wealthy.

Breath stuck in her throat. She studied Tam while he slipped into the water. The sight of him never failed to steal her breath.

~ * ~

While Tam had known she would be beautiful, that making love to her would be heaven, he never thought he would be unable to keep his hands to himself for the entire night then into the morning. He'd probably overdone the lovemaking. Now, watching her in the bathwater, he wanted to run the soapy rag across all of her. Relive the way she felt beneath his hand. If he didn't leave her now, they would make love again. He would be deep inside her.

A bigger bathtub would be purchased and sent here next time he was in London. When he first saw her in the hot water, he almost picked her up so he could sit down behind her. He had visions of soaping her breasts after that, more intimate places. To recreate those moments that sent them ascending into the sky, was foremost on his mind.

Did she love him? Even though she told him she fell in love with a commoner, when pressed, Kerrie didn't answer the question. If she said yes, he would not have been certain he could believe the words. Did he love her? Well, he wanted her more than he needed to breathe. He felt certain there was more than lust between them though passion raged. He burned, thinking about her. It seemed she had the devil's own time keeping her hands from exploring his body. She touched a fire in his soul. Seemed to possess his heart as well. The need to protect her at any cost ran rampant within him. Love was an emotion too hard to define.

His washing was unhurried. Tam enjoyed the heated water until it turned tepid. After they finished off the croissants, they would go for a ride. Her choice was to ride Briar or with him on Dex. Tam couldn't say that he didn't care what her decision would be. He wondered which choice would be hers. He hoped she would ride pillion with him. He wished for her to be close to him all day. If she rode in front of him, he would have easy access to all her beautiful lady parts. He would charm her. Sweet-talk. Seduce. She would fall prey to his coaxing words as well as the following actions.

The glade...he'd seen the drawing of the two of them naked, making love in that private secluded place on his land. The drawing was in the paper. Made the front page. Thank God the details of their faces were not good enough to identify Kerrie. With the drawing, it was obvious he was the lover. After news of their marriage was announced in the London Times, the identity of the lady would be clear. He hoped with a bit of time the scandal would blow over.

They were wed, the marriage consummated. When she found out who he was she'd be furious. There was nothing she could do to change her situation. He would never grant a divorce. In time she would never want to be separated from him. Hoped she would soon carry his child.

Tam thought he lost the man who attempted to follow them. Still wished to believe he did. The problem was that he captured her glorious curves to perfection. Her breasts. Her hips. Drew the tiny mole on her left buttocks. This man, whoever he was, either guessed at her generous breasts as well as hips or he watched them sharing an intimate moment. He would never have seen the mole if he didn't watch. A sick feeling entered his gut. His father told him all the papers had been burned. The papers in this household. What about the rest of London? The titter about them would circulate in all the men's clubs. There would be bets made. Money would exchange hands. If necessary, he would need to keep her isolated for a year. If he had his way, the man who was responsible would never have another job in London. He would need to discover the reporter's identity first.

Except for this one horrible setback, all his plans were coming to fruition. Everyone at this residence remembered to call him Mister Talmage. He had to laugh. Talbot had trouble swallowing the words behind his teeth. Even though he and his father were on a first name basis, it was all he could do to keep from calling him 'your grace.' The ruse could not go on forever. Soon, he would need to broach the subject with Kerrie. Tam understood the news would be better coming from him than as a surprise.

Riding Dex. Negotiating terms for her to follow on the training of the stallion. Somehow, he would have to figure out how to make good on his word to her. Tam thought he could allow her to supervise the training of Dex. Perhaps even the breeding. He would hire the best in the field to be at her disposal. She wanted to ride Dex. He would start the negotiations low then hope he wouldn't need to give away too much ground to her.

By the time he was dressed, she was sitting at the table eating a croissant. She grinned. Kerrie wasn't dressed in the riding habit he told her the maid laid out for her. Tam wasn't certain she owned one. He assumed the maid would do so because he told her they were riding. Kerrie was dressed in britches and a shirt. Beneath the fabric, the tips of her breasts evident, the rounded globes he'd come to adore were outlined by the fabric. She wore riding boots. When she stood, he watched the movement of her breasts beneath her shirt. Heat spiraled straight to his groin without one stop in between. He didn't need to close his eyes to recall the softness of her breasts. The way they tasted. If she did anything else that would heat him, they would not be riding this morning. Spending the rest of the day in bed with her would never be a hardship.

"That's not a riding habit!" he shot out, wishing she would follow a few rules.

She needed to conform so he could survive. He didn't understand why he yelled. Coming to her quietly would have been a better idea.

"No." She turned for him, showing off the delightful curves of her hips and butt. "Riding habits are for the sidesaddle. If I'm going to ride astride, I'm going to be dressed to do so. It's not safe to ride sidesaddle. You do like safe. No foolishness for me." She had the audacity to waggle her finger at him to put further emphasis on her point. "Don't wish to get caught up in too much fabric. As you told me, riding can be dangerous." Kerrie tilted her chin as if that movement forgave her for dressing as a man.

He didn't care. Liked to see her curves. It was just...just he didn't wish anyone else to see her delightful curves. Bloody hell, she threw his words back in his face. Damn, but he never gave how she rode the horse a thought. In this she might be right. Though he didn't like admitting to the fact. Backing down wasn't in his nature. When he rescued her, she'd been astride Dex. As a stuffy duke, he should have seen to her rescue. He understood to protest what she wore would be an argument he couldn't win. Decided he should only argue about things he felt were the most important. Things he would have the last say about. If he voiced his opinion about all the issues that he disagreed with, he would be arguing with her all of the time. He wished to spend his moments with her pursuing other more enjoyable pastimes besides quarreling.

His hand rubbing the tense muscles behind his neck, he spoke. Tried to keep his voice calm. Didn't want to see her bristle. "You can wear anything you like. Not that it's important what you wear as long as you are covered. When you ride, I want you to be safe. A sidesaddle looks awkward to me. Astride makes perfect sense when I take the time to think on the matter. Astride is not proper. I'll defer to your judgement on this issue."

Her eyes widened with what he supposed was surprise. "Do we agree on something? I like that. Perhaps it's a first negotiation." Kerrie flashed him a smile that was wide as well as brilliant. "Surprises me. Hope our future holds more agreements than arguments. Don't like turmoil in my life."

"Believe we will agree on quite a lot of things. I don't intend to become autocratic where it comes to your happiness. You are," he paused for emphasis. He wished to make his feeling clear, "very important to me. You are my wife. Shall we go?" Tam offered her his arm. She accepted.

As they walked to the stable, he took her hand in his, enjoying the feeling of her fingers encased in his. That simple touch sent fire to his loins. He brought her hand to his lips for a gentle kiss on her knuckles. Turned her hand over to place a tender kiss on the palm. They were small though her fingers were long. She was too delicate to ride Dex. No strength in her arms or thighs. "Do you wish to ride Briar or with me on Dex? You must understand what I would prefer. Nonetheless, this is your choice."

If she rode pillion with him, he would use the time to seduce. He had several places on their land to show her. Given enough time, he wished to make love in every spot that was important to him. He thought of all the erotic sensitive places he would explore, seduce. Grinned. Hardened in an instant. All it took were a few wayward thoughts about her lithe body for him to grow hard as steel. Never would he complain about the way she brought his sex to attention. His focus was on her. Her eyes. Her breasts. The flare of her hips. The length of her legs.

"Ride with you on Dex. For me there is no other choice. If that's the only time I get to be on him, I will always choose Dex first. I live to ride him. He does miss me. You know that. Don't you?" She paused, turning she tapped him on the chin. "I like the way it feels to have your hands around me when I ride in front of you. Touching me in all those private places you discovered. Remember what you did the other day. Where you warmed me. Heated me with sensual exploration. I wouldn't complain if you did the same today."

Her words thrilled him. How could he forget the way she twisted to give him greater access. Gave new meaning to excitement. He couldn't complain either. "Dex it is. We will ride together. I will explore. You will enjoy your pleasure. Mind you, when we reach the falls, I will need you. Nonetheless, if you are very, very good, I will pleasure you."

"Promise?" Her ensuing giggle of delight pleased him.

"Yes."

In a few minutes he helped her mount. He was behind her. With Kerrie's back pressed against him, they headed out. One hand rested on her hip stroking with tender meticulousness, the other held the reins.

"Where to first?" he asked as he pressed his lips against the nape of her neck, felt her small shiver of appreciation. He caressed, nipped, scraped his teeth across exciting spots, soothed with his tongue. Seduced. All the while feeling her animated response. He meant to set a storm brewing inside her. A tempest that could not be doused. One that would reach its completion in time.

This fine sunny day greeted them with its magnificence. Cerulean blue sky held a few wispy clouds. The sun shone bright sending heat to the surrounding area. The land in front of them was a vibrant green. A warm breeze sifted through the leaves of the trees. Small animals skittered in front of them to avoid the stallion's hooves.

"Did you wish to go to the glade where you took me two days ago? We could..." She left off as if too shy to say what she was thinking.

Tam understood what she was too embarrassed to ask him. He should wait until he could hear her say the words. Today, at least this time, he would make this easier for her. "Ah, you wish me to make love to you again. You, my love, are insatiable. I like that about you. Seems you can't get enough of this man's body. Don't mind though. Seems I feel the same about you. You've come to need your pleasure. I'm the man to fulfill your needs." He stroked her belly. Squeezed. A child could be growing in her womb. He hoped if not now then soon. His goal was to make her so ready for him before they reached the falls, she would beg him to enter into her.

As a precaution, he searched the land in a full circle. They wouldn't be newsworthy today. He hoped they wouldn't. There had been no scandal to nourish the gossip mongers. No rumors to feed to the ton that would create the newest *on dit*. They married. As far as he could see in all directions, there was no one following. There was no scandal to be reported about him along with his countess.

Her hands clasped his forearms. Long well-manicured nails bit into muscles. She tightened her fingers on him at his nip to her ear. Her nails slid along his arm. He placed kisses on the nape of her neck. She pushed against him, moving to press herself closer.

"Unfasten your shirt for me, honey." Tam bit with a light caress on her neck. "Kerrie..." he hoped he wouldn't have to ask her again. In time the discomfiture would lessen. Now, he understood encouragement was needed. "Unfasten the buttons, love. I know you want to. Believe you want me to stroke your breasts. They remind me of peaches. Pluck the tight hard buds. Would you like that? I would." The answer needed to be positive. He kept his fingers crossed.

She nodded. His free hand stroked her thigh to the apex, caressed. Even through fabric he felt her heat felt her moisture rain down to soak the fabric. If she'd worn a dress, he would have easy access to her dark secrets. He would test the honey. Hoped she reacted passionately to his exploration. If she'd worn a dress, he would have seen to her climax before they reached the falls. Perhaps he would have her open her britches for him. Deep in the back of his throat he stifled his groan.

"Yes. You know I would."

"Do I? You are so shy. Even after last night, your bashfulness shines through. If we weren't riding, I would touch your nipples with my teeth. Pull your breasts into my mouth. Suck the ripe peaches deep and hard. Could make this ride messy. I would enjoy tasting your darkest secrets again."

"Not when you are touching me. I'm not so self-conscious or modest. A few days ago, I never dreamed of a man touching me as you do. When your hands are stroking me, I forget about everything except the way you are making me feel. Everything is so evocative, mercuric."

"Do it," he urged. "No one save me will see you. Undo your shirt for me." His teeth grazed the back of her neck. I think you were hoping I would hold your breasts in my hands. You wore nothing beneath the shirt."

"Did you forget I would wear no underclothing for a month?"

He sucked air.

Kerrie looked around as if doubting him. He chuckled when two buttons were freed. He saw the rounded white curves waiting for him. Needed to see more. All of her breasts, the fullness he remembered. Heat flared. Surged to his loins. His arousal pressed against her backside.

"Not good enough. Though a tangible beginning. Every last one of them," he told her, his voice whispering across the back of her neck. Touching. He tortured himself. "All of them. Pull your shirt from your britches. Push the fabric away. Don't make me work too hard to please you. I won't appreciate that."

"I would not...all the buttons?" she argued with herself. Stated the question before a breathy little noise rippled from her kissable lips. He would have to wait to kiss her mouth. To taste her warmth. "It's..." she gripped his arm tighter when his teeth grazed the back of her neck. "Scandalous," she finished on a whimper as he paid more attention to her neck. "Outrageous. A nice girl doesn't...oh..."

"Shocking. Wicked. Do it, love. For me. For you...your pleasure as well as mine. We can make memories we will be able to tell our grandchildren about. We both understand you are naughty, not nice. Want the naughty you. Enjoy naughty. Wicked works too."

The erotic slowness of her fingers fascinated him. They opened one then fiddled with the next. Time passed while he watched, mesmerized by the sensual unveiling. Though he'd seen her, touched her, this was new. The adventure another beginning he would savor. Not too many seconds passed before her shirt was undone as well as hanging loose around her. Holding one breast in his hand, he gave full attention to the sweetness she offered him. His caresses were tender, gentle to the first one before moving to the other globe. He plucked the tight hard buds. Twisted. Wished he could kiss, taste the sweetness, enjoying the sounds.

"I need to touch you," she murmured, her voice soft, hoarse as her passion increased. Tempest seemed to ignite within her. "Want to hold your...in my hands.

Bloody hell, he needed that too. His arousal pulsed against his pants. "My sex, sweetheart. Say it for me. In a few minutes when we reach our destination. You can hold me. Say the words." From his vantage point he gazed on the play of her breasts, swaying with the cantor of her big stallion.

Holding his breath, he anticipated the word.

"Sex, your...sex. I need to taste you too. Want to pull you into my mouth. Suck you deep into my mouth. Taste."

*Bloody everlasting hell...!* "Ah...good, good between us you can say anything. Remember there is nothing to be nervous about when you are with me alone. Now your britches. Undo them, all the fasteners. Can't wait until we stop. Too long. Want to feel your white belly contract with my touch. Need to feel the heat between your legs, the dampness drizzling down on my fingers. The fire." He nipped again.

Tiny sounds vibrated from her in ribbons of pleasure of pure ecstasy. She did as he asked. He placed his hand on her belly. The soft roundness enchanted. They needed to reach the falls before he exploded. Feeling the contracting of her muscles, he dipped lower. She opened her legs further for his exploration. He put them over his thighs. Her head fell back against his chest. He saw the rose of her nipples pointed into the air hardening as he watched. He cupped her mound. Slid a finger into the soft damp part of her. He aroused. She arched. Seduced. She moaned. He explored deeper. She whimpered. Trembled. With infinite care he touched upon the tiny knot that would increase the raging passion within her slim body.

She keened. Moved her cute little butt against him. Pushed herself against his hard arousal.

Breathed in then out with little puffs of air as raw hunger filled her. "Tam...you're going to be the death of me."

He gave her the reins to hold. Focused all his attention to her seduction. When she splintered, shaking with the assault of her climax, he soothed the wild reaction with lightened strokes. Dex slowed. Came to a stop.

"We are almost there...to the falls. You are very naughty, my love. A naughty girl for her husband, a bad boy. I like that. Do you wish to receive more pleasure at my hands? I believe you do. You seem all dreamy...relaxed now. In another few minutes you'll be ready for a second round. This time I'll be inside you. Would you like to feel my sex inside you? Do you wish for me to fill you with my heat?"

They stopped in front of the falls. He helped her down before dismounting himself.

"You know I do," she whispered the words, her head falling against his chest.

The blanket was spread on the ground. He caught her in his arms then followed her to lay on top of the blanket. She fumbled with his shirt. He disrobed her then shed the rest of his clothing.

Tam fused his mouth with hers. Thrust inside her with his tongue. Penetrate then retreat. The mating was wild. So fast there was no time to breathe. In seconds they both climaxed. He rose above her, pushing damp strands of her long hair from her face. "Are you sated now? Would you like to try this again in another place?"

"What I wish for is to sweet talk my husband. Want to kiss you as I did last night. Wish to seduce you. Would you like that? I know I would."

As she mimicked his words, he found he enjoyed that too. "You can do whatever you like to this man's body. I will never tell you no." Tam paused, staring into the crystal clarity of her eyes. "However, we need sustenance if we mean to do this all day. My wonderful cook packed us a basket that would last for the entire time we are away. Believe Talbot was behind the instructions. He and my father will do anything that will give me pleasure. They understand how much enjoyment for me is wrapped up in your delicious body. They are also hoping for a little babe sooner than later."

"Sustenance? Baby? I'd like something to eat. As to the baby...?" She stopped talking, touching, tracing the tip of her finger along his chin. "I would like a baby. Your baby. Since I never intended to marry, I never expected to have a child. Everything about my life, my future has changed."

Naked, he rose. Strode to the satchel on his horse. Brought out cheese and bread then a skin of wine. "Drink."

She sipped. "It's delicious. I would have some of that bread and cheese. I am hungry. Didn't have much for breakfast. Here we are again..." she stopped.

"Still hungry for me?" He arched his brow.

She lowered her lashes before answering. "Yes."

Tam was both pleased as well as amazed when Kerrie didn't attempt to cover herself. She let him watch her, seeming at ease with her state of attire. They ate and drank. Made love again before he told her they were moving on to another place he had in mind. She was to leave all her clothing unfastened. Now that she understood why, she didn't act reticent. Her shyness was evaporating. It was nice to have her the way he wished.

The day passed too quickly. He showed her two more of his favorite places. The sun was near the horizon announcing the end of a day he'd remember forever. Kerrie was asleep on the blanket where they made love as well as filled their stomachs with food and drink. He wished he didn't have to wake her. Wished the sun wasn't setting. He knew when they reached home, his father with Talbot behind him would have questions. Would wish to hear every detail of their day. What they did together would not be repeated.

Tam woke her with tender kisses. Strategically placed sweet, hot kisses on sensitive skin. One more time before they left if possible. When her eyes fluttered open he was once more inside her. Penetrating, retreating, both hard and slow in her tight core until they both cried out. He held her. Reveled in the feel of her pressed close against him.

"We need to return," his voice was soft when he spoke.

"Wish we could stay here all night."

He did too. Nonetheless, the elements were against them. "You...we would freeze. We are without food. What do you think? We should go home then retire to our room. Let the servants tend to us. Would you like to soak in a hot bath? Eat our dinner in bed?"

"Yes, to all you said. Hot bath, food, wine then you. Heaven."

The rest of the week was spent in much the same way. Tam was pleased when no one in the home gave them away. Delighted, yet he understood he needed to tell her the truth soon. He was unwilling to lose the easy comradery they established since they were wed. When, not if, she discovered the lack of truth on his part, she wouldn't want anything to do with him. Kerrie would turn away from him. He couldn't bear for that to happen. He was falling in love with her. Hopelessly in love.

*I'm afraid, a coward bone deep. The thought of losing what we have together, terrifies me, turns my stomach inside out.*

Sooner or later, he would need to give her the bad news. As long as there was time, he couldn't tell her. She would despise him, his title, everything about his life. He was bred to be a duke. Being an aristocrat was all he knew. If he could, he would try to convince her a man with a title was not so horrible. *I'm damned if I tell her as well as damned if I keep the lie alive.*

This situation was untenable. The scenario was of his making. So far, he wouldn't change anything that happened between them. The week they spent together was heaven. Kerrie made an assumption that he didn't correct. There was nothing he could do to change the untruth he nourished by his silence. He was a man too close to the fires of hell. Tonight, he would tell her two things. One was the fact that unbeknownst to her, she was a countess and in time a duchess. Second, they were going to London for the week. He had work to do in the parliament. Needed to see to business that his father ignored or was unable to complete. His father had not visited London since he lost the use of his legs. Until now, Tam had not had anything to distract him. The long-needed vacation at the Montgomerie hunting lodge brought a wealth of disruptions to his mundane everyday life. A distraction he had come to cherish.

That night they were once more diverted by each other. The focus was on making love, giving as well as receiving pleasure. Exploring each other. By the time she lay sated in his arms, she was asleep. In the morning, he would tell her about the move to the city. During the carriage ride, he would give her the other news. If she was confined to the carriage, he didn't need to worry about her storming off.

It was essential for her to listen to his explanations as to why he never told her the facts about who he was. If he got lucky, she would understand then forgive him. If he wasn't lucky... Tam didn't wish to think about that last scenario. They spent a week making love. Even if she refused to come to his bed, she might be increasing. Enceinte. He smiled. The thought filled his heart. Earlier, she told him she wanted to have his baby. That might change with the news of his status.

Even if she was angry with him, Tam felt certain, with a few strategic kisses, he could charm her into his bed. After all the sweet loving, she would want him, need her pleasure. Would never wish to give up the ecstasy his hands provided. How long could she hold a grudge then refuse him? If he seduced, she would never be able to deny herself what he could give. If she allowed him to get close enough, he would charm her back into his bed.

~ * ~

Talbot sauntered into Robert's study a bright smile on his aging face. "We did it! He sounded as well as appeared jubilant. "We did it! Those two cannot keep their hands to themselves. Even when they leave that big bed, he is holding her. She has her head on his chest. He has his arm around her. Those two are in love. Mark my words, nothing will come between them, even the title."

He set the tray with the teapot along with scones on the top of Robert's desk before stepping back, his arms crossed over his chest. The smug expression uncontested.

"Did what?"

Robert sat back, his hand on his chest. He didn't feel all that well today. He'd hoped to see his grandchild born before he died. The way he felt this instant, he didn't think that would happen. In all this time though, he was pleased that he saw his son married as well as in love if Talbot was correct in his assumption. As much time as the two of them spent in Sterling's big bedroom, she must be well on her way to having a young Talmage inside her. This was everything we prayed for, he and Talbot.

"Well, you know, the staff came together. She never found out.

Everyone was able to keep the 'your grace's' from popping from their lips. Though there was a time or two I almost spilled all the beans. Now the newly wedded couple are on their way to London. If the news gets leaked, the fault will not be blamed on the staff here."

"I forgot. Pour me some tea, please. If I recall from the first time I met her, Sterling will have to do some fancy footwork to soothe her feelings. When the information comes to her, and it will, there will be bloody hell for my son to pay. The lady detests titles. Not the man though. It's obvious to anyone with eyes, she loves my son, the heir." Robert closed his eyes. His brow was sweating. His heart was beating hard. He sipped in as much air as he could grab. Breathe...that's what the doctor told him. Breathe long as well as deep to calm the racing of your heart.

"I'll send for the doctor," Talbot said as he turned to race from the room.

"Don't think doc can help this time," Robert said as the ache in his chest and down his arm grew. "Take care of..."

"I will. Treat them all as if they were mine, my son, Kerrie along with the new baby. You hang on now. It's not your time to go. You've got too much to look forward to. The little one will be here in no time...just nine months from now. You just keep breathing. Follow each breath with another one. You'll see. All will be fine. Think about your grandchild. Nine months in the making."

Another servant passed the room. Talbot handed out instructions. The man left on a dead run. "Doc'll be here before you know it. Can I get you into bed?" Talbot asked deep frown lines marring his aged forehead.

"I'll stay here,"

Robert let out a long sigh, relief pulsing through him. While the ache was intense, it seemed to be vanishing. He knew one day he would not withstand the attack on his heart. It was hell getting old. "I'm better. Pour me some of that tea. Put a little nip of brandy in it." Robert needed something stronger than tea even though that was one of the things his doctor told him to forego.

Talbot waggled a skinny finger at him, shaking his head as he did so. "Don't want to play a part in making your old ticker worse. No, you don't. Not on my watch. Doc says you're not to have spirits of any sort."

This time Robert's sigh was both exasperation as well as disdain. What did the doctor know? He was just guessing. "A nip of brandy might take away a minute or two of my life." Robert told his long-time butler and friend. Talbot helped pick up the pieces when his past collided with the present. "What difference will it make in the end? Tell me. I'd like to know." Robert gave up his cigars for the old doc. He wasn't about to give up his drinks. He needed a few pleasures in this life. Short as it was going to be. What was life without pleasure?

"Got to stay healthy for the baby's arrival. Which will give you more pleasure than a smoke or a brandy. Now you don't be giving up this soon. Before we know there's going to be a little nipper coming to stay with us. Could be the next Duke of Sherburn after Sterling or a beautiful little lady. You know how lovely Kerrie is. The babe would take after her mother. I'm certain of that."

Talbot was standing in front of the desk wringing his hands, gazing down on him. "Your son did his part. Found a wife he could love. You've got to meet him in the middle. Do your part too."

Robert cleared his throat while he held out his cup for Talbot to lace with the brandy he wished for. "Not giving up. I'll drink my tea then you can help me up to bed. Even if the Doc gets here, he will tell me what we know. No drink. No cigars. Eat right. Rest and get exercise. Walking is the best. What do they know? Walking is damn difficult for me. I'm going to have to have a shoulder to lean on."

"Yes," Talbot agreed, nodding his head. "We haven't been so good at doing that now, have we? I ask you if you are going to behave yourself. We will work together to give you a few more years. I've let you wallow in that damn wheelchair. You've got to get up and test your legs. You can always lean on me."

"Imagine there is no choice if I expect to greet the new marquis into the world. Think I'll officially give up the title. Not doing any of the work. Sterling is doing everything. Suppose untouched work is why those two left for London. Believe they would have stayed in bed another week if duty didn't call to my son. Two weeks in bed..."

"That's not something I know anything about. The young Lord Talmage doesn't tell me what it is he is about. Imagine you are correct in your assumptions."

With Talbot's help Robert made it to the bedroom then into bed. An hour later the doc arrived spouting all the remedies Robert repeated earlier in his office to Talbot. Robert decided he wanted to last a few years more. Wished to meet one grandchild then perhaps if we were lucky a second. Needed to see the Sherburn line continue. He would behave himself if only to insure himself another year or two.

"Talbot, in the morning you and I are going for a walk in the garden. Every day. Not going to give up my spirits though. Nonetheless, you may monitor the amount of brandy I consume. Furthermore, you may, with my permission, toss out all the cigars. They stink up the house. Don't purchase any more. We'll see if I might make some improvements on my health."

"No more red meat," Talbot waggled his finger at him. His scraggly white eyebrows tilting into the air.

"Yes. Chicken and fish it is." Robert made a disgusted face at the thought of no beef. He liked his beef a bit pink in the middle. "Maybe once a month."

"Once a month," Talbot conceded, "More fruits and vegetables," Talbot then added with a wistful sigh. "We'll both stay away from the sweets. You understand that will be more difficult for me than you."

"You do love your chocolate."

"Peppermint candies too."

"Want to see the next marquis. Get my advocate here tomorrow. I want to make the change as soon as possible. I will send a note to Sterling that I've officially abdicated my duties as the Duke of Sherburn. He will no longer need to put off signing official documents until he's spoken with me. My abdication will give me a few more years. Stress, you know. We've got to rid ourselves of stress. Both of us. A body doesn't need stress."

# Chapter Eight

Tam woke her with a swat to her bottom after tugging the sheets from her. Kerrie sat up, brushing the tickling strands of her hair from her face. She puffed a bit of air upward to push more hair away from her face. "What? That wasn't very nice!" She wanted to be furious with the blasted man. She couldn't. He was standing beside the bed, his grinning face looking tender, his lips twitching with unspoken amusement. No matter how hard she tried, she couldn't summon anger. She really was falling in love with him. The thought shocked her. She always thought that being in love with one's husband was the right way to go about marriage. It was what her mother and father had; a marriage based on love as well as commitment though the marriage didn't begin that way.

"Time to rise and shine, we're headed for London this morning. Get dressed. We leave in an hour." He tugged on the sheets covering her, grinning as they slipped lower with each jerk of his hand.

After this week together with the incorrigible man, she lost all modesty where he was concerned. She stretched, pushing her breasts upward, watching his gaze focus on her. Enticing him. She knew what she did. He would be hard, aroused. "You didn't tell me."

Kerrie lifted her arms, pulling her hair behind her head. Saw his gaze shift to her then downward as if wished to see more of her. Another yank and the sheets slipped lower. She smiled what she hoped was a siren's smile. She slipped her tongue along her bottom lip once then twice leaving a dewy trail of moisture behind. She didn't believe he could resist. The lip he would adore until it was fat from his attention. He'd nip then suck until she whimpered. Until her body quivered. She moved again knowing he would follow the dip and sway of her breasts. "I need a bath. Is there time?"

Her words were dark and rough with the desire she energized in herself.

"Vixen, sweet, darling witch," he whispered, his voice husky with the craving she also read in his eyes along with the growing bulge between his legs. "You know what that does to me. This time you are doing it on purpose. Believe I like to see you so brazen."

"Yes," Kerrie patted the bed beside her. "Tam...? I want you. Will you make love to me? If you don't..."

That was a semi-threat. She didn't know what she could taunt him with except withholding herself from him when he wished to make love to her. She inhaled a long deep breath.

He groaned low in the back of his throat. It seemed he couldn't stop staring at her. "No time. Wish there was. Waiting for you, love. Business calls to me. As to why I didn't mention the trip…" He paused stroking his chin, his eyes darkening as she continued to pose for him, thrusting her breasts out to entice. "Seems we got sidetracked a couple times last night. Can't get distracted now. Got to go."

"Alright. Have this your way. Though..." She focused on his crotch, saw the telltale bulge, larger now than the first time she stared. "If you can, have cook pack something for us to eat on the way. If you are in such a hurry, we can have breakfast in the carriage. Wouldn't wish to keep you from your work." Kerrie maneuvered her covers so they rested on her opened thighs.

"Good thought," he murmured while he toured her body, stopping on the puckered tips of her breasts, lower to even more intimate places which she revealed. "I'll leave you to bathe then dress on your own. God knows if I see you much longer like this, I'll tumble you back onto the bed. It's what we both want." He started to turn away from her.

She needed to stop him before he walked out of the room. "You want me. You know you do. What would another few minutes matter? Why, I do believe the way you've been watching me, ogling my body, I'm about to climax right now just from the ferocity of your gaze. Wouldn't you like to join me in the heat of my pleasure?"

She pushed the sheets lower. Her legs opened to him. Her knees were high and spread. She touched herself. Felt the small knub he showed her that would make her lose control even without his sex inside her. "You could come inside me."

Her smile grew when she heard his second groan. Thought he was about to succumb to her avid seduction. Watched him toss off his frock coat then the rest of his clothes. She continued to touch herself. Kerrie arched her body, revealing her secrets. Saw the way his eyes darkened with the need she generated. She was so wet. When she looked down, she saw the white cream of her raw hunger between her legs. She'd never seen that before. Her body quivered, pulsed. Inside she throbbed in anticipation.

Tam came down between her legs pushing them farther apart. She cradled him. He moved her fingers. Where they'd been he kissed, sucked and nipped that tender, sensitive jewel. His tongue entered her, darting in then out of her core. Penetrate. Withdraw. With deft precision, he moved up her body with kisses then nips. He sucked on one breast then the other. Nibbled on the tip of each, while the other hand replaced hers in her dark, secret place, massaging the nub that would leave her without breath. She trembled. Rounded her body to get closer to him. When his mouth captured hers, he thrust inside. The brilliant fragments of her climax exploded into his mouth. He absorbed the cries, the whimpers of pleasure. He yelled when he emptied himself inside her again. His weight covered her. She ran her hands along his back, stopping at his buttocks. Raked her nails up his long back, exhausted as well as weak from the violent end of their pleasure.

She was learning the power she held over him. Reveled in the fact she could bring him to this point of no return. Of course, he could do the same to her. That was fine by her. She pushed a lock of his dark hair from his eyes. "Thank you." *I love you*. She couldn't say the words to him.

As if nothing happened, he stood. Stared down at her. His expression looked as if he was all business. "Fifty minutes," he told her his voice tender. "I'll be downstairs." Tam turned his back. Washed himself then dressed.

With a heavy sigh, Kerrie understood she used up the extra time. She had fifty minutes. Best she hurry.

As commanded, Kerrie was sitting in the coach that would take them to London at the time ordered. She settled on the seat, plumping her skirts. Tam sat across from her. This was so different from their trip in this same coach on the night of their wedding. That night he couldn't keep his hands to himself. Today, he appeared preoccupied, morose. His lips turned down as if he was unhappy about something. She wished he would smile so she could drink it in. Kerrie adored his smile. Didn't understand what happened between this morning's seduction and now.

He alternately stared out the window then back to her with a strange expression on his face. One she couldn't fathom. One that was out of character. His eyes the color of dark pewter, simmering. He seemed angry about something, perhaps more annoyed. With every passing moment, she expected him to pull her onto his lap. He didn't. Tam stretched his arms across the back seat. Whatever caused his changed mood she must have been the catalyst. She didn't waste time when he wanted her to get ready. At least not after he made love to her. She was in the coach in forty-five minutes, not the fifty he gave her. On that score he had no reason to be angry with her.

If anything, she expected a comment or two about what she'd done. Her bold seduction of him which might have caused a ten-minute delay. Nothing to be so...so...uncommunicative. She liked the way he reacted to her this morning when she sought to go out of her comfort zone. Maybe that was what was wrong. If he didn't appreciate her beginning the lovemaking, he should tell her. She'd thought he would welcome the fact she was no longer shy or embarrassed until her teeth ached. That was what he told her he wished for. At least that was what she'd thought.

"Tam," Kerrie decided to approach the subject instead of waiting for him to say something. His silence coupled with not understanding was stretching her nerves thin as well as churning her stomach. She hated wondering what she'd done to create this situation. "Are you angry with me? I would know what I did. Was I too bold? Too brazen? Does that displease you? Thought that was what you wished for. If not..."

He reached over to touch her cheek. "No, I'm not angry with you. You were not too bold. I enjoyed you very much, every precious moment. The problem is...I'm in a quandary of my own making. Don't know how to get out of it without suffering the consequences. Never been a person to dodge consequences where they are deserved. Don't believe this is deserved. Been searching for a way to tell you something important. It's something you need to know. Vital for you to understand." He sat back, folding his hands on his belly, a wistful expression shadowing his eyes. "Just don't know how to ease my way into the conversation."

She waited for him to say something else. Instead of telling her this piece of news, he closed his eyes. He remained silent, a faraway expression painting his handsome face. When he opened them a few seconds later, he grimaced.

What to do?

"Just tell me. What do you think I'll do? Leave you?" she asked, wondering at the deepening frown, the arch of his brows. "I won't leave you. Ever."

"That's what I do expect," he murmured, his voice soft. "Won't let that happen though. Not when you hear..."

"This news of yours would need to be horrible for me to abandon all that we have together. I can't imagine anything so dire that would make me walk away from a marriage I adore." Kerrie was at a loss for words now as well as thoughts. He was insinuating something that was both baffling as well as annoying. Something so dire, she would wish for a divorce. "I cannot imagine anything you could say that would make me leave what we are beginning to build." She felt the need to repeat herself. If he didn't explain soon, she thought she might toss the pillow she was holding at the man. Her nerves were about to snap.

Tam wasn't forthcoming. His lips twitched. Dark circles formed under his eyes. Kerrie imagined when he felt the time was right, he would tell her. It was obvious to her that this thing he wasn't speaking about bothered him more than he cared to admit. She wasn't going to pressure him. Though he planted a bug in her head.

Patience.

She'd never been patient. Impulsive, yes. Wild at times.

Patient, never. Kerrie realized they were the antithesis of each other. Tam was known for his remarkable tolerance. The calm man who overthought everything. He'd been accepting of her spontaneous life since they first met. Well...maybe not so tolerant. When she did something he didn't like, he fixed the scenario to please himself.

Tam had been quiet during the short trip to London. After the first brief conversation, he said nothing. He brooded. Seemed nervous. As he stared out the window, looking pensive, Kerrie understood he had something important on his mind. Something he alluded to that concerned her. Still, he remained mute. She didn't know how to ask the question she needed an answer to. His demeanor was so different today from the man she'd come to know. Not once did he kiss or hold her. She expected they would have found themselves diverted more than once on this long, boring trip into the city. When he did look at her, it seemed he regretted something.

From that point on, silence reigned over the remainder of the trip. Most of the time he stared out the window. Brooded. Fear spiraled inside her, gave her the shivers. He told her she would leave him if she discovered what he was keeping to himself. Kerrie didn't believe that to be a possibility. While she never told him the truth of her feelings, she loved the intolerable man.

The carriage rolled up in front of a large brownstone. "We are here," Tam said as leapt from the coach to help her down.

Yes, they were here. Her heart shuddered. Kerrie knew from the previous conversation something she wasn't going to like was going to happen. She was about to learn something that would change her life forever.

Kerrie gave him her hand. He steadied her as she looked around the long, tree lined street to his home. Also, her home. The front of the house was lined with flowers as well as huge trees. They must have been there a long time. It was fall. The leaves were beginning to turn colors. Everything was changing. The last week her life shifted to something she never thought would be. She was also changing in a myriad of ways. She was a wife now. Could become a mother soon. Something she never expected since she never intended to wed.

"How long are we staying? What are we doing in the city? You never said."

She failed to ask the questions during the ride. Of course, he might not have answered. Just as Kerrie thought he wasn't going to tell her. Tam seemed so self-absorbed she didn't feel he wished to talk. He was inside himself so deep she would never be able to penetrate. She needed to understand what bothered him. If this problem did concern her, maybe she could help.

"Until I've seen to all the neglected affairs. Don't know an exact date. A month, maybe more. After that, if you'd rather live in the country, I'll make arrangements to have correspondence along with the necessary paperwork sent to the country home so I can work there. Imagine we'll have to stay here at least once a month for a few days. Will have to make occasional trips into town just as your aunt and uncle do. My father's duties have been neglected for years...since the accident. I've done my best to deal with the most important work. It's difficult to keep up with the responsibilities when I need to first run all the details by father."

"Why travel? You're not the same as Uncle Drake."

Her uncle had business with the ministry. He was a duke who needed to see to affairs concerning his status. She believed he was a member of parliament. Lords of the realm often were. They needed to attend when the parliament was in session. Whatever his duties were, she imagined he would feel obligated to see to them. Still, she meant to pursue this. Wished to know about her husband. "I don't understand. What is it that is so important? You never told me your line of work. Does this have anything to do with that?" Kerrie felt as if she groped to get some words from this man who was as silent as a stone. She realized she still knew little about the man she married. Who was he really?

Just as she asked the last question, the double doors leading into the foyer of his home opened. An older man, with thinning gray hair stood in the doorway and addressed them. He was tall, thin, his face narrow. His dark brown eyes welcoming them. He smiled, pleased to see the two. "Your graces." He nodded. "Happy to see the two of you. Heard you married, sir. Congratulations." Five servants stepped through the door.

Her heart leapt then stopped for a few seconds as she twisted over the words she heard in her head. Dazed.

*Your graces?*

Kerrie spun to look at him, scowling, her brows drawn together. Questions thundered in her muddled brain. She thought this had to be a mistake, possibly a bad joke. The servant had to be...this was a... She set her hands on her hips. "You all are joking." From that point forward her emotions climbed, soared out of control. "This ruse of yours is not funny! I will not put up with this!" Her fists tightened. She was beside herself. She looked to Tam for an acknowledgement to the joke. He didn't move, nod, tilt his head, smile that devastating smile of his.

His words rang in her head.

*You will want to leave me. You won't stay with me. There is something important I need to tell you.*

Tam's face held no expression. His gaze confronted her. Her body quivered, trembled as she sought the truth. Her voice shuddered. "Tell me this is a joke at my expense. This isn't nice of you." Her knees grew weak, legs wobbling. She needed to hold on to something. She leaned on the pillar nearby. Somewhere deep inside she understood the truth was being spoken. He would not joke about something this important.

Tam shook his head. Reached out to help steady her then drew his hand back as if he understood she didn't wish for his help. His expression too grim for the words to be a story. "No joke. Meant to tell you last night then on our way here. I couldn't find the words. Know how you feel about men with titles. Now though...I hoped the week we spent together would change your mind. Imagine you feel the same by the expression of horror I'm seeing on your face. Imagine nothing has changed."

Breathing was impossible. Tiny sips of air did nothing to fill her lungs. She wavered, praying that this wasn't true. She closed herself against the pain radiating through her in multiple waves. "You are 'your grace'?"

This wasn't a joke either, or he carried his amusement too far. He told her she would wish to leave him if she discovered what he kept from her. "You deceived me."

He was right. She couldn't stay with him.

His nod told her all her fears were true even before he spoke. His hands rested on her shoulders, held tight. He squeezed. She felt the pressure. His touch did nothing to reassure. "As are you, my countess. Since we are wed there is no way out of the truth." Now his brows drew together. His demeanor along with his voice changed. "You are a countess. I'm a marquis. When my father passes on his title, sometime in the next few days, I will be a duke. You will be my, duchess. Get used to the title.

It will be yours for life. If we have a son, he will become the next duke."

*No!*

Kerrie tugged in a long, deep breath of air. Her anger boiled, simmering inside. She needed to vent, to hit him. Needed air in her lungs. They were in front of servants. She couldn't hold back. "You lied to me!" She swallowed, gulping down the knot in her throat. "Should have told me the truth before we wed. Don't you think I deserved to know before committing to a life I would loathe? One that would never suit me!" She gritted her teeth against the fury coupled with despair. She couldn't stay with him. He couldn't be her husband. She would get an annulment.

"Come along now. It's time to meet the servants." He took her by her elbow then led her up the porch stairs introducing each of the people who worked for his family. Once they were inside their wraps were taken. Tam escorted her to the drawing room. "I will give you a tour of the house as soon as possible, though my London home is much the same as your aunt and uncle's. You will learn where everything is. You will run this household just as your aunt, the duchess, does for the duke, your uncle."

"Don't want a tour. Won't run your household. Don't know how. Never been taught. What I know is horses," she told him, understanding the words were a lie. "Not staying here, with you. You understand why. You knew what would happen. Told me as much when we were traveling." Kerrie sat on the edge of her chair. "I'm leaving."

"You can't." No emotion tinged his voice or his face. His tone was cold. Brokered no feeling. She felt ice touch her bones. The chill ran down her spine. "Won't allow that."

"I will!"

"Watch me. You are my wife. You will act the part even if you've come to detest the role of countess." His voice was harsher than she'd ever heard. His back was stiff, arms braced in front of him. His eyes were like ice chips. Cold. Determined for her to see things his way. "You will attend events with me, on my arm, a smile on your beautiful lips."

Kerrie didn't recognize the man. On trembling legs, she rose to leave. Her stomach churned. She could never be what he expected. Tam didn't make a move to stop her. He crossed his legs. Sipped his tea. He didn't like tea. She didn't know why that incidental piece of knowledge fluttered through her clouded head. She looked over her shoulder to see him giving directions to the butler or the under butler, she couldn't remember which one the man was. While he made the introductions, her mind was in a haze. When she reached the door, it was locked. She caught her bottom lip behind her teeth. Froze. Tam was making it physically impossible for her to remove herself from this home.

That little problem was never going to stop her. Stomping through the house, she found the back door. It was also locked. Kerrie threw up her hands, frustrated, furious. Emotions she never felt before raged. She imagined she might climb out a window. They couldn't possibly lock everything. After minutes of trying to find a means to leave, she found herself in the drawing room where a cup of tea was poured for her.

"We will have a late luncheon," his words calm, too cool.

His composure threatened her. "You will eat with me as a wife would. Do not speak of our argument in front of the servants. Your trunk has been brought into the house to our room. I will have paperwork to see to after luncheon. You will acquaint yourself with the downstairs as well as the upstairs maids. If you wish, I will hire a maid for you. We spoke of it earlier. You declined. Might need a lady's maid when we attend events. Unless you wish for me to help you into then out of your gowns."

"Fine!"

She seethed, her anger topping off. He would not have the last say in this. What did he mean her trunk was brought to his room? She had no idea. She did know.

She sat down, her back stiff. Sipped her tea. Tried a bite of the scone. Set the bread down. She wasn't hungry, not even for Tam. Everything they had together was a lie. Less than a half hour ago, she thought she loved him. She loathed him, his arrogance, his highhandedness and...his aristocratic hide. Curse his deviousness. He couldn't assume she would give in to his demands. He was just like all aristocrats she'd known. He was just like Uncle Drake. Never seen him highhanded.

Tam's legs were crossed. He had that lordly air about him she despised. The stuffy duke, the moniker fit. "I don't wish to be your wife. I'll get an annulment. You won't see me again. You can find a woman who wants a title. Your wealth. I don't need or want anything from you. Won't take anything." Kerrie searched for some way to break the terrible hold he had on her heart.

*I love him.*

*No!*

*How could I love him? A lord of the realm. He lied to me. Kept secrets.*

The thoughts shattered all she knew about herself. All she'd never wanted.

Tam barked his laughter before he schooled his features. His long fingers formed a steeple beneath his chin. He grunted before he spoke. "After all the times I've been deep inside your sweet luscious body. Heard your moans of pleasure when you climaxed. I left my seed inside you. If you recall, you seduced me this morning." He paused tapping his fingers together. "An annulment...no. An annulment would never be granted."

He shook his head, his smile feral. His fingers moved against each other as he pinned her in place with the intensity of his gaze. She shivered from the coldness he generated with the frostiness of his eyes. "You will remain my wife despite your hatred of the aristocracy. I'm not the man you hated before. Not the man you despised because he made assumptions that you would give to him everything he asked for without your consent. I courted you with gentleness. Gave you the greatest pleasure. Our marriage will never end—until one of us kicks up our toes. You will continue to lie beside me at night. You will accept me as a wife does a husband. You are mine, love."

"I gave you everything you asked me for. Everything! I gave you my virginity. You lied to me. I can never be with you again. I'll get a divorce."

"It was a lie of omission. Nothing you should get angry over now that you understand I'm not that person you recall. Be realistic. You might be carrying my child. A divorce would make our child a bastard. A label that would follow our child all his or her life. Besides, if you haven't guessed, I would never sign the papers granting you the end of our union. Despite what you wish, you, honey, are stuck with me until one of us cocks up our toes. For better and worse. Sickness and in health. As long as you shall live. Forever. Do you recall you promised before God that you would obey me?" He tapped his fingers on the teacup. "Perhaps we should begin this now, today. What do you think?"

The noise rattled her nerves that were stretched now to the snapping point. "Forgot nothing." Moisture clung to the back of her throat. Threatened to spill from her eyes. She wasn't going to cry in front of him. "I hate you."

"You despise who you believe I am. No, love, you don't hate me. You hate the fact I hold a title. Me...well...if I decided to kiss you, to stroke your breasts along with your other sweetest, wettest places in the most secret part of you, you would let me discharge my seed inside you. You would whimper as well as cling to me. You are no longer shy. I've seen, tasted as well as touched every sensual part of your lovely body. There will be no going back or denying me. You are my countess, soon to be my duchess."

Heat flushed her face. That was so mechanical, so distant so very frigid. Everything he said was true. "I can't live with you!"

She couldn't lie in his bed with him again. Could never allow him access to her body. Oh, God what if she did carry his child? The baby would...no, if she were pregnant, she would know.

*It's too soon to know.*

"You have nowhere to live besides with me. Nowhere to sleep except in my bed. All of the rooms will be closed to you. I will have my wife beside me at night. I will make love to her every night if the mood strikes me."

"No!"

"If you think for a moment your aunt and uncle would allow you to stay with them, you are sadly mistaken. If you believe you could go to your old home, your mother and father would send you back...to me. Your parents witnessed our marriage. Your father and mother gave you to me in a church in front of God as well as witnesses. They heard your promise to obey. There is no going back for either of us." He walked around the room to end up standing over her. "You are mine, Kerrie. That fact will never change. No annulment. No divorce. You are my wife."

~ * ~

Tam stood inside the door to their bedchamber watching her. His head throbbed while his heart pounded. Fear was what he felt. A terror he had no idea how to vanquish flooded him. He took his bath in a different room while he decided how he was going to approach his reluctant...more than unenthusiastic bride of a week. His lie was one of omission. He kept the truth from her. Held on to the secret that would ruin his life. Though he understood the impact. Kerrie never deceived him about the way she felt on this issue.

His body jerked in reaction to her words of hate. How could she spout that lie? She didn't hate him. Kerrie hated what he stood for. He couldn't change the circumstances of his birth. The woman didn't loathe him. She was hurt. Felt betrayed to the deepest part of her soul. She believed with all her heart he deceived her. If he'd told her about his heritage, she would never have given him a second look. If he informed her of his status, she would have laughed in his face. Her heart would have been hardened against him from the beginning. So hard, he would have never been able to break through the ice and never be able to melt the frost. Tam felt certain she cared for him. Wished she loved him. Thought if her feelings were those of love, they would get past this setback to their relationship.

As he got to know her this last week, he understood he wanted her for his wife. For him, there was no other woman. The decision was right for him, he hoped for her too. Didn't understand that his emotions for her would turn to love. He did love her. With all his heart he adored her, found himself besotted with her impulsiveness. Treasured the way her eyes shimmered then darkened when he teased her, kissed her, made love to her. How could she bolt so fast into his soul as if lightning hit him then abandon him as if he was nothing to her? Now he was faced with the hardest task of his life. To soften her hatred. To turn all that passion into love toward him. That was his goal.

In time, with enough faith, he would get her back. In the meantime, he was going to figure out how to sleep with his wife, make love to her without complaint. Tam understood she could be seduced. Understood, too, she would tell him no at first. He would need to find a way past that horrible word.

The certainty in his mind was that with a few strategic touches, she would once more melt for him. Give her body to him. Tam needed more than the physical act to sustain him. Her passion was uncontested. She heated so fast. Burned for his touch. The woman, his wife, was made for him. She was so beautiful. He adored everything about her even her impulsive nature that was so contrary to his.

He might have made everything worse when he had her clothing withheld from this room, his too. She would have searched for one of her nightgowns. Would have donned a shirt of his if he'd left clothing within her reach. While she was in the master chamber, she would have nothing to wear. The thought, in his mind, was a spark of genius. In their room, there was nothing for either of them to clothe themselves with. She would have the towel from her bath. The maid was instructed to remove her clothing as soon as possible.

This afternoon, every time she denounced him, he died a little bit more inside. His stomach turned sour. Lurched with her untrue words of animosity. Her reaction was what he expected. What he dreaded from the first. Now, he would do all in his power to change her feelings back to what they were. He would love her until she could do nothing else except love him back.

He pushed away from the door striding toward her. His smile set on his face was grim. He meant to approach the situation with cool logic. Hoped that would sustain him.

She was in his bed, curled into a tight ball facing away from him. He knew she wore nothing beneath the sheets except the towel. Tam lay down beside her. Set his hand on her damp hair. Lifted the covers to stroke her shoulder, to feel the silken texture of her skin. He set his hand on her hip, continued up the ladder of her ribs. He tugged on the towel loosening the fabric. She moved her arm back to push him away. He grunted.

With a fingertip, he traced the line of her spine to the crevice of her bottom pushing on the cloth barrier as he moved lower. Spread his finger over the roundness he found there. He adored her backside. Bent to place a tender kiss on each delectable cheek.

"The softness of you never fails to surprise me," he murmured while he took tiny nips before soothing with his tongue.

Her bottom quivered. He felt the beginning of the rise of passion within her. Kerrie could hide nothing from him. She wore her heart openly even though she wished to keep herself from feeling.

She tried to move farther from him, curling into an even tighter ball, exposing her backside more. "Go away."

"Never," his voice husky with the rising desire he felt watching her.

His kisses raked across her shoulders. He pushed damp hair from the nape of her neck, further sightseeing. She was melting for him while fighting the emotions boiling between them. Her body was no longer stiff. Her breaths were sporadic. When he touched her, he felt the trembling of her body. Saw the pulse beating rapidly at the base of her neck.

"You're despicable!" Kerrie cried out then let a long breath of air flow from her.

Her scent was erotic, all woman. His hands closed around her breasts. Tested the weight. Thumbs flicked across the taut buds.

Silken flesh.

The aroma of an aroused woman.

"You want me. Want that climax you've come to revere. I can give that to you. Give you everything you've ever dreamed about. Admit it, Kerrie, you want me to fill you. To become a part of you. Tell me you want that pleasurable ecstasy." He was still exploring with fingertips and tongue.

Tam knew she was wrapped in her towel for protection; he wasn't about to allow the material to provide that. The towel was no barrier to his questing fingers. He pushed the cloth down her back while he explored. It was loosening more, falling away in front. Soon the fabric would be gone. He wasn't going to sleep next to her while her hair was damp. Something would have to be done to change that fact.

"I know you believe I've done immeasurable harm. That I'm horrible. I'm not the villain you think I am. I'm a loving husband who wishes for his wife's hair to be dry before we go to bed. Don't wish for you to take a chill. Wet hair will never do. Come along." He tugged on the blankets. Grinned when he saw the white monogrammed towel falling around her. He'd pushed it down her back while he explored.

He pushed.

She pulled.

Between then and now, she brought it back so it was just beneath her armpits. "We'll sit by the fire. I will comb out your hair until it dries. We can watch the flames just as we did our first night together. Do you remember that night? Hmmm... I held you. Kissed you until you whispered soft sighs. You enjoyed that. You will enjoy doing so again."

"No...don't want you to comb my hair. Don't want you to touch me. Kiss me. Tam, you can't seduce me to your way. I... I won't let that happen."

Tam interrupted. "Your body tells a different story. I would wager if I touched you at the apex of your thighs, you would be hot, swollen, wet, ready for me to come inside you. To be joined with you. I've seduced your body. You will be prepared for me to leave my seed without pain of entry. What do you say? Should we test my theory?"

Without waiting for more conversation, a discussion he would lose, he scooped her off the bed then into his arms. Tam didn't want to hear anything negative. He meant to twist this encounter into a positive scenario. She didn't fight him. Kerrie could have struggled. If she'd fought him, she would have lost the towel. Deep down, Tam didn't believe she wanted him to stop. Neither did she wrap her arms around him to hang on. Her eyes were closed against him. Her fingers tight, holding the cloth covering her. He would deal with that in the ensuing moments. On his way to the hearth, he picked up her comb.

Reminded of another night, he set her down in front of him facing the flames. Vibrant colors shot up through the fireplace to the chimney, casting a haunting glow around the room. Pulling her against his arousal, he began to comb her hair. There were a number of times he combed his mother's long hair. He never felt like this. With each stroke of the comb, he grew harder, more needy. Burned hotter for this woman who stole his heart.

A slow easy seduction was called for tonight. Her willingness is what he sought. The best-case scenario would be if she came to him. The next best would happen if she didn't deny that she wanted him. He kept one hand on her shoulder while he pulled the tortoise shell comb through the strands spreading over her in single layers to dry. As the locks began to dry, they softened then curled. He moved her hair over one shoulder. The strands clung to his fingers. Stuck to his cheeks where the stubble from a day's growth tempted the strands.

He set his lips on tender sensitive flesh, on her nape, behind her ear. Felt shivers of heat flow through her. Her body trembled with mounting desire. Tam read her like a book. She could deny with her words until hell froze but her body told a different story.

"Does it make any difference to you that I don't want you to do this? That I'm telling you to stop," she asked her voice petulant. Wary. He heard the sounds of betrayal. "I don't want you in my bed or my life. Tam, you can't do this to me, to us."

"Should it make a difference? You're a little liar. You accuse me of lying when all I did was leave out a few facts about myself," he whispered against an ear. Touched with his teeth. Nipped then laved. Soothed with his tongue. Was delighted when he heard her soft sigh of pleasure. "You like this. Want more of what I can give you. Admit it."

He set a hand on her hip. Spread his fingers across her belly. Loved the soft feel beneath his hand. She tried to wiggle away from him. He would give her some distance. After a few moments, he would advance again bring her back to him. Always advance then retreat then advance again one more time until what he wanted was in the palm of his hands. She would not be able to tell him no.

Tam pressed his mouth against the pulse point at the base of her neck. Tongued the spot. Tweaked. Reveled in the response to him she couldn't hide.

"I don't want this. Don't want you to make love to me. You are a horrible man to insist." To his delight her bottom pushed against him as if seeking his hard arousal. She knew what she searched for.

"Who said I wanted to make love? Hmm... Seems you are making assumptions about my feelings. You hurt me when you told me you hated me. A husband doesn't recover right away from that horrific wound. Didn't you realize the pain of those words goes soul deep. I'm trying to adjust to your ever-changing feelings. Once, not too long ago, you told me you loved me."

Tam's hands ran down her arms then back to her shoulders. With his actions, the towel slipped, loosened. The fabric was no longer secure. He held her hands while he continued the slow seduction of his wife, his one true love.

The cloth covering her fell, hung on the tips of her breasts for a moment before descending to the floor. Tam did wish for her to be naked. Whenever possible, he would sleep with her wearing no clothing at all.

Kerrie whimpered. Sighed. She could never keep her feelings to herself.

His hand touched with shuttered reverence on the tip of one breast while he settled her into his arms on the way to their bed. The covers were pulled back. He set her down, stepping back to watch her scurry under the blankets. Kerrie pulled them to her chin all the while keeping her back turned from him. Seemed she was back to being a shy maiden. He needed her return to the way she was this morning, bold as well as brazen. Before she gained the unwanted knowledge he kept from her.

Tam disrobed then crawled into bed with her. He pulled her against him. His hand cupped her breast. Fondled. "Go to sleep. Relax, my love. Morning will come soon enough. If you wish, you can continue this falsehood between us that you've created. If you need for me to see to your pleasure, I will."

Against him, she was stiff. He set his hand on the curve of her hip, Caressed. Stroked. She wouldn't fall asleep. Tam understood she was aroused. Tense. Waiting for him to make love. Not yet. The scent of her was provocative. He would wait a few more minutes. Closing his eyes, he listened to her soft breathing. Flattened his hand across the rounded contours of her belly. Felt the jerking of her muscles as she anticipated his next move. Heard the sharp gasp of air, the small moan as her body, against her will, prepared itself for his entry.

His mouth passed across her nape. Bit. Laved the silken flesh. She shivered. Stirred against him. Kerrie no longer protested. Her body vibrated with building need. In one short week, he taught her what she desired, what he could give to her. How he could give her pleasure.

"Relax," he soothed, moving again to hold her breast in his hand. Skimmed his thumb across the hardened tip. "It's going to be just fine. You want me. I know you do. You don't hate your husband. You're angry. That's all."

Tam understood the convincing of his reluctant wife that he was not a despicable cad would not be easy.

Moonlight flowed into the room. Outside, the sky was dark, littered with brilliant stars twinkling in the night sky. Tam waited while he watched her. The stiffness of her shoulders began to ease, her breathing slowed. The last candle flickered then died. The flames in the fireplace became embers.

Kerrie slept in his arms. Turned to him as she did every night before this one. Her breasts pressed against his chest. One of her long legs slid across his thighs. She moved her cold feet along his leg. Without her knowing, her hands traveled down his chest, touched his sex. He claimed the tip of her breast with his lips. With gentle suction brought the globe into his mouth. Switched to the right breast.

Feminine noises whispered ribbon-like from her. Kerrie's hips moved, anticipating his entry into her hot sheathe. Pressed against him in her need, her body undulated. Begged for intimate attention. Arched. Shuddered. She was aroused. His hand slipped between her thighs, caressed with cherished precision the pearl that would arouse. Stimulate. "Please," she keened, a soft wail emanating from her lips. "I need you."

"That's it, love. Let it go. I'm going to come inside you now unless you tell me not to. Remember in the morning that you asked. You placed your fingers around my sex. Aroused me. Tempted as well as tortured me with the sweet promise of your love." He paused a few seconds, waiting for the hated words.

"Please, Tam. I need you." She whispered the words he needed to hear.

On top of her, he pressed her legs apart. Bent her knees. He claimed her mouth with his then filled her with his sex. The entry was slow. Meticulous. Gentle. Her core kissed his length. Pulsing. Throbbing with raw passion. He continued his assault on the tiny nubbin that brought her so much pleasure.

In then out. Fast then slow. She rocked him. Hard then harder still.

A soft sigh followed, a whimper after that. Soft feminine sounds of her arousal greeted him.

Her nails dug into his shoulders. She bit his shoulder. His hands beneath her bottom, he lifted her. Tam knew the moment she woke and knew what they did. She would not remember asking for this. He thrust hard. Deep to her womb. She cried out as her body climaxed. He sent his seed deep inside her womb. Yelled his pleasure. Fell on top of her.

"You are wonderful," he whispered to her. "Beautiful...all woman. A man could never ask for more than what you just gave me. If you recall, you begged me."

Kerrie's eyes were closed, her breathing still hard, fast. "Cad..." she said but the single word held no venom. The word was said with care.

Tam meant to ignore the comment but never the sweet dulcet tone of her voice. She might not recall that moment either. He was pleased. His patience paid off. Where she was concerned, perseverance always would.

"You are a delight, love. You moaned your desire. Your hunger. While I would have enjoyed this more if you cried out my name, the joining was acceptable for this marquis. I'm pleased with my countess. You were wonderful. The perfect mate for this humble man. Do you think you might have conceived this night? I will look forward to siring after me the next Duke of Sherburn."

She needed to understand she could never run from the title. While the title might haunt her, it was hers until she stuck her spoon in the wall.

He stayed inside her until he slipped from her. Pulled her once more into his arms. He held her in the silence of the night. Until morning there would be no more sweet talking. He would allow her the night of sleep, the time to become used to this new way life would be in the future. In time...

...in time she would learn.

Until her attitude altered, the nightly ritual would remain much the same. He dozed several times. Woke to the gentle sounds of her sleep. He pulled her closer, loving the feel of his soft woman in his arms. Her head settled on his chest. Her hand rested at his hip. If he was lucky, she might initiate their love play again.

When he woke, sunlight stole into the room. Streams of light were filled with dust motes. He found Kerrie's delectable little butt, pushed against his full arousal. His hand surrounded her breast. He rolled the hard tip between his fingers.

Tam caressed her. Kissed her neck. Tugged on a nipple.

When he heard her soft sigh of pleasure, felt her push against him, asking for his entry, he pushed inside. They climaxed hard and fast. The moment was messy. Silence greeted him. Tam believed silence was better than accusations. This time she didn't call him a name. Perhaps she was accepting the reality of this marriage of theirs.

After that mating, she continued the silence while he held her. He imagined there were no words. He was in full control of her sexually.

She might have the days. He would have the nights.

If she carried herself as a countess, the days would be hers. During the day he didn't intend to insist on anything from her. She would soon learn there would be duties for her to perform. How she did them or how well was up to her. Ella would be there for her, to help as well as guide.

Tam rang for a bath. Waited beneath the sheets for the servants while he continued to stroke his wife. Still there were no sounds of protest to hammer in his ears. Kerrie didn't stiffen. She might become resigned to this life sooner than he expected. He didn't want resigned. She was smart. With enough time, she would understand there was no escape. He wasn't like the aristocrat she'd come to dislike. Tam prayed when that time came, she would give herself to him as she did that first week of their marriage.

Once the water waited for him, he bathed. Felt the heat of her eyes on him. He smiled. Tipped his head her way. It was good she watched him even if there was fire in her eyes. Even if her thoughts were less than kind. He wished he could see inside her female brain. She liked to look at him when he wore nothing. That was a good strategy to deal with her. She would have no clothes. He would have none. They dealt well together in that state of *déshabillé*.

How long would this transformation take? How long would the nights be made of pretense held together by tender desire? He didn't believe she would tell him no again. She would accept him into her body when he asked. With the passage of time, she would accept her title. There would be an heir. Again, how long would this process take before she came to him, before he asked.

With the bath water, servants brought his clothes. He dressed in front of her. The silence made him smile. She must be plotting ways to get rid of him. If so, she would have her work cut out for her.

Hovering over her bed, he traced his knuckles along her bared shoulder. "Your bath will be ready whenever you ring for it. If you know what you wish to wear today, tell the maid who will be here to see to your needs. If not, the maid will call for the butler who will go with you to find suitable clothing. You may not take anything from the armoire except for your immediate needs."

He waited for a comment. Silence along with a scowl greeted him. "Nothing to say, love? No barbs to shoot my way?" he taunted. "No words of hatred? Nothing about aristocrats?"

"Why?"

"Use your remarkable wits to figure that question out. Now..."

Again, he stopped for a few seconds while he decided what to tell her. "I will be at my advocate's office this morning. Home this afternoon to see to the most important affairs. We've an invitation to a dinner party this evening. I imagine you have a suitable gown since you were decked out for the season. Pick out one of the gowns. If it needs pressing, the maid will be happy to do so."

Kerrie nodded, her eyes shooting fire. "I'm not going anywhere with you tonight. While you have made it clear I'll be in your bed, I will not play the countess to your marquis in the public domain."

"We shall see." He didn't have much to threaten her with. He would have to think on this matter. He wanted her company at all the places he was expected. "I imagine you will go. Life could be made unpleasant if you refuse wifely duties such as attending a simple dinner party with your husband. I will not be made to make excuses for an errant wife. Will not be humiliated by your absence."

"Whatever you might threaten me with, would it be more unpleasant than sharing your bed every night?"

The thorn embedded. He tried to ignore the pain her words inflicted. Things would change. "If I recall, I gave you that coveted climax. You begged me. Held my sex in your tiny little hands. You were not treated poorly last night or this morning. You wished for sex as much as I. If you'd said no...well...then you would not have found me deep inside you." Fighting for tolerance, he counted to ten. "I do expect you to acquaint yourself with the staff."

"If I don't?"

Good, she was talking. He didn't intend to answer that question. Since he didn't have a believable reply. "Good day, countess. I'll see you bathed as well as perfumed for the events of this evening."

Tam ducked the pillow she shot his way. A second pillow followed. Next, the candle holder. The covers slipped to her waist. He hooted with a bout of laughter. Decided there might be more pleasant ways to spend the early morning. He undid his tie. Tossed the snow-white cloth on the floor. Rid himself of his frock coat then his shirt.

"Tam! No!" She was on her knees, tugging the covers upward. Her breast reacted to the cool morning air. Swayed with each toss. Hardened. Tempted him beyond reason.

He finished tearing off his clothing. "Kerrie, yes!" Tam came down on top of her. His weight pushed her down. He placed his hands on either side of her head holding her fingers entwined with his. With his lips he found her breasts. Kissed. Suckled until she moaned and heaved with her need along with all the pleasure she desired. She bucked against him and cradled him between her thighs. He rocked her. She accepted everything he gave.

The loving, hot. Intense. Over.

Refusing to show her how she affected him, he stood as if nothing of importance occurred. Retrieved his clothes. Facing her he spoke. "Be ready for dinner, at seven sharp. If not, I will dress you. Carry you out of here. If necessary, carry you over my shoulder like a sack of grain into the home we are visiting. Don't doubt for a moment I won't! You will learn I've no shame where you are concerned."

Kerrie brought out his temper. A temper he never lost until she entered into his life. He schooled his features. Swiveled then strode from the room. Using as much restraint as he could find, he shut the door without a sound. He hoped she believed his threats. If she didn't, he would have to do what he told her. Violence was never something he resorted to. Bloody, bloody hell, she drove him to that.

Leaning against the door, counting to ten again, Tam remained in the hall concentrating on his breathing. Easy in then easy out. The woman would be the death of him. He couldn't believe he gave into his base desires. Seeing her naked, all he could think about was the heat of her body, the release of the sexual tension that encompassed them. Kerrie did that to him. Turned him into a mindless fool. A mindless fool driven by lust.

Drake, along with Ella, would be at the dinner party this evening. Tam wondered what tales of abuse his countess would relate to her aunt. He hoped she would keep their private life just that, private. Revealing what was going on between them in public was untenable. Perhaps he should pay a visit to Ella. Give her a bit of information that might soften the blow he anticipated.

Sweat beaded on his brow. While he didn't force her, she told him no once. Told him to stop. After that, the last two times there was nothing negative said. He could never allow her to ruin their lives with her ridiculous notions that she no longer wished to be his wife. He wasn't the aristocrat that set her mind against all of his persuasion.

She was his.

He was hers.

This was not the way he wished to continue with his married life. He prayed for what they had before they left the country estate.

In time...

He kept telling himself that a little time would solve all the problems existing between them.

She seduced him. Made love to him. Held his sex in her hands. Tam needed to get that same loving scenario back. Tonight, he would see what would happen. Tonight, he would understand just how accepting she was to him.

~ * ~

When Tam returned that evening, he half-expected to be met by a shrew. If so, he couldn't blame her. So much changed during the day. His advocate informed him that he was now the Duke of Sherburn. His father sent a letter abdicating from the title. Robert would always be the duke in Tam's mind. All the papers needed to be signed were done. He didn't know when he should tell her. Before or after the dinner. Ella and Drake would have learned about the change in status.

During the day, he purchased a new ship for the Sherburn fleet. Saw one ship off to China for silk, another to Virginia for tobacco along with cotton. Looking around the foyer, he wondered where his wife was. He had a half hour to get ready. His butler met him. Tam tipped his head in acknowledgment.

"Lady Kerrie?" Tam asked, still hoping to discover her whereabouts. Needed to determine if there would be a confrontation.

"Milady is waiting for you in the drawing room. A pre-dinner drink is also waiting. Would you like a bath? The water is heating. I had your valet lay your evening clothes out."

"Thank you, yes."

What the devil was going on? Sounded as if she caved to his threats. That wasn't something he expected. Kerrie was a fighter. She always thought she knew what she wanted along with what she didn't.

Twenty minutes later, Tam stood at the entry to the drawing room. Kerrie looked his way. While she didn't smile, she wasn't glowering at him. Her features were composed. Serene. It didn't seem she intended a fight. Expecting the unexpected, he continued.

"I poured you a brandy." Kerrie nodded her head to the sideboard where the crystal sat. Her words were slurred.

Ah, so that was the way the night would go. He imagined his lovely wife drank her fill while she waited. She was ready though. As always, she looked beautiful. Her chestnut-colored hair was piled on top of her head, held with combs the color of her gown. Except for her drunken state, he had no complaints.

Rounded tops of her breast were revealed by the fashionable low-cut of the bodice. Puffy little sleeves danced on her shoulders. He saw himself pushing those tiny sleeves to her elbows. Envisioned her breast popping free. Sucking on each beautiful tip. Nipping. The tender crests hard. Begging. He wished he could plunder all her charms this instant. If he was a brave man, he would sweep her into his arms then proceed to the bedroom.

"You look lovely."

"Thank you. As always you are handsome. The clothes suit you. As do the buckskins you like to wear."

Compliments, tongue in cheek compliments, Kerrie was taking his demand to act the role of countess to heart. While he sipped his brandy, she finished off her sherry. Her hands folded on her lap, she waited for him. Tilted her chin showing the long column of her white neck. His body tightened.

He tugged in Kerrie scented air. "Some news of importance..." Tam watched her. He was uncertain of what she would do. As it was, she surprised him.

"I'm certain I don't care about any new information you might confess to me. I will obey you. Care about you is a different notion. News about your endeavors will bore me to tears."

"Concerns your status."

"I would care if you told me you were no longer the marquis. I would appreciate that. Welcome you with open arms."

"Then you are in luck. Prepare to welcome me with open arms. I'm no longer the marquis," he told her deadpan, searching her eyes for a reaction to the news she would care about.

The amber of her eyes lit, shimmered. Her lips formed a tentative smile that faded. It seemed she realized what she asked for was what happened. Though this was not to her way of thinking. "You're the Duke of Sherburn."

"I am and you..."

"...the duchess." Kerrie tilted her chin and brought into her lungs a deep breath of air. Her breasts rose with fluid motion. "Will everything continue to get worse?"

"Shall we go?" He downed the brandy before holding out his hand.

"Your father didn't die...?"

"Abdicated."

"Oh. I'm glad he didn't die. I like him. Unlike my feelings for you."

Tam kept his hand extended waiting for her to acknowledge him. A bit wobbly, she stood. Accepted his hand. Her fingers were cold. He needed to laugh. Understood the best scenario would be to keep the bark of laughter as well as his smile behind his teeth. She would never take his amusement well.

"How much have you had to drink, love? Not that I care. If you mean to embarrass me, you won't. The only one who will be mortified is yourself."

He escorted her to the carriage waiting for them. This vehicle bore the Duke of Sherburn's crest.

"Don't know. Wasn't counting," she muttered. His hand on her waist, he guided her. "The sherry tasted good. Filled my empty stomach. Seems I couldn't eat. So, I drank. Didn't mean to get so tipsy."

"Did I tell you your aunt and uncle, the duke and duchess, will be at this dinner?"

Tam tossed the information out to see if he would get anything beyond icy disinterest. She should have first-hand knowledge of her uncle that would signal to her the man wasn't at all as she perceived men with titles.

"Nice, I'll have someone to talk to. How sweet of you to tell me. Did you invite them just for me?" she told him, a tilt to her head. "If you said something to me sooner, I might have thought on this evening with more favor. Might not have downed so much brandy...sherry," she corrected herself.

She'd been drinking brandy. The notion made him grin. The ride was short, silent from that point on. In her demeanor, he had no complaints. The fact she didn't wish to communicate with him was expected. The Mulligans had been friends of his father for years. Friends of his grandfather before that. This family had daughters...no sons. The title would be passed on to the oldest daughter's husband. At one time the elder Lord Mulligan hoped he would wed one of the daughters. He'd never felt anything except friendship for the girls. At times, even friendship was hard on him. They were both twits.

Tam was pleased to discover Kerrie said nothing to Ella about her feelings, how they changed. There was nothing for her to tell. He believed if Ella asked, Kerrie would have mentioned her distraught. That piece of information wasn't anything Ella had not heard before. Everyone understood before the wedding there would be hell for him to pay once Kerrie discovered his truth.

"She's holding up better than expected," Drake said to him after they retired with the men to enjoy a cigar, a customary cigar without the women.

Neither Tam or Drake smoked. They stood on the patio looking out at the night sky, sipping brandy, avoiding the smoke.

"Yes..." Tam agreed, unwilling to expose their private moments. "Better than expected."

"You don't have the look of a man on the second week of marriage. Should still be feeling the honeymoon."

"Didn't wish to return to the city. Liked the solitude of the country better. Business called. Needed to see to things that had been left far too long."

Tam leaned on the railing that led to the gardens then on to the gazebo. He thought perhaps when she was feeling more receptive to their lovemaking, he would make the gazebo at his home a favorite trysting place during the summer days.

"She knows..."

"Yes, she knows she is a duchess. Father abdicated. This morning I was given the news. Father is trying to live without the stress of the duties. He wrote that he and Talbot would walk every day. That will be hard for father given he has very limited use of his legs. Would cease with the cigars. There were other things he wrote in the letter. He wants to live to see his grandchildren."

"I wish you well. Understand you would never say anything untoward. I was surprised when Kerrie didn't take refuge with Ella when she learned that you weren't the peasant she thought you to be. I assume it would have been yesterday when you arrived."

"Told her Ella would send her back to me, her husband."

"My wife would have done just as you said. So would her parents," Drake said with a sharp laugh. "Kerrie is a smart girl. She will come around. Lyssa also has a title as does Nickie. She will realize how much she loves you. The title will become second nature to her. If she didn't love you, she would not have said her vows."

"I'm determined that she will soon see me in a different light."

# Chapter Nine

Three weeks passed. At night Tam comported himself as he did that first night in the townhouse. He allowed her no clothing in the bedchamber. He made love to her before they slept then in the morning after she woke. Sometimes he would wake her when he was deep inside her sultry warmth. Though she would never admit the truth to him, she adored him. Loved to have him inside her, to feel him fill her, while he sent mercuric magic through her along with evocative sensations. There were still things about him she would change. His arrogance, to begin with along with his determination to have his way in all things. He'd said they would negotiate. Not once did he keep his word on that score.

The maids brought gowns as he requested. If she would admit the truth even if it was just to herself, she didn't want the nights to change or the early morning hours. When he came to bed late, she would be awake waiting for him. One night, wearing nothing, she sat on the chair warming herself in front of the fire. He let his clothing fall around him, scattered on the floor. After he picked her up to set her on his lap, she straddled him. Their bodies joined while he orchestrated the magic that would fragment her world.

That night after the dinner party at the Mulligans, he helped her from the gown she wore. He tugged the sleeves down her arms to her elbows. Gave tender attention to her breasts before ridding her of all she wore. Captured her mouth with his.

The gown along with the corset were impossible for her to manage alone. He told her he would hire a lady's maid if she'd rather not have him remove her clothing. She snorted, understanding a maid to help her would make no difference in the final outcome of the night. Every evening as well as every morning, he made love to her...after she begged him...never before. A few times she pleaded until he gave in as if he didn't wish for the same outcome for the evening.

One night he handed her a wrapped gift. When she opened the package, she'd thought to throw the gift in his face. It was a sheer negligee. One he seemed delighted to skim the fabric from her body after she put it on. She wore the gown because it gave her a small measure of privacy. Even as sheer as it was, the fabric was armor. One more thing between him and his roaming hands. Not that the material proved a barrier. Not that she wanted the fabric to stop him.

Another evening, he gave her a ring to go with the wedding band he placed on her finger when they wed. The stone was amber. He told her the color reminded him of her eyes. He tried to be romantic. One night he brought dinner to the room along with a bottle of wine. She wore the negligee. He stripped off his shirt, wore buckskins and nothing else. Kerrie admired his body, the rippling muscles. He couldn't keep his gaze from roaming over hers. She couldn't stop looking at him.

Tam told her he wanted to return to the glade so they could make love there. He had fond memories of the isolated spot. Recalled the sweetness of the moments the day after they were wed. The weather was too cold now that it was the middle of October. The leaves on the trees were changing color, falling to the ground. This summer she hoped they would find time to visit then recreate the past.

Kerrie set her hand on her belly. Her monthly was late. That never happened before. She was always on time, give or take a day or two. She wasn't going to tell him she thought she carried his child. Not until he asked. Not until she was positive. He would wonder when she never told him she could not make love.

He would seek information soon.

Since he was intimate with her every day, he would notice. Tam would be watching for signs she carried his child. He wanted an heir. Last night he told her they would return to the country estate in a week. If she counted her days right, she understood she conceived one of the first times he made love to her.

He told her the nights were his.

His statement was true. The days belonged to her. The nights to him. She never saw him until the evening meal. He left after he made love to her in the morning. During the night he was warm, smiling after he brought her to a blinding climax. At those times, he would laugh then kiss her on the tip of her nose as if pleased with the events. Every morning when he said good day to her, his voice along with his eyes turned frigid. She would feel the chill throughout her body. The warmth they shared while in bed would evaporate with the beginning of the new day.

Kerrie knew he still harbored ill-feelings for her. She should tell him that she didn't hate him. Adored him. Even loved him. Somehow, she could not. Could not find a way past his blatant lies.

Tam showed her little to no emotion when he saw her at the beginning of the evening. He held himself in check as did she. Until he kissed her, he remained aloof as well as distant. From the beginning, he'd been right. She wanted him. Could never tell him no. She should have never told the lie that she couldn't keep.

Even now, thinking about Tam, she wanted him. Her body heated, ached in too many different places to count. He wasn't due home for another few hours. They would attend a ball at her aunt's home tonight. It seemed Ella was chaperoning another cousin. Tonight would mark her debut. She should know this cousin. She'd been so enamored of her horses, she paid little attention to the other families. They would attend to give the young girl moral support. There wasn't a single doubt in her mind that Ella had a husband picked out for her new charge. Ella had remarkable skill in that department.

Kerrie looked forward to the event. Enjoyed being seen with her husband. She wanted to dance with Tam. He would hold her close, too close. She would press against him, arouse him. By now she was well-versed in that department. If he wished to steal a kiss, he would whirl her onto the balcony.

Her personal maid's name was Mary. She was a sweet girl. Nonetheless, she took orders first from Tam second from her. The gown she was to wear this evening, he'd picked out. He made certain Mary understood the nightly ritual. After she bathed and was sweetly perfumed, the clothing would disappear. She tried bribing both Monney as well as Mary. Nothing worked. Kerrie didn't care anymore. All she wanted was a tiny bit of a say in the order of her life. Nothing more.

The loud banging on the front door brought the butler, Monney, to the door. Jerked Kerrie to focus on the door as well as wonder what the urgency was.

"He's hurt, bleeding from the bullet wound." A man outside the door told the story to Monney. "Got to get him inside. Got the bleeding stopped before we left the place."

Kerrie picked up her skirts, raced to the front door horrified to see her husband carried into the foyer. His right arm was soaked with his blood. "Dear God... What happened? Bring him inside."

She tried to think. Couldn't. Attempted to focus on what needed to be done. Her heart pounded. With her hand at her throat, she tried to suck in oxygen. What little she found seemed to burn on its way to her lungs.

*Don't faint. Not now when he needs me.*

Two burly men carried Tam into the house stopped at the staircase to the upper floors. "Where can we put him? Doc's on the way. The manager sent the message while we were bringing him home. Should put him to bed. Don't you think?"

"Yes, of course. Upstairs, I'll show you." Her heart caught in her throat, fluttered then started to beat again. Kerrie told herself she needed to stay calm. "What happened? Is he going to be alright?" she repeated looking from one man to the other.

If she didn't get a hold of her emotions, she would be no good to him. She wasn't a witless, helpless female.

"Some crazy man found his way into the club. Shot it up. Seemed he was angry about the rejection of his application. The duke wasn't the only one shot. The bullet went through the fleshy part of his arm. Nothing to worry about. When he went down, he hit his head on a table. He'll wake up soon, cursing a blue streak. He'll have a headache to beat all when he wakes. Arm will hurt like the devil for a couple of days."

"The doctor?" Kerrie couldn't remember anything. Did anyone mention the doctor? She was so worried. "He's going to live. Right? Is the doctor coming?" Her head was a muddled mess. "Monney, will you watch at the door? Send him up when he gets here. I'm going to stay with Tam."

Lord, she hoped Tam would wake up. She didn't know what she'd do if she lost him. She wasted so much time acting like a spoiled child.

Since she discovered his title, she never told him she loved him. There were so many times she could have said the words.

She didn't.

Neither did he. Wanted him to say them first.

"Yes, Doc should be here soon. Doesn't live too far from this place," one of the men said as they brought Tam into the bed chamber.

"Need to get him out of his clothes."

The man set Tam on the bed. He went to work, handing her each item. One man worked on his boots. They thudded when they hit the ground. For several seconds she felt as if time froze. She watched in a daze.

After she recovered from the shock, Kerrie scurried around, taking clothes when they were left on the floor as well as when the men handed them to her before setting them in the hall to wait for the maid.

He moaned. Tossed his head to the side.

That had to be a good sign. Didn't it? Her heart lurched to another stop. He must be waking up. She didn't wish him to be in pain. Moisture from unshed tears lodged in her throat. He wore nothing when the men put him beneath the covers. Kerrie didn't know if he had a nightshirt. He never slept with one. The doc still needed to see to his arm. No one thought it strange that he was naked except for her.

"Doc's here."

Monney stood in the doorway. Stepping aside, he let the man inside. "Ready to do what's necessary. Is Lord Talmage awake?"

Doc was older. His hair thinning as well as gray. He was short with a pouch for a stomach. He smiled as if that would reassure her. It didn't. His eyes were dark brown, his nose a beak coupled with a narrow chin that seemed to protrude in front of him when he walked. He carried his medical bag though Kerrie wasn't certain what he meant to do with it. He set the satchel on the table before opening it then peered inside. He rubbed his chin as if he was wondering what to use. Nothing the man did instilled confidence.

The doctor looked up, still seeming befuddled. Kerrie didn't believe the man knew what he was doing. That thought didn't comfort.

"Been told the duke was shot in the arm. Nothing to worry about,

Lady Talmage. Nothing to worry your pretty little head about. Was told your husband was shot though he wasn't the target. A couple of people went down before someone subdued the shooter. Heard tell it was the duke here who was the hero. Jumped right in then wrestled the gun from the man's hands. A real living hero. Because of him, no one died. Yes, yes," he cleared his throat. Pushed a long skinny strand of gray hair behind his ear. "A real hero, your husband."

"Don't know. You say he's going to be alright. He's not moving."

Her voice wavered; the words weak. She didn't wish for her husband to be a hero if it meant getting hurt. Telling him that would be first on her agenda when he woke. She would tell him just what she thought about his stupidity, jumping into the fray to grab the gun. A duke should never risk his life. Didn't he understand anything about his responsibilities? He was an irresponsible twit.

Drake gambled his life numerous times working for the agency. That was stupid, too. They were too important to be courageous. Ella always worried while he was gone. She would fret something terrible until he returned. Didn't they understand about wives who worried?

"Of course, I'm alright. Just fine..." Tam groaned as if the pain caught him off guard. "What happened?" He was trying to sit up, pushing against the mattress. The sheet pulled over him fell to his waist.

"Man shot you through the arm," the doctor said, then looked at her, his eyes narrowing. "Help me set him up. He's going to hurt himself more if he keeps trying to move without assistance. He's got to sit still. Need to make certain the bullet isn't still in the arm. Hope it went clean through. That would be best. Think it went straight in the front then out the back. The bleeding seems to have stopped. Give him some of that brandy. It will ease the pain and make him relax. When that's done, I'll help you get him into his nightshirt."

"Don't wear or own one," Tam said grinning at her, his eyes twinkling as if he recalled the exact reasons why. "Sleep naked with my wife. No need to put something on that's going to come right off. That would be a waste of time."

Heat raced through her. She set her hands on her boiling cheeks. Tam did that on purpose. She felt mortified to the tips of her toes. He was such a cad. The man enjoyed embarrassing her. He grinned again. No shame, no shame at all.

The doc cleared his throat glancing from Tam to her. "Suppose if I had a wife as fine as this lady..." He stopped as if he said too much. "Well then...in that case...I'll take a look. See just what needs to be done before the two of you can retire for the night. There's to be no hanky-panky this evening. Got to rest."

*Hanky-panky.* Dear God, he wouldn't, would he? He would if he thought he could.

Minutes later the wound was cleaned and stitched. Tam didn't make a sound during the entire procedure. Though he was sweating. His big body held tight, rigid so he could withstand the pain. His hands fisted while the doctor worked on him.

The doc turned to her. "Lady Talmage, you will send for me if there is any sign of infection. Keep him cool if he's hot. Warm him if he's shivering. Infections are going to be the biggest problem if one sets in. Though I have cleaned the wound most thoroughly. If he's thirsty, water will do. If he's hungry, stick to lighter fare. Soup will work best. He should be fine. Remember, no exertion, rest is the key to his recovery."

Kerrie found herself nodding her head, accepting the nursing job. She loved her husband. Should tell him she was tired of pretending to dislike him. She no longer cared if there was a title after his name or hers. He would tell her how stupid she'd been. Tell her too that he knew she didn't hate him.

What Kerrie understood was that she hurt the man she'd fallen in love with, with her hateful words. She wasn't proud of herself. Needed to make amends. The man was kind to a fault. He was always a warm, considerate lover. Even that first time when she said no to him, she wanted him. He charmed her stockings off. The man was right. She did cherish the climaxes. More than that, she cherished the man who gave them to her. Loved him for who he was, despite his faults, despite the title. He couldn't help who he was born to be.

Her husband looked dazed, a bit sleepy from the brandy he drank. The doctor gave him laudanum before he started probing for the bullet. When Monney showed the doc from the bedroom, she stood back from the bed. Her hands were clasped tight in front of her. She didn't know what to do. Food and water, the doctor told her was what he needed. Water. No more brandy for him.

What she needed was a full bottle of wine.

*No exertion. Lots of rest.*

"Come along, love." Smiling, Tam patted the spot beside the bed expecting her to sit next to him. His words slurred together. "Sit down with me. Suppose we will miss the ball tonight. Don't feel much up to dancing, even with you. I'll make it up to you. Know you wanted me to show you off this evening. You bought a new gown?"

Tam was making no sense to her. She wanted to dance, yes. To see Ella, yes. To help her cousin splash her way through the rakes who would pursue her. Seeing to her husband was far more important. He bought the gown, not her. "First, I need to get you something to eat. Are you hungry?"

Kerrie didn't want to sit by him. Naked as well as injured he was still dangerous. The glint in his silver blue eyes told her he was thinking about making love to her. His eyes shimmered with heat. The fire she saw was familiar. All too well she understood that hungry look.

"Ravenous for you," he said, his voice husky soft, always whiskey smooth. "Want you naked beside me. Need to touch every sweet, soft part of you."

"N-not in any," Kerrie gulped air. Swiped her tongue across her mouth. "N-no, not in y-your con-con-dition," she stammered, turning to pull the cord that would bring food along with drink to them. Monney would be in the room. He would not wish anyone to see them. She needed company until he fell asleep. The laudanum the doctor gave him would kick in soon. The man was irredeemable.

"Nothing to worry about. Just a flesh wound. I feel just fine. Invigorated. The little sleep I had has made me wide awake. Ready for you." He laughed at her look of chagrin. "You've got too much clothing on for my taste, honey. We need to remedy that deplorable condition. Come along now. It's your wifely duty to obey me. I need to see you naked."

She couldn't let him leave the bed to retrieve her. He'd hurt himself. She didn't want him to open the stitches. "No, not coming along for you. We are not going to do that tonight. You have to rest. Doc said you must stay in bed a couple of days. Said no hanky-panky. The wound might get infected. The stitches..." She broke off when she understood none of her words were having an effect on Tam.

"I'm fine. Nothing will happen. You worry too much. If you don't come along, I'll retrieve you. Seems to me, if you would do as I say..."

He was grinning, enjoying himself at her expense. That was no way to treat her. He chuckled. "If you would do as I ask, my wound won't open. Nothing will happen. If I have to retrieve you... You could sit on me. Do all the work." He lifted his shoulders, winced when the movement affected his arm.

"You were unconscious when they brought you here. You...you're not thinking straight." He was pushing the covers aside. Her husband would do as he wished. She held out her hands as if that tiny gesture would stop this man. "Don't you dare! Don't leave that bed or I'll...I'll..." she didn't know what she would do.

His right eyebrow slanted upward. "Hit my head on the damn table," he muttered. "Mortifying... I stopped the assailant. Caught the bullet meant for Jackson. Not fair, not fair a'tall. I'm the newest hero in the ton. My wife refuses to honor my wishes. Now, my love, come to me. I'm a hero," he repeated. "Don't you know? You need to appreciate me more. Take off those offending garments then you can lie down beside me. When you please me with this small request, we'll both be happier."

"Food is here," the upstairs maid said as she backed into the room. She curtsied then set the food on a table. "Anything else I can get you?" She looked at the two of them with a quizzical expression on her face.

*More laudanum.* She would need the entire bottle to put him to sleep. The man was so big. She might need two bottles. The doctor didn't give him enough. He was too bloody big. The man didn't realize what it would take to put him to sleep.

"Thank you," Kerrie said, her gaze moving from Tam to the food then back.

She imagined he might do as she said. He needed to eat then sleep. He still wanted her. Expected her to be naked in his bed for his use. She snorted. The sound far from duchess-like. She didn't care. When she turned back, the maid was gone. Most likely fled from embarrassment. She was alone with a husband who didn't understand he needed to rest. Making love to her was not rest. He would open the stitches. Would set him back.

"You could sit on me," he repeated. His husky voice of desire sent vibrations through her. "I would let you do all the work. Need to take those clothes off first. Can't make love to my wife if she is dressed in all that foolery. I'll watch." Again, he patted the place beside him. "Come along, now. Times a'wastin'."

She sifted in a deep breath of air to fortify herself against the task of discussing with her husband that he shouldn't overdo himself. He would never agree. His arms were crossed in front of him. A ducal stance she'd come to recognize. She had second along with third thoughts about telling him she didn't hate him that in fact she loved him. At this very moment, she...well...she didn't know what she wanted. What she needed was to feel his loving arms around her. Under the circumstances that wasn't possible. She needed to stay strong. His recovery was more important.

"Food first. When you please me by eating, after that I'll sit on you." Kerrie lifted the lids. It was obvious the doctor apprised the chef of the food he should be eating. "Soup then bread if you keep the soup down. After that we can discuss your other needs." She wondered if she told him she thought she conceived would his need for her change?

Oh...what if all he wanted from her was the heir? A wave of dizziness sped through her. She wavered. All this stress was getting to her. No...just when she was falling in love with him, she would think of something like that. All the blood drained from her.

"What's wrong? You look as if you've seen a ghost?" Tam asked his voice tender, concerned for her despite his issues.

"N-nothing is wrong."

She stepped toward the bed determined to keep the truth from him until she was sure about his feelings toward her. After all, it was only a lie of omission. Not a real lie. Besides, she didn't know for certain. "Let's eat," she said again, her concerns changing. "I'm hungry."

Pillows propped behind his back helped keep him sitting. The covers were around his waist. She followed the line of crisp dark hair to the top of the covers knowing what was below. Craving what only he could give her. Her tongue drifted across her lips as if preparing her mouth for his kiss. She would miss that tonight. This would be the first night since they wed that they would not make love.

"I saw that. Your little pink tongue wants to dance with mine. You want to touch me. Admit it. I watched you trying to look below the sheet. I'll show you mine if you show me yours." He looked as if he was laughing inside.

Bloody everlasting hell! He was horrible. A horrible, horrible man! Tam was right about her needing him. She squared her shoulders, understanding she was right in denying him. He was wrong. They could not make love for another few days. "If you weren't already hurt, I'd be tempted to put a bullet in your other arm," she bit out with sugar coating her words, pointing her finger at him. "Just be quiet and do what the doctor told you, you should be doing."

"You should eat too. I did have something at the club before all hell broke loose." If his long, drawn-out sigh was meant to make her feel bad, the ploy worked. "Come sit. Won't give you a hard time about your clothes. Understand what you are trying to tell me."

"Monney told me he sent a missive to the Montgomeries telling them we won't be there." Believing he had a change of heart, Kerrie sat beside him.

"Wouldn't be surprised if the duke stops by this evening or first thing tomorrow morning. Ella will need to stay at the ball," he murmured. "I would appreciate the gesture if you loosened a few buttons."

"If I did, you would ask for a few more then all of them. Admit it, Tam, you're never satisfied." Kerrie tried hard not to laugh.

"All true. I should do it for you. That way the unveiling will be done to my pleasure. What do you think? Should I take the matter out of your hands? You can tell me all your thoughts? Your opinion is always important to me."

Kerrie pushed his hands aside. Handed him a bowl of soup. "Bah! You never care about my view. I'm going to assume you can feed yourself. You're not going to need my help. Not that you would want it."

"Perhaps I'd like a bit more tender loving care from my wife. She has not been obeying me. You did promise. That was more than a month ago. Suppose the honeymoon is over. Did it ever begin? Ah, I do recall that first week of pure bliss."

Much to his delight, she snorted then gave in to his suggestion.

"That noise you just made is not duchess-like. You must learn to control your emotions." He watched the changing expression on her face. "Suppose I should ease off lest I get that bowl of soup poured over my head. I do know you, Kerrie. If provoked too far, you would retaliate with the first weapon you found."

"Very well. You've won me over." Petulant, perturbed, she held the bowl in one hand and the spoon in the other. While she tried to feed him, he unfastened the top two buttons of her gown. "Tam! Don't do that!"

Tam seemed to know his grin was smug. Understood also that she would take issue with the attitude. While he cared, wished she would stop putting her feelings on hold, he would proceed in his own way. "Don't stop. Keep feeding me. If you don't, I might pass on from lack of nourishment. You don't want that. You would need to revive me. Call for the doctor. Extra work for you, love. No need for that."

"Tam!" She jerked when his fingers skimmed over naked flesh. He was taking advantage of the situation. If he wasn't careful, she would indeed spill the bowl of soup on him. No, he knew she wouldn't. By the trembling of her hands, he would know she wanted this as much as he did.

"Take a bite for yourself. No, don't set the bowl down. For what I've planned we will both need sustenance."

Two more buttons were flicked open. He continued unhindered. Kerrie did as he asked. Sipped a spoonful of the chicken soup. Not bad fare for an invalid. "Damn, I went over what happened at the club. I had it all under control. I should not have been shot."

His thoughts caused her hands to shake. Even though a portion of her wanted to deny him, she would do as he wished. What else did she expect? Her alternative was to leave the room. He knew she didn't intend to do so. If he wanted her... Well...if he wanted her that much, she always let him do as he pleased. Doing so pleased her also.

"You're not wearing a corset. Thank you. It hasn't been a month yet. Do you wear your pantalettes?" He slipped the ribbons through the eyelets of her chemise. "This would have been easier if you...no, I like doing the chore myself. Your eyes are darkening. Don't know why you protested. You desire my body. Want all I can give you. No, don't tell me you don't. I know better."

The back of his hand brushed her nipple. She jumped. A bit of soup slid over the top of the bowl then onto the sheet covering him. "I protested because the doctor told me you needed rest. I was following his orders. You should do as he says. He told you that rest was the best prescription for what ails you. Having your way with my body does not entail rest."

There was a decided edge to her voice. One brought on by her frustration both sexual as well as emotional. "I'm content that you wished me to get better. There was a point when I thought you might want to see to my demise."

"Never," she murmured as his touch began to send heatwaves pulsing within.

"When were you going to tell me?" Tam's voice changed. Was now soft. Tender in the extreme. "Your husband needs to know all your secrets. Don't keep this from me, your loving husband."

"I don't know what you're talking about." Her shoulders stiffened, chin rising a notch.

"It seems you meant to deny this as long as you can. You might have been counting days. Just as I was. I'm making guesses. Perhaps you are too. I'm not going to consider the possibility that you might not have any idea. My Kerrie breeds horses. She would understand more than most women."

"Ah...I seem to understand. Caught up in a lie of omission, nothing for you to object to. It's not a real lie, now, is it?" Sarcasm clung to her voice.

He winced.

"Eat..."

She slipped the spoon filled with broth into his mouth to keep him from talking. If it was full, he couldn't toss out more words.

While he chewed the piece of meat she gave him, he pushed the fabric of both her chemise and gown to the side. He tugged on the sleeves until the corsage pooled around her waist. "You could help me, you know."

"I am. I'm feeding you. You hopeless man! What more do you want me to do?"

She ached for his touch to find more intimate places. Understood they should not be pursuing this. When the devil was the laudanum going to kick in.

"Wish for you to lie down beside me. Naked as the day you were born." His words slowed. Became sluggish. He was falling asleep. The laudanum took long enough.

The drug was taking effect. Thank you. Kerrie held a tiny sigh inside. Waited for confirmation. The feeling was both relief as well as regret. She would miss him tonight. She wasn't going to sleep with him, naked or otherwise. With nothing to wear except what she had on, she would curl up in the chair in front of the burning fire.

The servants would wonder. Kerrie didn't care what anyone thought. Monney would never enter into the chamber to retrieve her clothing that would not be left outside the door.

Tam's wellbeing came first. She wasn't going to risk his life because of his ridiculous notion he was hale and hearty. The doctor said rest. Whether he liked it or not, she would give him rest. If necessary, she would enlist Monney to help her keep the duke's voracious appetites in check. An audience would inhibit the man. No, he'd order Monney or Mary or whoever came into the bedroom out.

~ * ~

Tam woke to a pounding head along with an empty, cold bed. He was used to Kerrie sleeping on top of him, her body warming him. Her beautiful legs entwined with his. Sometimes she slept spooned up tight next to him. She wasn't even in their bed. Where could she be? He opened his eyes wider, searching. In his direct line of sight, he could see nothing. She needed to be in the room. He'd locked the door. Gave commands to the servants. She had to be inside with him.

His arm throbbed. Beneath his breath, he cursed. His brain was muddled. Foggy from the drug the doctor gave him. His mouth felt as if it was filled with sawdust. He groaned. Tried to swallow.

"Tam..."

Kerrie sat beside the bed on the side he wasn't facing. Good, she stayed by him. "Water? The doctor has been here to check on you. He says you look good. Your wound shows no sign of infection. You're going to recover with no problems."

With another healthy groan he pushed himself to a sitting position. "Feel as if a dozen horses ran over me. All of me aches."

He knew she'd been right last night. Didn't wish to think how he would feel if she'd given into his demands. He'd had every intention of making love to his wife. She wouldn't allow it. Put him off until he fell asleep.

"That good?" she questioned him with a damn smile on her lips.

She was laughing at him. Wondered what happened last night just when he was heating her body. She would never have refused him. He knew though they didn't make love. "Imagine how you would feel now if I'd let you have your way with me last night. You would be a fire breathing dragon."

Those were his thoughts. Was she reading his mind?

His wife looked too damn smug for his peace of mind. His arm hurt so bad he didn't have one urge to make love to his wife. It must have been the laudanum easing his pain making him act a fool. The thing was he recalled everything. He remembered last night while he tried to coerce her to give in to his wishes. He touched her breasts. The tight hard crests. He wanted to see to her pleasure. Fondled dark secret places only he knew. Only he tasted. Caressed. Had wanted to make her cry out his name.

Tam needed to have her tell him she carried his child. She was too irritated with him last night to tell him. She must have conceived one of those first times they made love. He would be so pleased when she could confide in him, when she trusted him. Needed her to do so. All the time he made love with her, she never gave her all as she'd done that first week. While she responded, he sensed the change. Felt the difference in every nuance of her body as he saw to her sexual needs. Physical needs were sated, not the mental ones. Always she kept something of herself back from him. She no longer cried out his name at the instant she fragmented into thousands of pieces. The magical enchantment of the mating was missing. Afterward, she would turn from him, giving him her back. She was angry with him. He understood. How to change that situation wasn't apparent. That was something he had no answer for.

He despised that reaction of aloofness. Needed that to vanish. Didn't know how to go about making her feel different about him.

What he wished for was for Kerrie to cuddle next to him. Set her head in the hollow of his shoulder. Run her hands down his chest. After the sex, the ensuing moments were often better than the physical release. The tender intimate seconds were cherished by him. Just as he treasured as well as adored his wife.

What would it take to get those sensations back? His hunger for her would never end. When he looked at her the dreamlike fascination of her person shone through. Looking at the cold expression on her sweet face when he left her in the mornings, left ice water in his veins. She was the same in the evenings when she greeted him for dinner or in their bedchamber. Once he kissed her, charmed her, she melted in his arms and flowed all over him like warm honey. It was then he knew the heat of her reaction.

If he told her those things, explained to her that he cherished her, adored her, loved her, she would toss the title back in his face. Kerrie would tell him how much she loathed him. He couldn't risk that. The pain was too great for him to take that chance. He would never make himself that vulnerable. Shaking his head in irritation, he couldn't tell her his feelings until life between them was different. He didn't see that happening any time soon.

"You didn't sleep with me, your husband," he accused, his stress over her emotions changing to anger with her for doing what she wanted. "After that damn drug put me to sleep, you could have crawled in beside me. You didn't. I didn't have enough strength to seduce you. You knew that."

"You're right. I didn't. Had your health at the forefront of my mind. Need for you to recover. Didn't trust you or myself." Once again, her smile was smug, self-satisfied. "Slept on the chair in front of the fire. Believed that to be better for you. I've your best interest in mind. You should understand that little pertinent fact."

"You've changed your clothes," he accused again, his voice too harsh for the circumstances.

She didn't need his permission to dress in the morning. There it was though, the words spurting from his mouth before he could stem them. "How? I didn't give permission for clothing."

"As per your orders, Mary retrieved what I asked for. Did undress then dress by the fire. If you were not so weak that you slept the day away you would have noticed. Been up for a few hours. You truly didn't intend for me to spend the day wearing nothing at all. Did you? You did sleep through the morning as well as the lunch hour. Drake told me he would visit with you this afternoon. If you didn't allow me out of this small prison as well as clothing, Drake would see me naked. Would you like tea? Something to eat. You must be feeling hungry. The doctor said you could have soft food."

"Hate bloody tea. No one is seeing you naked but me!"

He was in the worst mood. Never been worse than the night she told him she hated him. Everything between them needed to change before he lost his bloody mind. This constant deep freeze exasperated him. Maddened him. He tried to bring her around with sex. He gave all that he could summon. Still, the woman froze him out of her life. He didn't know how to proceed. He needed advice from a person with experience.

"Water then," she tried to soothe his temper. "Food will be here soon. After you've eaten you will feel better."

Tam hated that too. He pushed the covers away, swiveling on the bed to put his feet on the floor. "Going to get dressed. I'll eat in the breakfast room. Don't wish to be served in bed."

Bloody eyes, he needed to relieve himself. He didn't think he could do that by himself. Asking his wife to help was out of the question.

"Only if Monney decides to listen to your orders. The doctor told him to listen to me. I would do what is best for you. Rest means you must stay in bed for today. Tomorrow, if the doctor says you are recovering, we can go downstairs. In your present condition you might take a tumble. Would need to fetch the doctor again. You would suffer an impediment to your healing." She lifted her shoulders, her damn feminine shoulders. "A fall might set you back another week."

She sounded too damn superior. He wouldn't allow that attitude. Wasn't used to defiance. "I'm the duke!" he roared. One more time he found himself losing his temper with her. Damn her beautiful hide. He acted out of character. As the stuffy duke, he needed to temper his emotions. Keep them hidden inside. For the next few minutes, he needed to get rid of her. "Send Monney to me." She couldn't refuse him that request.

"I'm the duchess," she countered with a matter-of-fact tone tilting her head with defiance, a smug smile on her mouth. When the door opened, she turned to greet whoever was coming into the room. "Set the tray on the little table." She put a small bedside table over him so he could eat in bed. Kerrie uncovered the dishes. "Smells good for porridge."

If he didn't find some relief soon, he was going to shame himself. "Send Monney." Figured if he calmed his voice, he would get better results.

"Why?"

With her question, his temper flared. Felt heat flush his face. This was too much. "None of your bloody business!" he shouted at her, refusing to let this go.

He needed a man to see to his needs. Couldn't admit the weakness to his wife. It would give her one more thing to beat over his head so she could have her way.

"My, my...your mood is getting worse," she paused as she began to figure out his problem. "I'll get him."

Her face turned beet red with the revelation as to why he wanted his butler.

He heard the amusement in her voice. Despite her apparent embarrassment, she was laughing at him. It had been years since he felt this helpless. A multitude of years since he needed help relieving himself. He couldn't command his household. His wife had control of his servants, even the butler. This had to end. He was the damn duke! His fist clenched. If he could, he would hit something. The wall looked like a suitable place for his tantrum.

Damned at the moment to be at the mercy of his duchess. His wife.

She hated him. That's what she told him.

Tam found he wanted to throw the bowl of porridge at the wall. His stomach grumbled. "Did the doc say I couldn't have a real breakfast?" He stared at the thick mush. Wanted bacon and eggs, a few fried potatoes wouldn't hurt.

"No, your cook decided all by himself this is what an invalid should eat. He's seeing to your best interest as am I. In this, I had nothing to do with breakfast. I would have ordered a feast for you. A good juicy steak might be nice. Something you could sink your teeth along with your nasty temper into. Alas, I didn't say anything to your cook. His feelings would have been hurt. Anything to stop the growling along with the grumbling that seems to be getting worse as we talk. Did anyone ever tell you that you are a horrible patient?"

"Never!"

He was taking this out on her. He wished his life to be back to normal. He needed to be in control again. To command his household. Why the bloody everlasting hell did he step in front of a bullet. He never wished to be a hero. Didn't even care about the two idiots who'd been arguing.

"Would you like a bath? Could have one ordered for you provided you can get out of bed," she smiled at him, smoothed her skirts that didn't need smoothing.

Tam had other plans if there was to be a bath. Yet he also understood he was in no condition to play. Last night he felt different. It must have been the laudanum talking to him. This morning with no pain killers in his system, he hurt. Throbbed everywhere. Pain even between his toes as well as beneath his tongue. His armpits hurt. Didn't want to admit to anyone least of all his wife that she had been right.

"It wasn't my bloody leg that was shot. Not only can I get out of bed, I can walk to the tub." His smile was wicked. "You can wash my back."

He forgot the weakness pulsing through his body. He had trouble sitting let alone walking.

"Oh, here is Monney. He will see to...all...your needs. I'll return when all is done here. If you can manage, I believe Monney will help you down the stairs. A walk down the stairs might soothe that temper of yours. The doctor didn't say you should waste away in bed all day. Told me a bit of walking would be good for you. As you say, it wasn't your...bloody leg that was shot. I'm going to see to my visitors. Ones, you invited, by the way. You have no right to intrude upon my time. Ask people to visit with me."

He watched her sashay her pretty little rear out the door, her skirts swinging. He wasn't about to call her back. Kerrie was right about all she told him. He scooped up a bite of the gruel, he'd been served. Spit it back into the bowl. The taste was God awful.

Monney stood at the door opened by his wife. "Sir, you have need of me?"

"Help me to the water closet. My legs are unsteady, shaking."

Asking for help went against the grain. He wanted to be there when her guests arrived. She was right. He invited the ladies to be accompanied by their daughters. Tam thought it would be good for her to get to know some of the women she would be associating with. The mothers were all old biddies. Their daughters presumptive. All expected to marry a title. Personally, he didn't like any of them...except Ella and Elizabeth.

"Very well, your grace," Monney said, the tone bland as if he kept his real thoughts in his head.

"After that you can get me into the tub. Don't wish to fall on my face. Drown, for that matter. Bring me something appropriate to wear to the meeting with the esteemed ladies of the ton who you will be letting onto the premises in a half hour. We will need to protect the duchess against their babbling. Kerrie won't understand what is happening."

After taking care of his most pressing needs, sinking into the tub, Tam let the heat of the water soothe both his body as well as his nerves. With every second he felt stronger and more in charge of himself. Once down those blasted steps, he would take charge of his household. The ache in his head along with his arm was not so blinding. He wished she'd stayed to wash his back, to share the tub. The way he'd been acting, he would have a hell of a time charming her into his bed tonight.

"If you ask my advice, not that you would have reason to do so," Monney volunteered with a complacent grin. "Did see similar behavior with your father and his duchess. A man needs to appreciate the needs of his woman. Take care of her. See to her desires. Not just sex. There is more to life than fulfilling one's lust. If you see to her other needs, she will be more receptive."

"Advice I could use. I've made a mess of this. What is it you want to say, Monney? You are a bachelor. Maybe a single man with a wealth of perspective can shed light on what I'm doing wrong. Believe me, I'm befuddled at the thought of figuring this out on my own. All I've tried has failed to bring her to heel."

He grimaced at the last word. Would a wife understand that term? Would she take umbrage with the thought.

*Of course, she would. You dolt!*

*I'm a dunderhead.*

"Might I say this is in part the problem. One doesn't bring the woman he is in love with to heel. That expression is crass. Distasteful. A woman needs to learn that her man cherishes her. One brings his dog to heel. Not his wife."

To Tam the way Monney said the single word brought his thoughts into a different perspective. "To heel? Crass? Truly? What is wrong with the phrase? It seems necessary, if a man is to have the woman the way he wants her to be. To heel, a woman needs to obey her husband just as a dog..."

"Yes, sir, If I may say so again, a woman is not a dog. She cannot be brought to heel because a man wills this to happen. Most women will balk at the training needed to be brought to heel. She will not follow by your side with her tongue lolling out, panting for you to acknowledge her, waiting for a pat on her head or a treat for good behavior. A woman who thinks with independent thoughts such as your duchess can never be brought to heel. If that is what you are striving for, no wonder you feel as if you are failing. I imagine you wed this woman because of her independent nature. Don't suppose you wish to change that part of her which you fell in love with."

Those words uttered by a confirmed bachelor gave Tam reason to think on the matter. "Never thought of my wife as a dog! What makes you say that? To heel. I would never..."

Tam knew. It was his words. Is that what he wanted? A wife who would never question his authority? Never argue with him? He didn't know what it was he thought.

"Sir, is this a conversation we should have? I don't want you to..."

Monney rubbed his hand along his neck as if to ease building tension. Crease lines formed on his brow.

"Yes!"

Tam found himself still frustrated, still shouting. This time his yelling was at his butler not his wife. The advice might be sound. He still didn't know how to continue. How did a man get what he wanted with an independent stubborn wife? One who had opinions of her own.

"Well then, I want your promise I won't lose my job if I answer your question with my honest judgement," Monney said as it seemed he had more to say on the matter. "There are other things. If I'm going to be straightforward with you, you won't appreciate anything I've got to say."

"Didn't expect I would," Tam mumbled, feeling a bit put in his place. Damn, Kerrie thought he treated her as he would his favorite hound? He never wished to sleep with his dogs. "I'd never fire you over advice I've asked for even though I might disagree or don't understand. Go on. What other pieces of wisdom do you have to expound upon? I need to have something in my arsenal."

"You, yourself, said you wanted to bring her to heel. One cannot tame a woman who possesses such spirit as your duchess. She is too vibrant, too alive to subdue. You would never appreciate the new woman if you managed to squash her spirit. You must learn to ride the wind with her, to sway as well as bend with her ever-changing moods. She is unique. A one of a kind. There is no one like her." Monney cleared his throat with a pause then a look to the door as if he wished to escape. "And..." It seemed he didn't wish to continue.

Tam stood from the bath. Dripping, he found a towel to wrap around his waist. "Don't wish to tame my wife or make her believe she has no bloody say in what goes on in this household. She told me she hated me! Bloody everlasting hell! How does a man deal with that? I'd like to know. You've advice on that? How do I change her so she will love me? She loved me the first week we were married. She even said the words once."

Tam felt heat flush his face. That was much more than he should expound to a servant. He overstepped all boundaries between servant and lord.

"If I may be so bold, you should not take away her freedom to wear clothing or not. Making her set her clothes outside the door at night is appalling as well as demeaning. There is chatter among your servants. That is never good. Something stupid you ordered without thinking of the consequences." He held up his hands to stop the reply the man knew would be forthcoming. "I understand your clothing is also kept in another room. Nonetheless, that is solely to keep her from donning one of your shirts. Is it not? There is no fair play here. Your wife is at your mercy. That is not being reasonable."

"Don't want anything in the way when I make love to her. Don't wish to remove clothing. She needs to be ready for me. Eager." Tam looked up, the flush of heat deepening. "She would wear...one of those white virginal gowns that come to her chin if I gave her the choice. Don't want that. The first week we were wed..." again he said too much. The first week of marriage was perfect. Wanted those sweet moments back.

"This is none of my business though I would think if you told her that you loved her, the sentiment would go a great distance in curing your problem. A woman wants to know the man she married is in love with her."

*I do love her. I've never told her. Except that one time, she's never said anything to me about her feelings other than she hated me.*

"Why the bloody everlasting hell should I do that when she doesn't return the sentiment? When she hates me? She told me that! She told me she detests the ground where I walk!"

Tam slowly paced the room trying to calm his breaking nerves, his energy returning. Control, restraint, was what he needed where his fractious wife was concerned. He searched for the clothing that was supposed to be laid out ready for him. Found the appropriate attire. Still dripping and hopping on one foot then the other he managed to put on the dark blue pants. His shirt stuck to the dampness of his chest. He raked his hands through his wet hair.

"Again, this is not my place to say but I can tell you for certain, your wife loves you. She says it with her eyes every time she looks your way. You should be a man well pleased."

"She does?"

Tam was shocked then thrilled to the tips of his toes. He was still pushing damp hair from his face, astounded by his butler's comment. "Kerrie loves me?" He didn't believe the words. Not for one second. Wanted to believe with all his heart. "Why the hell hasn't she told me! No, she doesn't. Kerrie told me she hated me. Doesn't wish to be my duchess."

Monney lifted his shoulders. "Maybe she doesn't say the words because you don't. Someone has to break the ice. You do know she hated the title. Not you. Come to terms with that. Change the way you act toward your wife. When she understands you love her, she will come around. As it stands, she thinks you want her for the heir she will conceive and nothing more."

Ice, was what lay between them when she wasn't in his arms melting for him. He needed the warmth to extend past the bed, the night as well as the morning. Tam didn't want to spend all his time away from her just so he wouldn't feel frozen by her hate.

*Tell her I love her.*

"Good idea, Monney. Any thoughts on when I should do this?" When he was making love, she would never believe him. She would think it a ploy to get his way.

"Would be best if you showed her then told her you've had a change of heart. Tonight. Have her trunk as well as yours brought to the room. Give her a choice of what to wear during the evening hours. Maybe that virgin's night gown you spoke of or the flimsy negligee you gifted her with the other day. I'll have wine and cheese left on a tray for the two of you. A couple of bottles of your finest." He smiled that self-satisfied smile as if he'd done his good deed for the day. "Don't glower at her or yell. Remaining calm would go a long way to reassure her that you are thinking of her first. You of all people do know how to be calm. You are known as the stuff..."

"I don't yell!"

He didn't yell before she told him she hated him. Before he met her. Tam detested the smug look on his butler's face. The man didn't need to say another word. He sat down on a chair to put on the boots the man handed him. Where was his valet? The man was never there when he needed him.

As if Monney heard his thoughts, "You scared the poor man away. Suppose an apology would be in order if you expect better service. In your present mood the words might not have the desired outcome. More advice after that I'll let you go. Don't seek him out until your present circumstances with the missus is the way you like."

"Don't know how to be romantic." Tam tugged on his boots, grunting. Looking up, he spoke.

"Have that wine and cheese ready when it's time to retire. No sooner. After these ladies leave this afternoon. Don't know why I invited them. After we get them on their way, I'll bring Kerrie to the room for a bit of afternoon delight. Have those trunks in our chamber. Want to give her time to make choices."

"I'm certain you had good reasons for your little *faux pas*. Women do have a way of muddling a man's brain. As to your invitation to the guests, I am also certain there was a good reason. Though the invitations might turn out to be a huge mistake. Not at all certain your wife is ready for the unleashed hatred that might be hurtled her way."

"Hatred? These were women he thought he trusted with her. Don't recall why I did what I did. Just seemed right. Revulsion? Ella said I should introduce her to some of the ladies of the ton. Problem is...all these ladies have daughters. None of whom I like. Some of their daughters are worse than their mothers. The one thing and one thing only on their minds when it comes to choosing their husband is a title coupled with wealth. Which was why I always looked beyond these women."

"The doting mamas saw you as a prospective groom. The daughters as a title along with your wealth. You were worth a great deal to any woman looking for a husband. Now, you've been taken. You are no longer on the market. If I were you, I would protect Kerrie from the sting of their barbs. Protect her from the past, from the hatred spewed in the malicious gossip columns even in the front page of the London Times."

"He thought of the drawings he kept from her. Thought of all he'd kept away so she wouldn't be hurt. He was afraid he unleashed demons more threatening than the opening of Pandora's box. I don't know. Yes... This isn't going to go well. Is it? Would love to chase the ladies away before they arrive. We could put a note on the door as to the change of plans. Could say we went to the country estate. That would be good."

"Not well done at all the way I see it. Not after you and the duchesses were pictured in the London Times. Both naked. Arms as well as legs entwined and well..." He lifted his shoulders as if to emphasize his words. "If those pictures are brought up, your duchess will not fare well."

Tam grimaced at the implications he was imagining. These women would also have seen the drawing. He was recognizable. Her face wasn't. What didn't matter now would be the assumption that Kerrie was the woman in the drawing. The woman, as the caption read, he was cavorting with. The woman who didn't live by the rules. The woman who wasn't worthy to become a duchess.

Once more his anger surfaced. "I saw the drawing!"

Would he ever stop shouting? Tam didn't think so. Not until he had his life the way he wanted it to be. On an even keel, Kerrie, loving and in his arms, warm as well as tender, was what he needed. Her forgiveness more than anything. They wouldn't return to the country for another week. They needed more privacy to improve the relationship. Shaky ground would best describe what they had together. Their marriage was on unstable ground. Nothing was in order.

"Do you think the mothers and their daughters saw the drawings too?"

"Would be shocked if they didn't," was Monney's bland reply to his question. "May I be excused. Someone needs to be downstairs to allow the ladies entrance when they arrive. The duchess along with her daughter should be here first. Give your wife support if she needs an assisting hand. The hoard should be here any minute. As soon as you are ready, call me. I'll help you down the stairs."

"To run interference, don't you mean. Without a doubt they will attack Kerrie. She hasn't seen the drawing. Nor does she have any idea anything like that existed before we were wed. The sight will be a total surprise. Mortified might describe what she will feel. All the papers in both the Montgomerie residence and mine were burned. Destroyed so she wouldn't learn who I am." She would know why she didn't see the papers. Would blame me. All the headlines sported his title. This would be one more lie he would need to explain. He was sinking into a quagmire of his making. He didn't know how to swim his way out of this. Knew he could never have done anything different.

"I'm on my way. Don't know what I can do if those doting mamas you spoke of decide to attack. These women can be vicious. Their cannons loaded they will blast Kerrie straight out of the water. Your duchess doesn't possess anything malicious in her arsenal. Has no big guns in her armory. Wouldn't know how to use them if she did." Monney turned on his well-polished heel then exited the room with the intent to rescue his lady.

Tam was left to stare at the door, his mouth gaping open at all that had been learned. She loved him. Could his butler be correct? Well...even though it hurt to recount the words, Tam never believed she hated him. She even told him later that she disliked what he did...the lie of omission.

At night, Kerrie melted in his arms.

He always saw to her pleasure.

Was that enough for a woman to fall in love? There had to be more to this love thing. Didn't there? She agreed to the marriage even though she told him she never meant to tie herself to a man...a man with a title behind his name. Kerrie wanted to be independent. Free. Her freedom was important to her.

He told her he would negotiate.

So far in this marriage there had been no tender negotiations as he'd imagined, as he told her there would be. All thoughts of compromise changed when she told him she hated him. She didn't hate him. She loathed his title. After she saw the drawings, she would despise him...his lies of omission. The falsehoods that suited his agenda. He stole a huge gulp of air from the room. The scent of Kerrie lingered here even after his bath. The rumpled bed sheets reminded him of his wife. The way she looked stretched out on the mattress wearing nothing at all.

Fixing this was his first priority. Monney gave him food for thought. Though, telling her he loved her, even though he believed he did, would not happen until he felt more confident. Not, where she was concerned. He floundered. A fish out of water, flapping around on the ground with no oxygen to sustain him. That was the way he felt.

~ * ~

"The duke chose that slut over my daughter!"

She was talking to no one, only herself. Lady Mulligan stared between the luncheon invitation and the drawing of the naked couple cavorting in the secluded glade. Iris would never do something so lewd as frolic naked in the open where anyone would see her. She was a good girl. She was. Not like...not like that harlot. She had been taught to hold her favors until the wedding night. This commoner...peasant...knew nothing of moral values. She gave herself to the earl for the title along with his wealth. The woman was a whore...a slut.

Lady Mulligan tapped the engraved invitation on her desk, thoughtful. Her first inclination had been to decline the luncheon in favor of doing something less unsavory. Now, to confront that brazen hussy was foremost on her mind. It wasn't too late to abort the ill-conceived marriage. The duke must have discovered she wasn't a virgin the first time he pushed his rod into her. While she couldn't see the woman's face, it was obvious to anyone with a brain, the couple were the duke and his peasant wife. A duchess, bah, the woman didn't deserve the title. She was a commoner.

She would do her best to set the wheels in motion for an annulment...no it would have to be a divorce. Stirling Talmadge would divorce his wife of a month to marry her daughter.

Perfect!

Iris should have been the bride to Sterling all along. Her upbringing was proper and impeccable. She was just as stuffy. She would never let the man do anything untoward to her person before the wedding. The pair weren't married when the drawing was published. If he discovered her whoring ways that day, why did he say his vows? She must have her claws deep into him in some other way. Some unknown treachery must be behind the hasty wedding. The discovery would be worth her time. She meant to look into this woman's background.

"Iris, you look fetching this afternoon," she said, staring at her daughter as she stepped into the room to put a stop to her musing.

Iris whirled, her skirts billowing around her. "Thank you, Mama." She waltzed over to her mother, placed a chaste kiss on her cheek. "I'm ready to go. This luncheon will be so much fun. I will meet his duchess. She is lovely, don't you think? They seem to be a perfect match for each other."

Her daughter was far too gullible and naïve. She found herself shaking her head. Iris didn't hate the woman who stole the duke from her, the title along with the wealth. Why, it had been expected since they were children that they would become man and wife when she came of age.

"Come, we'll be there in a few minutes. We'll take the coach."

"The coach?"

"Don't want to mess up your lovely gown or your hair. Want to make a good impression when you meet the new duchess." Lady Mulligan slipped the drawing into her reticle. She had plans. Big plans. If she could humble the woman, she would enjoy the process. Wanted to see her eyes bulge when she presented the picture as proof the woman was a trollop.

They weren't the first to arrive. Lady Montgomerie and her daughter, Elizabeth, arrived in front of them, given entrance by the stodgy butler who was employed here. They were shown to the outside patio. Warm sunshine, unseasonable for this time of year, filtered through the overhead lattice giving the area a pleasant ambiance. Lady Talmadge sat next to Elizabeth, chatting and sipping on some drink. There were tarts and small cakes. Triangular cut finger sandwiches donned a plate that also held an assortment of cheese and meat.

Lady Talmadge rose, nodding her greeting. "I'm happy that you were able to attend this first luncheon of mine. Seems my husband along with my aunt decided on the invitations. Who was to come. This is perfect."

She shot her aunt a look that Lady Mulligan didn't know how to read. Though it was obvious there was some derision between them.

"Oh, this is so wonderful," Iris spouted as she smiled then spoke her warm greeting. "I'm so excited to meet you. I've known Sterling ever since I can remember. He's always been so sweet to me. You are very lucky. He's a wonderful man. A true gentleman in every conceivable way."

Her mother shot her a look that tried to tell her to act the lady. She was far too exuberant. She nodded to Lady Talmage.

"Call me Kerrie. I don't hold to the formality. We should be..." Kerrie looked to Ella who nodded her approval. "We could be friends."

Lady Mulligan whipped past Kerrie to greet Ella. Nudged her as she walked past. "Good afternoon, Lady Montgomerie. So, I have you to thank for the invitation? You understand this is nice, but my Iris was supposed to wed Sterling. They have known each other forever. Since they were children. As my daughter said, the duke was always sweet with her."

"Believe in their case the heart spoke up. These two are very much in love. Tam dotes on Kerrie. Would give his duchess anything she asked for."

Ella's voice was all sugar and spice. She smiled at Lady Mulligan as if that would diffuse her.

Lady Mulligan made a hrmf noise in the back of her throat. "Nonetheless, that drawing on the front page of the London Times should have put her on notice. A woman who would do such a thing should not be almost royalty. As a duchess she is down just a peg from the princesses."

"You are out of line," Ella told her, her voice cutting through the chatter around her. "I strongly suggest you change your tone. I am related to Kerrie. Her well-being is important to me."

"Mother!" Iris shouted, sounding shocked. "Lady Talmadge has turned pale. Oh, get the smelling salts, I'm afraid she might faint."

Lady Mulligan smiled, feeling as if everything she planned was coming to fruition. What else could go better. Soon Iris would be in line to marry the duke. "I'm certain the peasant is of sturdier stock than that. This is pretense. It isn't as if she is a true lady. Peasants don't faint. She is faking the distress."

Ella stood, her hands fisted. "Believe you should leave. Now!"

"Be pleased to leave the presence of that woman." She was pointing her finger at Kerrie. She drew out the paper with the drawing before tossing the London Times on Kerrie's lap. "A true lady doesn't do that. Cavort naked!"

# Chapter Ten

Kerrie stared at the picture in front of her, all her blood pooling into her feet. Lady Mulligan was right. She was sturdy. Made from hale and hearty parents who taught her to stand up on her own. They were commoners just as she was. Fainting was not part of her makeup. The drawing was well done. The artist captured Tam's handsome features to perfection. While her face was muddled, it was obvious the woman he was coupling with was her. They even drew the mole on her buttocks. This was not fiction. Whoever drew this was in the romantic glade. Watching. She felt as if she died a thousand times when her mind sorted out the picture to realize it was of her as well as Tam.

In the background, she heard her aunt ushering Lady Mulligan along with her daughter from the room. The commotion inside continued. The other women began to chatter their opinion of her along with the drawing. No one supported her or gave indication that they might be sympathetic except Ella and Elizabeth.

What Kerrie didn't understand was why Tam never showed this drawing to her. Why he kept the rendering of them making love from her. She doubted it was this morning's paper. Had to have been drawn weeks ago then published. Another paper was tossed down. The drawing depicted them riding Dex together. His hands were roaming, exploring her as he liked to do. Embarrassment didn't come close to describing her feelings.

Mortified.

Humiliated.

Her stomach churned. Somersaulted several times. She wanted to stand up, run, hide. Needed the peacefulness of the country life. Kerrie wasn't suited for life in the city among these people who took the first opportunity to shun her. She would never be welcomed into this arrogant group of titled aristocrats. All her opinions of people with titles were substantiated. She had to leave before everything got worse. The last thing she wanted was to make life crueler for Tam. She loved him too much to ruin him.

She imagined there wasn't anywhere she could hide. Her feet didn't work. Kerrie understood she couldn't stay in London. Had to go home where she felt comfortable. Where her life wasn't turned upside down. Must leave before Tam could stop her. He told her they would travel home in a week. She needed to do so today. Now!

Breathe.

Breathe in...breathe out. One more breath will help ease the ache. Nothing would stop the pain. Minutes ticked by, signaled by the grandfather clock near the door to the drawing room. No one was left here except Ella along with Elizabeth. Ella managed to chase the rest of the ill-meaning women from the premises. Silence engulfed all her thoughts. The shaking of her body didn't surprise.

A glass was shoved toward her. "Drink."

Without emotion, Kerrie sipped. The liquid burned on its way down. She sipped again. Coughing this time as it plummeted into her empty stomach. She did feel better. Finished the brandy before holding the glass out to ask for more. Fortification would help her get through the next few hours it would take to reach her home.

The glass refilled. She drank again. Let the heat soothe its way down her throat. Kerrie set the glass down. She turned to Ella. "Get Monney for me. I...just get him. Please."

She had so much to do. She would leave. Tam would be better off without her. Didn't need to pack. Left some clothing at the Montgomerie estate. She would send for the rest of her things once she got to Sherburn Hall.

"I'll go," Elizabeth volunteered then tore out of the room.

"Monney! Where are you? Monney!" Elizabeth called out. "Monney!"

Kerrie drug in a long breath of air. Taking control of the moment, she waited for the butler to emerge. She hoped he would treat her request without asking for Tam's approval. Her hands were clasped together.

Thoughts of Tam rifled through her head. He would be angry when he discovered she left him. She wasn't leaving him, just the degradation heaped upon her by cruel women. The bath had been ordered. He should be finished by now and dressed. He would need help maneuvering the steps. He was in no condition to argue or chase after her. She wondered if he even wanted to chase after her.

She had to leave. Had to disappear. Wished to leave before he could make it downstairs. Her heart raced while she waited for Monney, for Elizabeth to return to tell her the butler was coming.

For her, now that she understood what these not so good people thought of her, there was no choice. She couldn't go to another ball or dinner party. Couldn't go to the theater or Vauxhall Garden. Couldn't stay with the man she loved. Just couldn't. Not here in London. He could come to the city. She would never accompany him. Never!

*With the man I love.*

No! Needed to be gone before her husband stopped her. He would. Tam would tell her this was nothing to fret over. She could weather any storm. In a few days the gossip would be about someone else. That was what she wished for...to weather every storm that blew her way. Not this one, not this time. Now, she needed to figure out how to fight her way through the tempest surrounding her. She needed to come to terms with the naked depiction of her along with what people thought of her. To Kerrie it was clear the snobbish aristocratic women didn't believe she was good enough for Sterling Talmadge, the Duke of Sherburn.

She couldn't though. This was not the life she wanted. It wasn't the title she detested. It was what went with it. All these horrible things that accompanied the title. No! This was not what she wanted.

Snobbery.

Unkindness.

Cruelty.

"How do you put up with this?" Kerrie asked her aunt with whispered words then searched Elizabeth's expression. "You must have been ostracized when Uncle Drake took you to the hunting lodge. Everyone knew about the venture. Believed he compromised you. That was not at all well-done of him. He was horrible to treat you that way.

Tam didn't compromise me. Didn't take my innocence until our wedding night. He was a gentleman though he did...well...you saw the picture. He did other things."

Ella held her hands in hers. She met her gaze then answered her question. "Yes, as you must surmise, the first year was difficult. More than difficult. Horrible. While Drake was applauded for his brash actions, I was shunned. Your uncle did all he could to ease my way into the society I married into. I also am of peasant stock...a commoner...made from sturdy stock. It does the ton good. Interbreeding with the common folk never hurts. New blood so to say."

Kerrie was looking at her hands trying to tell Ella what was in her mind. "I'm leaving. After I'm gone, will you tell Tam what I did as well as why. Tell him I had to go where I wouldn't be forced to look over my shoulder for the verbal knives directed my way. Don't wish to spend the next week wondering what bit of horrific news will drop at my feet. I had no idea about those renditions of the two of us."-

"Where...leaving to...?" Ella questioned. Her head tilted to the right as if she was trying to see into her mind. "You're not going home? Are you?" There was both panic coupled with disapproval in her tone. "Your parents will send you back. There is no reason why you can't hold your head high. You've done nothing wrong."

"Home yes, but not what you are thinking. Going home to Tam's and my home. I feel comfortable there, in the country. Never been a city girl. Robert and Talbot are nice to me. Imagine they've seen those drawings also. Believe everyone there did their very best to keep them from me. They also hid the fact he was a lord of the realm. They liked me. Respected my position. They must approve of the match. I'm going home," she finished. "Home where I belong. Where I might be loved."

"I'm certain they have seen the two drawings. We all hid them from you before the vows were said. Both were in the London Times before the wedding. Drake had them all burned. Tam didn't wish to risk you're telling him no at the altar. He loves you enough to do all in his power to keep you from leaving him. Believe, in case you are wondering, that was your uncle's intentions when he propositioned me. Told me if I didn't go with him, he would never give me a second glance. Couldn't risk him abandoning me. I loved him the moment I saw him. It was as if I was struck by a lightning bolt. The French call the occurrence, '*coup de foudre.*' Love at first sight. That was what happened to me. Imagine that was what you also felt. If not, you would have never agreed to his marriage proposal."

"Yes, me too. I saw him and I found myself lost in the blue-gray shimmer of his eyes." Kerrie was having second along with third thoughts about leaving him. Ella was correct in her assumption that she was running away. She should stand and fight for the man she loved. Not today or tomorrow, there was no fight in her. At night, she would miss having his arms around her. During the days she never saw him. He always found reasons to stay away.

"Would you reconsider staying here? I would..." Ella shrugged. "I don't know what to do. I understand that you would wish to leave. The Duchess, the original duchess, helped me through all my hard times. The wedding was interesting. All my cousins and sisters were there."

"No, Tam would need to ask me to stay. He won't do that. In his brash way, he would command. Besides, I doubt if he wishes to meet with our departed guests." If Tam would ask her to stay, ask being the important word here, she would reconsider. There were other changes that would need to be made if she were to remain with him. Tam would never grant her a divorce. He did, however, say they could negotiate.

Let the negotiations begin.

Monney appeared with Elizabeth leading the way. "Found him at the top of the stairs. Was going to see to the duke. Told him at this moment you were more important. The duke could wait. Sounds irreverent but I'm used to the way mother deals with father. A person needs to learn what is most important at the moment."

"Thank you, Elizabeth," Kerrie said before turning her attention to the butler. "Please have the ducal coach in front of the house as soon as possible."

Monney bowed, "As you wish. Should I tell the duke?"

"No! No, I must not bother him. He's been wounded. Doesn't need distractions. Aunt Ella will explain to Tam everything he needs to know."

She paced, watching Monney for the betrayal she knew would

come. The man was adamantly loyal to Tam.

"It will take a few minutes to get the horses as well as the driver around to the front. He was not expecting to go anywhere this afternoon." Monney said his tone dry. "I might have to search for him."

"I'm certain summoning the man will not take that long. He is at the beck and call of the duke as well as...I assume, the duchess. Am I not the duchess? Summoning him now should not take long at all. Five minutes at the most." Kerrie was surprised to hear the authority in her voice. She didn't expect to take to the role this easily. "Do have the coach here in ten minutes. I'll be waiting outside the door. Not a moment longer."

"Ten minutes," Monney bowed again then turned on his heel heading for the door. Muttering to himself about the duchess.

He was grumbling now as he walked. Talking to himself. Not liking the command. "The duke's not going to like this. Not one bit. Not after he planned a romantic dinner for the two of them. He's going to be beside himself. Don't like it when he's angry. Takes his fury out on all of us. He yells. Don't like it when he yells."

"A romantic dinner?" Ella asked, looking at her with a quirky smile on her lips. "You are certain you want to leave. Romance between the two of you sounds nice. Earlier I heard rumors about your clothing being returned to you. Your husband might be turning over a new leaf, so to speak. His main objective might be to make his wife happy."

Kerrie snorted. She understood it was just a rumor. There would be no truth to that. Tam wouldn't change that much. "No. Tam doesn't realize how much the servants talk. He won't return anything to the room. Not as long as he..." She didn't know what she intended to say. "He believes I hate him. I...I don't..."

Unwanted moisture rose to her eyes. She tried to force the wetness to disappear. Tears ran down her cheeks. What he believed was her fault.

Ella reached out to pat Kerrie's hand. "You need to convince him otherwise. Since you did say the damning words, it's up to you to prove to the poor man you don't feel any hatred toward him. If you would like some well-meaning advice, ease his broken heart. Go to the man. Tell him you love him. Heard he's been yelling at everyone, even Monney he's in such a foul mood. Do you think that's because of you? I know with Drake if we argue, he's the same way. Yells at everyone in his employ. Never takes his anger out on me."

She stiffened her shoulders rejecting her aunt's advice. "Why? Why should I tell him an untruth?" Regretted the words as soon as she uttered them.

"Is it untrue?" Ella asked as she questioned with her eyes. "I believe you do love Tam more than you wish to admit. Have you forgiven the poor man for keeping the knowledge of his title from you? He has given you much you never sought or asked for. It was not his fault he was born to aristocracy. Are you willing to allow both of you to suffer the rest of your lives because of that one monstrous default he has no control over?"

"Yes...until today. Today I was met with every reason I despise; people with titles...except for a few. Those women were horrible. They said things... I can't forgive."

"There are a lot of titled people in your family. You cannot feel the same disgust for all of us. Besides, it wasn't Tam who said ridiculous things about you. It was doting mothers who thought their daughters were in line for the title you bear. Raise your chin. You are made of sterner stuff."

"My cousins and aunts who bear titles are cut from a different cloth than the women along with their daughters who visited this afternoon."

Kerrie understood her aunt was right about so many things. "Why did you invite those ladies? They came at your invitation."

"Didn't realize they were so conniving. The Mulligans have been friends with the Talmadges for years and years. I've the feeling though there is more here than I realized. After giving this some thought it was apparent Lady Mulligan fancied Robert. Your father chose a different woman for his wife. Now, she believed that her Iris should be the one Tam married. He chose you instead. She was furious she was thwarted twice. She hopes to make you an object of loathing. Really dear, you should stand and fight. Running from this will give your enemies more ammunition to fire at you. Blast them with all your cannons. Stand firm and they'll retreat. That's what I did. Though...it did take me some time to organize myself against the hatred."

Kerrie was shaking her head. "Don't have any cannons to blast at any one. No...not this time. I can't do that. I need to regroup. I was blindsided. Caught off guard. Now, all my emotions are out of kilter. All I once thought I understood is turned upside down. Maybe in time, I can do as you suggest."

"I will stand by you, your decision." Ella said as she rose.

Monney stood in the entrance again. "The carriage is ready and waiting for you."

"Thank you, I understand it's hard for you to go against what you believe the duke will wish. If you can manage this request, don't tell him for another fifteen minutes or so. He's injured. He won't come after me. He shouldn't. The stitches..."

The butler bowed. He remained silent while he escorted Kerrie to the coach. She understood that as soon as she was inside and the vehicle was trundling down the road, he would race upstairs to inform Tam. Assuming anything different would be a waste of good time. She didn't have fifteen minutes. She might not even have that, if Monney told him when she ordered the carriage.

In the coach, she covered herself with the lap rug that was kept beneath the seats. Kerrie leaned back. Closed her eyes, listening to the sounds of the horses. She wasn't surprised when twenty minutes later Tam wasn't there. Her assessment of the situation was right. She didn't know if she should be happy or sad about that. He didn't want her. All the rumors about a romantic dinner were false.

A few hours ago, he couldn't get out of bed by himself. Less than twenty-four hours passed since he became a notorious hero. Her husband wouldn't miss her until it was time to climb into bed with her. She paused trying to think with logic rather than the emotions which plagued her. "No, the man would miss her at night when he made love to her then in the morning hours when he did the same," she murmured as she thought about all the goings on for the last weeks. He never looked her way during the day. Lust drove him not romantic notions of love.

"Hold! Stop the coach I'm coming on board. Think I'll strangle my wife for this. Tie my horse behind. We're turning around."

Half asleep at the time, Kerrie jerked up in disbelief. She knew that voice. Knew the tone very well. Heard the strained tone. Tam shouldn't be out riding. He was supposed to rest. He could open the stitches.

*Tam...*

A wave of guilt swamped her as the coach rolled to a stop. Tam pulled open the door. With strain etched on his features, white lines around his mouth and eyes, he pulled himself inside. He lay back, his eyes closed. Tension lines were imprinted on his face. His breathing was shallow and quick, his face pale. The man was a fool. An idiot.

She leaned over. Reached out a hand to touch then quickly brought her fingers back to her lap. "Tam, what are you doing here? You're not supposed to be out of bed, let alone riding pell-mell across the countryside."

He grinned. The smile was weak. "What do you think I'm doing here? Bringing you home. My wife belongs with me. Where I am she will also be." The words were also tired. "Want to be in bed but not without you."

"You shouldn't be here."

Kerrie was shocked by his presence along with the pallor of his face. He never should have ridden after her. He was given permission to be downstairs this afternoon, not to ride for twenty minutes. He would have raced. She caused this.

"My wife isn't where she belongs." He shrugged his broad shoulders as if that wasn't nonsense. "Had to do something about that little problem. To bring her home where she belongs is the reason I went out riding."

He was looking at her. She was shaking her head to deny that bit of nonsense. "I'm going home. Can't stay in London under these circumstances." Kerrie tried for control of the situation. Failed. The coach wasn't going to move until he gave the order... Unless he ordered the vehicle back to London before he got inside. She did hear some chatter.

"I'm in London. You are staying with me," he gritted out through what appeared to be clenched teeth. "A good wife stays with her husband. I've plans with you for tonight. Didn't expect to have to come after you. This little escapade of yours has exhausted me. If you don't mind, I'd like to sleep until we return."

They weren't getting anywhere with this conversation. Furious with his arrogant assumptions, she shot back, "A good husband doesn't invite vipers into his home for his wife to visit with. Ella told me you approved the guest list." She leaned forward, pointing her finger at him. "A good husband doesn't hide things from his wife. Such as nude drawings...of her...with him. Imagine how I felt when the London Times was tossed under my nose a few hours ago. I was naked! Everyone in the town saw me wearing nothing!"

He had the good grace to grimace as well as flush a deep red as he ran his hand along the back of his neck. "I thought they were good people. Had no idea Lady Mulligan believed I would marry her daughter. Hell, the girl is more like a sister to me. Could never bed the lady. Besides, she's a bit of a twit. Don't enjoy twits. Thank God you're not a twit."

It seemed he was growing stronger. What the devil was a twit? "Does your arm hurt? Your head? Last time I saw you, you were in too much pain to leave your bed by yourself," she accused, pointing a finger at his chest. "Now, you certainly risked opening your stitches. I'm going to have to check them."

"You can do anything you wish to this man's body when we return." He grinned at her as it was becoming apparent he was regaining his strength.

Like it or not, Kerrie understood she was returning to London. The carriage began to move. She could tell it was turning. She was so close to freedom. Not freedom from her husband. Freedom from the other constraints that were put on her. She wanted to be more than a brood mare to him. Needed not a lot but a touch of freedom would help.

"What did Ella tell you about this afternoon?"

Maybe he should have all the information. He might change his mind about making her go with him. He could decide to leave London a week sooner.

"Monney told me more than your aunt. He has this way of knowing everything that is going on. I'm sorry about what happened. After the first week, I didn't think you would ever see the drawings. Didn't want you to see them. Knew you would be embarrassed. Devastated. Mortified. Didn't believe anyone at the luncheon this afternoon would want to harm you." His heavy sigh left her wishing she could forgive him. "It's obvious I was wrong."

"Another lie of omission?" she queried, her voice soft. "Seems you excel at leaving me clueless. If I'd known about the drawings, I might not have been knocked breathless when Lady Mulligan tossed the paper in front of me. I felt so humiliated. I was naked. All of London saw me with you, wrapped in your arms."

"How would you have felt if you saw them earlier? I'm guessing no different than now. If it's any consolation, I'm sorry. Thought beyond any doubt we lost the man following us that day. Dex raced his heart out to get away from the reporter. I was also wrong about that." He sucked in air then leaned forward, running his knuckles along her cheek. "I've been wrong about too many things to keep count of. Not used to being wrong."

"You thought wrong," she agreed with a shaky voice.

"I did."

"You don't plan on giving me a choice now, do you?" The question was pointless when she knew the answer. He would never turn the coach around again.

"No, no choice in this. There isn't a ghost of a chance I can ride back to London. The coach has to take me...us. I've a dinner planned for the two of us. Of all things it was Monney's suggestion. He's tired of me yelling at him. My valet is hiding from me. I don't yell at people, especially not my servants. Never have until now. No one will come see to my needs except Monney. He is so loyal he doesn't know how to stay away."

"I'm not hungry."

She turned away from the man who stole her heart the first time she saw him. *Coupe de foudre.* She needed to school herself against his easy seduction. She imagined she would once again be naked in his room. A dinner while they ate without the benefit of clothing. In this new atmosphere, she was still too self-conscious to be at ease with that scenario. The food always lodged in her throat. She had to wash it away with wine. Sometimes too much wine. Didn't like being tipsy all the time.

~ * ~

When he learned of Kerrie's departure, anger suffused his body so hard he shook. After Monney and Ella told him what happened he managed to calm himself. She didn't deserve to be chased from her home, from him by cruel, unthinking women. He was too furious to call the women ladies. What they were, were harpies. What he understood from the brief conversations with both Ella along with Monney was that Lady Mulligan hoped to stir up a hornet's nest of conflict. The lady thought her actions would result in a divorce. Nothing would cause him to divorce Kerrie or sign papers even if she wished for her freedom. He didn't believe she would want a divorce. She was so responsive when he made love to her. He was certain she carried his child. Tam wanted her to love him as he did her.

Now he was here, winded as well as in pain. His arm throbbed. He ached everywhere. Monney lectured him about riding after her. Told him she was only leaving London to go to his country home where she felt comfortable. Damn, he needed help to mount his horse. Felt like a damn cripple when he had to have a boost just to get his leg over the saddle to the other side. To make his way down the stairs, he had to lean the bulk of his considerable weight on his butler. Monney told him to let her go. Told him keeping her here would do him no good to force her to his will. His wife needed time to form some conclusions on her own. Being away from him would give her time to accept what happened. Accept the fact what they said was not his doing. She would be happier in the country with his father.

Tam couldn't do that. Couldn't let her go. He needed to be able to hold his wife, to reassure her. Ella told him she turned the color of death when she saw the reprehensible depiction of them on the front page. The scandal would vanish as soon as someone else did something foolish. Everyone would forget the horrible drawing. The gossip would end. Even this long after the event the rumors died to nothing. It was Lady Mulligan who stirred up the embers of gossip. She needed to give fuel to the fire for her own wishes. It was cruel in the extreme. What happened that afternoon was all his making. He needed to convince her that marrying him was a good idea. That was the only way he could think of to bind her to him more thoroughly than ever before. He wanted to give her so much pleasure she could never tell him no. If it was any consolation, his actions worked. She agreed.

He was here in the ducal coach with his wife. Their first conversations were queries. Now she was silent, staring out the window as the trees passed them by. Tam hoped the changes he made for her that Monney suggested would suit. Would end the aloof coldness between them. He'd been a befuddled fool with straw for brains. Before the night ended, he prayed she would tell him about her possible pregnancy. He understood it was too soon to know. She couldn't be certain yet. Even if she had been two months into the pregnancy the real possibility of a miscarriage existed. If that happened, he didn't wish for her to bare the pain alone. A missed woman's time didn't always signal the woman was enceinte. She could just be late. It had been more than a month since their wedding night. He made love to her more than once a day. Anyone with the tiniest bit of common sense would understand the very real possibility that she was increasing. That fact pleased him.

His Kerrie was smart. She bred horses. That in and of itself would give her more knowledge than the normal woman of her age and status...virgin status. She'd been innocent when she came to his bed. When she gifted him with her maidenhead, he'd been pleased...more than delighted he would be her only lover. Now, he hoped she would come to him again as she did in the early days. Would ask for him to make love to her. He needed that confirmation of their fragile relationship.

He knew when he asked her, she told him the truth. She didn't know. It wasn't a lie of omission as he jumped at that conclusion. Another month might pass before she felt confident enough to tell him she carried his child. She didn't trust him. He needed to change that way of thinking. Remembering Monney's advice, he thought all the confirmed bachelor told him would help the difficult situation that he single-handedly created. With all those thoughts sliding around in his head, he couldn't tell her how much he loved her. Not until he felt certain she didn't hate him. Monney also gave him that piece of advice.

"You..." she began, her breasts rising then falling, enticing all the male parts of him.

He needed to touch her so bad his hands shook. The soft rounded globes pushed from the top of the dress. Tendrils of curling hair framed her face. She was so beautiful. A Goddess. "You...should not have come after me. You are still too weak. You've hurt yourself. You're as pale as death. What you did is foolishness."

So damn eager to get away from the city, from him, she raced out of the house without a coat. She must be freezing. "You must have been..." Tam didn't have the right words. He didn't know how to apologize. He wronged her twice. "Frightened when the drawing was shown to you? I'm sorry," he repeated. Tam took his frock coat off then set it around her shoulders. "You should not have left in such a rush that you forgot a cloak to keep you warm."

He breathed in deep as he studied her. Her moods were becoming clear to him. He watched the changing expressions on her face.

Kerrie continued in the same vein. "Yes. Ashamed. Humiliated to the mortified roots of my hair. Couldn't believe I did that...we did that where anyone could see us. Draw a picture that would come back to shame me," she told him with blunt force. "I was so embarrassed. The man drew the mole on my..." she broke off seeming unable to say the rest of the words. Kerrie turned away from him to stare out the window.

"Yes, he did. I happen to love to kiss that mole. Cherish the tiny mark on your sweet butt. Furious, another man saw what is mine." Tam picked her hands up in his, rubbed his thumb over her wrists.

Relieved when the tiny shudder swept into her. It didn't seem she held him accountable for the drawing. That was one tiny step forward. She should though. He knew better than to tempt fate. Before Kerrie, he never did anything spontaneous. He was always predictable. To Tam it seemed when she was around, he couldn't think straight.

"Everyone in London as well as the surrounding area knows that..." She looked down away from his questing eyes. When she looked up, "You like to kiss my..." She couldn't say the word.

"The mole on your soft backside. Yes."

Inside he was laughing at her look of chagrin. His Kerrie still wasn't used to sex talk. In time, she might spout scandalous words to him.

He found he wished for her to do so. It would be amusing to hear what she might tell him when she was more comfortable with what they did in privacy. Her evolution would be amusing.

"They will forget." Tam tried to reassure her again. He traced the tops of her breasts, reveling in the satin finish of her soft, beguiling flesh. "By the end of next month there will be another scandal. There already is. Lady Mulligan renewed it for your embarrassment." Comfort was what he wanted to give her. Spouted words he'd said before.

A new direction of conversation might prove beneficial to taking her mind from the vagaries of today. "Should we negotiate a few things? I did give my word. We could begin now. I know I've been lax. Haven't lived up to what I promised."

Tam smiled at the way her eyes lit up. He was on the right track. Somehow, he would make her forget about this nasty intrusion into their lives. Would forget the title had nothing to do about his feelings for her.

"You did say you would negotiate. Didn't believe I would have to bargain for anything that didn't involve horses," she murmured, her voice becoming more vibrant.

"What did you have in mind, love?" He had a wealth of ideas. All given to him by his butler. He hoped once given they would bring her back into his arms the way she was the first week of their marriage. Before she discovered he was born to become a duke.

"What do you wish to bargain for? Name it and we'll talk. I'm in the best of moods. Would enjoy seeing to your every wish. So, ask away. Tell me what it is you would like to negotiate." he said as he thought about all his butler suggested. Tonight, unless she proposed something outlandish, he would give her everything she requested. He set his hand beneath her chin to tilt it up. Needed to see into the shimmer of her eyes.

"You would do this for me? Why do I think there is a catch somewhere? There isn't something you want from me if you give me something I ask for?" She fidgeted with her dress before staring at her feet. "Will you also ask favors? Don't know if I could reciprocate."

"Negotiate, love. That's all we're doing. If I ask for something you don't think you can give, you can refuse. That's what negotiations are about."

"I can?"

"Yes, of course. Though this isn't to be one-sided. There are things I would ask of you."

Her nervousness was endearing. Tam didn't wish for fear or for her to be worried about him demanding something from her in return. This was becoming too important to risk what he hoped would happen between them. "No catch. We are bargaining. That is all. It doesn't mean you will have your way in everything you ask. It also doesn't mean I might not ask for something in return. Promise I won't force anything on you that you would not appreciate."

"For starters..." She ran her tongue along the fullness of her bottom lip leaving dampness behind. He wished to pull her across the coach to sit with him. Wanted to taste her. Kiss her senseless. Recalled the wedding night from the Montgomerie estate to his home. The carriage ride was exquisite. "I would like to have free access to all my clothing. What you have done is humiliating and..." She looked down at her hands then back to him. "The servants must believe I'm witless. I can't even decide what to wear without help. None of that is true as you well know."

Tam never thought that. He doubted if the servants believed her to be so stupid she couldn't pick out her clothing for the day. He had more to make up for than he bargained for. He didn't intend to dig his grave any deeper. After a brief pause so she wouldn't be so unconfident of the next venture. "Done!" Tam adored the shocked look he saw in her eyes as well as the perfect 'O' her lips made. "Your trunk, as well as mine, will be delivered into the master chamber. Upon arriving, I will give the order to Monney. If you wish to don my clothes instead of yours, you may. Now I have a request. A kiss for each time I give you what you ask for."

He leaned across the carriage, set his mouth against hers. The kiss was light, a soft brush across hers. "Next?"

Kerrie appeared too shocked to say anything. Several seconds slipped by before she said. "I don't have to sleep without a nightgown every night? I want the choice." She looked so damn hesitant. "When do you want the next kiss? We can't just keep kissing."

Of course, they could. That was what he wished. "The choice is yours. I want to make the second kiss long as well as sweet. Want you to give me your tongue. Rub the velvet softness over mine," he leaned forward to bring her across the coach just as he'd thought about a few minutes earlier. Groaned when his arm didn't want to cooperate. After he gave up, he patted his thighs hoping she would understand what it was he wanted.

"This is up to me?" She made an unduchess like noise in the back of her throat. "It's only because of the gun shot. Otherwise, I'd be right where you want me. So, there is a choice?" She smiled; a wicked smile that made him wish to laugh.

"True to everything you said. Since I cannot lift you at this point in time, you have the opportunity to deny both of us a few kisses. Suppose I could move to your side of the carriage." To make his point he looked from her to his lap again. "As to the nightgown, you can choose what you do or do not wear to bed. Keep in mind you might not have it on in the morning when the sun rises. That's two more kisses you owe me."

"I can live with that."

When she smiled at him, brilliant, her eyes sparkling, his heart flipped. He needed her to smile at him just like that again. Tam heaved in a long breath of air. "I can live with that too. What else would you like?"

She moved over to do his bidding, sitting on him then placed her hands on his shoulders. "We could talk about the stable and how it will be run."

"A kiss first. You do owe me more than one." His hands circled her waist. He stared at her, touched the dampness of her mouth with his thumb. She opened for him when he caught her mouth with his, framed her lips. Pushed inside just as he'd like to push into her core. He deepened the kiss. His hands roamed the ladder of her ribs. The tiny female sound he loved to hear floated into his mouth. With his help the corsage of her gown slipped to reveal her milk-white jewels. "I want to taste all of you." Bloody hell, it had been two days since he felt her, tasted her. Felt her core milk him when he was deep inside. Wondered if she still wore nothing beneath her gown.

Kerrie responded, melting, joining him in the dance he orchestrated. He bent to suck one hard tip into his mouth. Teased the crest with tongue and teeth then turned his attention to the other breast. Tam moved back. Touched her nipples with his knuckles. Her heat sent a wildfire of temptation straight to his groin. "That's one. You owe me another. Later..."

Her breaths were hard, faster now that she was aroused. He understood that stopping at this juncture would be prudent. They would be home before he could give all of her the dedication she deserved.

"We could negotiate more but in a moment. I would like another kiss, one kiss from you. One that you orchestrate for my pleasure. You can do the honors." Tam couldn't hold his smile behind his teeth. She looked so damn flustered. "Kiss me like I've taught you. As we just kissed then I'll tell you what I've been working on some of the afternoons when I've been away from the house."

Tam needed to stay away from the house. If he'd been there, Kerrie would have been in his bed the entire day. When he finished this business, he thought he would take her somewhere isolated. The hunting lodge would be just the place for a honeymoon, relive the first tenuous steps of their relationship.

Kerrie looked as if she wanted that kiss then maybe one after that. "Alright. The second kiss is mine to give."

With a light touch she leaned into him. Followed that move with a gentle brush of her lips on his mouth.

If that was all she was going to do, he'd take over. He wouldn't allow her to get away with something so foolish as a faint skirmish of lips. Tentative and shy, she caressed his lips, sent her tongue into his mouth. Her scent captured him. The taste of her propelled heat waves pummeling into the hardest part of him. He groaned then decided he needed to control the kiss, deepening the contact, touching inside, sucking then rubbing his tongue along hers. She never denied him. His hand held her breast, thumb moving on her nipple once more.

When the coach slowed to a stop, he groaned low in the back of his throat. Brought the bodice of her gown to cover her, adjusted the fabric so no one would know what he'd been doing to her beautiful jewels. He pulled his coat across her.

His body tight as well as hard with its need, he adjusted his britches. They made it home. Now he had to navigate the rest of the evening. He meant to give her all the choices. Decisions were hers to make. That didn't mean he wouldn't try to steer her in the direction he wished to proceed. He planned to end the evening in bed. Hoped there would be no fabric between them when he got her there. If that wasn't to be, he would charm her nightgown away from her. She would understand she could never hide her beautiful body from the man who loved her to distraction.

He moved away. Touched her damp lips with a fingertip "I believe we've arrived. I would carry you to our room..."

"...but you can't. I want to know all about the stable. Over dinner? Before I left, I heard Monney mention something about a romantic dinner. Did you plan something?" Kerrie was curious. He appreciated her curiosity. Planned to use it to his advantage, subtly of course.

Tam hopped from the carriage then gave her his good hand to help her down. One more of her sweet smiles was ripping him into shreds. His nerves reacted. His body responded...tightened. He damn well planned to make love to his wife tonight. She could spout words about his resting all she wanted. The warnings weren't going to do a damn bit of good. He felt her tender response to the kiss. Understood she melted became liquid sunshine. That was one thing Kerrie couldn't deny...her body always wanted him. She needed him as much as he did her.

"The two of you are back." Monney met him at the entrance with a broad smile. It seemed he was watching for the coach. "I've taken the liberty to have that dinner you spoke of prepared. Would you like me to bring it up? It's ready. I took the freedom of picking out two of your favorite wines to go along with the splendid food your cook prepared."

"Give me a half hour," Tam said.

He held Kerrie's hand in his, tugging her toward the stairs. "We should go to our room. Change our clothing. Get comfortable." Perhaps having her clothing in the room would be advantageous. He could watch her undress then dress.

What would she put on?

Whatever she chose, he would take off.

He would see. In the master chamber, he let go of her hand. He motioned toward the open door to her dressing room. "See, your empty trunk is over there. Mary has put your clothing in the armoire. If you're inclined, you can make yourself comfortable before dinner is served. I will put on the black robe of mine. The one I haven't worn yet. So, you've never seen it. Don't wish for you to be uncomfortable." Perhaps he should have asked for dinner after he made love to his wife. After the carriage ride, he was ready for her. Needed her. Was desperate for her. Too much time passed since he'd felt her softness surrounding him.

Tam left her standing in the middle of the room, a blank expression on her face. After a few seconds of staring, she followed him. Touched his shoulder. He turned, his grin growing wider as he watched her bewildered features.

"You...you gave the orders before I asked. Why? There were no negotiations. You, I don't understand what is going on!" She sounded both indignant as well as furious. This wasn't what she expected.

"Why? I thought I was being a cad of the worst sort. Don't understand myself sometimes. Decided I didn't want you to hate me. Needed for other feelings to surface. Knew you didn't appreciate what I did with your clothing. I was a stupid man. Wanted to give you something...nice. Don't like finding out that I'm an idiot."

"You're not going to make me come naked to bed? I can wear anything?" Now, Kerrie sounded incredulous. "You aren't joking about any of this?" Kerrie waved her hand around the room before she stared at him.

Touching the tip of her nose with his finger, he spoke in the softest voice he could conjure under the circumstances. Instead of soft as he intended his voice was husky with his raging desire. He was amused as well as aroused by her look, by the thought of holding her in his arms tonight. His blood pulsed. What did it matter what she wore to bed? She would never wake up with the clothing on.

"Not joking. Need my wife to be happy. Don't you know?" Tam pointed to the clock. "You now have only twenty-five minutes to get ready for dinner. Monney will be prompt. The man always is."

He wasn't going to tell her half of what he was doing was his butler's ideas. Turning her, he swatted her delicious bottom. "Go! Change into something comfortable. Don't know what you had in your trunk.

Surprise me."

Kerrie's dressing room was separate from his. He tugged at his clothing. Naked, he donned a black robe with gold braid. The robe fell to mid-calf. As he stepped into the main room, he thought to peek into her dressing room. She'd closed the door. That was for the best. He did hope to be surprised by her choice. While she never refused his amorous intentions, since his reveal as the duke, she never started the loving. Kerrie wouldn't realize no matter what she wore, even a virginal white gown that covered her from her neck to her delicious toes, he would be aroused.

When she came through the door, she wore a lavender negligee with a matching robe. As she walked the fabric clung with love to her curves. He could see hints of her breast, her legs. Even the female mound at the apex. As he filled in the blanks with what he remembered, his imagination rushed to his groin. She was so damn beautiful. Tam didn't know if he could keep his hands off her until dinner time. The wonderful scent of her perfume wafted across the room. He inhaled Kerrie.

Trying to put thoughts of her naked in his arms from his fevered brain, he splashed wine into two glasses. Handed her one. He drank deep trying to keep his mind on the further negotiations they would have.

"I like your choice," he told her, his voice whiskey smooth and just as hot. "Did I give that to you?"

Tam didn't recall the gift. Wasn't certain... He'd never given her anything like this negligee. He made a note to remedy that. He should take her to a dressmaker here in London and have some commissioned. Anything she wanted. Any color she liked. Tam decided to ask Ella who the best seamstress was.

"Ella gave this to me for the wedding night. She told me you would appreciate me wearing this. In ways I feel..." she broke off pushing her hands along the silk covering her. "I didn't...wanton..."

"What do you feel? Wanton?" he asked, his mind reeling with the implications. Was she thinking of this evening as another wedding night? Tam hoped so. Beneath the robe he saw the tiny bows holding the gown to her shoulders. He stepped to her. Pushed the robe down her shoulder then kissed her bare flesh. The bows would come undone with one tweak.

"I feel as if I'm wearing nothing."

Tam couldn't tell her how true her words were. "Thank you for wearing this."

He caressed her shoulder before pulling the robe back to cover her. There would be time to play with the bows. Time to seduce. Time to charm. Now...more negotiations were in order.

"I know you better now than I did before. I..." She plucked at the skirt, her cheeks growing pink. "Perhaps I should change into something different." When she looked back to him, he sensed the sincerity in her words.

"No! No reason to take up time to do that. I like what you are wearing." *Like it a lot.*

"I do wish to please you. Don't like being at odds. Fighting. Tam, I don't hate you, never did. You've got to believe me. It was such a shock to discover that you weren't who you pretended to be. I reacted without thinking. I blurted the words without thinking. I could never hate you."

His heart jumped. "Hoped that was the case." He loved this woman to distraction. Loved the feel of her silken hair wrapped around him. The amber shimmer of her eyes. Believed he must have fallen in love with her the first second he saw her racing across the field. "So, shall we examine the truth? If you don't hate me...then...what are your feelings toward me, your husband?"

With the knock on the door, Kerrie scurried into her dressing room. He loved the fact she wore the negligee. Decided giving this wild impulsive woman the opportunity to decide her fate was the best way to approach her. Anger coupled with frustration had clouded his judgement. She pleased him. He didn't understand why he'd been so pigheaded with her. Kerrie was eager as well as reckless. Impulsive. He could deal with all those traits in a better way. It seemed she wanted him almost as much as he wanted her.

"Come in." Tam assumed the knock was Monney. He would have dinner ready for them. From here on out, the night would proceed in the manner he hoped.

"Sir?" Monney nodded to him. "On the table? Everything is as you ordered."

"Thank you. That will be all." Tam paused. "Thank you for

everything. You're a smart man, Monney. I'll have to remember that in the future."

He would recall everything if he were ever in need of advice. The man should get a raise. He would try to remember tomorrow.

One of Monney's silver eyebrows rose a notch. He smiled before backing away. "For this afternoon? I'm pleased things are going well for you."

"Very pleased," he said, his gaze drifting to Kerrie's dressing room door.

He could see her face. She was peeking at them. Her eyes huge.

"You're welcome. Will there be anything else?"

"Not tonight. All is as it should be." Tam looked to the dressing room door again. She'd closed that door. "Will see you tomorrow. You may retire for the night."

"You can come out now," he said laughing as she opened the door.

The soft rose adorning her face was beautiful. She was so damn sweet. He wanted to devour her, not the food. Wanted to spend the rest of the night pleasuring her, making everything all right. First things first. "Are you hungry?"

"Famished." Kerrie held out her glass, her eyes a shimmer in the night. She swept her tongue across her mouth in silent invitation. "Need more wine."

He poured more then pulled out a chair for her to sit. Dished up two plates. Tam found he was hungrier for Kerrie than he was for the food. Nonetheless, all that would happen tonight would be at her bequest. He wasn't going to initiate anything. Though he wasn't above a bit of charming subtleties. He could seduce her with little effort. He learned that piece of information a long time ago. If they negotiated again, she would owe him another kiss. He could capitalize on the kiss, explore tender soft parts. Taste her. Savor her beauty.

"Can we talk about the stable now?" Kerrie asked while she pushed food around on her plate. To Tam she looked nervous. "What role do I have in the workings of it? Can I ride Dex? Is he off limits? I need to train him. He understands my hand." Kerrie was beginning to babble.

Tam didn't wish for her nerves to get in the way of the

negotiations, of the seduction that was ripe in his mind. Nor did he wish for her to prattle on about things that would be obvious with his first words. She also needed to eat. "Yes, as to the stable, I've found a man for you to interview. He is well versed in the training of horses as well as breeding them. If you like him, you can hire him. The hiring and firing is up to you. If you don't believe he is good enough, I'll search for another man who might be more suited to your liking. The stable is yours. What your duties are is up to me. In a week, we'll be back at the estate. We can hash out the responsibilities then. I've been thinking. My mind is a blank slate. Will need your input."

"That's all good. What will I do? My duties?" She was tilting her head a bit sideways, biting on the same lip he needed to taste.

It seemed she didn't wish to let that topic go unanswered. Tam let out a heavy sigh. There were other topics that needed to be pursued. He wished he could tell her all she needed to do was look pretty. Didn't dare. Wouldn't want that woman. "Honestly? I don't know what I can allow you to do. I'm scared to death of you riding that beast of yours, Dex. The stallion is too strong for you. No matter how hard I think on the notion, I cannot get over that terror. When you're pregnant, I will also be frightened for the child. If you fell..."

He let that sentence fade. She could miscarry. He needed to protect her, his unborn child as well. Tam thought that a pregnancy might temper her actions.

"I am competent," she argued, her eyes flashing. "I've never had a problem with Dex. Never fallen from any horse. We know each other. Trust each other."

"As of today, you haven't had to pit your strength against his. Dex would win in every scenario I can imagine. That's why when something terrible as well as unforeseen happens we call the event an accident. Accidents happen. We will have to see. I suppose if you ride him only in the corral, I could give my blessing. That is...until you are pregnant. I would have to say no to every scenario involving that horse when we both know you are enceinte."

She struggled to square her shoulders. "While I don't wish to agree with you, I do. I will oversee the training. Don't have to ride him. Can be there when..." She blushed at the thought of what Dex might be doing when...a mare was bred.

She was adorable. "Yes, you can. As will I be there also. As to anything else that might arise that might prove controversial, we will talk about it when the time comes. You cannot be too close. Observation will be your role."

"That sounds reasonable."

"Are you finished eating?"

Kerrie mostly pushed food around on the plate. If they were hungry later, he would raid the kitchen. Tam gave all the servants the night off.

Kerrie nodded, "Guess I wasn't as hungry as I thought."

"Come sit on the bed with me. A kiss is what is owed now."

Along with whatever she will allow. If she tells me no, I'll have to figure out a way to change her mind. On his way, he picked up both bottles of wine. Tonight, he meant to spend making love to her.

"Do I have a choice?" she asked again, seeming to be seeking to negotiate further.

"Always, except..." he paused. "You do owe me a kiss. If you like, you can pick the place. Doesn't matter much to me." He could tell what was revolving in her head as she searched the room.

"I'd, well, I'd like to share the chair by the fireplace with you. I remember that first night, how we looked into the fire. Watched the flames leap. That was...nice."

The rug in front of the flames would be a perfect place to make love to his wife. He nodded. "I enjoyed that time as well. Thought it was more than nice."

When they reached the chair, he pulled her to sit on his thighs. Tam didn't know how slow he could be. He felt strung up tight, hard. Ached. Moving slowly with her would be wonderful. Letting her turn to liquid in his arms would make his evening.

"You wish for me to sit on you?" her voice was hesitant.

Almost as if she understood they would make love before the night was finished. For the first or second time, Tam didn't care. He wished for the entire night with his wife.

"If you like, yes. If not, we could stretch out on the fur rug. I would hold you. We could..." Tam liked that idea better. "Where would you like to sit?" He saw the slight smile forming on her mouth. Tugging on her lips was always such a delight. She didn't understand the subtle invitations she issued.

"The chair." Kerrie said after looking to both places several times.

Tam sat. Sipped the wine before setting the glass on the table next to him. A few seconds later, Kerrie sat on him. He pushed her hair over her shoulders. Brushed his lips down her neck. "You know I want you. You have no objections?"

"No objections," she parroted.

She nodded while he slipped the robe from her shoulders. The fabric pooled around her hips. Her body was revealed, all the beautiful dips and curves. With his teeth, he jerked on the tiny bow at her left shoulder until it loosened. Kissed her shoulder as he nudged the fabric away from her. The lavender material fell to catch on the tip of her breast. Just as he remembered, the nipple was a dusky rose. Hard. Tight. He followed the path of the negligee until he pushed the lavender silk from her breast. As he did in the carriage, he kissed then sucked the tip deep into his mouth. Her throaty moan of pleasure pleased him. Several seconds later he moved to her right shoulder. Repeated the process.

Kerrie wound his hair through her fingers. Pulled his shirt from his pants. Settled her fingers on his chest. His muscles twitched with the contact. Tam explored her leg, touched her, found soft wet flesh between her thighs. Her legs were shaking even while they were opening for him. She was inviting him to explore. Kerrie wanted him. The thought thrilled him. He needed this night after the ones before.

"Bed or the rug," he asked, his body hard as steel.

"Rug," she murmured. Though she was trembling, Kerrie stood by herself. The gown fell to the floor. She was naked for him. Standing, letting him devour her with his eyes. "I want you, Tam. Please."

She could very well be the death of him. After he led her to the rug, he stripped himself of his robe. After that he lay down beside her. He kissed her and sucked on all of her. Spread her legs so she was open to him. He saw the evidence of her desire. The tiny jewel that brought her so much pleasure pleading for his attention. With his tongue he touched and massaged. Her body arched, begging him for more.

Tam couldn't wait until she found her pleasure. He was ready to explode. The moment he pushed inside, she cried out. Her hot wet sheath milked his sex. He knew the moment her body fragmented with her desire. He exploded inside her. Falling on her, he braced himself with his forearms.

"I...I love you, Tam. Never hated. Never..."

*Kerrie loves me.* His heart swelled but he didn't return the sentiment. He wondered if the words were true. She showed him so many different shades of herself. God, he needed for her to love him.

"Tam?" She reached up to run her hand along his shoulder.

He kissed her mouth. "Let's go to bed."

# Epilogue

Three years later

Tam leaned against the rails watching his wife put the new mare through her paces. The stable prospered. Dex was sought out by many. He won races. Sired more horses. Time would tell if his bloodlines were pure. She was a damn good trainer. He was proud of her. A woman with exceptional skills. She learned from the best, her mother. He held his son, the heir apparent, in his arms who pointed at his mother.

"Mama..." The little man grinned, tried to get down to run to her. Tam held on to the wiggling bundle he loved beyond possible. "Want my mama! Now!"

The lad did tend to have a temper. He would need to teach him how to be calm.

"Not now. Mama is busy. She has to finish her work. It's almost time for your nap. Mama will play with you after that." Tam pointed into the ring. "Dangerous for you in there. Never go into the corral until I give you permission."

"Not mama? I want mama."

He sounded indignant. Determined. Entitled. Kerrie would tell him that was how her husband sounded when he didn't get what he wanted. He would tell her that fact was true of all men.

Well, where she was concerned, he certainly hoped not. It had been three years since their marriage, give or take a week or two. She told him she loved him that night. Thanks to Monney's help, they were able to solve their differences. He didn't have the courage to reciprocate the sentiment. He was so damn in love with her. Had been since he first saw her. *Coup de foudre*. That night was the last time she said the words. He couldn't blame her. She made herself vulnerable. He was unable to do the same to reciprocate the sentiment. Every time he came inside her, he needed to hear her words of love. Kerrie remained silent.

As did he.

That silence needed to end.

Over the years, three bloody years, he cursed himself for being a fool. Should have asked Monney for advice. Monney would have told him to say the words. Thoughts tormented him. That night had been an opening for something better between them. The cold evaporated for a short time only to be taken over by an ice storm of his making. Tam never understood why the words were so bloody hard to say. He needed to reply to her words of love. He just couldn't force the words from his lips. Tam needed to change that. He knew the truth of his thoughts. She gave everything, her heart along with her soul.

He was a coward.

She was pregnant again. This time he hoped for a little girl. One who looked just like his Kerrie. That night when he stopped being an autocratic fool, everything changed but not as much as he would have wished. She still held a part of herself away from him. It had been three years. Since that one moment in time, neither one committed to loving the other. To saying the words that would break the ice. Kerrie showed him in too many ways to count that she loved him. He tried to do the same.

From the corner of his eye, Tam saw Kerrie's approach. She was coming to take the boy to bed. Tam gave his son a quick hug then a kiss to his cheeks. He would have a few hours to play with the little man's mother. Today, telling Kerrie he loved her was at the top of his agenda. It was way past time to make the commitment. He prayed he had the courage to make himself so vulnerable.

"It's time for this little man's nap." Mary stood beside him; her hands stretched out to take the boy from him.

"Don't want to sleep!" he yelled, his voice carrying. He wasn't getting his way so he yelled louder. Not that doing so would help. "Not tired. Want my mama!"

"You have to take a nap, so we can play after dinner. Otherwise, you will fall asleep before I can toss you in the air, wrestle with you," Tam said, pushing a stray lock of dark brown hair from his son's eyes.

He watched as Mary left with the boy. Tam observed them until they disappeared into the back of the house. He turned his attention to his wife.

As soon as she finished with the horse, they were going riding to the infamous glade where they created a scandal that lasted a month then threatened their marriage. They rode there often. Tam was certain the last time they were at the glade was when she conceived their second child. That was two months ago. Kerrie promised to back off on her chores with the stable. She would not ride Dex even in the coral.

Financially, if the laws of his country concerning women were different, Kerrie would be wealthy, very wealthy. She was more than capable of managing her finances on her own. Was capable of dealing with the funds to run the stable. Tam didn't give his wife an allowance as most men did. He put her name on an account that was hers and hers alone. The bank manager frowned at him when he insisted that only her name be written on the account. That was another act that endeared him even more to his wife. As the money stood now, the funds were growing. Kerrie spent little on herself. She insisted that the expenses of the stable come from her income. She wouldn't take anything from him. She paid for the trainer as well as the breeder. She decided to hire two different men now that the stable had grown.

She dismounted walking toward him, hips swaying provocatively, smiling. She held her hands out to him. "Are you ready?"

Her gaze skimmed his body. Stopped at his crotch before going back to his eyes.

They planned the outing this morning when it became apparent the day would be sunny and warm. Tam helped her mount before vaulting on behind her. Her fingers wound around his forearms. His hand settled on her belly still flat though he felt certain in another month he would begin to see the signs of her developing pregnancy.

Today he had ulterior motives for taking his wife to this spot which held a wealth of memories for them. Once they dismounted, he spread the blanket on the grass. He snatched the bottle of wine from the basket. She handed him cups before pulling out the cheese and bread they brought with them.

Tam raised his cup to her. "To us, my sweet. To our future. To your stable." He paused for a few seconds, watching her. Needed to see her expression when he spoke the words that were too long in coming. "I love you," he blurted with no finesse.

Her eyes widened then shimmered with the pleasure his words gave her. She sent him a smile that went straight to his groin. "You've never said that before. Tam, I thought..." Now her hesitation surprised him. He didn't understand what that was about. She ran her sweet tongue across her mouth. "I thought..."

He cleared his throat so he could explain why it took him so bloody long to say the words. "I was a coward. I've loved you since the first time I saw you. Knew I had to have you. Realized in order to do that I would have to leave out the part of me that possessed a title. You were in my blood the moment I set eyes on you. Had to keep my secret in order to keep you. Rescued you even though you didn't need help. I love you so bloody much. I can barely breathe."

She touched her cup to his. "To, *coup de foudre*."

The look on his face he understood was a puzzled one. "*Coup de foudre*?"

"Love at first site," she murmured, then drank deeply. "I do love you so very much. Thank you for finally telling me, my secretive duke."

Coming Soon
by the Author
At Rogue Phoenix Press

*Beth's Enemy Her Love*
Naughty Book Seven


1841


White clouds billowed on the horizon, threatening a downpour, filling the space from the tops of the hills to high overhead, darkening even as he watched. A brisk breeze captured leaves on the trees surrounding the small lake, casting dancing shadows on the ground. Silver ripples from the remaining sunlight slanted across the water pulsing against the shore. The couple kissing by the water line seemed oblivious to the threatening storm as well as his presence. By his standards the kiss was chaste, not much more than a peck. Two young lovers who were trying out their wings. He recognized the young lady. She shouldn't be here unsupervised. He looked around for the ever-present guards. Some would call the men chaperons. They were and they were not. These men were hired to protect the lady's life not her virtue. Though their presence did both. The young woman took advantage.

Thad DuBois watched with caution born of experience knowing the duke's men could blend into shadows. Leaning against a boulder he tried for an air of casualness. Yes, he knew the young lady, Elizabeth Montgomerie. Wondered what her father, the duke, would think about her little tryst by the lake with her young lover. From what he knew of Drake Montgomerie, the man would not be pleased. Montgomerie was a man who expected perfection in himself. Thad felt certain the man would also expect the same from his children.

The young pup, Thad knew him also. Harry Sylvan had his hand on her rump feeling her. While he had no business watching this scene play out, he needed the lake water to clean a wound. Wished to rest for a few minutes before he finished the ride to his residence on the other side of the lake. He could wait these young lovers out. Couldn't leave without alerting the couple they had a visitor. Maybe he should present himself. Doing so would put an end to the groping by the young pup who didn't know how to charm the daughter of a duke.

To his surprise, she stepped away from the boy, shaking her finger at him. So, she wasn't as enamored of the lad as first appearance gave him reason to believe. It was possible the boy's kiss didn't melt her from the inside out or turn her into liquid honey. The girl should slap him. The boy had his hand on her ass. Perhaps she liked the feel. Maybe not. By all appearances now, he would go with the latter assumption. Leaving her standing by herself, Harry rode away. In every scenario, the lad should have escorted her home. Ah, but she had the guards to protect her. The boy would know…should know. Perhaps Harry was naïve.

Debating whether or not to make his appearance known, he held back a moment. The girl was beautiful. Intrigued him to the point he swelled. Thinking what the hell, he stepped forward. Something inside him wanted to show her how a kiss, a real kiss from a man, not a boy was accomplished. He grinned at himself. If he didn't miss his guess, he would get slapped for his forwardness. Decided the experiment was worth the sting.

She must have heard his near silent approach. Either that or the lady sensed his presence. Elizabeth swirled, skirts flirting around her slender ankles. Her hands beneath her chin, she stared at him. Drawing her brows together, she looked to the horizon. She could summon Drake's men with one word. Thad held up his hands. A gesture he hoped would show her he meant no harm. She would recognize him soon. When she did, she would back away or call out for her protectors. Thad was shocked when she remained silent.

"Lady Montgomerie…" He walked closer, unsure how he intended to proceed. "You having a little tryst with your young lover?" He couldn't stop the slow lazy grin from spreading across his face. Provoking her would bring out passion. "He's not a real man. Think, after that poor kiss, you understand that fact."

"Harry?" Elizabeth returned his grin. She shifted her feet. "Not that it's your business. He is not a lover. Not mine anyway. He has trouble taking no for an answer."

"Well, you're right, the kiss was a schoolboy kiss. A lover would give you a different type of kiss." His need to show her how a lover's kiss would feel overpowered his common sense.

Pleased with what he saw as her reaction, her entire body tightened with anger. A passionate woman he could deal with. He found he'd like to taste her. Devour her. Savor certain parts of her. Eat her up. She was a beauty. If her father knew what he thought at this instant, Drake would tar and feather him for his thoughts. The duke wouldn't want him anywhere near his daughter. Intrigued by her, his reputation be damned, he meant to carry this as far as this young lady would allow. She excited every male part of him. Just looking at her, he was at attention. Thinking with that part of him it would be prudent to ignore.

With flashing hazel eyes, she questioned, examined, even sent her brazen gaze down the length of him then back to meet his eyes. He was flattered. Her lashes fluttered closed as if she didn't wish for him to see her scrutiny. *Little flirt.* He held the laugh deep inside realizing she inspected his body just as he did hers. A young woman didn't show her thoughts to a man with this much audacity. She managed to steal his breath. He was so jaded; he'd never met a woman who could accomplish that feat. In the ensuing moments, Elizabeth became an open book. Elizabeth Montgomerie should learn to guard herself along with her vibrant emotions better. If a man could read those enigmatic hazel eyes, she would find herself lost.

To test his thoughts, he allowed his gaze to linger on the beautiful swell of her breasts, lower to the slim waist then the flare of her feminine hips. She seemed to understand what he was about. He sent her a half smile in order to encourage her further scrutiny of him. As if embarrassed, she turned away for a moment. When she met his gaze a second time, she sent him a slow sensual smile. Her lips parted in a soft mew. He saw the tip of her tongue. Thad wondered how much she knew. How much she understood about sex. Maybe she wasn't as naïve as he expected her to be.

His body tightened with raging need that couldn't be ignored, prudent or otherwise. He would have to think about that. She was still Drake Montgomerie's daughter. If he acted on his thoughts, he could be digging his grave.

"You're far too bold. While I recognize you, I don't know you. How dare you spout such nonsense about me?" The indignant tone of her voice came as a subtle surprise. Elizabeth understood the subtleties of manipulation. Her father must have begun teaching her from the moment of her birth. The man was treacherous. In flirting with his daughter, he was taunting danger.

"You know me. Know who I am. Don't you?" Thad stepped within a breath of air of her. Ran his knuckles down the long white column of her neck. With the gentle contact, her pulse raced. The breaths of air she inhaled were small short breasts as she strained to hide emotions that were as clear and unblemished as her face. He was pleased with her reaction to his bold advance. Testing her further today, yes, that would be a heady experience.

"What I say is not nonsense. I watched you kiss the boy. If you ask, I'll show you the difference between the kiss of a young pup and a man." He watched the darkening of her expressive eyes. She wanted the kiss. Thought to discover what he meant. He could read her mind as if it was a book meant solely for him.

The lift of her chin made him chuckle inside. "You're too arrogant by far. You don't know anything. I'll have you know who I kiss is none of your business." Elizabeth turned her back on him. Her skirt swirled around her trim ankles. She seemed to watch the ripples on the water. She wasn't going anywhere. He was pleased by her lack of fear. He half expected her to run from him.

"Yes." Thad set his hands on her shoulders. "You're right." Turned her. Needed to see her eyes when he spoke to her. "What if I wish to make who you kiss my business?"

"You're an assassin. You kill people," Elizabeth accused with an amused tone. Almost as if she didn't believe her words. "I shouldn't be here with you. You do know my father has men who watch over me. If I yell, they will be here in a blink."

"You are…" he paused thinking as he spoke. "Only get rid of little girls who talk too much. I can turn you into a woman." His thumb touched her bottom lip. The feel was soft, ambrosia to his soul. Wet. Hot as the fires of hell. He'd watched her run that pink tongue of hers across the tender flesh. Touched his thumb.

She sipped in a gasp of air. Started to turn from him again. Her hand flew to his chest. Touched. Brought her fingers away with a look of horror. Her eyes were wide. Shimmered. She appeared concerned. "You're bleeding!"

Bloody eyes, he forgot about that tiny matter. He shrugged with indifference. "It's just a scratch." He'd come to the lake to wash the blood from his chest before returning home. Found himself distracted by the woman. Distraction could get a man killed. "Yes." He continued, "A small matter. Meant to take care of it. Seems there was a diversion to my plans."

"No, no it's not a small matter. Who did this to you?" She started to unbutton his shirt. Her fingers grazed his flesh.

Thad stopped her, his hand on her wrist. "Not your concern," he said with heated force unable to tell her details or reasons. "I've been cut. Nothing serious. Needed to clean the wound. Just part of my work."

"You killed someone," Elizabeth was blunt, too candid, even though her face paled. In his line of work, he couldn't risk blunders of this sort. He made a mistake here. His lust for this woman got in the way of common sense.

"No…" Thad had to deny whatever she thought. His ability to stay out of Newgate relied on his ability to remain calm as well as indifferent in the face of adversity. This little lady was a titillating piece of baggage that could well be the end of him. One he needed to keep at a distance. Given time she would drive her father, the duke, half crazy. Maybe all the way senseless if she continued to take whatever she wanted.

"Oh…" Her voice trailed off as if she was disappointed in his renunciation. "I thought."

"You've heard stories. Sorry to disappoint. All the tales are untrue. Not a shred of reality in any of them. I've never murdered a living soul." Her disappointment was strange. Seemed Elizabeth wished to flirt with danger. Test her wiles on a dangerous man. There was more of the duke in her than her father would wish. To top it off, she was too curious by far. He liked that.

Her bottom lip caught beneath her teeth; she shot her hazel gaze his way. "Let me help. I can clean the wound. You might need stitches. I'm good at that. I've a steady hand. Been taught how to stitch wounds."

Before he could counter or deny that he needed help, she tore a piece of her petticoat then followed him, her expression one he didn't want to examine in detail. "No, you needn't. I'm fine. Can take care of myself. Have done so for all my life." In his present condition, her fingers on his chest would never be judicious. He did value his life. If the duke found out he was this close to his daughter, he'd shred his hide. The wound would never inhibit what he wished for with her. He still wanted that kiss.

"I see that. You've done so well. Unbutton your shirt. I'll take a look. Clean the wound so there is no infection." To his amusement, she expected him to obey. She was tapping her toe. Her auburn brows were drawn tight. The brows just a bit darker than her hair. "Well? What are you waiting for? Christmas? You've got a long wait ahead of you."

When he didn't move fast enough, he found she was flicking open the buttons on his shirt. He caught her hand. "I can do that." Her fingers on his chest might be a nice distraction to the slight pain the wound caused. He did need to clean the wound. Perhaps his original assessment was wrong. He should take what she seemed willing to give.

Elizabeth stepped back, waiting for him to finish what she ordered, her hands on those wonderful feminine hips he wished to caress. Bloody hell, he needed to stop thinking of Elizabeth as a woman he could have. He couldn't. That was that. Even the thought of that kiss, paled in light of who she was. He did give great value to his life. If the duke found out about this, he might never breathe again.

After he finished with the buttons, he pulled the tails from his britches then shrugged from the shirt. Holding it in his hand he waited for her to begin whatever it was she seemed to have in mind. He was curious where this was going. When her fingers touched his chest, he groaned. The sound was low, husky coming from the back of his throat. Lightening surged to his groin. His rod stood ready. Thad knew this had to be a monumental mistake.

"You'll live." She was so close to him he felt her breath murmur across his bared chest. Elizabeth dabbed at the blood until it vanished. A fingertip slid across the cut. "Stitches. You need them. If we go to the cottage…" Elizabeth jerked. Stared for a moment at the sky.

The loud crack of thunder boomed across the darkened horizon. Blue white lightening reached from the clouds to the ground. Sizzled. Rain poured down upon them. His horse reared on its hindlegs terrified then raced away.

Thad forgot about his horse. He ran to hers. Held onto the reins. "We need to find shelter." He didn't wait for her to agree or disagree, he tossed her on her mount then leapt on behind. "Is there anywhere we can go?"

"The cottage." Elizabeth pointed in the direction of the woods. He sent his heels into the mare. They raced the wind and the rain, the lightening along with the thunder. The distance wasn't far. They entered into a wooded area. The small structure stood isolated. He dismounted before helping her down. "Go inside. I'll be right there." To his surprise, she obeyed the command. He'd expected an argument that would include his wound.

Where were the duke's men? They couldn't be far behind. If those men found him alone with her, he didn't stand a chance of surviving. Thad took longer than necessary rubbing down the mare while he attempted to put what was happening into perspective. Unexpected as well as unwanted, he felt something for the woman-child. When she touched him, he almost drug her into his arms for the kiss he'd been thinking about since he first saw her kissing Sylvan. At that moment he felt a surge of jealousy that was out of character. He'd never felt possessive of women. Ladies were put in his path for one purpose. Nothing more. The bizarre feeling stuffed his head with unfounded emotions that needed to be dismissed.

By the time he walked into the cottage, Elizabeth had several items on the table. Among them were needle as well as thread then a bottle of whiskey. She opened it. Drank. Handed it to him.

"Drink up. Not the entire bottle. Just half. I'm going to stitch your wound. Looks as if three will do the trick."

"No."

"Didn't think you were a coward." She threaded the needle as if she didn't hear him. "Sit down. This will all be over in a matter of seconds. I'm a very good seamstress."

When she said those few words, he pictured needle work, not skin.

"You don't know what you are doing. I don't take orders."

She flashed him a smile that left his insides quaking and his sex throbbing against his buckskins. "I do. Father made certain I knew what to do. Ash too. He's never trusted doctors or surgeons as some call themselves. He tended to my mother when she was shot in this very room. Refused to call a doctor." She was humming between words. Her mood was casual as if she'd done this a thousand or more times. "He made mother stay in the room adjoining his. Didn't care one fig about her reputation. Isn't that romantic? They weren't married. The Duchess, the original Duchess, was fit to be tied. Papa wouldn't kowtow to her. Did what he wanted. He loved mother. Even acknowledging that fact, it took some time for him to admit to the sentiment."

By the time she finished her little story, Thad had downed half the whiskey. She was an audacious little thing. Spoiled. Spouted whatever came to her agile mind, most of her words nonsense. He found he enjoyed that side of her. When she poured whiskey into his cut, he thought he would jump out of his skin. "You could have warned me."

"Why?"

"So I wouldn't scream." This was a weakness he couldn't afford to show anyone let alone the daughter of Drake Montgomerie. Pain he could handle. It was the surprise that set off his nerves, leaving them in a tangled mess.

"Hurt that bad?" She laughed, the sound enchanting.

Found he wanted to hear her laugh more. What he wished for most was to show her how a man kissed. "Surprised, nothing else. As I said, a warning would have prevented the scream."

"Un…huh…" The needle entered flesh. In then out. Three times just as she told him. He drank from the bottle again. She took it from him before pouring more onto the wound. "You can put your shirt back on."

"What if I don't want to?" He pulled her between his spread legs hoping for that kiss he'd been dreaming about. His hands settled on her waist then downward to caress the swell of her hips. Her breasts were so close to his mouth he could almost taste them. Her scent sweet and clean filled his senses. That was what he wanted. A small taste of her. Needed to understand the flavor of the woman. The scent…Elizabeth smelled of spring…of daffodils and crocuses popping up from the earth to welcome the warmth a thunderstorm to his soul. She set her hands on his chest. Wished he dared put them on his erection. Tell her that was what she did to him. She might not understand. Teaching her would please him.

He stood, pulling her against him. Pressing her so she touched him. His mouth met hers. Captured her essence. Her taste better than the finest wine. He stopped for a moment, spoke still close to the lips he wanted to explore more thoroughly, the mouth he wanted to delve into. "Tell me to stop. If you don't say no, I can't be responsible for what comes next. This is your choice."

When she looked at him with wide hazel eyes all he saw was her acceptance. She wanted him. Needed him as much as he needed her. Understood what he wished. He could thank young Harry Sylvan for paving his way. Tonight, he would kiss her. Show her how a kiss was supposed to feel between a man and his woman. What came after that was up to the future. He wasn't a man to wait for what he wanted. If she gave him leave, he would take everything she offered. Everything.

Difficult as it was, he touched her with tenderness he didn't feel. Careful not to frighten her. Even though he might have guessed otherwise, he could tell by her hesitance this would be her first kiss from a man. Felt certain, despite her bold nature, she was untried except for a few chaste kisses from unexperienced boys. Didn't plan to shock. With possession, he held her, his hand holding the back of her head. His thumb sweeping the soft flesh on the long column of her neck.

Her heat swept into him. Heard the rush of her breathing as she tried to inhale air through him. His tongue brushed across her mouth touching, tempting, invading as she opened for him. He played. Danced as he brought her to his will. Experienced her. Her fingers wound behind his neck. Nails dug into flesh as he deepened the kiss. She clung to him. A soft sound of acceptance broke from her. His hands held her at the waist, knowing soon he would lower them to her sweet rump so he could pull her against him, show her how aroused he was. She might not understand what she was feeling. Wouldn't comprehend the intimacy she gave to him.

An insignificant whimper of pleasure on her part encouraged more bold actions. He smoothed one hand down her back. As long as she responded, he would continue teaching. He stood. Pulled her closer as if they were practiced lovers. Elizabeth pushed against him. Her breasts were lush, full, a woman's breasts. Not a child's or a woman too young for loving. Elizabeth was ripe. Ready to be cherished by a man. Her body was waiting to receive him. He wanted to be that man who would teach her more than how to kiss.

Thad had to douse that thought before it became part of his soul. He could never afford to give too much of himself away. His life didn't allow for a woman to become a permanent fixture. Elizabeth Montgomerie would need an enduring man. A steady man. One who could give her a solid home. A man who could continue to spoil her as she deserved to be treated. Pampering was what she was accustomed to. Drake would never allow him to have his daughter. Besides, he wasn't the marrying type. Never thought of settling down. What would he do if his life changed? If his work wasn't so important to him. For him, nothing would differ.

He heard his groan of pleasure. The deep rumble he didn't hold back. Wanted Elizabeth to hear how she affected him. He deepened the kiss. Touched deeper. Savored. Fought for control. Caught her lips with his teeth. Heated with her passionate response. She met his advance with one of her own. Pushed her tongue against his lips, imitating. Rubbed herself against his chest. Thrust her tongue against his mouth until he sucked her inside. The soft mew of pleasure delighted him. He pulled back to look at her damp swollen lips. Then look into her passion glazed eyes.

Thad was thrilled. Understood this needed to end before one of Drake's men skewered him through, barged through the door to put a stop to this seduction of their charge. He didn't understand why they left him with her this long. The storm couldn't be the reason. Even as the kiss deepened and he wanted to walk her to the bed in the other room, he knew he had to bring her home. His hand settled on her bottom. Squeezed. Tested the firmness. She moaned. Arched against him. Curled into his body. Begged him for more attention. Didn't step back to slap him as he half expected. To carry this seduction farther… With reluctance he left her lips. Let a long rush of air dissolve from his lungs. No woman had ever affected him so deep and so fast as this one.

Touching his forehead to hers, he spoke with tender words. "I have to get you home. Don't know why the duke's chaperones haven't come for you. Nonetheless, Lizzy, we need to leave. The rain has stopped. The storm has passed. There is nothing keeping us here." Thad was shocked when she stiffened then moved away from him.

"Don't call me that!" Her little fists were balled at her sides. Her rage obvious. Hazel eyes flashed fire.

He was shocked she might use her fist on him over something he said instead of how he touched her. Taken by surprise, "What?" he questioned. Thad was perplexed by the abrupt distance she put between them. The space wasn't caused by his hands on her rounded buttocks. She didn't smack him as he might have expected. Instead, she might be incensed with the nickname? Thad needed to clarify. "What did I say?"

"Lizzy!" Elizabeth turned her back on him. Walked away. "Nobody calls me that." She stood in front of the window, staring out into the darkness. "No one!"

He didn't like the sudden distance between them. Realized his mistake. Thad was beside her, turning her to pull her into his arms one more time. His mouth was a breath away from hers. "You don't want me to call you Lizzy. Elizabeth is far too long a name between lovers. Must be shortened." He lifted her chin. Saw hazel eyes blazing in his direction. He didn't wait. Taken by the thought of another man kissing her, he needed to make his point about the young pup. "If Sylvan can't kiss you like I just did, don't marry him. Don't settle for anything less than what we shared."

"We aren't' lovers," she denied them. "Never will be. You're right about him."

With straw in his head, he spoke without thought for his existence. "Not yet." He didn't understand where his confidence came from. What he knew was that he hoped someday they would be intimate. That day would be sometime in the future. As she stood in front of him now, she was far too young. Far too innocent for his jaded self. "Why don't you like the shortened name?"

"Lizzy sounds like a lizard." Her petulant remark gave him a reason to kiss her again to pull her into his arms.

"No lizards for me. Beth… do like the way that sounds? One syllable is all I can deal with when I make love to a woman. The name Beth is better than Lizzy…one syllable."

This time she didn't deny the name. Once more, his mouth framed hers. Touched inside. Sent magic into his soul. Beth enchanted him. He needed her. Couldn't have her. He was a fool to deny himself. "While I'd like to continue this…see where it would lead, I can't. Need to get you home, sweet one." Beth was sweet, heaven to this man who knew little about relationships. Long lasting relationships. This was a woman who could change that. His lifestyle would not allow this type of connection. He needed to get a hold of himself.

Elizabeth Montgomerie was out of his reach. The duke would never allow a man such as he to have anything to do with his cherished daughter. What he needed to do was get her home as soon as possible then put her out of his head. Later, after she was safe in the big mansion on the hill, he would visit his favorite tavern. There were several women there he could ease himself with. He could make plans. He had a new client. Could meet with the man to see what he wanted.

"Beth…where are your father's men. Don't you think they should be beating down the door? They've left me, a dangerous man, alone with you. His men will understand my reputation…who I am." Thad asked all the while wondering why he wasn't a dead man.

Her laugh this time sent a nerve throbbing on his neck. She swept her tongue across her lips, tempting. "I made an agreement with father that unless I was in mortal danger, the ever-present guards must keep their distance. You're right. They are out there. Waiting. I'm certain they know we kissed. Just as they know Harry kissed me. They also might understand that I stitched your wound. Before my feet are on the steps to my house, Papa will know everything they know. In spite of my displeasure, they run messages to him."

"I'm a dead man," he muttered knowing that fact for the absolute truth. "Maybe your father isn't home." Thad could always hope for a miracle. He knew the duke's reputation. While all he did was in the name of the crown, Drake Montgomerie was one of the most dangerous men in England. Maybe all of Europe. His reputation preceded him.

"I will tell Papa you were a perfect gentleman." She touched his cheek. Her fingers light. Sent his muscles rippling. Trailed the tip down his chest then across the stitches she sewed on his chest then his nipples. "You probably should put your shirt on before we leave."

His hand stilled hers. "I'm no gentleman…perfect or otherwise. Your father knows that for the truth. Drake knows who I am. What I do.

Whatever you do, don't lie to him. Always tell him the truth."

Her lashes fluttered a few times. "I won't lie. You are more a gentleman than Harry. I told him no. He didn't accept my refusal. Kissed me anyway. Doesn't a gentleman respect a woman's wishes? If you wish to learn the truth, I liked your hands where they were. Hoped for more. Not quite certain what that…more…entails. You could teach me. Would like to learn what you could teach me." She flirted with him, lowered her lashes then looked at him shielded by the thick fan of her dark lashes.

The answer to that question eluded him. He never thought of himself as a gentleman. His upbringing in France was questionable even though he was the son of a count. The bastard son of count DuBois. The man gave him his name so he would do things for him that were too messy for his hands. No other reason. His mother was English, an English whore. Had no idea as to her identity. Didn't recall much about the woman who gave birth to him."

"You never told me no. Don't delude yourself about my manners. Doesn't mean I would respect the no if the word went against what I wanted." He'd almost touched her breast just to see what she would do. He held off because he didn't wish to hear the word, no. "We could start over…a new beginning." He looked to the bed hoping to scare her into common sense…then again…hoping she didn't frighten easily.

"You're right. We need to leave the cottage. I'm…tired." Beth made a sudden swift change of subject.

Ah, so she wasn't quite ready to share the intimacies of a bed. He smiled. When he reached out to take her hand in his, she didn't stop him. He liked the way her hand fit into his. He was certain he was a besotted fool. Lust for him, never would override common sense. None of this would do. Building dreams around this lady would be as building sandcastles too close to the ocean. With the change of the tide all would be washed away. "We are going to ride to my home. It's not far from here to retrieve my horse. After that, I'll see you home."

"You understand I'll have an escort both directions. I don't need you to attend me. Father's guards will make certain I arrive home untouched."

"Ah, but you are not untouched."

He stopped her from leaving. His hand beneath her chin, he set his mouth on hers again, needing one last taste to hold him for the rest of his life. At this point, he felt certain he found the only woman he would ever be able to love. Well, he would need to believe in love for that to happen. "You will have me with you until I set you on your doorstep and you are safe inside. I would never allow a woman to find her way home alone. Despite the fact I understand your father's men are following me. Don't mind the reinforcements. Sometimes it's a wicked world out there. Your father has enemies. Men, who I'm certain would take revenge if given the opportunity. You, my sweet Beth, are the perfect target."

~ * ~

When Elizabeth stepped inside her home, the only person there was her brother, Ashcroft. He was sitting in one of the chairs that faced the fireplace, sipping a brandy. He looked thoughtful. This time of night her brother was usually with his mistress or carousing with friends. In the drawing room, she marched passed Ash to the sideboard, poured herself a brandy all the while her brother watched with an amused expression on his handsome face. She felt the hairs on the nape of her neck tingle. He knew. The messengers told their tales to her brother in lieu of their father who wasn't home this evening. She'd thought she'd been safe.

Ashcroft looked much like their father. His eyes were dark as was his hair. They would shudder then deepen from a very dark blue to almost black when he was displeased. His shoulders were broad, tapering to narrow hips. At the moment his full mouth slanted into a quirky smile. He seemed pleased with his thoughts now that he was no longer brooding. Elizabeth wished she could reach into his head then understand what he was thinking. She didn't want to be protected, least of all from her brother.

Elizabeth tossed the drink back before pouring another. She didn't wish to talk to anyone, especially not her older brother who was far too intuitive where she was concerned. In this case, Ash didn't need to be intuitive. He would know she spent a few hours in the cottage with Thad DuBois. She needed to think over what happened at the lake then the cottage as well as what she intended to explain to him. He would demand an explanation, an accounting as to the time spent with the man. Unthinking, she touched a fingertip to her mouth. Her lips felt swollen. Sore. She didn't wish to think about how potent Thad's kisses had been. Looking back, the sensation Thad DuBois evoked frightened her. When he kissed her, she lost all rational thought. She'd become immersed in the new searing desire surging through her blood so hot and fast the roar infiltrated her hearing eclipsing all other sensations.

He told her if Harry couldn't kiss her the way he did, she should forget about him. Elizabeth didn't need to be told that piece of information as well-meaning as it might have been. Perhaps his words of caution were also a bit self-serving. He put his hand on her bottom. She liked the way his long fingers caressed and tantalized. He pulled her so close she felt the hardness of him. Wasn't certain what it was. Had a guess. Didn't appreciate the fact she'd been sheltered her entire life. There were things about man and woman relationships she needed to understand.

Elizabeth turned to look at her brother. The thought of questioning him about what she felt against her belly flashed through her head to disappear with just as much speed. If a girl couldn't ask her brother about sex, who could she ask? Certainly not her father or her mother. Though she did give her mother credit for enlightening her about a few things. All of which she ignored tonight. If she gave Ash any indication of what was on her mind, she would never be let out of this house again. Her protectors would never allow her space if her father did send her somewhere. Worse, she would never be allowed to see Thad again. Her father would know him for the assassin that he was. Everyone knew what Thad DuBois did for a living. He was hired to kill.

She wished for another kiss.

"Two drinks? Hard night, Sis?" Ash asked as he sat back down in a chair in front of the fire the crystal glass that held his brandy resting on his hard belly. "Want to talk about what happened in the cottage? I'm a good listener."

She did and she didn't. Talking to someone impartial would be nice. Ash would never be neutral. Tomorrow, she'd see if she could go the distance to Lyssa's. Her cousin would be unbiassed. She could ride there or take a carriage. First, she would need to make sure Lyssa was in residence. Though she and Kane rarely went into town. There was also Kerrie. She could see her. Answer all her questions. They were closer in age as well as distance.

"No…yes…not with you. You wouldn't understand. I would be embarrassed. You would tell father. He wouldn't let me out of the house.

One thing after another." Elizabeth fumbled for words. Didn't have the foggiest notion what she wanted. No, she did know. She wanted answers. Needed to see Thad again. Kiss him one more time just to see if the kiss would elicit the same heady response. Two more times. See what came after the kisses. Even now her breasts tingled as if in anticipation. He never touched her there. She would not have denied him.

"Try me?" That quirky smile grew. He was wicked to taunt her so. He lifted his glass her direction, saluting her. "Never thought you had in it you. You've always been Daddy's little girl. Someone kiss you? Harry? Didn't think the lad had it in him to kiss you so hard that your mouth appears ravished. Your careful hairdo slipping from its pins. You still appear as if you are under his spell."

Elizabeth sipped in a quick breath of air. Her hands flying to her mouth. How did he know? Her hands shook. "Yes…not Harry. It wasn't Harry. Don't even like Harry." She didn't wish for her brother to think she would allow that boy to kiss her like that. When Harry touched her, she felt nothing except denial. His touch made her skin crawl. She loathed the man.

"Who then? You must tell me. If not, I'll have to have a talk with father. Anything else happen besides a kiss or two? I would know the truth." He motioned for her to sit down in the chair next to his. His stance no longer so relaxed as it had been before. "Since father isn't here, it's up to me to discover the truth."

Too much restless energy surged inside her. She paced the room. Yes, Thad put his hands on my butt. I felt him hard against my belly. She whirled around, her mind reeling. "I can't say. Though I'm guessing you know who I was with. The duke's men would have informed you since you were the only male home."

Ash nodded his head, staring at her. "Would rather hear the truth from my little sister. Want to be able to trust her. Hope she will listen to reason along with my brotherly advice. If not Harry, tell me who initiated you to a man's kiss. I'll speak to him. Would ride there tonight."

"No, you won't. It's not going to happen again." Ash's life could be in danger if he confronted Thad. Though she didn't think so. Thad denied being an assassin. That renunciation didn't mean anything.

*If he can't kiss you like that, don't settle. Don't marry him.*

She'd never intended to settle for Harry Sylvan or marry him. The boy had always been a nuisance. He teased her. She chased him when he embarrassed her. He didn't make her heart sizzle or inflame her senses. Thad did. Elizabeth understood from watching Lyssa along with Kerrie, Thad was right about the kisses. If she ever married, passion would have to soar, take her to the moon then beyond. Her heart would have to ignite. Elizabeth wanted everything life would give her then more. Wished for a real love one just like her parent's.

"Who is this guy? Did he hurt you?" Ash walked to her. Stopped her pacing as he separated the drink from her hand. "Sit down. Admit to his name then we can talk. I'll give you advice. You'll most likely ignore the guidance."

"I'm not hurt. He was." She said too much. Maybe he didn't know. It was possible the men didn't report to Ash. Possible, too, he arrived home just before her. There might have been no time for more exact information to exchange hands.

Elizabeth swallowed hard. If she told Ash she stitched a knife wound, he'd guess who was kissing her. Ash would intercede. She didn't need anyone's help. This was her battle to win or lose. Her problem to solve. They made no plans to see each other. Unless a coincidence occurred, she might not ever run into this man again. The thought left a feeling of despair in the pit of her stomach. Maybe she should ride to his house. He just lived on the other side of the lake.

She wasn't going to see Thad DuBois again. There would be no plausible way to do so. When Thad left her here with the door open, he chose a different path. There could never be anything between them. They didn't say goodbye. He set her down on the porch step. Waited for the door to open then whirled on his horse. Standing in the doorway Elizabeth watched him ride from her life.

"You're going to need to enlighten me. He was hurt? How? You belted him a good one for kissing you? That's my sister. Always fast with her fists." Ash was laughing at her. His eyes twinkled with humor.

"I'm not going to see him again even though I like him. Yes, I tended to a wound. The cut was nothing serious."

"This unknown man ravished your mouth. You should be certain mother doesn't see you. Even more certain father doesn't get a good look at your lips. They aren't home so you're in luck on this score." He tossed back the contents of his glass. As if this conversation affected him as much as it did her, he splashed more brandy into the crystal. "Do you want another glass? I'll indulge your whims tonight since you've been so frank as well as open with me." The note of sarcasm in his voice didn't go unnoticed.

"This is private. Ash, I'd like to leave this incident alone. There is nothing more to say."

"Father's men will know who it was you saw. You weren't at the lake all this time. The storm was fierce. You needed to take shelter. The cottage is a lover's retreat. Been there a few times myself. Bloody hell! You've only turned eighteen. You didn't…he didn't toss your skirts." He leaned forward. The amber liquid in his glass threatened to overflow the crystal. "Did he?"

Elizabeth found herself shaking her head at him. Found a momentary reason to smile at his assumption. Doubted if she would have stopped Thad if he did take her to the bed. "Just a kiss…a very nice kiss. One I'll remember for a long time. Is that enough information for you? I would retire to my room."

"Not until you tell me who kissed you. He touched you too. Where? I can tell by the deep shimmer of your eyes along with the blush of color on your cheeks when you speak of this man. Bloody everlasting hell! You're in love with the bounder! How long have you known him?"

Her face heated with the flush of embarrassment. Knew as the conversation with her brother continued this would happen. The air turned hot. Sizzled. Elizabeth sunk into the chair. Exhausted. If she tried to walk up the stairs then to her bedroom, her brother would follow. Ash wouldn't give up until he got all the information he sought. The difficulty here was once one question was answered, the response would lead to another query in a never-ending circle.

"I'm not in love with anyone." Though, Elizabeth did admit that she could fall into love with Thad in a heartbeat.

"This unknown man did touch you where he shouldn't. Admit it. You're as red as the flames in the fireplace. Where? Where did he set his lecherous hands. I don't intend to give up until I know. Rest assured, one way or another, I'll discover the truth."

What Ash said was true. He was as ornery as a dog with a new bone. Would wrestle with the thought, never stopping the interrogation. It would be easier to blurt the truth then be done with the cross-examination. Giving up was not a characteristic of her brother. She delivered a long slow breath of air while she thought about giving out the private information. Lifted her shoulders in silent resignation knowing Ash would learn the truth he wanted her to tell him before he retired for the night. All he had to do was talk to one of their father's men. He could walk outside. He'd rather torture her.

"Thad DuBois." Elizabeth sucked in air. Held her breath. Waited for the yell of outrage…the accusations. Instead, she was greeted by an eerie silence that stretched her nerves to the snapping point. While a second ago when she said the name, she'd been looking at her interwoven fingers that rested on her lap. Her knuckles were white from the tension. With a start, she looked up. His back was to her. She couldn't read any information in his face.

What the hell?

Ash was pouring himself another drink. He'd taken her glass. Filled it then held it out to her. "Thought we were telling the truth tonight. You afraid to admit you let Harry do more than you wished? No, Harry would never have need of your gentle stitches." His lips thinned as if he was afraid, she did speak true. "Drink up. If what you said is true, you're going to need the fortification. I have to tell father. You understand that don't you? Thad DuBois is a dangerous man." He drank again. "Don't wish to believe you. See by the way you're looking at me you speak true. You never were a good liar. Always saw through your words."

"You don't need to tell father anything. It was just one kiss. Can't you keep this a secret?" She could continue to ramble. Tell him she wasn't going to see him again. She'd said that already. "Don't want papa to know. Don't wish to be kept a prisoner in my home. Need to have some freedom."

"You know what DuBois does?" Ash's voice was gentle now. His tone one of grave concern. "He's treacherous."

"Our father can be treacherous." She tried to counter the accusation.

"Do you know how he makes his money?"

She was going to divert his line of questioning. Sipping in a charged breath of air. "I've heard gossip, rumors. Been taught not to listen to the gossip. Rumors have a way of not telling the entire truth." Thad was the most handsome man she'd ever seen or met. He was an Adonis. The man would know how beautiful he was. Maybe that was part of his charm. He told her he only killed little girls who asked too many questions. She stopped asking. Yes, she knew what he did to make his money. True, she didn't care. Still wished she could see him, talk to him again. He was the most fascinating man she'd ever met.

"Dear God, he's an assassin! Don't you understand?" Ash pinched the bridge of his nose, his eyes squinting together. "He might target you. You cannot trust this man! He will hire out to anyone willing to pay for his services."

Elizabeth snorted, acknowledging that Ash spoke from rumors he'd heard. There was no fact in what he spouted at her. "Cade is a bounty hunter. The way I see this scenario is that there isn't much difference between the two men. They are both dangerous as is our father. The family accepts Cade. Our father looks out for us. From what I gather, you tend to be following in father's footsteps. That fact makes you just the same. Dangerous!"

"For the right amount of money, he might target you. Cade is paid by the English government. Our father is also as am I. The government doesn't hire people to kill," Ash repeated, this time his voice slow, modulated as if that would make a difference to her. As if she was too enamored of the man to understand all the implications.

She wasn't enamored; at least not yet. She was interested. Curious about him. He intrigued her senses. When she was with the man, she felt heat zing through her as if sparked by flames. "Why on earth would he do that? Target me? I'm nothing. Besides, if I was a target, I wouldn't be talking to you now. I was alone with him while I stitched a wou…" Good God, she was a blabbering idiot. She was about to give credence to part of his accusation. He'd been injured. A knife wound. He didn't get that without some type of confrontation.

"A wound he most likely got when he killed someone or tried. Perhaps that person got the upper hand." Ash was quick to give his opinion to enlighten her. He pointed a finger at her, shaking it as if that would help make the accusation true. "There is no proof because he disposes of the bodies. How he does it so easily… I have ideas but I'm not going to enumerate on all the possibilities. Take care…Elizabeth. Don't see him again if you value your life."

Her stomach somersaulted at the thought of bodies being disposed of with no trace left behind. She found herself shaking her head, unwilling to accept all Ash pointed out to her. While at the same time understanding there might be some validity to her brother's statement. Elizabeth intended to stay firm on this topic, on his accusation. She was not going to cower in fright. If she wished to see this man, she would. Well…he would have to extend an invitation. "I'm not a target. Even for revenge, no one would take their hate out on an innocent female. No one wants revenge on mother for what my father has accomplished in his work. That leaves father to keep us sheltered. He keeps all of us well-guarded. Even you." Now, she found she was trying to convince herself. "I'm not going to see the man again."

"You can't rely on that. DuBois comes and goes as he pleases. You have the distinct habit of visiting the lake. Thad lives nearby. He could get to you anytime he wished."

"I can…I can change my habits." She meant to be just as stubborn as her brother. Even though she wished for something different, seeing Thad again was out of the question. Doing so would never happen. Not in this lifetime. She stiffened her spine, deciding that was the only capitulation her brother was going to receive from her. Defending herself along with her actions was out of the question.

Ash had that way of looking at her that never failed to unnerve her as well as send her temper to flare. Her brother perfected that look when they were children. He was tapping his finger on his chin. The look in his eyes smoldered. That was when he tossed out the question she couldn't refute. "Doesn't Lady Lenore have a ball scheduled for next week? The man receives invitations to all the events. Seems he is there more often than he is not. He attends most in his father's name. Count DuBois, have you forgotten? He and our father have never been on the best of terms."

Her brother did seem to have an answer for everything. "You go to so many," Elizabeth tried for syrupy in her tone. "How would you know? Besides, seeing the man at a ball, is not at all the same as seeing him at the lake." Seeing him in the cottage where he kissed me…touched me where he shouldn't.

"Alone at the cottage…" One of Ash's dark brows shot up confirming Beth's thoughts. Another annoying habit of speculation. He got that from their father. "Elizabeth, I'm worried about you. You've got to understand this is not a game. At least not one you can ever win. Father would never allow you to marry the man if the relationship ever got that far."

Elizabeth disliked the drift of his queries. He questioned whatever she spoke about. She was no longer a child he could dictate to. For her there were no thoughts of wedding him. She was just curious about her feelings for the man. That was all. "I'm not going to see him again unless it is something like that, at a ball. Never seen Thad before at the entertainments father and mother allow me to attend. Doubt if the man is interested in *débutantes*. That's what this ball is…one for the coming out of young ladies. You won't be there unless mother insists you put in appearance to support me. Neither will Thad."

"He might if he believes he will see you there, dance with you. Thad DuBois is intelligent. He would never have kissed you, risked that intimacy, if he hadn't been taken by your beauty…or…what he believed you could give him."

There was nothing she could give this man. She possessed no sway with her father, if that was what Ash implied. "Thad will not be there." She meant to remain stubborn in the face of his arguments. "Truly, if he does attend, I won't speak to him. Won't dance with him. His name will never be on my dance card. You needn't worry." Elizabeth understood she lied through her teeth just so her brother would stop harping at her.

"Shouldn't you address this man you only met this afternoon as Mr. DuBois. Oh," he tapped one of his long fingers on his chin. His grin turned feral. "I forgot. You've kissed the assassin…the bounder. You've allowed him to hold you in his arms. What else? Where did he touch you?"

He was back to that. She wasn't about to let on what happened or didn't happen between them. Those were facts her father's men wouldn't perceive. "You don't need to learn everything. I'm keeping that a secret."

He poured a third glass of brandy. "If it were me doing the kissing, the seducing, I would hold your butt with my hands. Pull you against me so you would comprehend how much I wanted you. Was that what he did?"

Unable to stop it from happening, her face heated. She gasped in a tight-fisted breath of air. Her brother probed too far. She was shaking her head, willing the flames to disappear. Wishing her face would cool. She would stop giving away her secrets. Ash would see her cheeks. He would know what she wished to keep private. His grin unnerved her. She felt her nerves stretching, snapping.

"No!" The next move happened from instinct. Traveled back to their childhood. She held a pillow next to her chest. The next moment the soft cushion became a missel directed at her brother. The projectile flew for a beat, hit the hand holding his brandy. Liquid splashed over then onto Ash. His cuff was soaked. Her mistake was evident in the hard chisel of his jaw. He didn't intend to let the result of her temper pass.

"Now you've done it." His voice was calm, mortifyingly controlled. That was when she knew she was in huge trouble. Ash set the glass down. He moved toward her. His strides long, filled with purpose. "You deserve a child's punishment! I've been tolerant. Tried to give good arguments coupled with some much-needed advice. Help you judge the situation. You've ignored everything I've said. Now you've drenched this shirt. I'll have to change before I go out tonight."

Unwilling to waist valuable time, Elizabeth raced toward the door. Her brother caught her by her arm before she could slip through the small opening. Turned her to face him. His hands on her arms tightened. She felt a moment's panic. Not that it would have mattered if she'd been able to pass through the door. He was faster, more agile. He would have had her before she reached the stairs. Bending low, he caught her up onto his shoulder. Walked with her back to the drawing room to stand in front of the chairs.

"You need a spanking," he muttered reiterating his previous statement as he tossed her on the chair where she'd been sitting. Father has spoiled you. You take too much for granted. He directed a finger toward her. "I can tell by the look in your eyes you don't intend to be practical about this situation. What are you going to say if DuBois asks you for a dance? If he holds you too close? He could dance you into a secluded corner. Steal another kiss. Would you create a scene? Go with him? You want that second kiss. I can read you like a book. I've known you for so many years. You are unable to hide anything from me." He sipped in a long deep breath of air. "I don't know what else to say to you."

Seizing her win, she expected him to either give her that child's spanking or tickle her until she couldn't move. Elizabeth was pleased he gave his threat more than one thought. His voice lost the sting of anger. What she heard now amounted to silent resignation. "If he asks me, I'm going to say yes. It would be impolite to refuse. He won't ask. You've nothing to worry over. Thad will never attend a débutante ball."

"You have to learn how to say no to that man. Somehow, you've stirred up a nest of hornets. Bloody eyes, you didn't say no at the cottage. A girl has to learn when to tell the man she is with to keep his questing hands to himself." Ash kneeled down beside her, placed her hands in his. "I'm worried about you. Truly, I am. I'm not playing at being autocratic. It's not the kiss that has me sweating. It's the person you're interested in who frightens me. Listen to me. You have to stay as far away from that man as possible. Don't go to the lake. Don't go to the cottage. You must go to the balls. In that there is no choice. You never need to accept a dance with him."

"Mother didn't stop our father from taking all he wished for before the marriage," Elizabeth pointed out with a matter-of-fact sigh.

"That's different. He wasn't an assassin."

Without admitting Ash was right, she did agree with him. Danger radiated around Thad. That was part or most of the attraction she felt. "Do you intend to tell Papa?" she asked afraid of the answer.

"Not yet. Against my better judgment, I'll wait. See what transpires in the next few days. Be good. Be careful. Don't do anything you might find you will regret. Bloody eyes, don't fall in love with this man!"

Doing so, falling in love with Thad, might be far too easy. With her, he was so gentle. Tender. "You know there is no proof that he kills people to make his money." Not understanding why, she defended him. "Doesn't there have to be evidence of a crime? Fact that a certain person committed said crime? You've tried him then found him guilty all on your own."

"That's because there are no bodies to be unearthed. No trace of the person who has disappeared. Seems not only is he the handsomest man in all of London, he is also the most devious. The truth…the man is good at what he does. Right, there is no evidence…not irrefutable proof. Yet…" Ash paused then pouring them both more brandy. "Yet…people hire him to get rid of people. That isn't rumor. Cold hard fact is that he accepts pay for the purpose of ridding the world of…people."

"I've heard rumors," Elizabeth admitted, rehashing all her brother's words. "I never felt afraid of the man. Believe there would have been some fear if he…if he was a cold-hearted murder. Don't you think?"

"He wasn't there to hurt you. You're right in your assessment. The man was smitten with you. Either that or he wished to see how much of yourself you would give him. If what you told me is true, he respected you to some extent. While the kiss was natural…"

"I liked the kiss," Beth was quick to say. She smiled at her brother understanding she'd won his silence. "Wished for another kiss. He stopped that from happening by telling me he had to take me home. Even though he understood father's men would see me home, he insisted."

"That you enjoyed the kiss was obvious on my first sight of you. Your mouth is even now red as well as swollen. I'm glad you told me the truth. If he approaches you again, we have to let father know. We can't protect you if you keep secrets. If he contacts you in any way, you must tell me or father. Can you agree to that?"

Elizabeth didn't want to agree with him or with anything he spouted. Knew her brother would be relentless in pursuing his wishes. While she wanted to see Thad again, she did need to admit the man was dangerous. One could say the same of Ash along with their father. Tara found love with a man who was a bounty hunter. That was dangerous work. Though that man worked for her father. If the truth was told, she was surrounded by dangerous men. Men like that excited her.

Thad DuBois, from what she heard, was a free agent. He worked only for himself. No, that wasn't true. Thad also worked for his father, Count DuBois. Would Count DuBois want revenge against her father? Would he use her? Elizabeth didn't believe any of that nonsense. When they were together, the count and her father seemed to get along. What did she know about any of the intrigues going on in London.

"If, at a ball, he asks me for a dance, I won't refuse. He would believe it strange on my part after I let him kiss me. That would make him wonder about my motives. Won't allow him to dance me into a corner for another kiss even though I would like that."

"One dance, one dance that is all that's allowed under any circumstances. Don't allow him to find a dark secluded corner of the balcony. It's a bit too cold to spend time outside. Thank goodness for winter." Ash was pacing now, talking, instructing her.

"One dance," she agreed even while she dreamed about his arms around her, the scent of him, the warmth of his male body next to her. She hoped he would hold her closer than what was deemed appropriate. "Are you going to attend?"

The loud groan from her brother gave her, her first reason to smile since she returned from the cottage. Ash hated débutante balls, débutante rehearsals…everything débutante. After his lecture, he would feel honor bound to protect his little sister. Attendance was necessary.

"I will be at Lady Lenore's soiree. Just to make certain you keep your promise."

"I didn't promise anything."

~ * ~

Thad spent the week with Beth ever-present on his mind. Night as well as day, he couldn't keep from thinking about her. At night, his dreams focused on her. The brief kiss escalated in the shadows of his mind, searing his body with lightning swept desire. Didn't wish to constantly think about her. Needed to maintain a clear, level head when he met with Grisham Monthaven.

This man couldn't be trusted. Grisham sported an evil agenda. One Thad wished he could sort out. While he put out feelers, he wasn't rewarded for his efforts. He sent Jacque, his trusted friend, to following the man hoping to ferret out a few more details. All he was able to discover was the fact the man had no past. Everyone possessed a past. A life that could be used against them or for them.

Thad harbored misgivings a mile deep. For a brief time, thought to tell him he wouldn't see him or entertain any adventure he might request. Grisham Monthaven spelled trouble. He needed something to hold over his head. A means to keep him quiet if approached. The money offered to him for the job tempted. Seemed to override his instincts. The job would be an easy one. An older woman…to be brought down to her knees because of petty revenge. For a moment, he felt sorry for the lady along with all she would lose.

He brought in a deep breath of air, reminding himself he needed caution with every decision. As far as he could tell the job could be carried out with ease, the monetary reward exorbitant. He along with his men would be careful. Intended to take every precaution. The task would be completed before the ball. He could return to see Beth. If allowed by her male chaperones, a dance.

There were opportunities presented when he rode by the lake in hopes of seeing her. She was never there waiting. Didn't expect that to happen. Thad was certain she'd been warned away from him. Any self-respecting father or brother would feel impelled do so. Understood when he brought Beth home the other night, Ash was waiting for her. What he didn't know was how much of their escapade her brother knew about. This first meeting was by chance. The coincidence would never happen again. He needed to orchestrate a second meeting.

After several days of careful deliberation, he decided to see the man offering the job one more time. Might indeed take on the task that he offered. Needed a diversion from thoughts about Beth. There was no better way than work to take his mind off a woman. Take his mind off the way her mouth felt beneath his. Her scent…evocative…titillating. The touch of the rounded, soft curves of her breasts pressed against his chest. The feel of her curved derriere as his hands explored places, he had no business sightseeing.

Beth never told him no. Instead, she purred softly, ripples of that female hum coming from deep in the back of her throat. She pressed against him. Tried to move closer when he kissed her. Held the back of her head with his hand. She met his tongue with hers. Pulling away before he knew her secrets better was next to impossible. Thad shook his head as if the gesture would rid him of thoughts of Beth. Needed to keep his mind sharp. Focused on the business at hand.

The challenge of his job, the daring, the excitement, those were all things he craved. Thad met Grisham at the Boar's Head Inn. This tavern was where he did all his business. The owner was trustworthy. The maids he kept loyal to his cause with attentive consideration to their needs. No one here would betray him. His meetings were kept secret. He paid the hired help well, treated them as if they were queens. Bedded the serving wenches with dedication to their needs. Never left a woman unfulfilled. The people who worked here would do anything for him.

They kept what they guessed about his secrets, secret.

Now, he waited for Grisham Monthaven in the side room he used for all his business ventures. Here there was a table big enough to accommodate him along with Jacques, his most trusted retainer along with his client. For his convenience a side door would lead outside. A man could leave this establishment without walking through the common room. A carriage for his use always waited within easy reach. There were no windows. Thick planking on the walls along with the door, kept whatever was spoken in the room private. As the door opened, Thad stood to greet the man who was here to hire him to dispose of an unwanted female. Watched the man as he paused a moment framed by the open door. Took stock of him. The eyes of this new client of his held the slant of betrayal. For the right price, this man would sell his mother to the devil.

"Grisham," Thad said as the owner led the man into the back room of his establishment before pulling out a chair. A serving girl followed with a tray holding ale along with meat pies. "Have a seat. What is it you have in mind?" Thad thought the man looked familiar. Couldn't place him. This man, Grisham, had led a hard life. Lines around his mouth and eyes aged him as did his weathered skin. White streaks touched his dark hair. Grisham was gaunt yet he carried himself as if he owned the world. That stance told him the man came from aristocracy. He seemed to have fallen on hard times. Though…Grisham wouldn't be here if he didn't have the funds to meet his requirements. There was much to learn about him if he were to become his client.

Grisham looked around. His brows drawn together in concentration. He tapped his fingers on the table seeming hesitant to carry out the business at hand. "Can this place be trusted. Need complete discretion. Don't have a mind to end up in Newgate or on a ship bound to a penal colony." His prospective client set the cane he walked with beside him on the table. While it appeared, the man needed the staff to walk, Thad would bet there was a sword at one end. A bit of protection for this frail man if he needed to defend himself.

"Everyone here is faithful to me. There are no prying eyes or ears that would deceive me. Now, I don't have a great deal of time to waste. If I agree, want to take care of this matter before the end of the week. What is it to be? Tell me what you need. Who you want me to dispose of then pay me. Half now then the last half when the person has disappeared. No questions about how or where. No questions at all." Thad leaned forward. His eyes focused on this new client. "You understand. If too many questions are asked, they won't be appreciated. There will be consequences. Discretion in the key to this type of business as well as its success. The less you know the better for both of us." Thad understood most requests were meant to do away with an unwanted person. "Who is it you detest enough to never see in this lifetime?"

Again, his client drummed his fingers on the table, touched the handle on his cane several times as if thinking about the sharp pointed tip at the end. Nervous energy twitched at him. His brows drew together. Concentrated. His lips formed into a sneer. After he looked up, he spoke, his voice a rumble of hatred. "My wife…my ex-wife. She divorced me twenty-two years ago. All these years I've wanted to see her pay for her crimes against me. She abandoned me when I needed her. She must pay. Now is my chance to get even. Revenge can be splendid. Don't you think? I want her to know it is me who has sent you to her. She won't recognize my last name. Tell her Grisham sends his regards. She will understand that I've reached out from what she believed was my grave to do away with her." His hands were clenched tight, quivering. The lines of his mouth were drawn. Age lines around his eyes made white with the malice he felt. He seemed to clamp down so tight on his jaw Thad could hear his teeth grating.

Thad had no intention of learning about her crimes against this man who harbored hatred in his soul. Came back from the dead, did he? Interesting thought. The less he knew or understood about his victims, the better. If he learned too much, he might sympathize. "Her name?" he queried beginning to lose patience.

"Mary White. The woman remarried. Had two sons. Forgot about her two daughters she conceived with my seed. Went right on with her life as if I'd never been a part of hers. Wrote me off, she did. Could have tried to save me. There was enough money to bail me out. Didn't come to visit before they set me on a ship to Tasmania. I saw her at the docks the day I left the country. She was smiling as if saying good riddance." He waved his hand in the air. "Now I say, good riddance to her!"

"Where does she live? I'll send a message for her to meet me. Will let you know when it's done. Other than that specific piece of information there is nothing else for you to learn." Thad rose having collected all the information he needed for a successful business venture. He never shook hands. Waited for the payment. Grisham pushed over a bag filled with gold coins. Thad emptied it on the table, never trusting the men or the women who came to him. If he was underpaid, he would have to do something about that pertinent fact. His client's understood retaliation along with underpayment would be deadly.

Once Grisham left, Thad knew his man, Jacques, would follow discreetly. It never paid to trust anyone. When Jacques returned, they would exchange information about the man. He needed to learn as much about his clients as possible. Grisham carried a wealth of secrets, ones he needed to know before business could be conducted with any success. Thad must know all of a client's secrets. Anyone who could order this type of blow was a man who could never be trusted. Spent time in Tasmania, he'd said. Must have been sent to a penal colony. Never heard of anyone escaping from an institution of that sort. What did he do to warrant that punishment? He didn't think the crime had anything to do with his quest for revenge against his wife. There must be someone else involved. Montfort wasn't his last name. Discovering his true identity became first on his list of must-dos. He would take care of the wife after he learned a few more salient facts.

Thad, leaned back lacing his fingers behind his head. One of his favorite ladies who worked here brought him a glass of ale. She set her butt on the table in front of him. Leaned over showing her charms in hopes of enticing him to her bed this evening. He smiled at her then shook his head. Since meeting Beth, he…he'd been celibate. It had been less than a week since meeting her, kissing her. She entranced him. He wished to have many more sensual encounters with her. Must figure out a means to get passed her ever-present guards. Perhaps he should focus on Mary White. He wanted to be done with this client so he could attend the upcoming débutant ball.

Damn, since kissing Beth he wasn't interested in other women. Couldn't even get an erection looking at the rosy tips of this lady's breasts. For a few seconds the woman stared hard at him. After that she sighed, softly shaking her head.

"Damn, but you've got it bad for some special lady. Who is the gel who has you wound into so many knots you don't care about your pleasure? I can help you forget her at least for a short time."

"Doubt that could happen."

## *Dream About Lyssa*
### Naughty Book Two

When Lyssa Andrews sees the earl sitting behind his desk scowling, she knows she will someday put a smile on his face. The handsome brooding earl isn't playing the same game. He resists her outrageous comments and questions until she is ready to give up. Lyssa didn't come to London with the intent to find a man. Now, though, she is willing to chance love with the stodgy earl of Blackmore.

Raised by the Sioux when his father sought adventure then fell in love with a Sioux maiden, Kane has been betrayed once by a white woman. He isn't about to give his heart to another, especially one who is as white as newly fallen snow. Despite his best efforts, he can't deny Lyssa's intoxicating effect on him. Now Kane will risk his very life to protect the innocent beauty who has seduced him with her tender love.

## *Deke's Magic Kiss*
### Naughty Book Three

She would risk everything to become a practicing doctor

Annie Lundin's dream of practicing medicine and a life of dignity and self-sufficiency vanishes in the small Kansas Territory town of Denver City. When the men of the town refuse to become her patients, all she has left to fight for is her practice. She is thwarted from every direction. She didn't mean to fall for the dark, handsome sheriff. Didn't mean to ask for his help. Annie needs Deke Sullivan to protect her from the dark secrets that follow her from Boston. In return she offers all she has—herself.

He would stop at nothing to win her love and trust

Raised by the Cheyenne, Deke Sullivan was churlish, overconfident, and dangerously handsome. His life changed when his Irish grandfather discovered him. He was sent to West Point, fought the

Seminole in Florida as well as some on the planes where his loyalty was divided. A woman is the last thing in the world he needs. Especially a woman who belongs in Boston, not the rugged Rocky Mountains. He has commitments that don't include a woman. The moment he sees Annie her intoxicating beauty changed him forever. Love has a way of changing the rules.


## *Chasing Still Water*
### Naughty Book Four

The single kiss behind the church changes Chauncey Lakeland's life forever. At that moment, Chauncey knows Still Water Runs Deep is the only man she can love. Someday she will prove to him she can be courageous as well as bold. She decides that when he leaves for Dakota territory she will follow. Chauncey has every intention of being with this man she just met. She isn't going to risk losing him. No matter what it takes, Still Water Runs Deep will be hers. Now, she is willing to take a chance on love with the Sioux warrior who kissed her then stole her heart.

Still Water Runs Deep, a Sioux warrior, is a man intent on living true and loving deep. His greatest challenge will come with the woman he is destined to love. In Chauncey's stubborn determination to follow him into Sioux territory despite the danger, he realizes the fire in her soul. Wrapped in her arms he discovers both his heaven and hell. Even as she risks her life to be with him, he must keep her with him.


## *Chasing Still Water*
### Naughty Book Five

Without lies...

A woman with no guile, with adoration in her heart for the only man she believed she would ever love. Tara once loved with purity and passion. Shared all that she was. Then she learned the agony of irrevocable loss—along with the unexpected permanence of death.

Without trust...

Case Ferguson has known only animosity as well as treachery from women. Scarred, embittered, Case becomes a solitary aloof man— swearing never to allow himself to have faith in a woman again.

Passion for all time...

When Tara and Case meet there is a haunting quality of misjudgment between them. Desperate to get past his disparaging ways, she understands his vulnerability. Tara is willing to gamble what proud reticent Case cannot. With tenderness and understanding she brings trust along with love to an anguished soul who believes in neither—though she fears in her heart that by loving Case she will lose him. Just as she lost her first love.

*VISIT OUR WEBSITE*
*FOR THE FULL INVENTORY*
*OF QUALITY BOOKS*:
*http://www.roguephoenixpress.com*

# *Rogue Phoenix Press*

*Representing Excellence in Publishing*
*Quality trade paperbacks and downloads*
*in multiple formats,*
*in genres ranging from historical to contemporary romance,*
*mystery and science fiction.*

www.ingramcontent.com/pod-product-compliance
Lightning Source LLC
Chambersburg PA
CBHW060350260626

47160CB00006B/2265